GEOFF C............. ....
BETWEEN HIS HANDS . . .

. . . and pulled her toward him. "Look at me, love. Do you want me to kiss you?" He read her look of indecision and, in a moment of insight, knew why she could not answer. "Lying is a sin, Faith."

For a split second, she was tempted to swear. She might have succumbed had she not been so sure that in her heart, she was committing another sin altogether.

"So is lust," she answered.

He laughed softly, but not unkindly. "A wish for a simple kiss is not lust, love."

"What is?"

"Something far more potent, I assure you. Something to save for another day. For now, what do you want?"

His face was still inches from her own, and she could see a faint shadow where he had shaved earlier in the day. There was a force about him, a warmth that drew her, and she closed her eyes again. "Kiss me if you please, Geoff."

She was unprepared for the strong wave of heat that engulfed her at the tender touch of his lips to hers. Her first instinct was to pull away, but he still held her face between his hands, then slipped one gently to the nape of her neck. His mouth moved softly against hers, as though he had all day to accustom her to the feel of it, and at last, she relaxed, her own lips softening, yielding. When he pulled away, she felt as supple and soft as the cloth upon her lap.

"Are you sure this is not lust?" she asked.

BOOK YOUR PLACE ON OUR WEBSITE AND MAKE THE READING CONNECTION!

We've created a customized website just for our very special readers, where you can get the inside scoop on everything that's going on with Zebra, Pinnacle and Kensington books.

When you come online, you'll have the exciting opportunity to:

- View covers of upcoming books
- Read sample chapters
- Learn about our future publishing schedule (listed by publication month *and author*)
- Find out when your favorite authors will be visiting a city near you
- Search for and order backlist books from our online catalog
- Check out author bios and background information
- Send e-mail to your favorite authors
- Meet the Kensington staff online
- Join us in weekly chats with authors, readers and other guests
- Get writing guidelines
- AND MUCH MORE!

Visit our website at
http://www.kensingtonbooks.com

INTO HIS ARMS

Paula Reed

ZEBRA BOOKS
KENSINGTON PUBLISHING CORP.
http://www.zebrabooks.com

ZEBRA BOOKS are published by

Kensington Publishing Corp.
850 Third Avenue
New York, NY 10022

All Kensington titles, imprints and distributed lines are available at special quantity discounts for bulk purchases for sales
promotion, premiums, fund-raising, educational or institutional
use.

Special book excerpts or customized printings can also be created to fit specific needs. For details, write or phone the office
of the Kensington Special Sales Manager: Kensington Publishing Corp., 850 Third Avenue, New York, NY 10022. Attn.
Special Sales Department. Phone: 1-800-221-2647.

Zebra and the Z logo Reg. U.S. Pat. & TM Off.

First Printing: June 2004
10 9 8 7 6 5 4 3 2

Printed in the United States of America

Chapter 1

1671

Small and elegant hands, roughened by work, turned the smooth ball of brown dough onto the flour-strewn table. It was with certain strength that they set to a practiced, rhythmic rocking—flatten, fold, turn, flatten, fold, turn. The yeasty smell of the dough mingled with the aroma of a hen simmering among herbs over the fire, and soft light filtered through the windows.

Faith Cooper worked the mixture with graceful determination. This was perhaps the most satisfying task she could perform when her mind was in turmoil. Her frustration flowed from her fingers and into the dough, allowing her to maintain the calm demeanor she had cultivated so carefully throughout her life. Generally, she was very good at it, the illusion of pious tranquility, but this time, merely keeping her hands busy and her face serene did not chase away the doubts in her head.

Aaron Jacobs was a fine choice, she told herself, squelching a sigh. He wasn't a handsome man, but his face was pleasant enough. He was a good Christian with a successful wood mill. To be sure, marriage to him meant that she would live the rest of her life as she had lived it thus far, docile, obedient, unquestioning. If she felt it was a masquerade, what did she expect? Well she knew that very few men in Massachusetts would accept anything else from a wife.

It was time to stop dragging her heels and grow up. She was one year shy of a score and had already turned down four offers of marriage. George Mayfield and Roger Smith were wealthy, but older than she would wish in a mate. Josiah Wells was more of an age, but he had always been cruel as a boy. She doubted that as a man he was any different. Paul Geddes had no head for business. Aaron was a perfect husband by all reasonable standards.

A sharp rapping upon the door of her family's clapboard house broke her gloomy contemplation, and for a moment, she was relieved for the distraction. Quickly, she dropped the ball of dough into a bowl and spread a cloth over the top to let it rise. Wiping her hands on the broad apron that covered her deep brown skirts and checking to be sure that her hair was neatly tucked into her linen cap, she answered the door with a smile that faltered, then froze. The somber clothes of her visitor could have belonged to any man in the village, but the formality of his dress and authority in his stance were unique.

"Reverend Williams!" Faith exclaimed. "You honor us. Were my parents expecting you? They're in my father's joinery if you will but wait a moment."

The clergyman raised his hand in curt acknowledgment. He was well over two score in years and singularly unremarkable in looks. Lank, graying, brown hair fell to his wide collar. His eyes, a nondescript shade of blue, scrutinized her carefully, lit with some emotion that she could not name, but that left her feeling slightly queasy.

"Nay, Miss Cooper, I would speak with you awhile first, if it is not a bad time."

In truth, she had no wish to spend long in this man's presence without the comfort of her parents. Whenever she encountered him at meeting or in the village, he regarded her too steadily. A slight smirk would pull at the corner of his lips, as though he knew some dark secret about her. Still, she could hardly refuse hospitality to her own minister.

Carefully arranging her features to affect a calmness she did not feel, she replied, "I have no pressing business. Will you come inside?"

In the three months that Owen Williams had held the position of minister in her Puritan village, he had yet to pay a mere social call on anyone. It was much discussed among their neighbors that he found ample opportunity to chastise his flock for the slightest transgressions. She had no doubt that his censure would at last be felt here, in her home, as well.

Still, the only sign of her apprehension was the slight wariness in her striking, aqua blue eyes. "I have tea warming by the fire, and I baked gingerbread just this morning. Would you take refreshment?"

"Aye, I would," he replied.

Making no attempt at common pleasantries, he swept past Faith, who held the door open for him. With disdain, his eyes swept the immaculate keeping room. It was large, and the furniture sparse, though well made. One side held a spacious oak table and chairs as well as a cupboard and sideboard. The other held a bench and several high-backed wooden chairs in front of a generous hearth crafted of local stone. A small, leather-bound Bible sat open on the bench. Steep, narrow stairs led to the second level and the sleeping quarters. Those, too, spoke of the craftsmanship of the cabinetmaker who lived there.

Faith fetched sturdy earthenware dishes from the cupboard and served the offered refreshment, all the while acutely aware of his eyes on her.

"I'll speak plainly, Miss Cooper," the reverend began. "Aaron Jacobs tells me that he has spoken with your father about the possibility of taking you to wife."

Faith brought her own cup of tea to the table and sat at the opposite end. "Aye, my father has spoken of it to me."

"I am told other offers have been made for you."

"Aye, that's true."

"How comes it, then, that you are nigh onto twenty and still unwed?" He took a bite of gingerbread and made a face of tight displeasure. "A bit dry," he commented.

Faith ground her teeth at his criticism, one implied, the other direct, but gave no outward sign of her indignation. If it was her marital status that bothered him, she had just resolved that problem in her own mind.

"My parents would have me happy in my union. None of the others suited me, but I have decided that Goodman Jacobs and I are an acceptable match."

A pinched smirk flickered across his features before they resumed their stern scowl. "None *suited* you? You find Goodman Jacobs *acceptable*? I see you are a finicky miss, then. What kind of father is it who lets his daughter make such a weighty decision for herself, and what kind of daughter does not seek to please her parents?"

Faith ducked her head in a manner suggesting meek deference, though 'twas another thought altogether that caused her to shield her face. Well she knew that her eyes were the very mirrors of her thoughts, and at the moment, she was furious that the minister would so grievously overstep his place.

"My father is a good man and a strict parent, Reverend," she protested. "He would not hesitate to admonish me for contrariness or arrogance. I assure you, had my parents shown some preference in my choice, I would have submitted to their will. It is only, as I said, that they wished for my happiness."

"I heard what you said. Do not be impertinent, girl!"

Anger flushed Faith's cheeks, and she again dropped her gaze to the table, hoping that he did not see. Later, when she recounted this tale to her parents, she would have no shameful outbursts to confess. Striving to be ever the mistress of her emotions, she murmured, "Forgive me, Reverend, I meant no disrespect."

"This pretense works on these simple villagers, Miss Cooper, but you will find that I am not so easily gulled. Your neighbors think you as pious as you are comely, when 'tis clear you are prideful and vain. Still, you cast your eyes down and flutter your lashes, and they mistake your affectations for divine grace."

His attack left the girl speechless. 'Twas true, no others had guessed at the temper she masked in her meek manners. And her faith in the austere theology of her church was, of late, riddled with doubt, but she did her best to hide these flaws and live as an upright Christian.

Though her conscience pricked her for the deception, she protested. "I—I know not what you speak of. I am an industrious and obedient daughter. And truly,

I have refused the others only because I thought our characters would not suit in marriage."

"Aye, *your* character might not! You think yourself too fair for the others who would offer to be your husband. You seek a young man, one ill prepared to enforce the dutiful obedience you obviously refuse to accept as your place."

Faith tightened her fingers around her heavy clay cup. "I assure you, Reverend, I shall strive to be a dutiful, Christian wife." But even to her own ears, the words lacked conviction. The minister only snorted in disbelief, and with rather more sharpness than she intended, she said, "I do not understand what I have done to so displease you. Do you not wish me to marry Aaron Jacobs?"

Relief flooded her when her parents chose that moment to open the door and greet their visitor. Her father, Jonathan, was a solid man. His dark blond hair, streaked with silver, brushed his shoulders. His wife, Naomi, was the source of Faith's delicate features. Like Faith, she kept her hair neatly contained in her linen coif and wore a serviceable gown of dark wool covered by a wide apron.

The minister dismissed Faith with an imperious wave. "Goodman and Goodwife Cooper, I would have a word with you. Your obstinate daughter's presence is not required."

Both Faith and Naomi gasped at the minister's blatantly rude comment, and a glimmer of indignation crossed Jonathan's face.

"Obstinate, Reverend?" he asked. "I must confess, you bewilder me. Our Faith has ever been a most biddable girl. It seems you have yet to meet any young person in our village who meets with your approval."

"You are lax in this village," Williams replied. "But no matter, I see no evil here that cannot be set quickly to rights."

It was clear by the look upon his face that Faith's father did not relish the conversation to come. In a tight voice he commanded, "Faith, your brothers are in the joinery. Our young David has done a fine job helping with the cradle for your unborn niece or nephew. He and Noah would have you see it, I'm sure."

She dropped her gaze and curtsied, but her deference seemed only to annoy the reverend, who gave her a skeptical glare. Once outside, she hesitated a moment. Faith seldom disobeyed her parents, but urgent curiosity got the better of her, and she lingered at the window, watching and listening through the glass.

"I bid you welcome to our humble home, Reverend Williams," her mother began. "I apologize if our Faith offended you in some way. Was there some disagreement?"

"To be sure, this is no idle visit, Goodwife Cooper. Indeed, I am here because I have concerns about your daughter."

"Pray tell, what concerns are those?" her father asked. "I have heard nothing but good report of her in our village."

"She is sorely led astray, I tell you, and may well lead others down her crooked path."

"Have you heard some vile rumor? Whatever it is, I assure you, our Faith is a pure and pious girl. Surely it is a misunderstanding."

"Is it a misunderstanding that she has turned her nose up at every covenanted Christian man who would be her husband?"

The couple exchanged baffled looks. "She has not yet chosen to accept any offer that has been made, but I assure you, sir, her reasons were sound. She was ne'er a flighty or capricious child." Outside, Faith gave hasty thanks to God for her father's defense.

"She is a fair maid," Reverend Williams pressed.

"Aye, she is," her mother replied.

"See you no danger in that? A fair female with no man to claim her is a sore temptation to honest men!"

Jonathan paused and looked long and hard at the minister, who bristled under his scrutiny. "If they are so tempted," he said at last, "then I must question their honesty."

"They are but sons of Adam, and a girl such as yours is no less than a daughter of Eve. What honest reason has she to reject the authority of a husband? She is a woman, fully grown. It is long past time that she submit herself to an upright man."

"I am her father, and she submits herself to me. What say you to that?"

"I say that you are a man who does not show the proper respect for the clergy! Further I would say that you are blinded by a parent's pride."

Naomi narrowed her eyes and stopped the argument. "Have you an upright man in mind, Reverend?" At his terse nod, she continued. "I think it is not Aaron Jacobs, although he has recently asked."

"Nay, Goodwife Cooper, it is not. Goodman Jacobs is too naive, too trusting. Like the rest of this village, your daughter has duped him into believing her a saint."

"And what is she?" Naomi pressed.

"I have told you, she is bold and a temptress!"

"Who is it that she so tempts?" her father asked,

his voice tight with anger. "What man comes to you and casts a shadow upon my daughter's reputation with his own impure thoughts?"

The minister's face flushed scarlet before he barked, "That is unimportant! It is clear to me that she will require a far firmer hand."

Faith's stomach tied itself into a sickening knot at the minister's mention of a firmer hand. Only last Sabbath he had castigated the congregation for its leniency with their children. "He that spareth the rod hateth his son!" he had thundered, though there was nary a child present who had not felt the wrath of an angry parent upon his backside. The adults of the town were not brutal, but neither could just accusation be made of softness for their children.

"Have you a firmer hand in mind?" her mother asked.

"Aye. I have come to believe that the only man here who will remain unaffected by her comeliness is myself."

Him? The minister had come to suggest *himself* as her future husband? Never could she hold her tongue and bow her head day after day in this man's presence! Never would she find the grace and peace of mind she sought! Her church taught that one's life's path was preordained, but surely this was not God's will. Surely she must have some say in the matter!

"There is naught I would quail from doing to keep her upon a righteous path," he continued. "I have been a widower these four years, and my wife left me no child for comfort. Your Faith is young and strong and, with proper instruction, can be made into a suitable wife and mother, God willing."

Faith's heart began to hammer in her chest, and she

pressed her hands to her breast as if to muffle the sound. She feared to contemplate the meaning behind his ominous words.

"You?" Jonathan's voice was deceptively mild, and the minister's face twisted into a self-satisfied smirk.

"Aye. I would be willing to take on the challenge."

"The challenge of a fair wife who is known to be kind to her neighbors and faithful to her church? How generous you are, sir. How blessed our fair village to have such a spiritual leader."

Missing the other man's sarcasm, Owen Williams nodded. "Well, then, it is settled. We will be wed next month when the weather warms."

Jonathan replied in a measured tone, "I think not. You may be the new minister here, but I will decide who weds my daughter. I cannot think what has caused you to form such an ill opinion. Perhaps it is because you know her but little." At Williams's look of haughty disbelief, Jonathan's self-control slipped. Raising his voice, he concluded, "I would see her wed to a man who may come to love her as God intended, not one intent only upon squashing her beneath his heel!"

Faith's breath caught in her throat. Surely her father pushed too far, though she was deeply moved by his loyalty. This man was the village minister and fast friends with the governor of Massachusetts! He would be a powerful foe if her father angered him. The knot in her stomach tightened, and her knees felt like water.

Naomi placed a restraining hand on her husband's shoulder and in a placating tone said, "My husband is protective, as is his fatherly duty, and we care deeply for our daughter, of course. She is our only girl. Give us time to consider your offer. We would not be hasty in this matter."

Williams gave her a doubtful look. "Might I ask what there is to consider? Have you some better offer?"

"Better suited, I think," Jonathan snapped, and Naomi's eyes widened at the audacious response.

"I will not be rejected like a common farmer! I offer her a life of comfort and not a little prestige. You could do no better by her. As the minister, I have a sacred duty to look after the welfare of this village, and I say that Faith Cooper must wed and that I am the safest choice. I will leave it to you to inform her, but know this: I will not compromise in this matter."

Naomi's hand rested lightly upon her husband's rigid shoulder. "This is very sudden, and I think Faith hoped to accept Aaron. Will you not give us time to accustom her to the idea?"

"You spoil the girl as I will not. Be that as it may, she is yet your concern. Do as you think best, but tell her soon. I bid you good day."

Chapter 2

The reverend turned abruptly toward the door, and Faith fled to the side of the house, not a moment too soon. She leaned against the wall and tried to catch her breath, listening to the minister's horse as it methodically plodded back to the main road. When Williams's form disappeared down the path, she returned to the front of the house, halting when she saw her father waiting at the door.

"Did you see your brothers' handiwork?" he asked.

It was a sin to lie. Faith wrapped her arms about her waist and said, "Nay. I watched at the window."

Jonathan's face looked grim. "I told you to go to the joinery."

"I didn't want to disobey. You suggested that I go there, but the Reverend Williams and I had spoken before you came, and I did wonder what he sought. It seemed to concern me."

Not missing his daughter's pale and anxious face, Jonathan said, "Come in, child. We must speak on this."

Faith followed her father back into the softly lit interior of the house, where her mother waited by the fire. She idly basted the hen in the pot, but a worried frown creased her brow. Faith's hands had gone cold, and she trembled, but she assured herself that her parents would look to her welfare.

"She heard," Jonathan told his wife.

"I see." Faith's mother gave her a cross look for her transgression, but compassion softened it before she could entirely shame the girl.

"I listened at the window." At her parents' stern faces, Faith dropped her gaze. "I meant no harm, but clearly his business concerned me."

Jonathan took a deep breath and a long look at his daughter. "Have you any notion why he might think ill of you?"

"Nay, Father! I cannot think how he came to believe me anything other than a dutiful Christian."

"It may well be that she is not at fault for his opinion of her," Naomi said to her husband. She cast an anxious look at Faith and then back to Jonathan. "He seemed to rather dwell upon her tempting honest men."

"Aye, I caught that, as well," Jonathan replied. "But he is a man of God."

"Of course," Naomi agreed. Then she added, somewhat hesitantly, "Still, there is something about him that does not sit well with me."

Jonathan nodded grimly.

It took all of Faith's self-restraint not to tear her hair out at their exchange. "So we defer to him in matters of our very souls, even though he inspires no confidence?" she asked.

"This problem is not so simple, Faith," Jonathan said. "We survive in this harsh land by God's grace alone. We must think well on it ere we challenge the authority of the church. You are young yet. In time, you will understand."

Once, it had seemed to Faith that her father had an answer for her every question. Now, quite the opposite of his sentiment, it seemed that circumstances had been much simpler when she was young. It was age and experience that complicated things.

Naomi shook her head sadly. "We have been fortunate here, Jonathan. We have ever had upright leadership. It is understandable that this bewilders Faith."

Faith turned her hopeful gaze to her mother.

"Then you understand?"

"Aye, child, I do. But your father is right. All of us have sacrificed much to build this colony, based firmly upon God's law. We cannot weaken it from within by defying our own government."

She took a deep breath and offered Faith a weakly apologetic smile. "It is an honor to be asked to stand at the side of the man who leads our church and our village. Reverend Williams is new here, and mayhap we are, as yet, unused to his zealousness. And it may be that he will soften to you, once he gets to know you."

"Nay, Mother, you cannot mean this!"

An angry hiss escaped through Jonathan's teeth. "You will not speak that way to your mother! This defiance is most unlike you."

Faith closed her eyes and forced her features to relax. She had learned long ago to smother her anger, swallow any argument. In her mind she beseeched God for patience.

"Forgive me, Father. I am distraught."

Jonathan sighed and sank onto the bench, next to the open Bible. "Perhaps your mother and I should discuss this first."

Faith folded her hands serenely so that only an astute observer would notice that her knuckles were white or that her jaw was tense from gritting her teeth.

Naomi sat in one of the straight-backed chairs and spoke with her accustomed candor. "Nay, let her sit with us. She must understand the whole of the situation. Faith, I think the minister is set in this course."

"Aye," Jonathan concurred, although he scowled. "And there are those who will support him. We know well that three of the men she has refused are bitter, and George Mayfield and Roger Smith have considerable influence."

"And of course," Naomi added, "there's always the governor."

Jonathan gave his wife a skeptical look. "Surely you do not think that the governor will trouble himself over our daughter's marriage. We are not such important people, Naomi."

Leaning forward, she replied, "If it is put to him as a matter of Owen Williams's authority being placed into question, do you really believe he will not defend his friend?"

"Then you truly believe Williams will win her sooner or later?" Jonathan asked.

She leaned back again, a look of defeat in her eyes. "I believe so, and I think it is in Faith's best interest that we anger him not in the course of this thing. It would not go well for her. We must look to God here."

The tears that had stung Faith's eyes could be denied no longer. She knew that she must plead or rage, and that anger had never moved her parents. Whatever the cost, she had to change their minds. "Please, I beg of you, do not marry me to a man who thinks so ill of me. I will marry Goodman Smith or Mayfield if it will soothe them and gain us their friendship."

Jonathan rubbed his hand across his eyes. The slight slump in his shoulders and his steadfast refusal to look into her eyes spoke all that was in his troubled mind.

"We may yet soften his heart. Your mother is right. Once he comes to know you . . ." But he let the sentence drift away, unfinished.

Naomi rose to look out the window. Her eyes scanned the forest beyond, as though she sought something far in the distance. "There is, perhaps, another way."

Hope lit Faith's anguished face. "Anything, Mother!"

"It is not your consent that concerns me." Naomi turned to Jonathan. "We can send her to my sister."

He bolted from his seat and thundered, "Out of the question!"

"For Faith's sake, can you not release your harsh judgment of Elizabeth?"

"No one wants Faith's happiness more than I, but we are talking of her immortal soul!"

"She is strong in her beliefs, and Elizabeth is still a Christian, after all."

"A Christian? She's a *Catholic*, Naomi!"

Faith barely registered anything beyond her mother's first statement. Her mother's sister? In all of Faith's life, her mother had never spoken of a sister. Her grandmother, God keep her immortal soul, had spoken of two miscarriages and a young son lost on the journey from England to the Caribbean island of Cigatoo. They had tried to settle the island with others of their faith, but it had been impossible to farm, and they had come here, to New England. By then, her mother had already married another of the island's settlers, Jonathan. No one had spoken of any other family members. In a daze, she took her mother's place in the chair by the fire.

"They are Anglican now," Naomi said.

"What?"

"Jamaica is English now, Jonathan. They were allowed to stay because Elizabeth is English, but her husband, Miguel, had to convert."

"So it is that easy for Elizabeth, is it? Be set firmly upon the path of righteousness, but convert to Catholicism for the sake of a mere man, and when the political winds blow another direction, convert again." He began to pace in agitation before adding, "And how do you know all of this?"

"I wrote her," she said, and her voice dared him to challenge her. "Sixteen years ago, when the Spanish were defeated and Jamaica fell to the English. I wanted to know if she was well. I received her reply a year and a half later. We have not written since, but I believe my daughter would be welcome at Winston Hall."

"Jamaica?" Faith's timid inquiry brought her parents' attention back to her. "You have a sister in Jamaica?"

Naomi smiled and moved back to the fireside near her daughter. "Her name is Elizabeth Fernandez de Madrid y Delgado Cortes." When Faith simply blinked, her mother laughed. "Thank goodness she followed English custom and merely took his last name instead of adding her own to the mix."

"How can you make light of this?" Jonathan interrupted. "When it became clear that our tobacco farms would never be successful on Cigatoo, we stayed in the Caribbean until we could find passage to New England." He paused, crossing his arms. A disgusted look marked his austere features. "While we were there, Elizabeth took up with a Spaniard who owned a sugar plantation on the island of Jamaica."

Taking a step toward him, Naomi replied. "Oh,

Jonathan, you make it sound so sordid. She fell in love with him. She married him. She did not 'take up' with him."

His face did not soften. "She became a Catholic."

"His church would not marry them otherwise."

"And what is his faith to him that he could cast it aside when the island changed hands?"

"Wait!" Faith cried. "Scripture tells us that we must judge not, lest we be judged. Perhaps it is not our place to condemn—my aunt." How strange that sounded to her, an aunt!

"Nay, Faith, you are grasping at straws. I will not send my daughter half the world away to be cared for by an idolatress!"

Naomi interrupted. "It is as I told you; she is Anglican."

"Fine, then a woman who mistakes a political faction for a religion!"

Faith barely heard her father's objections as her whole mind wrapped itself around this one hope. "Mother, do you really think she would have me?" To ease her father's worries, she added, "Perhaps I could find a suitable husband there. There are still Puritans in the Caribbean."

"Enough! I am the master of this house, and I forbid it! When we left the Caribbean we agreed that Elizabeth's name would ne'er be spoken in this new land. Naomi, it was foolish of you to have broken that silence. We will put an end to this discussion right now. God willing, the morning will put a fresh face on this matter. For now, let it rest!" Silence followed her father's outburst, and after a pointed look at the two women, he stormed out of the door in the direction of the joinery.

Naomi went to the kitchen to quietly cut onions for the stew pot while Faith punched down her bread dough with more force than usual. She divided it and placed each portion in its own pan.

"Perhaps I should not have offered false hope," her mother said at last.

In a small voice, through a tight throat, Faith whispered, "Will you speak with him tonight?"

Naomi sighed. "Aye, I'll speak with him."

Afternoon faded into evening, and the males of the Cooper family left the joinery. Seven-year-old David and twelve-year-old Isaiah, both towheads, playfully splashed each other at the pump outside as they washed away the day's sweat and sawdust. Naomi clapped her hands and firmly reminded them that the spring evening was too chill for such play. They traipsed in noisily behind Faith's twin brother, Noah. With a happy grin, Noah accepted a small pail of stew and half a loaf of bread to take home to his wife, who was heavy with their first child. His hands full, he shook a stray lock of blond hair from his face.

"I thought I'd deliver that sideboard tomorrow, Father, if you can spare me from the joinery."

Faith's spirits lifted. "Are you bound for Boston, then? May I go with you?" Boston was always exciting, and it would be a pleasant diversion from her woes.

"I'd welcome the company," he replied. "The hours get long when I'm riding alone."

"Aye, that's a fine idea," Jonathan agreed. He exchanged a quick glance with his wife that said they had much to discuss while Faith was gone.

Noah left, taking his mother's food and his sister's promise to be ready to go early the next day. At dinner, David and Isaiah were subdued. The tension between their sister and parents was palpable, and in a home where discord was most uncommon, it dampened their usual boisterous natures. The meal was a quiet one, punctuated by the clatter of dishes and the occasional strained cough.

That night, Faith blew out the candle next to her bed and stared up at the pitch-black ceiling. "Dear God," she prayed in a fervent whisper, "grant me deliverance, some means of escaping this terrible fate. I beg you, I will try harder, do anything! Please, show me the way!"

In the keeping room, Naomi knelt by the waning fire, glad that her husband and children had gone upstairs and that she had a few moments to herself. Like her daughter in the room above her, she spoke her heart in her prayers.

"Dear Father in Heaven, for many years now my church and my family have been blessings beyond measure. I am deeply and profoundly grateful. But now, my two greatest blessings are entirely at odds. We need Your guidance! I sacrificed my sister for You, once. I beg of You, Holy Father, do not take my daughter as well."

Knowing that God saw into her heart, she made no attempt to stop her tears. "Faith has been foundering for a while. I have sensed it. And yet, she seeks only to please us and to obey You. This test is too much, and I fear that we will lose her! In the darkest moments, I fear that You will lose her, as well. It is not merely her comfort I look to. It is her soul.

"And Jonathan's, too," she whispered, uncertainly. "I have never seen him so torn. How can he choose between You and his child's happiness?

"I know it is not *my* will that must be done, but *Thy*

will. I have no doubt that you have a plan for my girl, just as you did for me. But I cannot hide from You my dearest hope that Owen Williams is not a part of it, that you will send her another, even as you sent me my Jonathan. But if he is—if she must endure this trial—help her to keep her faith. Hold her, keep her, protect her in Your love. Amen."

Chapter 3

Rambling buildings of brick and wood surrounded Boston Harbor, a veritable forest of masts and tightly furled sails. The timbers stood tall against the pale gray sky and deep greenish gray of the ocean. Mammoth ships rocked and creaked in the lapping waves. The smell of salty sea air mingled with fish, though occasionally a faint hint of spices would waft through, a ribbon of tangy sweetness amid the earthier scents.

Faith loved coming to town and the port, where the wide world beyond their little village was displayed in wares brought by the ships and the men who sailed them. People came and went around her in the chilly spring air, and it was easy to believe Noah when he told her that Boston had nearly two thousand people living in it!

She was always careful to keep her eyes modestly downcast, but she walked among them listening to their foreign tongues. Sea captains and other men of importance wore elegant coats and frothy lace, far more adornment than the sumptuary regulations of most Puritan villages permitted. Faith dreamed of England, where everyone was so refined. The ships now in Boston Harbor would carry timber, sugar, and all manner of products from the New World up the Thames to London. She tried to envision that faraway city, one that she knew dwarfed the port she currently explored. Mayhap some of those things would find their way to the king. It seemed to her that London was exactly the opposite of her village. It was a city full of changes and chances . . . and choices.

For a bare moment, she allowed herself to imagine such a life. She would open her wardrobe and ask herself, "Shall I wear this pink gown today or perhaps this lovely yellow one?" She would walk among the shops and dare to choose some exotic scent from the Far East to dab behind each ear. And gentlemen would court her. She would choose a man she could love, not merely accept a man who was suitable. A dark cloud smothered her lovely fantasy. It seemed that she was not to be allowed any choice at all in her husband.

Noah brought with him a beautifully wrought sideboard that had been commissioned by a shipmaster's wife, and while Faith strolled through the market outside of the Boston Town House, he delivered the piece. She had promised her mother that she would pick up sugar and salt, but as she made her way through the crowd, she found herself distracted by a bolt of peacock blue silk. Glancing guiltily to either side, she reached out to finger the luxurious fabric.

It was just at that moment that Captain Geoffrey Hampton spied the pretty little Puritan maid who wistfully caressed his merchandise. He tucked his hat beneath his claret velvet-clad arm, revealing a head of thick, light brown hair.

What a shame, he thought. He knew women well enough to know they had a weakness for lovely things, and here this one was, primly ensconced in a plain, russet wool skirt and bodice and modest linen collar.

"Captain Hampton?"

The seaman tore his eyes from the girl to look impatiently at the merchant he had been trading with. "Aye, forgive me," Geoff replied. "I lost my concentration for a moment."

The merchant wore somber clothes, and a wide collar proclaimed him a member of the same religious sect as the woman. Shaking his head, he looked at her. "Aye, I see what you mean. I cannot fathom what her family is thinking to allow her on the docks unescorted. You there!" he called to her. "I doubt me that is on your shopping list!"

The girl looked up at him and flushed. Whether 'twas guilt or anger, Geoff could not tell, and she fled before he could determine. He was sorely tempted to take the man to task for speaking so harshly to her, but he smelled money and a sizeable sale.

"I must say," the merchant said, resuming their previous conversation, "I didn't expect to see you here, what with so much gold for the taking in Panama. Surely you were there for the raid last winter?"

His question did nothing to soothe Geoff's irritation. "Aye, so I was. But the Spaniards had taken most of the treasure from Panama City in earlier ships. As for what was left—Captain Henry Morgan saw to the loading of it, and most of the gold went with him and his cronies. We were fortunate to have been left our vessel. As fate would have it, we encountered a small Spanish merchant ship in the Windward Passage between Cuba and Hispaniola."

"The source of this fine merchandise?" His companion gestured broadly at the array of items that surrounded them—casks of rum, bolts of silk, spices, costly trinkets that had once graced fair Spanish women.

Geoff smiled humorlessly. "He was outnumbered four to one when we boarded, so the captain was most generous with us."

"'Tis sure the Spaniards will be cursing your names for years to come."

"Aye, I suppose so. For now they'll be busy enough rebuilding Panama City. The entire place is naught but ashes now."

The merchant chuckled. "Well, however you may think of Captain Morgan, the king is sure to love him. More gold for England's coffers, less for Spain's. My wife insists that buying from privateers is the same as stealing. By my reckoning, you're God's way of diverting funds from the Catholic Church, corrupt old whore that she is."

"Well, it would be a lie if I said that I cared about the politics of it," Geoff replied. Somehow he doubted that the merchant cared much about the politics or religion either. They were convenient excuses for profiting from plunder. Mayhap Geoff was little better than a pirate, but at least he was honest about it. "Still, Morgan could never have done it alone. Show a brave Englishman your favor and take some of this off my hands."

He spent the morning haggling with merchants and giving the earnings over to Giles Courtney, the ship's quartermaster, to be divided up later. They sailed on the morrow, and he intended to enjoy the afternoon and evening. Boston lacked the vast array of entertainment available in Port Royal, Jamaica, but there was sure to be a willing wench somewhere.

In the back of his mind he could not rid himself of the merchant's hypocrisy or the maid's blush at having been chastised for so little a sin as admiring a bolt of silk. Hell of a curse, that, to live in Massachusetts. On a lark, he held back one item, and he tucked it beneath his arm as he strolled, his brown eyes with their golden flecks scanning the crowd.

Beyond his view, Faith wended her way through the throng, listening to blends of Dutch, English, and a bit of Portuguese, when a heavy Cockney accent caught her attention.

"Aye, it's been a profi'able journey, but oi'm fer gettin' back to Port Royal. The rum's cheap and the wenches willin'. The fair ship *Destiny* sails at dawn, and oi'll be 'ome with gold in me pockets."

"Is yer cap'n all they say?" his compatriot asked.

"Aye, fair to a fault, but 'e foights loik the very divil. Le' me say, it's glad oi am to be on 'is side. Oi'd loik not t'meet 'im at the other soid of 'is cutlass."

Faith froze and fought to stem the impulsive thoughts that flooded her rebellious mind. A ship bound for Jamaica that sailed on the morrow! She had asked God for deliverance—was this it? Nay, to follow such a mad path was to disobey her parents and her church! She would have to travel half a world away to a woman she hadn't even known existed until yesterday! Mayhap she would only be turned away, stranded in a foreign land.

Sugar and salt. She was here to buy sugar and salt, not to find passage to Jamaica. Besides, she had no coin to pay her way. And he said the captain fought like the devil. What manner of man was this? She could hardly place her trust in the stranger she had heard the man with the Cockney accent describe.

Spices and seasonings abounded among the street hawkers, and when she was quite certain she had found the thriftiest bargain for the items she needed, she took out the coin to pay for them. The seller had a fresh shipment of cinnamon, as well, and Faith was reminded that she had used nearly the last of theirs on gingerbread the previous day, so she added it to her purchase. She could see her family's wagon from the street stall, and since Noah was nowhere in sight, she decided to walk a little longer.

Destiny. The name of the ship rang in her head like a bell, and again came the niggling question whether this was the answer to her prayer. She told herself that she simply wanted a breath of sea air when she wandered out onto the wharf, not leaving until she found the small, elegant brigantine. The sails of the ship's two masts were furled, but in her mind, Faith could see them filled with wind out upon the high seas.

Perhaps half an hour later, Faith placed her bags into the wagon. She did not notice the golden-eyed sea captain who stared at her through a tavern window. He had nearly given up looking for her, but now, he rose and gulped the last of his rum. Tossing a coin to the serving wench, he strode to the door.

Faith, however, never spared the tavern a glance. She simply turned to Noah when he walked up behind her to place a small set of carpenter's tools next to her purchases.

"For David," he explained when she gave him a curious glance.

Forcing herself to stop thinking of the ship, she turned to her twin and gestured to the tools. "For a seven-year-old?"

"A common age for an apprentice."

Faith sighed. "I suppose it is. He still seems so young to me."

Noah looked across the street and waved, then told his sister to wait while he greeted the friend he had spied. She gazed longingly at the ships anchored in the harbor, picking out the twin masts she knew belonged to *Destiny*. In but a few weeks that ship would sail into warm waters and dock at an island that had never known a hard, cold winter.

She thought back to her parents' tales of the time they had spent in the Caribbean. Tales of lush, colorful flowers and bright, loud birds. Springtime in New England had its own charms, to be sure. But on this day, the sea and sky were a leaden gray, heavy colors reflected in the skirts and coats of most of the people who came and went down the busy street. Caught up in these thoughts, it was a moment before she saw the man who had come to stand beside her.

Geoff gave her his best smile, one that had served him well with the fairer sex, but she only looked at him in confusion. So much for dazzling the girl with his charm, he thought to himself. It was pure folly to be standing there with her at all, but he noticed that she was yet even prettier than he had first realized. And ere she had spied him, there had been such a look of longing in her eyes as she stared out at the harbor. 'Twas a look he knew well, for he had seen it in the eyes of many a fresh-faced cabin boy seeking adventure on the high seas. He doubted not that just such a look had lit his own face from time to time.

"Aye," he said to her, "the smell of the sea and the line of the horizon, they stir the blood, do they not?"

Faith gaped at him in wonder. Had the man read her very mind? Hastily, she searched her memory for any recognition of the handsome stranger before her. He wore a fashionable coat of rich velvet, the shoulders of the garment stretched taut by the shoulders of the man. The hem of the coat and an elaborate gold vest flared over trim hips, brushing the tops of serviceable, well-cared-for boots. Elegant lace spilled from the neck of his shirt and the wide cuffs of his sleeves, the delicate froth only enhancing his masculine features and competent hands. His hair, surely his own rather than one of the wigs worn by men of fashion, fell over his shoulders in thick, light brown waves streaked golden by the sun. A low-crowned, wide-brimmed hat with an outrageous ostrich feather topped his head. Surely she would have remembered if her father or brother had done business with such a man!

He turned gracefully in front of her. "Do I pass inspection?" he asked.

Faith blushed. She had been staring, no doubt. Gathering her dignity back around her, she replied, "Forgive me, do I know you, sir?"

"Nay, I am Captain Geoffrey Hampton. I could not help but notice you amid my wares outside of the Boston Town House earlier, and I fear my customer chased you away ere you could make up your mind. I have a small token of apology." He pulled a length of the stunning blue silk from beneath his arm and offered it to her with a courtly bow.

She raised her golden brows in alarm and looked all around for possible witnesses. "You are too bold! Well you know I cannot possibly accept such a thing!"

He gave a dramatic sigh and placed his hand over his heart in comic affectation. "It wounds me to see so fair a maid in such a drab gown. Perhaps, then, just for a petticoat?"

Handsome he might be, but who did this popinjay think he was? Faith strained her neck in an attempt to sight her brother, but her heart sank when she recognized another familiar form striding purposefully in her direction.

"Please, sir, you will leave at once. You compromise me by your very presence!"

"Faith Cooper!" the Reverend Williams's voice bellowed. "Who is this man you meet so boldly at the docks? What business have you with him?"

"I have no business, Reverend. This man accosted me!"

"Accosted you? With this silk?"

Geoff stepped between the girl and the irate clergyman. "I must accept full responsibility. I have a sister in England with just this maid's coloring. I did but ask if I could view the cloth against her skin. She was just in the midst of giving me a sound dressing-down."

The minister narrowed his eyes suspiciously, and his gaze swept Geoff from crown to toe. "Think you that we are so provincial that we can be deceived by the likes of you? This woman is to be my wife! Keep to your dockside harlots and leave good Christian women alone!"

Geoff looked at the girl. Her face had flushed a deep red, and her chin dropped to her chest. Something tugged inside of him, and he lifted that chin to look into her eyes. Her demeanor might have appeared utterly subservient, but in her gaze he saw unexpected mettle. A damned shame, he thought, this extraordinary woman with that irritating little man.

"Unhand her!" the minister shouted.

Dropping his hand, Geoff pulled himself up to his full six feet and looked down at the other man, clearly four or five inches shorter, then back to the woman. A damned shame, indeed. It was sure this wench would never know a moment of pleasure at the preacher's holier-than-thou hands, and perhaps more shameful, he didn't believe the man had the good sense to enjoy her much, either.

"Forgive me, miss. I meant to cause you no trouble."

Something powerful welled in Faith's heart, a consuming urge to seal her fate. Though she was sure to pay for it later, she dazzled him with a friendly smile. "You've caused no harm that was not already done, good sir. I wish your sister joy in that new cloth. She will look most fetching, and you shall doubtless be called upon to protect her from the attentions of many a devilish rogue."

The nasty little man next to him sputtered, but the captain could not spare a glance from the girl. She would put the fairest angel to shame. Heaven help her betrothed, for this one had a will of her own, and her eyes were those of a woman who had made a momentous decision.

From the corner of her eye, she spied Noah, who quickened his steps. Faith had recounted the previous day's events on the way into town, and she was sure that her brother would realize that his sister, Owen Williams, and a handsome stranger were an ill mix.

"Good day to you, Reverend Williams," Noah said breathlessly. "I hope there's been no trouble here."

"It is as your sister says, no harm has been done that was not done before. I see that I shall have my work cut out for me. No matter." His chilling blue gaze settled on Faith. "I shall have you back upon the path of righteousness. Make no mistake about that."

The other two men glanced at each other uneasily, but the minister's cold stare and foreboding words did not touch their intended target. She had well and truly made up her mind; one way or another, she would never marry this man.

They arrived home shortly after the dinner hour and sat at the table with their parents, even before the dishes were all washed. Noah, clearly worried for his sister's welfare, repeated the afternoon's events to their parents. The conversation held little interest for David, as he sat by the fire playing with a wooden horse, but Isaiah listened intently, his eyes wide with concern.

"Why does the minister not like Faith?" he asked.

Naomi raised her eyebrows at her husband, and he set his jaw before he turned to his son and replied. "The minister did but misunderstand the situation. He does not dislike Faith. In fact, he's to be her husband." Jonathan seemed to try to inject a sense of cheer into the words, but failed miserably.

Faith sucked in her breath but held her tongue. She knew that if she said one word, she would be entirely unable to stop herself. Instead, she rose abruptly and set to washing the dishes her mother had scraped and stacked earlier. Anger made her careless, and she immediately chipped a heavy earthenware pitcher.

Naomi joined her, and carefully taking the pitcher from her daughter's hands, she pulled Faith away from the task. "Isaiah," she said, "take David to bed. It wouldn't hurt you to get a good night's sleep, either."

"But, Mother," little David protested. "We have but finished dinner."

Isaiah shushed him and took up the wooden horse. "We'll play awhile, and then I'll read to you. How about First Samuel, Chapter Seventeen?"

Even through her anger, Faith had to smile. What a little man Isaiah was becoming. He knew that David never tired of the story of the king for whom he was named and Goliath, the giant he defeated. But as soon as the boys disappeared upstairs, the softness that had touched her heart hardened again.

She turned abruptly to her father and, despite years of Biblical proscriptions against challenging her parents, asked, "So after all this, I'm to marry him anyway?"

"It was a misunderstanding, Faith," he replied tersely.

She looked to her mother next. "He accused me of encouraging strange men on the docks of Boston Harbor!" she pleaded. "Am I to spend the rest of my life being so 'misunderstood'?"

Naomi shook her head. "I know not what to say to you, child. Ours is a small world here, our choices limited. We must hold fast to our belief in God's plan, though at times it may be beyond our ken."

But there was a much wider world beyond Massachusetts, Faith thought to herself. "And that is to be the end of it?" she asked. "You will do nothing to seek another way?"

Jonathan ran a rough hand through his graying hair. "I went to Aaron Jacob's saw mill today."

"Aye?" Faith prodded.

"He has withdrawn his offer. It seems he is no longer sure that the two of you will suit."

"He only says that because Reverend Williams has told him to!"

"George Mayfield and Roger Smith are of similar minds. I have no doubt that 'twill be the same no matter whom I speak to. Name for me a man in this village who will defy Williams in this."

"I can name the man who should," Faith answered, and though her voice was hardly more than a whisper, it carried loudly in the quiet of the room. She looked at him, her eyes filled with reproach. "Will you not speak for me, Father?"

Unable to meet her gaze, he studied the back of his hand. "I will not pretend that I like the path this has taken, but it is not for us to question God's will."

"This is not God's will! 'Tis the will of Owen Williams!" Faith cried.

"He is our minister!" Jonathan shouted back. "His will and God's are one and the same. Mayhap he is not so far wrong. Mayhap I have been lax if my daughter thinks to raise her voice to me."

Faith stared at her father in openmouthed disbelief. If it had come to this, then there seemed but one choice left to her. God help her if she chose wrongly. Before she could foolishly speak her mind, she turned and fled up the stairs to the little cubby that served as her room.

Naomi watched Faith's flight before turning hard eyes upon her husband. "Do not tell me that you cannot conceive what distress would cause our Faith to speak so to you."

"She is my child, and you my wife. I will not be questioned and defied."

"This is not like you, Jonathan."

He moved to the fire and sank into a chair. His

voice lacked its usual strength and carried a heavy weight. "How can I abide your questions when I have no answers, Naomi? What would you have me do? Williams is not so old that we can hope for his death ere Faith has passed a marriageable age. Who will care for her when she is older? It cannot be we two, forever. Besides, she will want a home of her own, children . . ."

"Aye, and rightly so. She will make someone a good wife and be a fine mother, but not with this man. You know as well as I that she will never find contentment there. Perhaps if we looked to another village," Naomi suggested.

"With Williams so well connected to the governor? I tell you, Naomi, I have examined this from every angle. There are forces at work here that we cannot comprehend."

Naomi sighed. Jonathan was right about one thing. No one in the colony would dare to cross someone with Owen Williams's influence. "Will you not even consider—"

But before she could finish, Jonathan barked, "Never! Do not bring it up again!"

With another glance up the stairs, Naomi fought the tears that threatened. "We will lose her, Jonathan. I tell you, we will lose her. I cannot bear what my mother bore. It nearly killed her when she left Elizabeth behind, never to speak to her again. I know what the loss of my sister cost me."

Jonathan rose and took his distraught wife in his arms. "'Twas Elizabeth's choice. She chose that papist above her family. But Faith is a good girl. In time, she will accept her fate and make the best of it. You underestimate her."

"It is you who underestimate her," Naomi said. Sick at heart, she bid her husband good night. For a moment, she paused outside Faith's door. Well she knew what doubts plagued the child, but having no comfort to offer her only daughter, she moved on to her own bed.

Chapter 4

Far to the east, out on the Atlantic Ocean, there was another who, like Faith, knew that his only hope lay in divine assistance. He sailed upon a ship called *Magdalena*, bound from Spain to Cartagena, the heart of the Spanish Main. She was a small ship, a carrack, but Capitán Diego Montoya Fernandez de Madrid y Delgado Cortes loved her as though she were a proud galleon. Perhaps he did not own her, but she was his to command, and he took his post most seriously.

He knelt at the ship's rail, his hat on the deck, baring black hair that fell past his shoulders. Memories of a cool, candlelit cathedral back in Cadiz conjured the smell of incense in the ocean wind, familiar, soothing. He closed his dark eyes and envisioned the statue to one side of the golden altar, where the Savior's face held utter confidence in His Father's power and love. On the other side, the blessed virgin looked down upon Diego with an expression of infinite understanding. But she was not the Mary to whom Diego prayed in quiet but fervent Spanish.

"Santa Maria Magdalena, do not leave me. I am ready to captain this ship, I am. I have been second-in-command for a very long time. The saints have been very good to me, and I am most grateful. But it is a lot of responsibility, and the sea is fickle. I ask your help, because the ship is named for you, *Magdalena.* Diego is not perfect, but neither were you, eh?" He chuckled a bit, as if he and the reformed sinner were old friends, but his merriment was feigned and didn't last.

"Maybe I am a little afraid. Our captain is dead of a fever that I pray does not linger on our ship. I lost many friends in Panama City. So now I'm not so sure as I once was. You think I am a coward, maybe? I admit, I am a little worried, but I am not a coward. I will challenge these pirates who steal the gold from our ships and cities. Gold that should go to Spain and then to the Church. I will make you proud."

He crossed himself and stood. Men's lives rested on his decisions, as did his employer's cargo. An employer who did not know that Diego was now the captain of his ship.

Even as she quietly led one of her father's horses down the darkened street in the middle of the village, Faith wished that she had had the nerve to press one last kiss to little David's brow. She walked past Noah and Esther's house and felt a wave of pure rage at the unfairness of it all. Likely as not, she would never see her twin brother's child. Like her, the child might well never know that he or she had an aunt.

But the rage didn't last. If she were entirely honest with herself, there was a sense of adventure that quickened her pulse every bit as much as her anger and nervousness. Once she was beyond the village, she mounted the horse and rode as fast as she dared toward Boston.

She tried her best to focus upon the sound of the horse's hooves on the packed dirt road, ignoring the rustling of night creatures in the forest that flanked her. When she was a child, she had been told many a tale of the witches and demons that stalked the woods at night. Such stories were not merely told as fairy tales. They were intended as very real warnings about the dangers that lurked in the wilderness that was, as yet, untouched by the light of God's Word. Long ago, Faith had begun to question such wild stories, but on this night, ever so aware of the many sins that she had taken upon her soul, she eyed the dense blackness. It would not have surprised her to find that burning red eyes peered at her from the roadside.

At last, she reached the outskirts of Boston, unmolested by any agents of Satan. Quickly, she tied the horse to the little fence that surrounded one of the churches her father had helped to build pews for. Surely the minister would recognize the mount and see to it that it was returned.

Even in the dark of night, Faith was able to find the ship *Destiny*. Though she suffered a thousand doubts about her reckless plan, she had no doubt at all that this ship was the answer to her prayer. How else might it be that she should learn of her aunt in Jamaica, then stumble upon a ship leaving just in time to take her there? Surely this was certain proof that God never intended her to be Owen Williams's bride!

Her confidence wavered as she looked up the tall side of the intimidating vessel. The watchman leaned upon the rail where a lantern sat and cast flickers of light and shadow across his face. What came next? How foolish she felt. Surely even a novice to the sea would have assumed there would be some watch and that she could not stride, bold as brass, onto the deck of the ship. Under her arm, she had tucked her best summer dress of indigo cotton along with a clean shift, coif, and apron. She also carried with her a metal pail that held six tallow candles, a striker and flint with which to light them, and a small quantity of food. She planned to make her way to the ship's galley late at night when they were under way. Would there be some unconsidered complication there, as well?

Another man came to the rail, and after exchanging a few words and a laugh, they both turned and vanished from sight. There was no time to contemplate further consequences. Faith pulled her shoes from her feet, wincing at the cold ground beneath them, and ran silently up the gangplank. No sooner had she reached the top than she saw the two men across the deck, and she quickly ducked behind a barrel. She curled up tightly, pulling her skirts in beside her. Behind a veil of clouds, the moon glowed dully, and Faith watched the lantern light as it moved across the deck, certain her short breath and pounding heart would reveal her presence to the two men. They returned to the gangplank, speaking softly.

"'Tis a wonder the cap'n'll wait fer 'im," the watchman pondered. He held the lantern aloft and seemed to gaze somewhere out into the dark docks beyond.

"We cannot sail without our carpenter, that's sure. Well, I'll keep a sharp eye fer 'im. Ye can turn in now," the newcomer suggested.

It was a marvel that they could not hear her heart hammering in her chest or the blood pounding in her ears. Looking sharply through a pale mist, she realized that her breath was coming out in little puffs of steam, and she worried that it, too, might give her away. Clapping a hand over her mouth availed her naught, for the steam simply drifted from her nostrils instead. So she breathed as little as possible and watched from the shadows as the first man descended a ladder to the lower decks of the ship. The new watchman lit his long pipe, filling the air with the pungent scent of tobacco, and hummed softly to himself. By her best reckoning, Faith thought she had a bit more than an hour until dawn. By then she had to be safely tucked away in the hold or she would surely be discovered!

Faintly, at first, she heard the strains of a drunkard's ribald song on the dock below, but it came louder, until the watchman called down to the caterwauling man. "Ahoy there, Ken Taylor, ye drunken fool! We're to sail in a few hours' time! Whoa there, a few steps more and ye'll be in the drink! Wait there a minute and let a friend get ye on board."

The man clenched his pipe tightly between his teeth and mumbled a few choice words around it as he descended the gangplank. The invisible drunk called out a hearty welcome, the sound of which cut through the quiet night like the serrated edge of a knife.

Again the hand of Providence seemed to have given her a brief opportunity, and Faith took it. She bolted across the deck and descended the same ladder she had seen the first man go down. It was surprisingly dark below deck. A bit of weak moonlight spilled through the hatch, but there was neither a lantern nor candle lit anywhere. She paused, listening intently.

Merciful heavens, she thought, *what have I gotten myself into?* She could barely make out the dark shapes that surrounded her, but the sounds were unmistakable— snoring! She might not be able to see, but there was no question that she had stumbled upon a goodly number of sleeping sailors! She didn't move, fearing that she might trip and make some noise in the dark, but above her she heard the watchman dragging the inebriated Mr. Taylor to the hatch. In the meager light from the opening, she made out a clear passage to the wall, and she raced to it, pressing herself against it in the shadows.

The two men made their cautious way down the ladder, the watchman carrying the lantern. They moved away from her, keeping her out of its halo of light, but affording her a glimpse of her surroundings. Indeed, the floor was packed with slumbering men, none sober if her nose was any judge of them. Still, there was something of a path among them, and she should be able to make it to the next hatch and into the hold when the two new arrivals left. To her dismay, the sailors weren't the only living occupants of the lower deck, and she stifled a scream at the rat that scampered quickly over her stocking foot. Perhaps this would be more difficult than she had anticipated.

The watchman tried to settle the carpenter into a relatively comfortable spot and resume his duties on deck, but the drunkard wrapped his arm around the other man's neck.

"Stay awhile yet, Lucy. There's a lovely gold coin in it fer ye," he mumbled in a sing-song voice.

"Lucy!" the watchman muttered. "Do I feel like yer Lucy to ye?" He took the man's hand and put it on his whisker-stubbled face.

"Well," the carpenter slurred, "ye're a might hairier than I thought. Ye don't smell as good, neither." He heaved a plaintive sigh into the watchman's face.

"Ugh!" the watchman cried. "Ye're a fine one to be talkin' about smells, Taylor. Now lemme go."

The one called Taylor peered up at his companion. "Ye're not so fair as I thought, either."

"Sleep it off, man."

Taylor mumbled something else, and as quickly as that, he was snoring with the rest of the crew. Faith had been certain that the commotion would wake those around them, but no one stirred. The watchman muttered a few more profanities, then ascended the ladder back up to the deck.

The moment his feet disappeared through the hatch, Faith stepped quickly through the darkness in the direction of an opening that she hoped led to the lowest level. She had been sure of her direction, so she was completely stunned when she kicked something and it gave a muffled curse.

Tears stung her eyes, and she didn't dare move. She fought to keep her breathing silent and felt sweat trickle down her sides and between her breasts as she waited for the sailor she had roused to fall back into a deep slumber. When she tasted blood, she realized that she had bitten her lip in agitation. At last, she heard his breathing grow steady, and with considerably more caution, she picked her way to the hatch.

Greater courage it required by far to descend into the darkest bowels of the ship. Though she could see nothing, she recognized all too well the scurrying and squeaking that carried to her sensitive ears. Rats! Dearest God, how many? A damp, musty smell drifted up to her, and the air around her felt clammy and stagnant the farther she descended. She paused on the rungs of the ladder and conjured in her mind the cold, fanatical eyes of the man who would be her husband. This alone gave her the nerve to continue her descent.

At the bottom, she dared to strike a light, stifling cries of terror at the hundreds of little creatures that swarmed around her until she lit her candle and the beasts became shadows that darted beyond its illumination.

The hold was crowded with barrels and crates, but she found a nook that would serve her well. The candle seemed to hold the rodents at bay, but she dared not leave it lit long, risking discovery. Finally, she screwed up her courage and blew it out. At first, she sensed rather than felt the horrid beasts, but soon they ventured forward, squeaking and skittering. Constant motion seemed her only defense, and while she shooed them away, she found it easier to deal with them by thinking of other things.

It seemed unreal. Days before, the course of her life had been certain if unsatisfying. She had tried to be a dutiful and obedient daughter, and she had truly cared for the others in her village, gladly giving them what help and kindness she could. Of course, her theology taught her that mere good works did not move God—it was divine grace alone that saved the souls of the righteous. She had always hoped that with that, and with proper self-discipline, she would vanquish her doubts and weaknesses. Now it seemed that she had been counting on grace that belonged to her family members alone.

The thought of her family only deepened her misgivings. It had been all well and good to flee from Reverend Williams to an exotic island far away. But there was another side to this venture. She was leaving behind a home and parents that had sheltered her all through her youth. David and Isaiah would grow to manhood without her. Noah, the twin brother she had cherished all her life, would father children she would never meet. She was turning her back on the church that had guided her every step, and for what? To venture out upon a wide ocean that could well swallow her whole? And if it did not, she could find herself friendless upon an island peopled by pirates and ne'er-do-wells.

There in the dark, surrounded by rats, she utterly doubted her place among the elect. And yet, even that basic tenet of Puritan theology buckled in the dankness of the ship's hold. How could her life's path be preordained when she had taken such bold strides to forge her own way? Mayhap God had provided the means, but it was she who had found the courage to answer the call.

She felt a little better, contemplating her own bravery, and the ship rocked gently in the harbor. At last, her mind succumbed to the past two sleepless nights. Rats or no rats, she drifted into dreamless slumber.

When she awoke, the ship rocked with a violence entirely unlike the gentle sway that had lulled her to sleep. The hold was still dark, though the dimmest light fell from the hatch. Suddenly aware of the creatures that roamed freely across her prostrate form, Faith jumped up, and they scampered to safety. The boat pitched, and she fell against a crate, trying to steady herself and gain her bearings.

She had just thought to seek her provisions when the first faint inklings of nausea hit. She would have to wait for it to pass. Nevertheless, she sought her pail for good measure and gave a soft cry of dismay to find it empty! The wretched beasts had devoured everything, even her tallow candles!

Frustrated and overwhelmed, she curled into an

abject little ball in her space between the crates. Had she seriously mistaken the significance of the ship and its name? This didn't seem to be her deliverance at all! The turmoil of her thoughts mimicked the pitch of the vessel, none of which helped her queasiness. She groaned as she realized that she could no longer keep the meager contents of her stomach, and she reached hurriedly for her pail.

At first, seasickness left her merely miserable, but as the hours passed she became parched. Her throat burned; her empty stomach heaved until her back and ribs ached torturously. Doubled over with ruthless cramps, she lost the strength and will to brush away the rats. Through her dry, cracking lips she began to pray.

"Dear merciful God, please let me die. Take me from this earthly torture. Bring me to Your heavenly home, or if it be Your will, the fires of hell, but deliver me from this infernal, pitching torture chamber!"

Apparently God was not moved. Her heart continued to pump, her lungs to draw breath, but she found it increasingly difficult to keep her eyes open or to think. She passed in and out of dreams in which beautiful angels beckoned, only to have their glowing countenances replaced by a leering Owen Williams. Small forms flitted over her—tiny demons sent to torment her!

Occasionally, lucid thought broke through, and she knew that the day was passing. She was consumed by thirst but had neither means of quenching it nor any confidence that she could keep water down if she had any. It seemed impossible that she could make it through the night. The light from the hold waned, and with the darkness, one last rational thought seeped through her muddled brain. Every muscle aching, she dragged herself to the bottom of the ladder. Despite her impassioned pleas to her Maker, Faith was possessed of a strong will to live, and that impelled her up the ladder onto the level above.

Chapter 5

The ship's cook, Thomas Bartlett, stared in the dim light at the apparition that crawled from the ship's hold and collapsed in an untidy heap. He scratched his balding gray head, and then his substantial paunch under a shirt that might have once been white.

"Who are ye," he asked, "all drunk and dressed in women's clothes?" He crept up for a closer look. "Blimey, ye *are* a woman." Wrinkling his nose in distaste, he added, "And a sick one, at that."

With an anxious look around him, he left her where she lay and lumbered up the ladder to the deck above.

The sun had long ago sunk into the water, and a patch of stars twinkled where the clouds parted in the deep black sky. From time to time, the moon broke through, and its reflection danced upon the oily darkness of the ocean. One man played the fiddle while another, as accomplished a vocalist as he was a sailor, sang a lusty tune in a rich voice. None of this gave Thomas pause. He quickly found the quartermaster, Giles Courtney.

Giles stood at the helm, brown hair tied back in a tight queue that defied the wind that tore at it. The authority in his stance left no doubt that this was a man with nearly as much power as the captain himself.

"Ho there, Thomas!" he said. "You look as though you've seen a ghost!"

"I may have, Courtney. I may have!" The cook led Giles below, stumbling over the explanation of how he had come upon the girl who lay in a heap just above the hold.

Giles knelt next to her and pressed his hand to her throat. "She lives. I'll carry her to the captain's cabin. You go and fetch the captain!"

Thomas did as he was bid, glad to wash his hands of the responsibility. Giles lifted the woman's inert form and carried her aft to his friend's cabin. Once there, he set her gently on the bunk, lit the lantern affixed to the cabin wall, and studied their unexpected passenger. Her face was pale and drawn, and she smelled of sweat and sickness, but there was no doubt that clean and well, she'd make a fair sight to behold.

He shook his head grimly. A woman on board a ship of unruly men was bad enough, but a pretty one was sure to be trouble. He wondered what the cap'n would make of her. By the look of her dress, she was a Puritan, and likely a virtuous maid.

That might offer her some protection from men who respected such qualities, but Captain Hampton was a different story. He and Geoff had been friends since they were mere cabin boys, and Geoff had always thought women to have but one purpose. There was but one thing for it, Giles decided, and he bent down to scoop her up and move her to his own quarters. Ere he could do so, the arrival of the ship's commander stopped him.

Giles and Geoff were of an age, a score and seven

years. Both wore boots and breeches, and like Giles's, Geoff's hair was pulled back into a queue. But the resemblance ended there. Where Giles's eyes were gray and serious, Geoff's were nearly gold and held a perpetual hint of recklessness. Giles's deep brown locks would never dare escape the ribbon that held them in place, where strands of Geoff's lighter mane had pulled free in several places. Despite all of this, the captain appeared the elder, his features sharper, his mouth more cynical.

Geoff strode purposefully to the bunk, a question upon his lips, but he paused when he saw the woman who lay there. A look of recognition lit his eyes.

"What is it, Cap'n?" Giles asked. "Do you know this girl?"

"Aye—well, nay. That is—we've met, but I do not know her."

The cryptic answer did little to sate Giles's curiosity. "What on earth do you suppose she was doing in our hold?"

Geoff tilted his head and gave her an admiring look. "I think I have a notion, old friend."

"Don't hold back! What's this about?"

The captain only smiled slightly. He reached down and pulled the limp coif from her head, then freed her shimmering locks from their restraining pins. "Ah, Giles, this one's made for where we're bound." He twisted a nearly silver curl around his finger. "Her hair, it puts me in mind of a fine, white beach in the moonlight. And well I remember the color of her eyes, blue as the Caribbean itself."

Giles set his jaw and crossed his arms. "Hold there a moment, Geoff. I'll not argue that she's a lovely little thing, but she's hardly given you leave to run your fingers through her hair. I was thinking perhaps she'd do better in my cabin."

Geoff laughed, and though 'twas a sound that usually lightened Giles's serious demeanor, now it did but rankle. The cap'n's laughter died down to a chuckle. "Your cabin, indeed. Doubtless you'd find some nobler purpose for laying hands on the lass."

"Actually, I thought we'd share your cabin and give her a bit of privacy."

Geoff seemed to ponder the idea earnestly, but he couldn't fool his oldest friend. Giles knew Geoff would find some excuse to disagree.

"She'll be safer with me," Geoff said at last. "No man would dare breech my door. And much as I like you, old friend, I've no wish to be your bunkmate this voyage. This arrangement is better, for I'll protect her well."

"Protect her, will you?" Giles asked.

Geoff gave him a dark scowl, one he saved for crewmen who crossed him and the captains of vessels they seized. "'Tis my decision as cap'n," he said, "and 'tis final."

Unintimidated, Giles frowned back. Geoff seldom pulled rank between them, and he didn't appreciate the fact that he had chosen to do so now. It looked to be a stormy passage, indeed!

Faith continued to drift through unreal darkness. At first, she was caught in a complete void that neither light nor sound could penetrate. Then the blackness erupted into flames, and she stood on the bank of a lake of fire. She was consumed by thirst, but the molten lake offered no relief. From the darkness beyond, Satan tempted her in a voice she vaguely recognized from somewhere, though she couldn't quite place it.

"Here, love, take a little sip," he cajoled, holding a chalice of some evil elixir to her dry, parched lips.

She knew she should resist, but when the cool liquid touched her mouth, she swallowed against her will. Sweet, cool water flavored with rum trickled down her raw, burning throat, but it came from the devil, indeed! He gave her enough to whet her craving, but not nearly enough to quench her prodigious thirst.

"More," she croaked, heedless that its price could well be her soul.

"Nay. I know you've a powerful thirst, but you must go slowly to keep it down." He reached over and tenderly brushed a tendril of hair from her brow. The touch of the devil was soft, not at all the searing brand she expected.

She still could not see his face for the flickering shadows of the inferno around them, but he wore an ostrich feather upon his hat. "How odd," Faith murmured. This was hardly the horned and cloven-hoofed image of Old Scratch painted by the passionate preachers who had warned of his trickery.

At intervals, she floated slightly from the darkness that enveloped her to partake of more liquor-tinged water, and in time, her throat was soothed and she fell into a peaceful sleep.

She awoke more fully herself and found herself in a room lit by a window through which filtered soothing, gray light. Beneath her was a soft mattress in a fairly roomy bed that was bolted to the floor and against the wall. Still, she rocked, but it did not seem as violent as before, or she had grown accustomed to it.

She sought to familiarize herself with the rest of the chamber, but her gaze was arrested by the alarming sight of a man seated at a heavy desk, his unshod feet propped upon its scarred surface. He appeared to be sleeping, and though she could not recall where she had seen him, she knew that they had met.

Either he slept lightly or slumbered not at all, but when he opened his eyes and grinned at her, she knew at once who he was. He looked altogether different without his hat, his hair pulled back. The lace cravat and velvet coat had given way to a plain, loose-fitting shirt, its collar left open at the throat. He had doffed the boots and left his legs and feet bare from the knees down, sinewy calves resting casually on the desktop. Nonetheless, this was unmistakably the sea captain with the silk!

"Awake, are you?" he asked.

"Aye," she answered nervously as she sat up. "This is your ship, then?"

His brows shot up in puzzlement, and he lowered his legs. "Aye. Did you not know that when you came on board?"

"Nay. I knew only that this ship, *Destiny*, was bound for Jamaica, and I have a need to go there."

"You wound me," he teased. "I did think 'twas my devilish good looks and chivalry that lured you here. But tell me, now, what's in Jamaica?"

Faith hesitated. Perhaps it was unwise to tell him everything. In truth, if she never arrived, no one would know what had become of her. Even should her parents think to look for her in Jamaica, it was most unlikely that they would trace her to this ship. If he knew that, it might not go well for her. Instead, she thought it prudent to change the subject.

"You gave me water," she said.

He smiled, but the expression served only to make him look a bit dangerous. "Not going to tell me? So be it. We'll be at sea at least three weeks, possibly four. Neither of us is going anywhere, and there will be more than enough time for questions." He shrugged with catlike grace. "For now, aye, I gave you water. You were sore in need of it."

"Is this your room?"

"It is. Only the quartermaster, Giles, and myself have our own cabins. The rest of the crew sleeps where they can. A man may lay claim to one of the hammocks, but he's likely as not to lose it gaming."

His answer certainly raised its own problems, but Faith wasn't ready to contemplate them. At the moment, he was addressing her kindly and didn't appear immediately threatening.

"Are you not angry with me, then, for sneaking on and stowing away in the night?"

"Well, if you were a man, your welcome would be altogether different," he conceded, his golden eyes sweeping over her.

A jolt of fear raced through her, and she looked away. To her horror, she realized that her own clothing had disappeared, and she was covered only by an oversized man's shirt made of white lawn. The neck was not completely fastened, so it slipped over one shoulder, and the hem reached only the middle of her thighs, leaving her legs exposed amid the tangle of bedclothes. With a small gasp, she tucked them in and pulled the sheet to her chin.

"Modesty?" he chuckled. "'Tis a fetching trait in a pretty wench, but who do you think washed the sickness from you and changed your clothes?"

Faith's entire body went hot with shame, and she thought that surely fear would make her sick again. Oh, what could she have been thinking? She had boarded this vessel knowing nothing of its captain and crew. They could have been pirates for all she knew! He didn't look like a pirate, though. She had seen them at the harbor, a dirty, hairy lot. Still, his hard, lean face seemed suddenly sinister. She clutched the bed sheet in her sweaty fists.

He rose from the desk, appearing to fill the room with his tall form and broad shoulders. "Good God, woman! Do not look at me like that! Most women think me a handsome fellow, and I'll have you know I've yet to have to use force to get a wench to share my bed."

This pronouncement did little to calm Faith's consternation. "But you—you saw me!"

"Don't trouble yourself over it. It was no chore, I assure you, and I wasn't about to leave you in my clean bed as you were. Your dress was covered in rat filth. I doubt me 'tis even worth saving."

"I have another in the hold."

"In no better shape, I fear."

"They're all I have! I'll wash them myself, but I must keep them!"

The captain seemed to ponder that a moment. "Aye, you could do that, but laundry must be done on deck, and what will you wear while you do it?"

An image popped in her mind of herself in the lawn shirt, washing her clothes while a shipful of men watched on. Tears stung her eyes, and she buried her face in the covers.

"Now, now, love, I was only teasing." He sank onto the mattress next to her, and she scuttled backward to the wall with another gasp.

"Damn!" he muttered under his breath, and he stood up and crossed to the window. "'Tis a good thing you found your way here, and not on board some other ship. For God's sake, girl! Did it never enter your mind what you risked stowing away on a ship of men far from land and female company?"

Her cursed willfulness flared inside of her. She had been through too much to be chastised and sworn at. Without a thought for the consequences, she snapped, "I didn't think they would ever know I was there, and I wish you would not do that!"

"I promise, I'll stay all the way over here," Geoff replied.

"Nay, not that. Well, aye, stay over there, but I wish you would kindly keep the third commandment." He stared at her incredulously, and Faith thought that surely she had pushed too hard. He had not done her any harm, thus far, and it would not do to anger him, so she did as she had always done when faced with another's displeasure. She cast her eyes down and whispered, "If you please."

"What the hell is the third commandment?"

"What? What sort of Englishman does not know his commandments?" She risked another glance at him and saw that he regarded her with one brow lifted in disdain.

"The kind of Englishman who captains this ship and decides your fate. Humor me. What sacred commandment have I broken?"

Another chill of dread made her shiver. Keeping her voice and manner meek, she replied, "Thou shalt not take the name of the Lord thy God in vain."

Geoff snorted. "He's your god, you keep his commandments. Me, I've no use for him or them." He strode to the bedside and lifted her chin in his hand. "And why do you do that?"

She tried to pull free, but he kept her chin in a gentle yet firm grip. "Do what?" she asked.

"You did it at the dock, too, when that pompous, overbearing preacher interrupted us. You tuck your chin down and go all meek and mild, but in your eyes there's something completely different. Why do you hide yourself?"

Was she really so transparent, then? No one had ever seen it before, but first Reverend Williams and now this man had divined rebellion in her.

Instead of answering, she sought to change the subject again. "I have forgot your name," she said.

For a moment, he contemplated her face, and his eyes narrowed in suspicion. "All right," he said at last, "we'll drop that, too, for now. I am Geoffrey Hampton, captain of this fair vessel, and you are Faith Cooper."

"How did you know? I'm sure I never told you."

"'Twas how your betrothed addressed you. How likes he your trip to Jamaica? Is he to join you there, stowing away on some other ship?"

Faith dropped her gaze to the sheets.

"Damn it! Look at me when we speak, Faith Cooper!"

She gasped in alarm, but fury surged through her, as well. Who did this man think he was to speak to her so?

When he spoke again, his voice was treacherously soft. "Do I frighten you, Faith? Well I should. But I anger you, too. I like a wench with a bit of fire in her. I take it your affianced husband didn't approve. Prefers his women mild as milk, does he?" She glared at him, and he laughed. "Go on. Tell me about your holy husband-to-be."

"Throw me into the ocean, if you will, but I'll not

return to that man!" Embarrassed by her own passionate outburst, she looked away, but then looked right back for fear that he would yell at her again.

"So, 'twas not exactly a love match, was it?"

He spoke gently now, smiled sympathetically, and Faith found herself suspicious of the sudden change. Still, it would do no good to try to pretend otherwise, and it was a sin to lie.

"Nay, not for either of us."

Geoff shook his head in disbelief. "Your betrothed did not wish to marry you?"

"He wished to marry me, but 'tis sure he never loved me. He didn't even pretend to like me. Now, why would a man do that, set his mind to marry a woman he didn't want?" she wondered aloud.

"Mayhap 'tis true he didn't like you, but he would have to be made of stone not to want you," he answered.

The compliment brought a blush to her pale cheeks, but again, she dropped her gaze. "You are too bold."

"What now, Faith? My words please you, and yet you would hide from me."

She tucked her chin shyly against her shoulder, causing silky strands of flaxen hair to spill forward. "Pride is a sin," she replied.

Geoff rolled his golden brown eyes cynically. "Spare me. Nothing wrong with a wench who knows her worth."

"A woman's worth lies not in her face!" Again, she realized that she had responded more sharply than intended. Again, she cast her eyes down, only to bring them up quickly before he could comment. What was it about this man that made her so forget herself? More calmly she added, "I mean, her value is in her obedience to God and her family. Which means I am of no value at all."

The captain's tone was as sharp as hers had been. "That preacher is not God!"

"Nay, but he is one of God's own men, and I have scorned him. I—I do not like him, not at all. There, I have spoken it! I do not know how this happened to me. I've long curbed my rebellion and my tongue, and now it seems I shame myself at every turn." She looked up into his clearly irritated countenance. "Forgive me. I do not mean to trouble you with my woes. You have been so kind already."

"Do you really believe all your sanctimonious prattle?" he asked, shaking his head.

She knew not how to answer. She had never before spoken to anyone who questioned the teachings she had learned from infancy. It struck her as dangerous, this conversation with a man whose heretical words mirrored too closely her own thoughts, of late. Despite her worries, she spoke her mind.

"He does not strike me as godly," she admitted. "And honestly, sometimes I think I confuse thinking I ought to be ashamed with actually being so." Giving voice to these thoughts left her somehow lighter inside, and she felt a sudden, odd trust in this man who listened without shock or dismay. "What think you of that?" she asked, lifting her chin defiantly.

"I think, Faith Cooper, that you are a singular woman. And," he added, "I'm thinking that I'll have to see that you do away with shame altogether someday soon."

Chapter 6

Giles might have missed the heavy footsteps of the captain behind him on the deck but for the sullen looks upon the faces of the men who had gathered 'round him to voice their complaints.

"Cap'n," he began, his voice all business, any warmth of friendship banished. "Word of our new passenger is out, and there's some question as to what's to be done with her."

"And you've explained that the decision's already been made?" Geoff asked.

"I have," Giles assured him. "But there are those who would contest it."

Geoff met and held the gaze of each man who surrounded him. Many an enemy had likened his golden orbs to a lion's in battle, and one by one, the men looked away. "Then which of you will step forward and voice your questions to me, instead of sniveling to my first mate?"

Pete Killigrew stepped forward. He was a bandy-legged sailor with long, greasy hair, rotting teeth, and a nose that was at once grotesquely humped and skinny. He sailed for profit, not patriotism, and he made sure all who met him knew it. Though he stood directly in front of his commander, he studied the main mast behind the man and grumbled sorely, "Keepin' 'er fer yerself, are ye, Cap'n?"

Geoff kept his face carefully bland. It was this complete absence of emotion that had chilled the blood of his enemies, even before his cutlass had spilled that very blood upon the decks of their ships. He raised his left hand, from which dangled a weighty cloth bag.

"Take this, Giles," he said, but his eyes never left the face of the man who questioned him, "and add it to the crew's profits from this voyage."

Giles opened the bag and let the handful of rich gold doubloons pour into his palm. It was a small fortune, no doubt!

"That's to pay her passage. She's my affair now, and of no concern to the rest of you."

In terms of the crew's immediate discontent, Geoff's gesture soothed Giles's worries. The men might well have preferred the woman to the gold, but none could afford to raise the ante. Paying for her would seem, to most, a fair enough way to settle the matter.

The morning's orders were issued, and the men set about their tasks, some busily, some indolently. Giles joined Geoff at the helm, gesturing away the crewmen who loitered there.

"You're an unrepentant rake, Geoff," Giles challenged quietly. "Lord knows we've wenched together often enough in the taverns of Port Royal, but a virtuous Englishwoman's a different story. She's no whore, Geoff, and I'll not have it said that we're pirates and rapists here. She's protected by the very Crown that we serve under the king's marque."

Geoff's brows shot up in genuine shock. "You know me better than that, Giles. The girl's safe with me."

"Would you have me believe you can keep a tempta-tion like her in your very bed and yet seduce her not?"

The grin that crept across his friend's face did little to allay Giles's concern. "You said that we're not rapists here, Giles, and I'm with you on that. Seduc-tion is another matter entirely."

"'Twas me Old Thomas came to when he found the girl. 'Twas my care he gave her into," Giles protested. "I cannot stand by and do nothing when I know that you mean her mischief."

Geoff raised an authoritative hand, halting further objection. "I am the captain, and even would you and the crew vote me down over this, I've paid her way. She stays in my cabin, and I'll be the one who's re-sponsible for her."

'Twas clear by the look on Giles's face that he had no intention of letting him pull rank again, so Geoff let the command slip from his tone. In friendship, he appealed, "I mean her no mischief, Giles, and I've no taste for force. If it makes you feel better, I'll swear to you now that I'll not do a thing to her that she doesn't want done."

Giles narrowed his eyes in suspicion. "I'll not abide by 'her lips said nay but her eyes said aye,'" he warned.

A slight smile tugged at the corners of Geoff's seri-ous lips. "If I do not hear her speak her desire with her own sweet mouth, I'll not lay a hand on her."

With a shake of his head, Giles said, "I'll wager all my booty from this voyage the girl wouldn't know what to ask for. Do you swear it, then, that you'll do nothing she does not directly ask you to do?"

Geoff stood a little straighter and put his hand over his heart. "I swear it."

Giles grinned in spite of himself. "And what will

you swear upon? The devil's had your soul since you were six!"

Geoff laughed out loud, and the two men's joviality cut the tension between them. "Aye, well, there's that," he said. "I'll swear it as your friend and as a loyal Englishman. I'll take nothing from the lady that she does not consent to give." He rolled his eyes in mock chagrin. "God help me," he added.

"God help you, indeed," Giles replied.

As soon as Captain Hampton left, Faith placed her bare feet carefully upon the chilly floorboards of the cabin and tested her legs. They wobbled, and she felt weak; but she found they would support her, so she wrapped the sheet about her waist to cover her legs and explored the room.

Dark wood paneling and furniture gave it a cozy, masculine feeling. Though the glass in the large window was too thick for a clear view, the mere thought of the unfettered ocean and sky soothed her troubled soul. The cabinets were unlocked, and with a twinge of guilt she perused their contents of heavy, leatherbound books on navigation and neatly rolled charts. She unrolled thick, ivory vellum to reveal a beautifully wrought map of the coast of the Spanish Main.

From the desk, she picked up and hefted a shiny compass made of brass. It was solid and cold in her hand, and she idly turned it to align the needle. Also upon the desk rested some instrument with three metal rods fixed at two angles, each topped by wooden curves along which slid some sort of marker. The larger curve was inscribed with a mysterious grid, while the other was labeled with degrees. Fastened to the bottom was a small, brass square with a slit. She picked it up, turning it this way and that, but could determine no practical use for the contraption.

"'Tis a backstaff," said a voice from the door, and she nearly dropped it in surprise. "A navigational tool. Did I frighten you?"

She turned abruptly back to the door and to the stranger who stood somewhat formally in its frame. "Well, you startled me, that's sure!" she said.

Though she was instinctively afraid of anyone she met on this fearsome journey, she could not help but note that this man had a kind face. He was perhaps as old as the captain and wore his hair in the same queue, but his face was soft and kind, rather than hard and lean. His eyes were the same soothing gray that spilled through the cabin window from the sea and sky beyond. He was a bit shorter than the captain, as well, and the cumulative effect was far less intimidating.

"Forgive me," the man apologized. "The door was ajar, else I would have knocked." He stayed just outside the entrance, and Faith pulled the sheet more tightly about her. "I am Giles Courtney," he said, "the first mate and quartermaster here. I brought you to this room actually, but I don't suppose you remember that?"

"Nay. It seemed I was below, thinking I could never climb the ladder from the hold and would die there; then I was here with the captain."

She did not speak it, but wondered if he had assisted in changing her clothes. The thought brought a stain to her cheeks, and she fixed her eyes upon the tool in her hand.

"Aye, I thought you'd not remember. You were out cold when we found you."

"We?"

"The ship's cook found you first. If you'd not made your way up that ladder, we'd not have found you in time. 'Tis glad I am to see you well and comfortable. You are comfortable, then?"

Nay, Faith thought, *I am most assuredly not comfortable.* But to the sailor she replied, "Aye, at the moment."

Giles smiled mildly at the uncertain look in her eyes. "I see Geoff has been his usual forthright self. Frightened you a bit, has he?"

"I seem to be a stowaway upon a ship with a man who mocks the Almighty without a thought of divine retribution. I am at the mercy of the sea and your captain, and I have done nothing of my own accord to secure God's grace. Why would I have cause to fear, Goodman Courtney?"

"Call me Giles, please, and with regard to God, well, Geoff and He have never been on the best of terms. If you hope to win a soul for the Lord, you'll fight a losing battle there, Faith."

She started to bristle at the use of her Christian name, but was struck by the irony of her circumstances. She sighed and gave him an uncertain little grin. "Nay, Giles, I'm in no position to admonish anyone in the name of God."

He gestured as though to entreat entry, and she nodded, sitting at the desk. He moved with the same confidence as his commander, but without the arrogance, and it struck Faith that she had, indeed, studied the other man's every move. Why?

"How came you on our ship?" he asked. "Are you in some trouble?"

"Aye," she admitted without thinking, but shook her head at his knowing nod. "Nay, not of that sort! I assure you, I am a virtuous woman! I was . . . no longer welcome in my village."

Giles said nothing, but patiently waited for her to add what she would.

"I seem to have gotten myself at odds with our new minister. I am bound for Jamaica and my Aunt Elizabeth."

"And the rest of your family?"

Faith sighed and toyed with the backstaff before her. The question was a natural one, but it brought with it a pang of regret. "This was my mother's idea," she explained. It wasn't a lie, not really. "My father disapproved."

"Ah, so that is why you did not simply book passage upon a likely ship."

"Just so." She swallowed against the guilt that tightened her throat. It was a lie of omission, no better.

"Where upon the island lives your aunt?"

Where? In truth, she had no idea. How large was this island? She chose to elude the question, again forcing back regret for her dishonesty. It was but one among a host of newly committed sins. "She and her husband own a sugar plantation. Winston Hall."

"Aye, I know of the place." Giles scrutinized her, and she felt her pulse quicken and her palms turn slick. She wanted for practice at this business of dissembling, and she thought sure he saw straight through to her heart and knew her to be a fraud.

"There now, you see, Giles, she is yet in one piece," Captain Hampton called merrily as he swept through the door. "I have refrained from swallowing her whole, however tempting a morsel she may be." In one hand he carried a steaming plate of eggs and dried beef, in the other a tankard of warm milk.

The smell of food drove every other thought from Faith's befuddled mind. Her stomach had been empty for well over twenty-four hours, and she rose from her seat, salivating.

"Breakfast?" she asked, a bit too eagerly.

Geoff teased her a bit, waving the plate under her nose. "Hungry, are you?" he asked. He laughed at the almost pained look on her face and offered her the plate.

Self-restraint aside, she grabbed it, muttered a quick blessing, and took a healthy spoonful even before she sat again. Her eyes closed, and a throaty sound of ecstasy slipped through her lips as she swallowed. Her attention was completely absorbed by the meal, or she would have noticed that both men watched her in pure fascination.

I must be mad, Geoff thought. Her full lips glistened with grease from the eggs, and the pale waves of her hair tumbled down her back away from her angelic face. Her golden lashes rested against her pale pink cheeks in pure delight while she daintily popped a finger in her mouth and savored the flavor that clung to it.

How did one get a virgin to ask for things she didn't know about? He glanced over at his friend, who laughed silently, sure proof that he had read Geoff's thoughts.

"I see she has a healthy appetite," Giles observed.

"Aye, for food, anyway," Geoff sighed.

The spoon paused halfway to Faith's mouth, and she ducked her head, embarrassed by her own lack of manners. "Forgive me. I was just so hungry, and the food is delicious. How do you carry enough eggs for all the crew?"

"We don't," Giles explained. "On deck we have chickens. We eat the eggs for the first part of the voyage, and the hens as we near the end."

"And the milk?" she asked, draining the last of it from the tankard the captain had brought in with the plate.

"We keep goats, as well," Geoff answered.

"The deck must be a merry place, indeed! If someone could just rinse out one of my dresses, I'd love to go up there. I've never been out on the ocean before."

The two men exchanged uncomfortable looks. Her fate had been an easy enough matter to decide when only one other besides themselves had seen her, and he only in the dark. Still, the journey would have them at sea nearly a month. They could hardly expect to keep her below deck the whole time.

Giles spoke first. "Ken is washing out her things. He'll set them out to dry in the wind. The wool will take a goodly while, but the other will dry soon enough."

Geoff's face took on a grim expression. "Aye, too soon, to be sure." He turned to Faith. "I'll see what I can do. Make sure you wear one of those caps, and keep your eyes downcast. I'll order the men to leave you be, but I doubt they'll hold for very long. Remember that every smile, every word, will be seen as encouragement. In the end, I don't want to have to kill any of my own crew over you."

They were easy enough instructions to follow. What he asked was a demeanor she adopted every time she left her house in her village, but it had always been to protect her reputation only. She had never truly feared the men around her. Her earlier feeling of dread returned full force. "What manner of men are these?"

"Ordinary men, Faith. Men who know they'll be a month at sea without women. Men who would find you a temptation even were they surrounded by willing wenches with common looks."

"What would they do?"

"With enough drink, who's to say? At best, they might beat me senseless and game for you, at worst throw me overboard and share you."

Again she looked to Giles to confirm what she had heard and was terrified by his nod.

"Are you pirates, then?"

"Nay, Faith!" Giles protested.

"Privateers!" Geoff corrected. "The king has granted us a letter of marque to harass the Spanish, and we pay our fair share of profit to the Crown. Still, we're not navy here. The discipline is not so harsh, and the men more likely to have minds of their own. Most of the crew are honest Englishmen with respect for a good woman, but there are those with fewer scruples, and after a night of drink, the line between the two gets a mite thin."

When the captain had left her earlier, Faith had begun to relax. It had seemed that Providence had guided her to a safe haven. Now her newfound security slipped through her fingers, and the food that remained on her plate lost all appeal. "I see."

"Speaking of the crew," Giles interrupted. "One of us had better be up there."

"Aye," Geoff said. "I'll join you shortly."

"Welcome aboard, Faith."

"Thank you, Giles. And thank you for saving me."

He smiled shyly, but at his captain's frown, he made a hasty exit.

"One more thing, Faith. When you're on deck, 'tis

best if you—well, if it appears that we have a somewhat closer relationship."

Faith's aqua eyes grew round. In a voice hardly above a whisper, she asked, "They think I'm your whore?"

Geoff scratched his head and tried to think of how to soften it. "I've laid claim to you for myself. It was for your own safety!"

She studied a long scratch in the surface of the desk. "What does that mean, 'laid claim'?" she said, never lifting her eyes.

"Most will assume we're lovers."

Her face burned, and she kept her eyes carefully focused on the scratch. "But they will be mistaken."

"I cannot abide it when you will not look me in the face, Faith!" He was glad he had insisted, for he saw not the look of fear he had expected. Her face was red, but her eyes flashed with challenge.

"You said that you do not take women by force, Captain. If that is so, then anyone who assumes that we share a bed will be mistaken."

"You will call me Geoff. We'll hardly convince anyone that you're taken if you call me Captain." The golden glints in his eyes twinkled, and the genuine smile that lit his face chased away the sinister look he carried when serious. "Besides, it will be no mistake. I cannot leave you here unguarded at night, and I'm not thinking to sleep with my feet upon my desk each night!"

Again, Faith felt her momentary calm rocked by a sense of alarm. "Surely you do not think to sleep here, with me?"

"Aye, there's nowhere else. 'Twill be an exercise in self-control, but I'll manage."

"Nay, Captain! What you suggest is out of the question! I'll sleep on the floor, then. I do not wish to trouble you."

He reached across the desk and lightly traced the line of her delicate jaw, sending strange fluttery feelings down her throat.

"You will trouble me no matter where you sleep, but I cannot put you onto the hard floor. I promise, I will be utterly trustworthy. Or is it yourself you do not trust, fair Faith?"

She looked anxiously, first at his broad shoulders, then at the bed that had seemed so large and comfortable. It appeared to shrink before her very eyes. "I cannot sleep in the same bed with a man."

"Well, if you insist, there's no need to sleep much at all."

Her gaze flew to his, but she could not tell if the merry twinkle in his eyes said he spoke in jest or in hope. "Have you an extra blanket?"

The humor left his face, and he again looked the part of cold-hearted pirate. "I give my word, you are safe from any unwanted advances, but neither of us will sleep on the floor, Faith."

She couldn't help it, but whenever she was faced with someone's displeasure, she lowered her eyes and could not entirely find her voice. Besides, at a moment's caprice he could become quite intimidating!

"I only meant that one of us should sleep above the bedclothes," she said. "The layers of cloth will keep our bodies separate."

Geoff felt a quick stab of guilt for glowering at her. "I didn't mean to cause you fear. That's a fine idea. A bit of a disappointment, but sure to do more to preserve my sanity. Look at me, now, I won't bite."

She peeked shyly through her lashes, filling Geoff's

head with images that were bound to do little for his self-restraint.

"Good, then. I have duties to attend to above. It will be a while 'til your clothes are dry. Can you keep yourself occupied here?"

Relieved that the conversation was at an end, she nodded. "I am still weary. Perhaps I'll just nap." Perhaps if she napped, she would be too well rested to sleep at night. Perhaps then she would sit up and read until dawn.

The thought of her lovely, white flesh warming his sheets sent Geoff tripping for the door with a brief nod of farewell. Perhaps, on deck, he could work himself into an undeniable exhaustion. He would need to be weary to the bone to survive this night.

Chapter 7

Two days had passed since Diego Montoya, captain of the Spanish ship *Magdalena*, had made his humble plea to the prostitute-turned-saint for whom his ship was named. In those two days, his prayer that the late captain's fever would leave the rest of them alone had been answered. The answer was no.

There were no leeches on board the ship, so the surgeon used his bloodletting instruments, moving from one patient to the next with the red-stained blades. Each crewman only worsened, moving inevitably toward the sea, sewn in a pure white shroud. Diego himself felt dizzy, his coat and vest too warm to bear. The ship's doctor noticed when Diego pulled the offending garments from his body and wiped his hand across his damp brow.

"Here," the physician said, pulling one of his knives from his latest patient's arm. "Perhaps if I bleed you now, before the fever can get you in its grip, I can spare us the loss of another fine captain."

Diego eyed the bloody object and shuddered. Perhaps he was a coward, after all. "No," he said, "I am fine, truly. Bloodletting leaves one weak, and I cannot be weak now. My patron saint, she is looking out for me."

"It may be your only chance."

"No. I will be fine."

He closed his eyes and prayed silently. "Santa Maria, you must help us. Cleanse us of this disease. Protect us from pirates. I will fight bravely if I must, but we cannot fight if we are sick, our numbers depleted. Please, as you washed the feet of the Savior, wash our decks of this fever."

He made the sign of the cross and opened his eyes. Blood flowed from the arm of yet another crewmember at the surgeon's slice, and he felt his faith flag. Who was he, Diego Montoya, a mere second-in-command, to captain the ship through such calamity? Another wave of dizziness swept over him, and he was tempted to retreat to his cabin to seek much needed sleep.

"Capitán," a small voice prodded, and Diego turned to look down upon his cabin boy, Galeno. "Capitán, I don't feel so well." The boy's brown eyes were glazed with fever and wide with fear, and Diego knew that now was not the time to indulge his own weakness.

Before the physician could lay his besmirched hands upon the child's sweaty brow, Diego instinctively pushed Galeno behind him. "I will put him to bed in my cabin. It is too soon for such drastic measures."

Galeno followed docilely and snuggled into the covers on Diego's bunk. "Are we all going to die, Capitán?" he asked.

The boy's simple question gave voice to Diego's own fears, but he forced a broad smile. "No, Galeno, we will not all die. Look at me. I am not going to die. And neither are you. You stay here and rest, because you have many duties, and I need you to be healthy again."

The boy looked somewhat assured, enough so that he closed his eyes and let his face relax. Diego's own thoughts of lying down to rest had all but vanished. His fever and exhaustion were unimportant now. Too many people depended upon him, and there was too much work to be done by too few hands.

Faith had no idea how much time had elapsed when she awoke to a soft tapping on the door. The light that spilled into the room from the window seemed dimmer, but it hadn't been terribly intense at any point, so it was of little help. She checked to see that she was sufficiently covered as she called out, "Who is it?"

"'Tis me, Thomas, the ship's cook. I've supper here for you, if you're of a mind."

The mention of food caused her stomach to growl in response. "Aye, thank you and come in."

Thomas was a portly, jolly-faced fellow who looked near three score in years, though Faith suspected he was somewhat younger. He stood, plate in hand, and gaped at her. "Lord have mercy," he whispered.

Embarrassed, Faith again surveyed the sheets and the neck of the borrowed shirt to make sure that she was decently covered.

Thomas shook his head as though to clear it from a blow and set his concentration upon arranging her supper on the desk. "Sorry 'bout that, miss. I didn't mean to stare, but ye're uncommon pretty. 'Tis glad I am there's no one aboard who can match the price the cap'n paid for ye. We'd have a fight on our hands, sure."

Her heart skipped a beat, and Faith was certain she hadn't heard the man correctly, or perhaps she misunderstood his meaning. "The price the captain paid?" she asked.

"Aye, miss, a bag of gold doubloons. Course, the cap'n doesn't drink as much as most, and he never gambles. He spends a bit on wenches when he can, but there's little else he does with his booty. I imagine he can afford more than that if there's a need."

Her head swam at the thought. How many doubloons had there been? She assumed her aunt and uncle to have some means, for sugar plantations were known to produce considerable wealth, but they were yet strangers. She could never ask them to repay such a sum! She looked up at the cook, who looked back with a worried expression.

"Have I upset ye, miss? The cap'n said ye knew the whole of the situation."

"Nay, you've done nothing wrong, Thomas. The captain told me that he had paid for my passage," she answered breathlessly.

Thomas blushed and said, "Forgive me, miss. 'Twas a crude thing to say. O' course the cap'n paid yer passage, he didn't pay fer ye. Why, ye're not a slave nor a whore—er—horse, nor nothin' like that." He gave her a nervous smile and nodded his head with its thin wisps of gray hair. "Ye just eat up, and I'll be down soon."

He left in a dither, and Faith paced the cabin furiously, unable to touch her plate. She could never raise enough money to repay the captain, and a man like him did not part with that much gold with no expectation of a return. What was it Thomas had said, he only spent his money on wenches? She could only imagine what they did to repay him, but she knew that was impossible for her.

She stood at the window and found she could just make out the gentle swells of dark waves as they moved against a somewhat lighter sky. Still, it seemed darker than it ought, and she wondered if the ocean would pitch them about and make her sick again. She couldn't shake the feeling that she was the source of some divine amusement. It seemed that every time she concluded that her situation was not intolerable, that God had, in fact, granted her a reprieve, it took a turn for the worse! Reverend Williams would assure her that she was but reaping the rewards of her evil behavior.

She could almost hear his supercilious tone. "Do you see what becomes of a woman who scoffs at her Commandments and thinks herself above a very minister!"

"I did not scoff at the Commandments! Granted, my father did not want me to do this, but I am honoring my mother's wish."

"Your mother did as a dutiful wife should," the illusory voice preached. "She and your father agreed that you would wed me. They said as much when you returned from Boston."

Faith buried her head in her hands against her imaginary accuser. "But it was my life! I had no choice but to disobey them. I could not live with you, you hated me!"

"Nay, Faith, it was you who spurned me! A plain-faced, plainspoken man of God was not enough compared to a dashing ship's captain in a velvet coat and lace cravat. Even now, you pretend righteous indignation, but in your heart, being in his debt and lying in his bed gives you shameful thoughts!"

"Nay, that is not so!" she cried aloud, uncovering her eyes in the empty room.

He was not there. Of course not, she told herself. She had left Reverend Williams far behind. Where, then, had that accusation come from?

The door creaked open behind her, and Faith nearly jumped out of her skin, sure the horrid clergyman had somehow boarded the ship. She felt no relief at all to see that it was the captain followed by the cook.

"Can you not think to knock!" she cried, more shrilly than intended. She was too distraught even to care that she had shouted at him. Thomas quickly scuttled in and looked quizzically at her untouched food. "Take it!" she snapped. The older man looked at his commander in confusion, but did as Faith bid him and retreated.

Geoff simply smiled. He had no idea what had raised her ire, but she was a fetching sight, indeed, when she was angry. Her pale cheeks bloomed with roses, and her eyes shot sparks. "'Tis my own room," he answered calmly, "and I'll see naught that I haven't seen before." His eyes traveled slowly over the sheet that covered her as though it were not there.

Refusing to fall prey to his attempt to embarrass her, she placed her hands on her hips. "That's entirely unfair, and well you know it!"

"Aye, it is," Geoff agreed. He moved as if to unfasten his breeches. "Mayhap I can put us on even ground, let you see all I have to offer as well."

She grabbed at her linen shift and indigo gown that were draped over his arm. "Nay, 'twill make nothing even at all, since I have no intention of offering you one thing that you saw. May I have my clothes, please?"

He moved the garments just beyond her reach and with a roguish grin said, "There's a price."

"Ah!" she cried. "I knew it! You know I haven't even the usual amount required for passage, much less a bag of gold doubloons! You did not 'lay claim' to me!

You bought me! Well, I didn't ask you to! I didn't want you to. And I don't want to be your, your—whore, or wench, or whatever you call it! I don't!"

He held his hands open in gentle supplication. "There now, love, don't fret. I haven't asked you to do any such thing, have I? All I've asked is a decent night's sleep in my own bunk without feeling guilty for putting you out of it. I had thought to ask to accompany you on your stroll about the deck, but if that's too much, I'll not press you."

"Aye, that's all you've asked for now, but you cannot tell me you weren't expecting more."

He dropped her clothes upon the bed and gave her a serious look. Oh, she hated it when he looked like that! He was scary, and masculine, and something else. And it made her feel small, and vulnerable, and something else. Something that defied description sent tiny jolts of alarm through her. She ducked her chin and shut her eyes, but his low growl reminded her that she angered him when she did that. It took all the courage she possessed to fix her eyes on his.

"Did your father beat you that you cringe and hide every time you show a little spirit?" he snapped.

She lifted her chin in defense of her father. "Certainly not! He raised me to be a proper Christian woman and to keep my place, but 'tis sure he never beat me!"

"What does that mean, a proper Christian woman?" he sneered. "What was your place in that ivory tower that religious zealots call Massachusetts?"

How was it that this man could hit the mark with her so unerringly? He gave voice to the very questions that had been plaguing her. Refusing to let him see the cracks in her fortress, she lifted her chin and replied, "I am the mistress of my emotions! I am not controlled by passions like anger, and . . ." She searched for another example.

"Passion?"

"That's base."

He moved slowly toward her, and Faith was struck by how very confined the cabin was. "Do you never have feelings that are 'base,' Faith?" he purred.

"I'm human," she stammered, backing up, though she held his gaze, "and wickedness is our nature, but through God's grace we can rise above our wickedness and find purpose and joy!"

He stopped less than a foot away from her when her back came against the barrier of a cabinet door. "And have you found that, 'purpose and joy'?"

"What?" she asked. She could feel the heat of him, breathe the masculine scent of sea and sweat. She glanced to the side, seeking escape.

He placed a hand on either side of her, blocking any retreat. "What was it you sought when you crept onto my ship in the dark of night? What do you think you will find in the warm, sultry air of Jamaica?"

"Jamaica?" she asked. How had the conversation ended up there? She was befuddled, her mind wrapped in some hot mist that emanated from the man whose heat surrounded her. Faith stared into his golden eyes, and they bored into her, seeing into the darkest part of her heart.

"Jamaica is not the cold, emotionless land of the Pilgrims, love. It is a violent land, a land of passion and death, where men throw away fortunes for a night's pleasure and slaves die for the sugar to make cheap rum." His voice was deep and intense, and his eyes devoured her.

"You confuse me," she whispered, looking at his bare feet but a step away from her own.

He pulled her face back to his. "You are confused, Faith, but not by me. What do you want?"

She turned and gazed out the window at the gathering darkness. She braced herself against the cabinet and realized that the ship was rocking more intensely. "I do not know. I only know what I do not want."

"That's a start."

She turned to face him and pushed him away, ducking beneath his arm. "I do not want a man who hates me. I do not want to spend every minute of my day trying to be perfect, dutiful, obedient, only to be told that I am wicked all the same. I do not want to owe you more money than I can ever repay, and I do not want to sleep with you because of it."

He continued to look at her, now with that unreadable expression he often adopted, but she didn't feel a need to look away. It was enough that it was not a look of disapproval. It was *that* that had commanded her whole life, fear of disapproval. Fear that she might not fit the conception everyone held of her. Fear that really, deep inside, she was a fraud.

Geoff sighed and crossed to sink onto the bunk. This was why he avoided respectable women. They were impossible to understand. "I don't want you to sleep with me because of the money. I've given tavern wenches baubles worth five times that, just to see the pretty smile they cause."

"Just for a smile?" she asked skeptically.

He grinned, and she relaxed. "Well, I always get more than a smile, but I'll have you know I'd have gotten their favor without the jewels. A coin or two is plenty for a man of my skill!"

He so resembled a puffed-up peacock she couldn't help but laugh. "How comes it, then, that I find you so very resistible?"

With a wicked smile and a careless shrug, he answered, "I cannot fathom it. Mayhap it is because you know not what you're missing."

He moved to rise, and she retreated to the opposite side of the desk. "Nay, stay where you are! I did not ask for a demonstration!"

Smugly, he stretched back out upon the mattress. A lock of gilded brown hair had come loose from its queue, and his skin was dark where the sleeves and collar of his loose, white shirt fell away. The sight of his tanned, bare legs and feet suddenly seemed painfully intimate, and she felt her cheeks grow warm.

"What thoughts bring that color to your fair face, love?"

Tired of ever being at a loss, she used a weapon that had never failed when a boy in the village looked at her too boldly. "Whatever would your mother think, Captain Hampton?"

To her amazement, he only laughed. "She would think you were a fool to pass up a prime opportunity."

"I think not!"

"She was a whore, Faith."

"Captain, you mustn't speak so of your mother!" She cast an anxious look upward, half expecting lightning to strike the main mast of the ship.

"If I called the woman a bitch, love, that would be disrespectful, although I've described her that way from time to time. As it happens, I do but state a fact. She may have been expensive and well-educated, but a courtesan, as she preferred to call herself, is a whore, nonetheless."

Faith was not entirely ignorant. The Bible referred to harlots, and she had heard vague rumors about some of the women who frequented the docksides of Boston harbor. Still, such a thing was only a concept, far removed from her reality. She could not even imagine what his life had been like. She had grown up in a happy, wholesome home with loving parents. Why, did he even know who his father was? She did not ask.

"How awful for you," she murmured.

He sat up and rested his arm across his knee. His casual air of belonging emphasized that the bed she had come to think of as hers was, in fact, his.

"What is so awful?" he asked. "I grew up knowing what men and women have to offer each other—no pretense, no pretty frills complicating it. It was all very straightforward, and no one got hurt."

"Did you ever ask your mother that? If no one got hurt?"

"Well, if there was pain involved, the price was much higher," he teased, but was disappointed to see that he had only confused her.

Dear God, she really was naive! Still, it intrigued him. What would it be like with a wench who had never known a rough hand, who had never known any hand, save his? He shook his head to clear it. It would hardly do to get sentimental. He had seen men go soft for innocents before, but sooner or later, innocence was lost.

As he looked at her, his eyes darkened, and his face fell serious again, though somehow not so frightening. "I wouldn't hurt you, Faith. If 'tis joy you seek, I can give you that." His gaze sent heat pouring through her.

So this was temptation, she thought. It was, indeed,

a powerful force. "Where is your mother now?" she asked.

"Dead."

"How?"

He paused, and whatever storm was building between them abated. "The pox."

Her breath caught in her throat, and she looked at him with pity in her eyes. Softly, she replied, "But no one ever got hurt, did they, Captain?"

Chapter 8

If the storm in Geoff's body had calmed, the squall that swept in on the ship did not. The rain was cold and the sea turbulent, but it was short-lived. Faith postponed her trip to the deck above and concentrated on keeping down what little food she had eaten. She lay in the dark, still wide awake, when the motion of the ship steadied and Geoff returned, carrying a single candle in a lamp. She closed her eyes and forced her breathing to remain steady and deep.

Clothing rustled faintly, and something wet snapped when crisply shaken. More rustling, another snap—was he naked? She squeezed her eyes tightly shut and fought the urge to bolt from the bed and flee the room altogether. Only the knowledge that the floor beyond the cabin was littered with disreputable men stopped her.

In the candlelight, Geoff draped his wet pants over the back of the chair and smiled at the blush that stole across her cheeks. She was a prisoner of her own ruse. If she weren't pretending to sleep, she could insist he don dry pants, at least. As it was, he took roguish delight in lying naked on top of the covers next to her, pulling the extra linen and blanket across him.

"Sleep well, love," he whispered.

Faith lay perfectly still. His warmth gradually

seeped through the thin barrier between them, and his breathing fell into the genuinely relaxed rhythm of slumber. He smelled faintly of rain, sea spray, and male sweat, and she could feel the hard muscle of his arm pressed against her, even though she had edged herself clear against the wall.

Whenever she had thought of sharing her life with a man, she had thought of a home of her own, children, and a place at his side in a church pew. She had not thought of the place she would occupy in her husband's bed. Lust was a sin, and marriage did not make it any less so.

But what did Geoff mean, he could give her joy? What was this strange feeling that tugged at her stomach? She wanted to touch him, feel the flesh of the arm that invaded her space on the mattress. Was it evil to want such a thing? Her mind was a jumble of questions, but at last, she drifted into an uneasy sleep. In her dreams, shame forsook her, and she ran her hand decadently over the sensuous bulge of skin and sinew.

Geoff came instantly awake. Dawn had barely begun to gild the seascape beyond the thick glass window, but the molten heat of reality roused him from the comfortable warmth of dreams. Faith's hand had fallen softly inside the crook of his elbow, but then it moved boldly upward, her dainty fingers splaying themselves across his arm until they rested upon his shoulder. She moved closer, pressing her face against that same shoulder. In her sleep, she smiled slightly and breathed deeply.

He stifled a groan and dearly regretted his decision to come to bed nude, her effect on him being far too evident. Perhaps he could ease himself from the bunk and dress without waking her. Still, the feel of her pliant body through the sheets enticed him to linger a moment longer. A moment too long, alas.

Faith's lashes fluttered, and for a moment or two, she was content to enjoy the warmth and evocative scent that permeated the air around her. Where was she?

With a shriek she pushed against the unyielding form beside her. "What are you doing?" she gasped.

Geoff winced at the noise and sat up, wrapping the covers around his waist and carefully centering the excess fabric. "Sleeping! What are you doing? Changed your mind, have you? 'Tis a woman's birthright, I'm told." He smiled lasciviously, and his eyes caressed her.

Faith looked about her and realized that somehow, in the night, she had rolled away from the wall. She didn't know exactly what had happened, but it appeared that she was the one who had breached the space that should have remained between them.

"Forgive me! I do not know what came over me." She gathered the bed linens to her breast and scooted backward. Unfortunately, in her haste to gather her own sheet, she had caught the corner of his, and came dangerously close to pulling it from his hips altogether.

Quickly, he stayed her hand. "Have a care, love. You'll get an eyeful more than you expected that way. Of course, I have no objections if you'd like to continue to explore."

"What?" Her breath caught in her throat, and she blanched. "Oh, dear God, did I actually touch you?"

"Watch out, love. Was that the seventh commandment you just broke?"

"What?" she cried, her face horror-stricken.

"You know, 'Thou shalt not take the name of God in vain.'"

"That's the third commandment!" she snapped.

He laughed at her pale face. "Oh, this is interesting. Shy Faith is like to bite my very head off. Pray tell, what is the seventh?" He reached over to toy with a curl that fell over her shoulder.

She gave his hand a bold slap and brushed the curl away herself. "It is of no importance."

"A commandment of no importance? Ha! Not for you, I'll wager. Speak, else I'll give you my sheet after all," he teased, moving as though to pull the cover away.

"Adultery!" she cried, turning her red face to the wall. "Thou shalt not commit adultery!"

He chucked her softly under the chin, making her jump. "No danger there. Neither of us is married."

"Fornication is just as bad!"

"Well, I vow this, when we get around to that particular sin, you shan't sleep through it. If you could do that, I'd have to resign as captain and take up dressmaking! 'Twould be a point of honor."

She kept her face to the wall, but not merely to hide her burning cheeks. Truth to tell, the thought of Captain Geoffrey Hampton, lap covered in silk and lace, wielding a needle and thread, brought a smile to her lips.

"Put your clothes on!" she commanded, stifling a giggle.

"Sensible girl. What a pity."

She listened again to the rustle of clothing and spoke, if only to cover the embarrassing sound. "Can I go above today?"

"Aye, and bathe, too, if you like. There, I'm covered."

Faith peered at him, unable to disguise the look of longing the notion of a bath brought, and Geoff could not help but wish the look were for him and not bathwater. "We've barrels full of rainwater. You can scrub with saltwater, then rinse in the other. 'Tis cold, for there's no practical way to heat it, but it feels fine."

A short while later, Thomas brought in a small tub and two large buckets, one of opaque saltwater, the other crystal clear rainwater. She smiled her thanks as he left, then hastily stripped. Geoff had spoken truly as the modest bath raised gooseflesh over her, but it felt wonderful to get truly clean. Using the water as carefully as possible, she found she even had enough to wash her hair. Shivering in the cool cabin, she hastily dried her body and donned her shift, the fabric dragging reluctantly against her damp skin, clinging to the moist places on her back and between her breasts. Water trickled from her hair, leaving the thin cloth sheer where it molded to cold, taut nipples.

Next, she took the bath linen to her hair, pulling it over her head and rubbing vigorously, the fabric rustling in her ears and blocking her sight. If not for that, she would have noticed Geoff's return. As it was, she did not see him when he leaned against the door, clearly enjoying the view.

"If you'd like, you can go on deck and let the wind dry it," he offered helpfully. Faith screamed and held the wet cloth to her breast. He only chuckled when she turned away, blushing furiously. Fortunately for him, he thought, she was unaware that her garment clung as enticingly to her backside as it had the rest of her.

Her clothes were a rumpled mess, but they would have to do. The collar was far too wrinkled to wear, so she cast it aside, though it left a slight V of throat exposed that would have been modestly hidden.

On deck, fresh sea air filled her lungs like a balm.

The sky had calmed, and a circle of light penetrated the gray that hovered over the ship's masts. Green waves lapped the tall, wooden hull of the ship, and though the wind chilled her, it felt wonderful after the stuffiness of the cabin.

As Geoff and Giles had told her, there were cages of chickens that clucked incessantly and three goats that roamed at will. Geoff led her directly aft, scowling away any curious sailor who ventured too close.

As he watched the pleasure of crisp, clean air and freedom wash over his unexpected passenger, Geoff found his imagination drawn to the prim little notch at the neck of her gown. He thought of the two small, perfect breasts that had pressed against her wet shift when he walked into the cabin. He hadn't intended to interrupt her, thought he had given her more than enough time, but neither did he regret his premature arrival. Two perfect handfuls, he had thought when he first undressed her and again that morning. How to get her curiosity piqued beyond endurance? He was not generally a patient man, but however long it took, he would know the feel of all that he had seen.

Geoff had given Faith an ivory comb, and she used it now, trying to work the snarls from her hair as it blew in the sea breeze.

"Here, let me have that," he said.

"Nay, Captain, I've not finished."

He caught her hand and tugged at the comb. "Not 'Captain.' Geoff. Say it, Faith." Their eyes locked. He was serious again.

"Geoff," she replied.

"There, that was not so very hard, was it?" He put his hands on her shoulders and turned her back to him, then patiently began to coax the tangles from the strands of moonlight and quicksilver that trickled through his fingers. When she would have pulled away, he wrapped his hand in a damp lock. "Which commandment would that be, love?"

"Commandment?"

"Thou shalt not let a man comb thy hair."

"The Lord is not mocked."

"He has mocked me all my life."

No one had combed her hair since she was a very little girl, and she was surprised at how heavenly it was, though it was so simple an act. She ceased her protest and allowed herself to enjoy its tenderness. "Do you not believe in God at all, Geoff?"

"I do not trouble myself with it. If there is a god, he thinks little enough of me. Why should I think of him?"

"Do you not wonder what's to become of you when you die?"

"I know what's to become of me. They can fling my skin and bones into the ocean and feed the fish. If I owe anything in my life, 'tis to the ocean I owe it."

"You've no desire for heaven nor fear of hell?"

"Heaven, hell—they're like love and forever, Faith. They're fairy tales."

"You do not believe in love? But that's so sad. Have you never been in love?"

Geoff felt an unpleasant twinge at the wistfulness of her voice. It had not occurred to him that perhaps there had been some man, someone other than the odious preacher, who had shared Faith's life before him. "Have you?"

She gave a little sigh. "Nay. Before the whole predicament with Reverend Williams came up, I had thought to marry Aaron Jacobs. He is a good man and kind. I hoped we might come to love each other someday."

"Have you ever known anyone who was in love? Not for a day, or a month, or even a year, but forever?"

"My parents." She imagined them now, worried sick. Before grief could overwhelm her, Geoff's cynical tone interrupted her thoughts.

"Do they love each other, or are they simply two people, cut from the same cloth, reaching for the same impossible goal?"

"They care for one another. They treat each other with respect and kindness. They suit each other in every way."

"Is that love?"

"Aye, I think so."

"Sounds lukewarm to me. I've a taste for passion, for the thrill of a moment. Give me the heat of battle, a fervent tumble with a willing wench, a storm and a ship beneath me. They're here and now, Faith, not some vague promise that may never come true. Suppose you spend the rest of your life not doing all those delicious things that your god says thou shalt not do, and then when you die 'tis just over? Life is short, love, and much of it unpleasant. I take what I can when I can, and if I burn in hell, it will be without regrets."

"But I've followed the teachings of my faith all my life, and I've been happy, for the most part."

"Faith, you don't know what happiness is."

She looked over her shoulder into his face, weathered by wind and by life. His eyes could twinkle and laugh, but they didn't just now. When he chose, his face revealed nothing, but lurking in his eyes there was sadness, and the lines around his mouth spoke of pain. "Neither, I think, do you."

For a long time he combed the knots from her hair while Faith absorbed the sea around her. The sky was the same leaden gray it was in Boston in the winter and early spring, but it was different here. Bigger. Everywhere she looked was gray sky and green water, and though it seemed she should feel some trepidation at the vastness of it all, she didn't. She felt unencumbered, as though the world was too far away to matter. Here there were no looks of scowling disapproval.

Well, aside from Geoff. He was impossible to estimate. At home she had always known just what was expected, but the meek and mild manner that had pleased her family and neighbors made him cross.

At last he finished, but he continued to run the flowing strands through his rough, brown hands, and she was content to let him. He leaned close until his breath tickled her ear, and in a tenor voice that melted her every resistance, he sang:

> *"Amarantha sweet and faire,*
> *Ah brade no more that shining haire!*
> *As my curious hand or eye,*
> *Hovering round thee let it flye."*

"What a beautiful song," she murmured, knowing well she should stop him.

"'Tis by a man named Richard Lovelace. There's more."

"More?"

He smiled and skipped a few verses, moving to his favorite.

> *"See 'tis broke! Within this Grove*
> *The Bower, and the walkes of Love,*
> *Weary lye we downe and rest,*
> *And fanne each other's panting breast"*

"Geoff!" She tried to pull away, but he held her fast.

> *"Heere wee'l strippe and coole our fire*
> *In Creame below, in milke-baths higher—"*

"Those cannot be the right words!" She pulled harder.

"Why, they are, indeed, love." He chuckled at her flaming cheeks and finally let her go.

"'Tis a wicked song!"

"The sight of you brings me wicked thoughts." He reached for her again, and she moved quickly away.

"We've tarried here too long. What will everyone think?"

"Exactly what they must think if you're to stay safe with me."

"I'm not sure it wouldn't be safer to take my chances!"

"Put your hair up in that awful cap, and I'll let you be the judge of that."

She quickly put her hair in the pins Geoff had taken from her that first night and tucked the knot neatly into her coif.

"Remember, do not be overly friendly. Mere kindness might be misinterpreted." He waved to Giles at the helm.

As he had instructed, she kept her hand in the crook of his arm and her eyes down as they walked the length of the deck. She was acutely aware of the growing silence and cast a furtive look about her. The men were rough looking, unkempt to be sure, but they didn't strike her as dangerous. She quickly reassessed them when one strode boldly over to them and openly leered at her.

"So, this is the woman ye bought out from under us, is it, Cap'n?" he said.

"You'll keep a respectful tongue in your head, Killigrew. The matter's been settled, if you'll recall. I paid her passage, that's all."

"Aye, ye paid a king's ransom. I see why, now. When ye tire of her, I'll be happy to reimburse ye some. Not all, seein' as she's slightly used."

Geoff's fist shot out in a blur, and of a sudden the man writhed on the deck, blood seeping through the fingers he held over his mouth and nose. Faith gasped and recoiled in horror, though she was unsure whether it was from the man's disgusting insinuation or the violence of Geoff's response.

The rest of the crew seemed as shocked as Faith. Clearly, it was most unlike their calculating commander to react so impulsively. When the captain turned to another sailor, the man stood to attention, his old navy training kicking in lest he be next.

"When he can stand, have him clean off this blood," Geoff barked.

"Aye, Cap'n."

"Anyone else have anything to get off his chest?" he asked, his rock-hard gaze sweeping the assembly.

The gathering became instantly busy. There were ropes to splice, sails to mend, animals to tend. The fact that there would be weeks in which to accomplish these tasks did nothing to alleviate the sudden sense of urgency.

Giles, who had bolted from his place at the helm, took in Faith's pale face and wide, stricken eyes. "Best you go below now, Faith," he said, and she nodded meekly. She had had more than enough adventure for one day.

"Interesting response, that," Giles commented dryly to his friend, once Faith was gone.

"He had it coming," Geoff protested. "He—" Suddenly, he realized the absurdity of the sentence that had nearly spilled from his mouth. *He insulted Faith.* Since when had he broken the nose of one of his men for making a lewd statement to a woman, even one in his company? Oh, he was gentleman enough to defend a woman, but so violently? Never. "It was the second time he challenged me over this," he amended.

"Was that it?" Giles inquired, but gave his friend a knowing grin. "It's glad I am to be here to see this."

"See what?" Geoff asked, his voice edged with irritation.

"To see you meet the woman who could finally get under that thick hide of yours."

When his nose finally quit gushing blood, Killigrew bent to the task of swabbing the deck, but under the surface he seethed. "So what if the rest o' us don't 'ave the Cap'n's means to pay fer the tart?" he asked one of his shipmates. "It don't make a crime to look."

The man next to him shrugged. "'Twas the offer to buy 'is leavings what got yer nose broke," he stated matter-of-factly. "She's got 'im by the cock, that one. Wouldn't surprise me none if she 'asn't let 'im do nothin' with 'er, yet. Got 'im all worked up with no relief."

Killigrew licked his thin lips. "D'ye think so? If the wench were mine, I'd toss 'er skirts over 'er 'ead and take my relief. Mind ye, I'm not finicky, but it's sure I wouldn't mind bein' the first to 'ave at 'er."

"Well, if ye figure it out, let me in. I've no qualms about second 'and goods," his colleague replied. He eyed the bloodstained deck. "My qualms is the cap'n. Next time it'll be the cat-o'-nine-tails."

Killigrew smirked contemptuously. "Well, a lot could 'appen to a man on the open ocean." He cast a sullen glance toward the portal to the lower deck, where the cap'n had gone chasing after the frigid bitch. "Arrogant prick. The satisfaction of runnin' 'im through would be well worth it, wench or no wench, virgin or not!"

Chapter 9

The night was torturous for them both. Faith could hardly sleep for trying to make sure that she did not repeat the mistake of rolling against him unaware. Geoff hardly slept for hoping she would roll against him unaware. To her infinite relief, he had taken to wearing breeches to bed, but his chest and arms remained disturbingly exposed.

In the morning, Faith had not yet turned away as he rose from the bed, and her breath caught audibly in her throat when she laid eyes upon his back. It was deeply scored by numerous wide, puckered lines that stood out in stark contrast to the rest of his dark golden skin. He dropped a shirt over himself and turned to her with that guarded, nearly emotionless look of his. For once, he said nothing when she dropped her gaze and remained silent.

He left, and she donned her cotton dress. Gathering her skirts about her, she struggled up the ladder and through the hatch onto the upper deck, acutely aware that there was no way to negotiate the ladder without exposing a bit of leg.

Geoff had cautioned her about being too friendly with his crew, but that didn't seem to include Giles, so when Geoff was busy at the helm, she stood at the opposite end of the deck and spoke at length with his friend.

"'Tis a fine day," Giles observed, as they gazed up at the patches of blue that broke through in the clouds overhead.

"Aye," Faith agreed. "And 'tis peaceful up here on the deck when the sea is calm."

Giles chuckled, his gaze sweeping over the raucous men that surrounded them.

"Well," Faith amended, "'tis peaceful if one overlooks the gaming, swearing, and drinking."

"Aye, and the chickens and the goats."

"Them, too." The two of them laughed at the absurdity of the conversation. After a moment, Faith sobered. "At home, idle hands were the devil's workshop, and one was expected to be always busy. Indeed, there was much to do, helping my mother with cooking, baking, laundry, caring for our few animals. I only meant that it seems so peaceful to have nothing more to do than enjoy a lovely day."

"They worked you hard, then?" Giles asked.

"Oh, nay! Everyone worked hard. I never minded much, for we worked together. Mother and I tended the house and garden. Father and the boys worked in the joinery."

"He was a carpenter, your father?" At her nod, he asked, "Do you miss them?"

"Fiercely," she answered. She told him of her family, her brothers and her village. He told her of his family, as well. His father had been a shipbuilder, but he had died when Giles was young. His mother and sisters had stayed in their little cottage, eking out a meager living. But he had signed on as a cabin boy with one of his father's old friends. He still saw them when he could, though it was rare.

"Our past makes us very much what we are," Faith observed.

"Aye, it does that."

"You and Geoff," she prodded, "you're close friends, but you're very different from one another."

"Aye, well, as you said, it is the past that makes us. We've done a fair job of wasting our youth together." He gave her a little wink, but fell serious again. "But our boyhoods were altogether different."

"I don't wish to give the wrong impression," she began. "Your captain has been a gentleman, I assure you."

A little smile tugged at his lips. "There's not many would dare accuse him of that."

Faith smiled, too. There was no doubt that Geoff was unaccustomed to self-restraint. "To be sure, I do not ordinarily look, but it is difficult when two people share a space." Her face was beet red, but she was determined to continue. "How came he by the scars upon his back?"

Giles's smile faded. "Geoff has been at sea since he was a lad of ten. In his early years, he worked for a captain who was a harsh taskmaster, impatient with a cabin boy whose inexperience might lead to an occasional mistake."

"He was beaten for mere occasional mistakes? Were they so serious?"

"Nay, a spilled breakfast tray, not enough rum in the captain's water. It was no better when he first signed on as a regular crewman. It made of him a meticulous sailor. He thinks of every possible consequence in a heartbeat before he acts, and unerringly chooses the best course. He's a fine leader in the heat of battle, and he's never lost a man who obeyed his orders. That calculating disposition of his reduces Spanish merchant captains to cowards once we board. It means we seldom have to kill anyone, which suits me."

"I cannot fathom why he would have stayed at sea when his first experiences were so cruel."

Giles shrugged. "You must consider his choices. They were much the same for any boy with no father to follow. I was fortunate, for my father had friends to look after me. Life at sea, no matter how harsh, was better than Geoff's life in London. The kind of people he met there would have used a handsome young boy far worse."

Faith's brow furrowed in confusion. "How so? What could be worse than brutal beatings?"

Gazing down into her innocent, earnest face, Giles seemed at a loss to explain. "You don't want to know," he said, at last.

"Surely his mother would have protected him."

"I think Geoff's mother was very little like yours or mine."

"He told me that she was a—a—"

"Courtesan?"

"Aye," she answered, relieved not to say it herself. "But surely she loved him, just the same."

"I swear, there was never a time in my life when I was as innocent as you, girl. 'Tis not a bad trait, but the world will play harshly with you."

He shook his head at her quizzical look and continued. "Geoff talks little about his mother. It sounds as though she was very beautiful and entertaining, but she could be harsh and angry as well. Once, when she'd had too much drink, she told him she had tried to rid herself of him before he was born, but only bled enough to scare herself out of trying again." He paused at Faith's gasp. "Shortly after she told him that, he heard her speaking with a nobleman who wanted to, ah—well there's no way to soften the sound of it. He wanted to buy the lad for the night."

"Buy him for a night? What would a man do with a lad for . . ." She stopped, and her face went ashen. "You cannot mean . . ." But she couldn't finish the sentence.

"She turned him down," Giles added, "but there was enough temptation on her part to worry Geoff. He thought that perhaps someone would yet find her price for him. 'Twas then he found a post as a cabin boy. He saw her only thrice after and didn't much mourn her when she died."

"There are people who would do such a thing to a child?" She sought Geoff's commanding form with her eyes and tried to imagine him as a boy. What had he been like ere he learned that life would treat him so harshly? Mayhap he had always been so bold, so strong, having learned early that he had no one to depend on save himself. Was there not still some softness inside of him?

Giles read the look she cast toward the captain. "I've told you too much, Faith. They say that that which does not kill us makes us stronger. Geoff made it through. He's master of his own fate now, successful and respected by his men."

"But there are hurts inside of him that, like his back, will forever bear witness to all that he has suffered. He has no faith in God or humanity. He doesn't even believe in love."

"I doubt me there is much that can be done to soothe those hurts now. He has in me the love of a loyal friend, but when a boy reaches manhood having never been freely given the love he ought, he must give up wanting it to survive."

"Nay, he's not given it up; he's only buried it! He's sad, Giles. Do you never see that?"

"Ah, Faith, don't go thinking you'll make it all better for him. You'll only get hurt. He wants you, maybe even likes you, else he'd not be so patient, but he'll make you no promises, and in time he'll move on."

She watched the man they discussed as he stood at the helm, the wind tearing through his unbound hair with its glints of gold and molding his shirt to his muscular torso. He appeared to be engaged in a serious discussion with one of the crew. Giles was right, of course. It wouldn't do to think softly of Geoff. In such close quarters that meant certain disaster. He nodded to the crewman and left him at the helm so that he could join Giles and Faith.

"You're looking far too serious here," Geoff said when he reached them. "And, Faith, your fair skin is no match for this sun and wind. Your nose is turning pink!"

"Aye, I suppose I should go below, but it does get so dull."

"Make use of my books if it pleases you."

"That's very kind of you, but they're all on sailing. I try to pay attention, but my mind wanders."

Geoff smiled slightly. "There's a volume or two of poetry in the cabinet. I'll be down in a bit and keep you company awhile."

He turned to Giles, and all trace of merriment vanished. "Dobbes has gone betting with money he doesn't have again," he said. "There's three or four men want to run him through with their cutlasses."

Giles crossed his arms and scowled. "Damn me if it's

not tempting to let them," he said. "You cannot tell me you're not bloody sick of saving his sorry hide."

"Aye, well, 'tis a sickness with him," Geoff said. "I can hardly let the crew have at him. Still, I've done him no good so far."

"What will you do?" Giles asked.

"As usual, find him some extra duties, something noxious and worth the extra pay he'll get to pay his debts." He sighed, his face a mask of grim resignation. "And this time, give him forty lashes. There's nothing else for it."

Faith sucked in her breath, and his gaze flickered across her. "Go below. You'll not want to watch this." With long, purposeful strides, he headed across the deck where a group of surly men obviously awaited the captain's decision.

She looked to Giles, who only shrugged. "He's saving the man's life, Faith." Then he turned and followed his commander.

Effectively dismissed, Faith descended the ladder into the dimly lit space below. She searched the cabinet until she found a volume of poetry by a man named Robert Herrick. Sinking onto the bed and turning its leather cover over in her hands, she contemplated what might be inside.

"I see you've found something," Geoff said as he came into the cabin.

"Aye," she said, a bit hesitantly.

His eyes sparkled mischievously. "That's one of my favorites. You should enjoy it."

She looked up at the ceiling, thinking of the drama that must have unfolded above. "The man, Dobbes . . ."

Geoff shrugged. "Mayhap he will think twice ere he

gets himself into this predicament again. His mates are out of patience with him."

"Why do they bet with him if they know he cannot pay?"

"'Tis not their job to watch after him. What would your people do with a gambler?"

"The same," Faith admitted.

"Let's speak on more pleasant things." He gestured to the book in her hand. "What do you like to read?"

"I've never read anything that wasn't religious. My primer as a child was based upon the Bible. 'A is for Adam. In Adam's fall, we sinned all.' When I became old enough, scripture was all that was allowed. My parents always felt poetry and plays to be a frivolous waste of time, even wicked."

Some mysterious mirth danced beneath the surface of Geoff's face, but he simply said, "Well, Herrick is an Episcopal minister, if that soothes your worries."

Instant relief appeared on her face, and he almost felt a bit guilty. Almost. "Save it awhile, though. I've something else to help you bide your time."

He handed her a slightly battered package wrapped in brown paper, and she pulled it off eagerly, then stopped as though she had been caught doing something very, very naughty. It was the silk, the exquisite silk that had somehow played a part in setting her on this tumultuous journey!

"Oh, Geoff, 'tis beautiful, but I truly cannot accept this."

"Why not? No sumptuary laws here forbidding ornate dress, no self-important clergy to disapprove."

"'Tis—" she paused, running her hand over its luxurious texture. It spilled across her lap like the waters that surrounded them, and she felt—covetous! "Well," she amended, "I've read the Bible many times, and it seems to me I've never seen any proscriptions against silk."

"No 'thou shalt nots' about pretty clothes?"

"Nay, only pride and vanity."

"Venial sins! God made you to wear a gown of this silk, I assure you," he coaxed.

"My other gowns are a shambles," she vacillated.

Wickedly, he added fuel to the fire. "You can hardly meet your aunt for the first time in either of them. Winston Hall is a prestigious plantation." At her surprised look, he supplied, "Giles told me. Now, why would you tell him the reason you were bound for Jamaica and not me?"

Faith absently rubbed the heavenly fabric against her cheek and closed her eyes. "I didn't know if I could trust you," she answered dreamily.

"But you trusted him?"

She opened her eyes, and he was pleased to see a trace of humor in their fathomless depths. "More than you," she said with a smile that was almost saucy.

He smiled back, the price of the silk more than repaid in this new facet of his little Puritan maid, for he did, indeed, feel something akin to possessive with her. "Wise woman."

"What a pity," she replied, mocking his words of the previous morning.

He knelt with one knee on the bed and held the silk back to her face, bringing his own within close proximity. His golden eyes pinned hers of blue-green, and his breath was warm upon her face. The fabric was a bad influence, indeed, for instead of moving away, Faith merely closed her eyes and waited.

Geoff waited, too, though it cost him more than she

would ever know. When she opened her eyes again, they were filled with hurt confusion, but she said nothing.

"You must ask, Faith. I gave my word."

"Your word?"

"I swore to Giles that I'd do naught for which you didn't ask."

She looked away and shook her head. "I do not know what you mean. Whatever would I ask you for?" Even as she uttered the words, she felt a pang of conscience. She knew exactly that for which she longed.

Geoff caught her face gently between his hands and pulled her toward him. "Look at me, love. Do you want me to kiss you?" He read her look of indecision and, in a moment of insight, knew why she could not answer. "Lying is a sin, Faith."

For a split second, she was tempted to swear. She might have succumbed had she not been so sure that in her heart, she was committing another sin altogether.

"So is lust," she answered.

He laughed softly, but not unkindly. "A wish for a simple kiss is not lust, love."

"What is?"

"Something far more potent, I assure you. Something to save for another day. For now, what do you want?"

His face was still inches from her own, and she could see a faint shadow where he had shaved earlier in the day. There was a force about him, a warmth that drew her, and she closed her eyes again. "Kiss me if you please, Geoff."

She was unprepared for the strong wave of heat that engulfed her at the tender touch of his lips to hers. Her first instinct was to pull away, but he still held her face, then slipped one hand gently to the nape of her neck. His mouth moved softly against hers, as though he had all day to accustom her to the feel of it, and at last, she relaxed, her own lips softening, yielding. When he pulled away, she felt as supple as the cloth upon her lap.

"Are you sure this is not lust?" she asked.

"Nay," he replied, his voice rough. "I'm not sure of that, at all." He rose and ran a hand through his hair, his face troubled.

"Did I displease you?"

He gave a strangled laugh. Nay, she had pleased him far more than he had expected. He did not look at her again until he knew he could face her with a light smile. "'Twas a fine kiss, love, but I've no time to dally, and you sorely tempt me. You'll find scissors, needle, and thread in there as well." He nodded to the package that lay open on the floor. "I hope that will help occupy your time."

"Aye, between this and the book, I'll be fine."

A shadow passed over his face, but quickly evaporated. "Save the book awhile, love. You'll have plenty to do with the dress."

When he left her, she was enthusiastically spreading the fabric across his desk, which somehow brought to mind the thought of her skin sliding as lightly across his body. Still, there was more to the turmoil inside of him than the simple anticipation of bedding her. He had made her happy, and he could almost believe that should she remain stalwart in her purity, her happiness was enough.

The thought brought him up short. What was it about the wench? Damned if he wasn't beginning to like her! Oh, wouldn't Giles be ever-so-smug about that? He allowed himself a wry grin at his own expense. So he liked her! Even Faith would be hard-pressed to find the sin in that.

In the cabin, Faith set about carefully measuring and tracing a pattern with a light heart. She had never met anyone like this captain who seemed two completely different men. He was at once a hardened cynic and a gentle romantic. Oh, she well knew that the gift was but a part of his campaign to seduce her, but there was something else there. She could feel it like the timeless movement of the ocean.

Mayhap he was a rogue. Mayhap he was nothing like the good and pious men she had known all her life. But neither did he ask her to be anything but what she was. In his rough way, he was honest and kind and generous. It occurred to her that just as there was a world beyond her small village, so was there a goodness beyond her small understanding of goodness.

Chapter 10

For the seventh time on this one voyage, Diego closed his eyes and bowed his head over a shrouded body. The priest, who had accompanied them as a passenger to the New World, chanted sonorously in Latin, swinging his censer and, through some miracle, bringing Diego's patron saint to him. In the darkness behind his eyelids, he could see her! She was beautiful, dressed much like the mother of God in all the paintings and on all the statues, but darker, with jet-black hair and full, red lips.

"Fear not, Diego," she whispered in a lilting, foreign accent. "This will be the last taken by fever. You have been brave and strong. Yours has not been an easy journey, and it will be harder yet."

For a moment, he was speechless. His first instinct was to fall to his knees, and it was a moment before he realized that he was already there. He remained dimly aware of the priest's voice and the scent of incense. His heart pounded, and his mouth went dry. Who was he to be visited by a saint?

"Santa Maria," he begged her in his thoughts, "more trouble we can do without. I do not know how much more I can get us through."

"You are a man of generous heart and great pride. You will do whatever you must. But I warn you to remember this: sometimes what you wish for most is not meant to be. Take care of your men. It is not yet time to play the hero."

Alarmed, he opened his eyes, and she disappeared in the blinding sun that bounced off of the snowy linen shroud before him. He glanced around at the men who surrounded him. They were respectfully silent, fearful of all that had befallen them, but none seemed as if he had seen a saint on their ship.

Diego wiped his sweating palms on his breeches. The sun, that was it. He was still fighting the effects of illness himself, though he had never fully surrendered to it. The heat of the sun and the last vestiges of fever were toying with his mind. This was no time to fancy himself a visionary.

Still, he could not help but hope that she spoke the truth when she said that this man would be the last to die. Of course, she said that the journey would be harder still, but that it was "not yet time to play the hero." Now, what did that mean? Females, even female saints, were a mystery to him.

Faith and Geoff supped together, and he taught her to play backgammon. He told her that the men placed wagers on this game and asked what she might stake, but she only smiled and shook her head at him. The water was always flavored with rum, as it took little time in the ship's barrels for it to begin to taste a bit off. Tonight he poured the libation more liberally.

"Are you hoping to inebriate me?" she asked.

"Is that a sin, too?"

"Aye, it is," she said, as she took a healthy swallow.

She showed him her progress on the gown, and he explained how the mysterious backstaff worked.

"You see, you stand with your back to the sun, like so," he said, standing behind her to guide her hand, "then look through here."

Faith giggled. "There is no sun in here."

Geoff looked all about the cabin, as though the fact had escaped him. "True enough," he admitted, but he stayed behind her, his hands still holding hers. "We'll have to make do with our imaginations."

"I think that you do but seek an excuse to stand so close together."

He gave her wounded look, but he could not keep the sparkle from his eyes. "Me? Stoop to petty excuses to touch you?" His large, callused hands covered her own white ones, though they were strong and work roughenéd, as well. "You have fine hands," he whispered in her ear, sending a thrill down her spine.

"So do you," she replied, slipping her hand from beneath his to caress with one finger the veins that raised his dark flesh along the back of it.

He turned her smoothly to face him, and she had to tilt her head back to look up into his eyes, placing her hands on his shoulders to keep steady.

"Do I always have to ask?" *What has become of me?* Faith wondered silently, but her heart beat more rapidly in anticipation.

He didn't answer, simply pulled her to him and took her soft lips to his own. She knew what to expect this time and welcomed the rich, melting sensation that flowed from her mouth to her limbs. Her hands tangled themselves in his hair, and she pulled him closer, wanting something more, but not sure what.

Geoff tore himself away before he lost every last

shred of self-restraint he possessed. "That'll do, love. We've a whole night to make it through."

Faith smothered her disappointment and changed the subject. "Why do you call me that?"

"What?"

"'Love.' You say you don't believe in love, yet you call me by its name when you tease me."

"Believe me, Faith, it is not I who is teasing. Nevertheless, 'tis just a word. A pet name."

"I wish you wouldn't call me that, not if you don't mean it."

"Don't start getting sentimental, love, uh, my sweet. Is that better? Why is it women like you cannot simply enjoy a little pleasure without turning it into something ridiculous and complicated?"

"Women like me? Ridiculous and complicated?"

"Oh, now don't get cross." He smiled winningly, but she refused to be taken in. "I meant no harm." He took her hand and pressed his lips to her palm, causing a pleasant bolt of sensation to race from her hand through her arm and straight to her heart. "I mean to have you, that's sure, but not under false pretenses. We'll have a good time, maybe be friends, but we'll part ways in Port Royal."

Faith pulled away from him and moved to the window. In the dark there was little to distinguish sea from sky but the moon that wavered murkily behind the glass. She did not want to be friends and part ways. She thought perhaps she wanted him, too, but she couldn't help it; she believed in forever.

She didn't dare look at him. Surely her heart was in her eyes, and he would scowl and scold her. Instead, she glanced around the room with a light smile. "Yes, we'll have a very good time, we two good friends.

We'll play backgammon and chess. Perhaps I'll tell you Bible stories. They are quite exciting, some of them. I could tell you about Mary Magdalene. Surely she's a woman from the Good Book whom you could admire."

Geoff gave an exaggerated shudder. "Bible stories? We have a very different notion of a good time, you and I. But I confess, you have my attention. Why would I like this Mary Magdalene? Was she not the so-called virgin who gave birth to Jesus?"

Faith shook her head vigorously. "Nay! That was Mary—well, just Mary. Mary Magdalene was a prostitute. A repentant sinner who served the Lord ere he was sacrificed."

"Repentant sinner? Nay, she's lost my interest there. I think she's one prostitute I would do better to avoid."

In fact, he decided it best to avoid temptation altogether. The thought of listening to Bible stories from the very lips he had yet to taste enough of was too disturbing. Likely as not, he would silence her in ways that would take them straight to bed, with or without her elusive consent. He gave her cheek a chaste peck and hied himself to the deck, where no one would simultaneously preach to and tempt him.

Hours later, when Geoff came to bed, Faith lay awake, unable to sleep. He seemed more awkward than most nights and gave her a toss when he fell into bed beside her. Within moments it hit—the smell of rum. She knew enough to know she could never trick him into believing her asleep.

"Are you drunk?"

He heaved a pungent sigh. "Aye."

"The cook said you didn't drink."

"Not often."

"Is it because of me?"

"Go to sleep."

"Did I anger you?"

"Faith, I've drunk all this so that I can sleep with you next to me. Now shut up and let me sleep, else I'll do what I was trying to avoid!"

Faith wisely closed her mouth. She wasn't sure how far she was willing to let this go, but she was certain she wanted it to stop before he did. She relaxed, growing accustomed to the steady sound of his breathing, the comforting warmth of him. This was depraved, she told herself sternly, but in truth, it did not seem so. It seemed so utterly right, so completely natural. She did not hold herself rigid against the wall, but allowed herself to fall into a deep, dreamless sleep.

She must have been tired, for when she woke he was gone, and the room was filled with light. She pulled her gown over her shift, slipped on her shoes, and raced above into the bracing wind as she tucked her hair into her coif.

She recognized Geoff's broad form, even as he leaned over the deck rail. Whatever was he looking at? "Good morning!" she called.

When he turned to her she knew a sudden sense of alarm. He didn't look at all well! "Geoff, are you all right?"

"Have you never encountered a man after a night of drink?" he asked crossly.

"Nay." He looked positively green, and Faith feared that he had quite poisoned himself. "Is it serious? Did you truly drink so very much?"

"Aye, I'm like to die," he groaned, but then laughed weakly when her eyes widened. "Nay, I'll live. I've no stomach for it is all. Especially rum."

"Oh."

He shook his head at her disapproving look, then clapped his hand over his eyes. "Don't preach. God is punishing me enough, to be sure."

Giles came to her side and gave her a merry grin. "'Tis good to see the captain faring so poorly."

"Excuse me?" she asked.

He winked at her and replied, "Means he's keeping his word, and that you're sticking to your guns. 'Tis about time he met a wench who didn't tumble into his bed after a single look."

A frown pulled at the corners of Faith's lips. "How many women have tumbled into his bed?"

"Now, Giles," Geoff protested, "you're doing me no good here. She'll think I'm a rake."

"You are," Giles supplied cheerily.

Fine for them, she thought to herself. To her it was no laughing matter. The thought of him with other women hurt more than she cared to admit, and left her wondering what he thought of her. Did he find her lack of experience unsatisfying? Perhaps if she knew what she was doing, he would not need to drink himself into a stupor. She could do something that would please him for the time being.

A niggling guilt tugged at the corner of her mind, but she brushed it aside. She had committed so many sins already, what was one or two more? Besides, Puritan theology taught her that the actions of mortals did not move God. Those among the elect, chosen for salvation, had been chosen before birth. If she were truly graced, she would not even have these strange desires. For a wicked, wicked moment, she pitied those so chosen, for they would miss out on this exhilarating, befuddling experience.

She silently argued with herself as the two men spoke of mundane matters, and was still trying to harness her wayward thoughts hours later, when Geoff joined her for the midday meal.

He slowly chewed the dried beef in front of him, grateful that his nausea and headache were abating. The woman in front of him toyed with the food on her plate as though she were the one who had imbibed too heavily the previous night.

"Something's troubling you," he said.

She looked up at his words and seemed to search for something very important in his face.

"Is it yesterday?" he asked. "I spoke too bluntly. I made it sound as though all I cared for is your body."

"Isn't it?"

"Nay, and that's the very thing. I've never had a woman for a friend. I think that would be the perfect lover, a woman you liked who liked you."

"But not love."

He shrugged. "Of a kind, but even friends can't spend every minute of every day together. They wear on each other. I shouldn't want to pledge myself to Giles for the rest of my life."

"But you'll be friends for life."

"Aye, but 'tis different."

"How so?"

"Giles can make his own way in the world. 'Tis not your fault, but you'll need a man. You're not made to take a series of lovers, and no man who marries you will share you with me. We'll have to part, sooner or later. Still, I like you. You're not like any other woman I've known."

Whatever response Geoff expected, it was not the one he got.

"Will you kiss me, as you do other women?"

"What?"

"I think there is something more. I sense you hold something back, and you seem unsatisfied. I would know what it is that you withhold."

The wait for just such a request had long tried his patience, yet now he hesitated. "I warn you, Faith, 'twill take more than a kiss to satisfy me."

"You have spoken plainly with me, and I will do the same. I cannot promise you more than this kiss. Still, I have asked."

He smiled at her implied demand. "I promised I would do naught but what you ask for; I did not promise to do all that you ask."

"Do you not want to kiss me? 'Tis a sin to lie." She smiled back, an enticing little smile that brooked no denial.

They rose from their respective places at the desk, eyes locked, tension vibrating in the air between them. He closed his eyes and tried to imagine her a mere tavern wench, an easy night's pleasure, but when his lips touched hers, the illusion would not hold. Her mouth was eager but untaught.

"Part your lips for me, Faith," he murmured against her, and when she did, his tongue dipped delicately to savor this first sweet taste of her. She sighed softly and stood on her toes, pressing herself full against him, and he pulled the coif from her head to bury his hands in her hair. Instinctively, she turned her head slightly, giving him full access to her, and he deepened the kiss, thrilled when her tongue responded tentatively in kind.

The blood roared in Faith's ears, and she knew not whose breath was whose, only that it came hard and fast. Her fingers splayed themselves against the hard heat of his back beneath his soft cotton shirt. When he would withdraw, she cried out softly into his mouth and pulled him back to her. She might well burn in hell for the feelings Geoff had ignited; she would have her fill and make it worth the price.

Geoff ached. He wanted to touch her, taste every inch of her, bury himself in her, and just at the moment he believed she would let him. He had to make her think. If he took her now, she would feel nothing but regret after.

He pulled forcefully away and spoke, his voice thick with desire. "What is it you would ask of me, my sweet? Do you want me to make love to you?"

An "aye" nearly tripped from her tongue, but a moment's reflection stopped her. Make love? Aye, she wanted that, and no less. "Nay. Forgive me, I did not know it would be so—"

"Powerful?"

"Aye," she said, her voice laced with awe.

"I told you, lust is a powerful thing."

"Aye, it is," she said, moving away from him.

And so it was. When he held her in his arms and pressed his lips to hers, desire seemed to drive every rational thought from her mind. But even when he was not touching her, she loved every moment in his company. He was a scoundrel by every rule she had ever known, but she admired him. He could be as serious and responsible as the most staunch Puritan man, but he was witty and playful, as well. He laughed easily, and she found that with him, she could, too.

It wasn't that her family had been entirely lacking in humor. She thought wistfully of David and Isaiah's childish antics and of the gentle, good-natured teasing between her and Noah. Even her father could engage in some jest if the circumstances made it too hard to resist. But as with all other things, humor and fun were to be had in moderation. At the appropriate time, and in the appropriate place.

Geoff cared naught for moderation. Work, play, food, flesh. He embraced and savored all that life had to offer and encouraged her to do the same. At times, she would think of the huge, irrevocable step she had taken when she had left home, and she would be nearly paralyzed with fear. But then he would sweep into the cabin, or appear on deck, and she found his reckless sense of adventure contagious. With him, she felt she could do anything.

"I'd give a gold doubloon for those thoughts," he said, interrupting her ponderings.

"What?" she asked, giving her head a little shake.

"For a moment, you looked so stern that I thought you must be contemplating the fires of hell. But that was a lovely little smile, just at the end there. Tell me 'twas thoughts of me that put it there." He grinned rakishly at her.

She tried to frown at him in mock disapproval, but the corners of her mouth would not comply. "You are a terrible, wicked man, Captain Hampton."

"Thank you," he replied.

Chapter 11

Faith lay atop the covers on Geoff's bed, transfixed by the volume of Robert Herrick's verses. She had not begun it earlier because the dress had occupied much of her time, but her fingers rebelled at last, and she sought a chance to relax. The book was anything but relaxing. In it were verses gently chiding young virgins to "Gather ye rosebuds while ye may," for life was short and youth quickly spent. There was verse upon verse dedicated to a woman named Julia. Verses extolling the merits of every part of her body. Verses that made Faith wonder wickedly if perhaps Geoff might see "strawberries half drown'd in cream" in her nipples as Herrick saw in Julia's.

It was little wonder this poet was a favorite of the man whose bed she shared. In one composition, he spoke of how he loved to woo but had no wish to wed. He had somehow managed to make his appetite for many women seem romantic rather than depraved. All this, written by a minister? She knew that she should set it aside, that her parents had been right. Poetry had no place in the library of an upright woman. Just reading it had made her tingle and awakened strange cravings. It had aroused an immoral sense of curiosity.

She closed her eyes and buried her face in the pillow that smelled of Geoff, allowing images of him to drift through her head. In her mind's eye she could see his hair as the wind swept it about his lean face, envision his broad, dark shoulders and back when he peeled off his shirt. She imagined his eyes, intense and golden, and it took all of her will to keep from running her hands over the front of her bodice, thinking of his hands, large and strong.

She sat bolt upright and flushed guiltily when he opened the door and walked into the room unannounced.

"Geoff! You startled me."

"Sorry, my sweet. Were you napping? I thought to let you know the weather looks a bit untamed, and we'll soon be rounding Cape Hatteras. 'Twill be a rough day at sea today." His gaze fell upon the book that lay open next to the pillow. "Ah, you were reading, then?"

She rose hastily and became absorbed in one of the many wrinkles in her skirt. "You said they were written by a minister."

"They are," he defended. "Even a minister can appreciate the pleasures of the flesh. You see, Faith, 'tis not so very sinful."

Could that be so? It was tempting to believe him. After all, marriage was consummated by such pleasures, and what was the meaning of consummate? To perfect, to complete.

Nay! She did but seek to justify her weakness! "Such verses are a bad influence," she said with a frown.

Interest lit the gold dust in his eyes. "Are they? What influence have they over you?" Her blush deepened, but she said nothing. Geoff closed the space between them like a lion stalking a nervous gazelle. "Tell me, Faith. Tell me of their corrupt influence."

"They are lewd," she whispered, without conviction.

"They are erotic."

Erotic. It was a word she had never heard before, but somehow it brought to mind the whisper of her scissors as they sliced through the silk Geoff had given her. It was a word that seemed to fit the smell of him, the heat when he pulled her into his arms.

Geoffrey watched the play of emotions on her face. The poetry had given her knowledge she hadn't possessed, awakened urges she hadn't known lay dormant within her. The realization filled him with urges of his own, ones that had been simmering just below the surface for far too long. He sighed in pent-up frustration.

"Why must you complicate it, Faith? Why can you not lose yourself in it?"

She lifted her gaze to his. Lose herself, indeed. Her whole world seemed trapped in the light of his eyes. He took both of her hands in his and pulled her to him, his mouth brushing hers, his teeth lightly catching her full, tempting lower lip. The slight growth of beard upon his face rasped gently against her as he continued to kiss her along her jaw and down her neck.

"God, a man could drown in the taste of you. You're sweeter than any wine. We thirst for each other, my sweet, and we could quench each other, as well, if you would only let it be enough."

She opened her mouth to stop him, but nothing more than a sigh escaped. He captured her mouth again, drinking as though she were, indeed, the wine of which he spoke, and she drank, too, as though she would die of thirst. His hands moved, traveled down her bodice just as she craved, spreading liquid heat in their wake.

She didn't think, banished thoughts from her befuddled mind. Her own hands slid over the soft cotton that covered his hard, muscular chest, then journeyed on over his shoulders and down his arms. He caught one hand and placed a lingering kiss on the sensitive flesh of her palm, then pushed her sleeve up, bestowing kisses up the inside of her arm, warming the blood in her veins.

"Geoff," she whispered. She had no idea what she had intended to say. Whatever it was, he cut it off when his mouth returned to hers. He pulled her full against him, filling her with aching desire.

"Tell me you want this," he whispered fiercely against her ear.

She wanted to. She wanted to drown in the waves that washed over her, but she couldn't find her voice. Geoff looked deep into her eyes and read the indecision there. With a groan he kissed her again, more deeply, more intensely. "Let go, Faith. Give in. Tell me you want this," he repeated.

"I want—"

He didn't release her when Giles pounded on the cabin door. "Cap'n, we'll be needing you above. You've no time to tarry."

"Damn," Geoff swore softly under his breath. "In a moment," he called to Giles. "Faith—" he began.

Relief and regret mingled as she pushed him from her and regained her senses. "You're needed above."

Geoff frowned darkly as he watched the passion abate from her expression. "We are not finished here, Faith. I'll be back tonight, and if you're asleep, I'll wake you."

With that he turned abruptly to attend to his duties on deck, and Faith wondered which storm would prove more violent, the one that threatened to toss the ship into a fevered pitch, or the one that raged inside of her.

She stayed several long hours in the cabin below. The ship heaved violently upward, then slammed down again with bone-jarring force. Anything that was not securely anchored down fell to the wooden floor and skittered back and forth across it. The window offered no comfort, pounded by waves, wind, and rain. It was surely a miracle that it did not give beneath the onslaught. She had not been so terrified since she had huddled in the pitch-blackness of the ship's hold, surrounded by rats. Even then she had not had this horrible sense that the ship would fill with icy water at any moment. Sooner or later the wood would splinter and crack under the force that smacked relentlessly against it.

Unable to bear staying in the cabin alone, Faith braved the passage beyond. She knew that she wasn't to be alone with the crewmen, but no one paid her any mind. There was noise and confusion enough to mask her presence. The lower decks were packed with men and animals brought in from above to weather the storm. Chickens raucously protested being tossed about in their cages, and the goats were in a truly foul temper, biting and butting anyone unfortunate enough to be thrown in close proximity to them.

Faith stumbled to the hatch and clung fiercely to the ladder, hardly daring to breathe until she opened the trap door at the top of it and stumbled out upon the deck. Ice-cold rain drenched her instantly, and the wool of her gown became impossibly heavy, so that when her feet slipped upon the wet deck, she could do naught but go down.

"Faith!" Giles called to her above the gale. "What are you doing up here? Go below before you're hurt!"

"Nay!" she called back. "'Tis worse down there!"

"'Tis bad enough to 'ave 'er on board in a storm like this!" Killigrew complained. "Rotten luck, a woman on a ship. Send 'er below!" Under his breath he grumbled, "Like it don't already stick in our craws to think of the cap'n's privilege without 'aving the wench underfoot at a time like this."

The ship careened, and Faith slid, fear wrapping icy fingers around her heart as the rail rushed toward her. She ripped her nails digging them into planks of the deck, but to no avail. She didn't have to look to know that it was Geoff's hand, sure and strong, that pulled her to her feet and back to safety. When she found the courage to look up at him, his face was dark with anger.

"You can't be up here!" he called. Water poured from his hair, cascading over the clothes plastered to his body, and it occurred to Faith that if the deck was not safe for her, neither was it safe for him.

"You are up here!" she shouted.

"I've no time for this," he shouted back. He hauled her unceremoniously to the aft mast and wrapped a rope about her waist. "Stay here," he instructed and strode across the slick deck as though it were dry. The crew quickly hulled the vessel, furling most of the sails so that the ship could drift with the wind, rather than allowing the wind to fill them and tug the vessel on her side.

Rain and waves washed over Faith and the deck in torrents, pouring from the roll of sail above her with enough force to drown her if she didn't actively seek air. Geoff stood firmly at the helm, steering them through the storm as best he could, while Giles kept order within the chaos of men who had remained above to work.

The two men labored tirelessly as the rest of the crew cycled in and out, up and down from the safety of below deck. Giles beseeched her to go below as well, but though she was frozen, tired, and frightened, she had to see for herself that the waves that crashed around them did not sweep Geoff into the vast and careless ocean. She was useless and a distraction to the man who caused her such worry, but she couldn't bring herself to leave.

Geoff glanced over to the foolish woman who coughed and gasped under the canvas. Whatever discomfort she suffered was her own doing, but it riled him to realize that it didn't stop him from wanting to go and wrap his arms around her. When he thought of her sliding swiftly and inexorably toward the rail, he knew a coldness beyond the biting rain and wind. Over and over his mind replayed the scene, but he saw another ending, her small frame swept over the side to be swallowed by merciless waves. He shook his head to clear the image. This was no time to chase nightmares, not when there were dangers real enough to contend with.

In time, the storm finally spent the greater portion of its fury. It settled into a steady rain and churned the sea less brutally. Geoff turned the helm over to another and retrieved Faith from the mast. When they gained his cabin, he shut the door and immediately set to stripping the sodden dress from her shivering body. She tried to push him away, but her frozen limbs held no strength.

"Geoff, about what happened earlier," she began through chattering teeth.

He glowered at her from beneath scowling brows. "At the moment this has nothing to do with what happened earlier. The damned thing is pouring water all over my floor." He picked up the dripping mass, opened the door, and called out to a crewman beyond. "You there! Take this. Hang it out to dry when the storm clears."

She stood in her linen shift, pulling the wet, clinging, sheer fabric from the front of her and trying to maintain some semblance of modesty.

"These, too!" he barked, causing Faith to turn curiously. She was too stunned to speak. Before he could pull the blanket from the bed and wrap it around him, she caught sight of his compact, naked backside, the skin oddly white from waist to knee. She forgot all about her own state of undress until he turned back to her. Whatever he had opened his mouth to say to her died, even as his eyes heated.

There were no preliminaries, no pretense of gaining permission. He crossed the cabin floor and grabbed her roughly by the shoulders, fastening his mouth to hers hungrily. His skin was as cold as hers, his mouth searing in contrast. "Do you never think before you do a thing?" he demanded when he tore his lips from hers.

"Are you telling me to think now?" she asked. She tried to think. She knew that she should stop this before it raged out of control. Watching from the mast above she had been torn between the firm belief that if God saw fit to spare them she must repent and sin no more and the overwhelming desire to hold Geoff in her arms and give him all that he could ever ask.

"Nay, not now. Of all times, not now," he answered hoarsely. He tangled his hands in her wet hair and kissed her again, taking the breath from her and making her dizzy. His hot mouth left a scorching trail as his kisses drifted down her neck. Resistance was impossible. Her body and heart defied her conscience. She let her head fall back, offering him the length of her throat, and he did not stop, even when he reached the top of her shift. Instead, he tore it from neck to waist, the fabric rending effortlessly in his fingers.

"This is about what happened earlier," he said firmly.

Vaguely the thought crossed her mind that she hadn't exactly shifts to spare, but he pushed it away like so much flotsam on the tide. His mouth tasted lightly salty, and his hair smelled of rain. His kisses moved down over her neck and shoulders, sending seething heat through her limbs as he lifted her up and eased her onto the bed. As though to prevent any protest, his lips returned to hers, and he pressed her to the mattress with his weight. The feel of him made her heart pound, and she knew that she was powerless against the current that swept her away. She had found a part of herself she hadn't known was missing and could not let it go if she had wanted to.

The cold that had gripped Geoff throughout the storm dissipated quickly as he melded his flesh to hers. Her mouth was warm and sweet, intoxicating as rum, and her sighs ignited white-hot flames inside him. He hadn't meant it to be like this. He had meant to take his time, torment her as she had tormented him, but the fear of nearly losing her drove him. He had never lain with a virgin, and he knew that he should be gentle. There was pain, and usually some fear, but the ardent wench beneath him seemed anything but frightened. Her hands pulled at him in wanton invitation. Still, there was a small technicality to dispense with.

"Say it, my sweet," he urged.

"Aye, Geoff," she moaned.

"Aye, what?"

"Aye! Aye, I want you. I want this. I have never known such wanting!"

He gave in to her then, fastening his mouth around her taut nipple. Her gasp of pleasure brought a tightening to his loins. The inside of her thigh felt like silk to his questing hand, though the wet softness at its highest point was more enticing still. Slowly he slipped his finger into the tight sheath hidden among the moist folds, and sweat broke out across his forehead as he held himself in check. His gaze drank in the sight of her alabaster form writhing among the sheets as he rhythmically stroked until her back arched gracefully and she cried out his name.

The moment she seemed to return from the abyss, he covered her pliant body with his, insinuating his knees between hers and spreading her legs wide under him. He braced himself with one hand, using the other to gently caress her, tracing her breasts and stomach as he sought her entrance with his hardness. The heat, the wetness, was nearly more than he could bear, and he fought the urge to bury himself, press onward to his own climax.

Faith moved her hips against him. She had no idea it would be like this, that there would be this screaming, driving need to be filled with him, yet he drove her mad as he took his time. At last, fill her he did. She felt a resistance inside of her, and he fell upon her, his mouth claiming hers completely and swallowing her cry of pain when he thrust deeply and took her maidenhead.

He would have stopped, allowed her to accustom

herself to him, but she would have none of it. The discomfort of his invasion was nothing to the agony of her need, and her hips moved of their own accord, pressing against his in urgent demand. He withdrew slowly, causing moans of tormented desire to rasp in both their throats. His next powerful thrust wrung yet another cry from Faith, and though he feared he had hurt her, the rapture on her face said otherwise. He quickened the pace, and when he felt her tighten around him he found his own release, pouring himself, body and soul, into the sweet, all-consuming essence that was Faith.

At last, he regained some sense of himself and looked down into the blue-green ocean of her eyes. In the flickering lamplight, they were wide with wonder, gazing earnestly back at him. "What think you of the wages of sin?" he inquired softly.

"Sin? Oh, nay, Geoff. 'Twas no sin. 'Twas a gift. The most precious, most perfect gift! It was not the pleasure only. It was you, and the wholeness of it, and . . . Ah, there are no words!"

The change in him was so abrupt, Faith could not fathom what happened. When first he looked down upon her, she had seen it all in his eyes, too. The rapture that went beyond anything that could be spoken. Now he shut down with that emotionless look that chilled her so. Had she said something wrong?

He rolled away, and the warmth of their loving evaporated like mist upon the shore. "Geoff?" she called uncertainly.

When he turned back to her, the look was gone, replaced by a casual grin. "Do you see what your 'thou shalt nots' would rob you of? You'd never have known what you were missing."

Unable to bear the hurt in her eyes, he rose from the bed and pulled dry breeches from his sea chest. He had to leave, go above into the bracing rain. He had to think of something other than the one truth that washed over him like a solid wall of icy seawater. Through all the years, through all the women, he hadn't known what he'd been missing.

"There's sure to be damage. I'll go take care of my duties and be back soon. You get some rest, lo—" He stopped himself. It was just a word, a pet name, and he had promised not to use it.

It hadn't escaped Faith. He hadn't slipped and used the endearment at all before now. Was that because he felt something, or because it was what he called all the others? Perhaps what happened was nothing special. Perhaps it was always so. Still, she felt certain it would not be the same for her with any other. She had not merely wanted a man; she wanted Geoff.

Chapter 12

Diego's patron saint had proven herself, so far. As she promised, no others fell to fever, and the last of those who had suffered were rapidly improving. Little Galeno recovered quickest of all, bouncing back in the way that only the very young can. Diego couldn't decide whether his vision was blasphemous, holy, or merely a hallucination brought on by fever and weakness. It was probably the latter.

She had also said there would be more trouble, but all was well, and soon they would be in Spanish waters off the coast of Cuba. He hastily crossed himself. Was he a fool to tempt the hand of God? These were the most dangerous waters of all! This was the route taken by galleons, floating low under the weight of gold that flowed from the Spanish Main. Because of this, it was a route plagued by pirates. His was a small ship, of little consequence compared to the treasure fleets, but her cargo and crew were not worthless.

The men who surrounded him went about their duties with the same cautious optimism that Diego himself felt. He worked hard to keep the edgy sense of foreboding that plagued him deeply buried. He was their leader, and they looked to him to assuage their own fears. They had been through much and served him well, for all that he was not the captain to whom they had originally pledged their loyalties. He could not let them down.

"Santa Maria," he whispered softly into the warm gulf breeze, "perhaps we could forego these other hardships of which you spoke. You said there would be another time to play the hero." He closed his eyes, half expecting her to appear to him again, and he was both relieved and disappointed when all he saw was the backs of his eyelids.

When Faith awoke, the cabin was unfamiliarly bright. Geoff was not next to her, and she had no idea whether or not he had ever returned. She rose, wincing at the tenderness between her legs, letting her glance skim the droplets of dried blood upon the sheets. She could almost have believed the whole incident a dream if it were not for the physical evidence. Once she had dressed and tucked her hair into her coif, she mounted the ladder determined to face the day.

Nothing could have prepared her for the sight that met her eyes. At first she felt disoriented by the blinding light, and she closed her eyes against it. Then she blinked and gasped in awe. Above her, the sky had been washed clean to a dazzling azure offset by merry yellow sunlight. The ocean had gone from murky green to brilliant blue, and the breeze that caressed her was warm and delicious.

Geoff couldn't help himself. He watched her, the look of disbelief followed by wanton pleasure. In the dark of night he could easily promise himself that he would never touch her again. In the light of the sensuous Gulf Stream sun, he knew that he would take all that he could get ere he left her in Port Royal.

She scanned the deck and found him. He smiled at her, and whatever coldness he had left in her heart the previous night melted. She spread her arms and whirled in a spontaneous gesture of delight.

"It is a miracle, is it not?" Faith asked.

As much as he wanted to believe it, Geoff only shook his head. "'Tis no miracle, Faith. 'Tis calm, blue waters reflecting the clear sky above. What you see is but the nature of these climes."

"And 'tis our nature to be moved by them," she insisted. "Mayhap that is the miracle."

"Mayhap," he agreed, unwilling to spoil the moment and having no argument. "Mayhap."

Faith ducked her chin sheepishly. "I must seem so very silly to you. Of course, you've seen this many times."

"Aye, Faith, I have. Still, one can experience a thing over and over, and with the right person, 'tis all anew."

She cast a questioning look through her lashes, and her heart gave a little flutter at the seriousness in his eyes. He meant more than this new aspect of the ocean.

They walked to the rail, and she leaned comfortably against him, letting the wind blow her troubles into the endless jewel of the ocean and sky. She had almost expected the storm to renew its fury the night before, when Geoff had left and she had had time to contemplate the magnitude of the choice she had made. All this beauty, the perfect contentment she felt in his arms, it all seemed but a benediction. Perhaps God understood that these were special circumstances. If this was, indeed, meant to be, there was time to set things aright.

The crew seemed lighter of heart, as well. They laughed more readily; tempers flared less often. The one with the fine tenor voice broke into song, and Geoff hummed along softly. The tune was unfamiliar to Faith, who knew only hymns, so she simply enjoyed the music and the breathtaking loveliness of the scene.

Only the one called Killigrew continued to nurse whatever resentment he held. He watched her intently, and she liked not the look in his eye.

Giles cautioned her about the effects of so much sun on skin as pale as hers and led her back to the cabin below. She flushed brightly when she saw his eyes travel to the rumpled, bloodstained sheets. Hastily, she tugged the covers up and smoothed them neatly.

"You've no cause for shame," Giles said softly. "And besides, I had no need to see the sheets. 'Twas on your faces above."

"You must think me loose," she protested.

Giles only smiled. "You? Nay. Geoff has always had a way with wenches." At Faith's sharply indrawn breath, he hastened to explain. "Forgive me! 'Tis just a word. I've been too long in coarse company and don't always think before I speak. You are a lady, Faith, and a virtuous one."

She blushed again, and her eyes were drawn back to the bed with its incriminating linens hidden from view.

Guessing the path of her thoughts, Giles leaned against the desk and addressed her firmly. "Virginity and virtue are not the same thing, you know."

"Not entirely," Faith acceded.

"Not at all," Giles replied. "Damn me! I almost feel like I should call him out over this. Did he hurt you?"

Unable to meet his earnest gaze, she shook her head. "He kept his promise to you," she confessed.

"Well, then," Giles answered with a little grin, "I shan't run him through with my cutlass, after all."

Finally, she looked him in the face. Perhaps she was a little embarrassed, but she wasn't truly ashamed. "I love him," she explained, and as she did so, her throat tightened and tears welled in her eyes. "It wasn't merely lust. I think I could have resisted that."

With a weary sigh, Giles pulled himself up so that he was sitting on the desk. "You cannot love him, Faith."

"But I do! You cannot know what it's like. All my life I have felt like a fraud. I have never measured up to what I was told a good woman should be. But Geoff, he makes me feel whole. He makes me feel worthy. I can think, be, breathe when I am with him."

Giles nodded. "Aye, he's a good man, Geoff. He is forthright and honest, and accepts people for what they are, even as he expects them to accept him on the same terms. So, in his honesty, Faith, what promises has he made to you?"

She broke her eyes away from his. "He needs time, that's all. Everything's changed now. Ere we reach Jamaica, he'll see that we must be together."

Sliding off the edge of the desk, Giles came toward her and took her hands in his. "You are very young, and you'll grow much in this journey of yours. But Geoff is a man, fully grown and set in his ways. I only hate to see you hurt."

"And you believe that to be inevitable?"

"Men like us, adventurers and libertines, we're not the ones for women such as you."

She gave his hands a little squeeze. "You're no libertine, Giles Courtney."

"Well, I'm no gentleman, either. The Caribbean is not Massachusetts, Faith. You'll find the freedom you seek, even with a more stable husband. It's more

broad-minded even than Europe, so this affair will do
little to spoil your chances of finding the right man."

"You think I've made a mistake, then?"

"Perhaps not. Perhaps, after a while, you will look
back and treasure this time. Your mistake is in believing
it will last."

In the weeks that followed, Geoff and Faith took all
they could from the fair seas, warm rains, and each
other. Now that they had reached more temperate
climes, Geoff hung blankets on deck to shield her
from prying eyes, and she bathed in seawater. Letting
the rain caught in a tarp sluice over her, she rinsed
the salt and sweat from her, while Geoff took his place
at the crow's nest, keeping watch over the sea and her,
neither a sight he could ever tire of.

It was on such a day that Geoff called out to the
men below, "Ship off the port bow! Faith, dress and
go below!" He hastily climbed from the crow's nest
and began his descent.

She obeyed without hesitation, but called up, "Is it
an enemy ship?" She couldn't imagine who their enemies were. It seemed that Geoff would be on friendly
terms with most pirates, and they were protected by
the Crown.

By the time Geoff reached the bottom of the rig-
gings, she was dressed and pulling down the blankets
that had afforded her privacy. There was no time to
dry her hair, and water soaked the back of her gown,
making it stick uncomfortably to her.

One of the sailors climbed up in Geoffrey's place,
and after a long look through the spyglass, he sang
out, "Spanish! A carrack, Cap'n, merchant ship!"

The crew raised a general shout of enthusiasm, but Geoff swore under his breath and turned to Giles. "We'll hold our course and let her pass."

The one called Killigrew stood but a few feet away, and his eyes lit with fire. "What are ye talkin' about, man? She's sittin' low in the water, ripe fer the takin'."

"Not this time," Geoff responded tersely. "We've enough from the last one. We all have plenty to keep us in drink and women when we get home."

"Oh, ye've enough fer a woman, that's sure." Killigrew swept her with his eyes and a nasty sneer. "'Tis she who's makin' ye turn coward. Well, the rest of us 'ave no wench to keep us satisfied, so 'tis gold we'll be takin'. Ye can be the captain ye're paid to be, or ye can take a swim and we'll choose another."

There were shouts and murmurs of agreement, and even Giles turned his palms up in a gesture of defeat. "If we don't go after her, they'll mutiny. Faith's no safer that way."

Killigrew still assessed her, licking his lips in anticipation, and Faith squelched a sudden urge to vomit.

When Geoff faced her, it was with cold, blank eyes. He pulled her roughly away from the odious sailor and spoke to her in a harsh whisper. "Go below, Faith. In my desk, you'll find a flintlock. If it is not Giles or I who come to get you, you must use it."

"But of what use is it against a mob?" she cried.

The barest trace of tenderness and regret slipped through his defenses, and his throat constricted around his words. "For yourself. You must use it for yourself."

She stared at him in disbelief and choked on a sob.

Giles softened it a bit. "If the Spanish win, you can claim you were kidnapped. They might show mercy.

But if 'tis Killigrew and his men, believe me, Faith, you're better off dead."

"Giles?" she asked, seeking reassurance.

He laid a gentle hand on her shoulder, and all at once, she thought of Noah. This day might well seal her fate. If Geoff and Giles did not prevail, it was very likely she'd have no chance of ever reconciling with her family.

"Have faith," Giles assured her.

"You'll protect him?" she asked.

"We have ever guarded each other's backs."

She nodded, and he turned away to serve his captain and his friend.

Geoff was already shouting orders. Cannon and flintlocks must be loaded, the red flag hoisted. She was loath to leave, but Giles firmly led her to Geoff's cabin. Once there, she opened the desk drawer and found the flintlock, a lead ball, and a small pouch with acrid, black powder. As they approached the Spanish vessel and fired a warning shot across its bow, she discerned how to load it. By the time they had drawn alongside the other ship, she felt sure she knew how to use it.

Suicide was a mortal sin, but as both Geoff and Giles had told her, she would have little choice. The thought of Killigrew and the others' vile hands upon her, profaning the act that had seemed sacred in its own right with Geoff, was enough to spur her on. Besides, if she had to kill herself, it would be because Geoff was dead, and even heaven would be hell without him.

Chapter 13

It was almost automatic, really. He had been through enough battles to give all the right orders and yet still allow some part of him to dwell upon the woman who waited below. Cannon were fired across the merchant's bow, and none answered back. At first he thought it was the easy surrender that kept his blood from heating as it always did when he and the crew took a Spanish ship. Nay, 'twas Faith. She had brought out so many surprising feelings that he was hardly shocked to realize that he had no desire for this battle, and that it went beyond his concern for Faith's safety.

He knew that one of his greatest strengths in combat was that while he wanted to live, he did not care if he died. It gave him a lethal combination of daring and self-preservation. Now, he had to live. He was, quite simply, not finished, and it was this thought that he carried with him when his crew swung their grappling hooks across the space between the two ships, pulled alongside, and boarded the Spanish carrack *Magdalena*.

Capitán Diego Montoya Fernandez de Madrid y Delgado Cortes pulled his sword from its sheath. He knew that his carrack could not outrun the larger, faster brigantine, and there was no question that *Magdalena* was outgunned. He could not challenge *Destiny* across the water. Still, the valor in his men's hearts could surely prevail above the pirates' evil intentions. Hand-to-hand, he thought they might well stand a chance.

But his optimism did not last. Pirates swarmed *Magdalena*'s deck, and though his crew fought as bravely as he could have asked, they were no match. Diego scanned the fray, his brown eyes alighting upon a tall, golden man who fought with the grace of a cat. Their captain. Without hesitation, he plunged forward. Perhaps, if he could fell their leader, they might still stand a chance.

Geoffrey neatly parried the thrust of a Spanish sword, his own cutlass slicing through the sword arm of the man who had challenged him. The merchant crewman screamed, slipped on his own blood, and fell heavily to the deck. Even as a young cabin boy, Geoff had always had an unerring sense of impending attack, and he spun just in time to avoid another Spaniard's advance.

On a naval vessel, one always knew which of the crew was its captain. On a merchant vessel, it was often not as clear. Now, as Geoff gazed into the determined eyes of his opponent, he knew that it was his counterpart with whom he crossed blades.

"*¡Entregue!*" Geoff shouted. He knew little Spanish, but a few words were essential for a privateer. "Surrender" was one of them.

"Never!" the Spanish captain rejoined, and Geoff had to grin. Apparently his foe had picked up a little English, as well.

Their blades struck against each other over and over again, their clanging lost amid the cacophony of metal clashing and men crying out in pain or glory. The two were well matched, and while one might gain the advantage for a while, the other would quickly take it back. In turn, each would reach up to wipe away the sweat that stung his eyes and tasted of salt upon his lips.

Abruptly, a horrifying sight struck Diego's eyes, distracting him from the battle. Galeno had taken up the blade of a fallen crewman and was hurling his small body straight at one of the pirates!

"*¡No, Galeno, espere!*" he called out. Then, next thing he knew, his sword was wrested from his grip, and the Englishman's sharp blade was pressed against his throat.

"*¡Entregue!*" the man repeated threateningly, his golden eyes glittering in the afternoon sun.

"*¡Pare! ¡Pare, ahora!*" Diego shouted.

The crew around him took up the cry. "*¡Pare! ¡Pare!*" And one by one, they dropped their swords. Silence fell over them, so that the only sound was Galeno, kicking and yelling in the iron grip of the Englishman he had sought to attack.

Diego felt sick. He had made a terrible mistake. If he had surrendered immediately, perhaps they would have had a chance. Now the whole crew would be slaughtered, even the boy, all because of his foolish pride.

Giles gave the squirming lad a stern shake. "Leave off, little man!" he thundered, trying to keep his face serious. "Geoff, tell your man there to call off his puppy."

"*¡Pare, ahora!*" Diego ordered Galeno, and the boy went still, though his face was mutinous.

"You speak a little English?" Geoff asked.

"I speak perfect English," Diego countered.

"So maybe the first time I told you to surrender, I should have spoken English. Apparently it's your Spanish that's wanting."

"The crew obeys my command," Diego said, ignoring the slight. "They have no choice. Do whatever you will with me, but spare my men. They were only following my orders."

"Did you know what ship you crossed?" Geoff asked, his face devoid of any emotion.

"Aye. The ship is *Destiny*."

"Had you heard of it?"

"Many such ships plague the Caribbean," Diego replied. "More than one by that name."

Geoff pressed the blade a little harder into the man's throat. "Know you what fate awaits those who would defy Captain Geoffrey Hampton?"

"What fate awaits any who are defeated by your kind?"

Geoff's smile did not reach his eyes. "Those who surrender keep their ships; those who fight receive no quarter."

Diego closed his eyes, and in the sea breeze the voice of a saint echoed. *But I warn you to remember this: sometimes what you wish for most is not meant to be. Take care of your men. It is not yet time to play the hero.*

"Many honorable Spanish capitáns have died on pirate blades, though they handed over their cargo for the lives of their men," he protested. "I did but act to protect those in my care. Have you no trace of honor to which I can appeal? You are a captain. You know where the responsibility lies."

"Aye," Geoff replied, "I do. I have responsibilities of my own. In many ways, the safety of my men relies upon my reputation. Few men are as foolish as you. Most surrender, sparing my crew the danger of battle. I prefer it that way."

Diego had never felt so utterly helpless in all his life.

Irresistibly, he glanced again at Galeno, who was still in the pirate's firm grip, but whose angry face was now filled with fear. Again, a voice from the past whispered. *Are we all going to die, Capitán?* His mouth went dry.

"You could torture me," he choked. "If my men carry back a truly terrifying tale, your reputation as a ruthless killer goes unchallenged."

A little smile tugged at the corner of the Englishman's mouth, and Diego's gut twisted and cramped in sheer terror, but he would not beg for mercy. He would do whatever he must to protect those who depended upon him.

Geoff had to admire the man. Right now, he was scared enough to soil himself, but he kept a brave face. This was a true leader. The kind of man he probably didn't want to run into again, especially not if he gained a larger vessel and crew. But he was also the kind of man who commanded respect.

Scanning the deck of the carrack, Geoff felt a twinge of regret for the handful of men whose lifeblood ran across its planks. Did any of them have wives? It was a thought that had never troubled him before. He was merciful to those who chose not to cross him, and that had always been enough to soothe whatever conscience he had. Some might say he had ruined Faith, but in truth, 'twas the other way 'round.

"What is your name?" he asked the Spaniard.

"Capitán Diego Montoya Fernandez de Madrid y Delgado Cortes."

The name struck Geoff as familiar, though he couldn't place it. He was sure he had never encountered this man before. "Well, Capitán Diego Montoya et cetera, et cetera, as it happens, I've no taste for blood today."

"What's this?" Killigrew shouted. "Ye're not goin' to let 'im off, Cap'n! 'E knew what 'e was up against, an' 'e made 'is choice. Run 'im through and we'll take what we want. Then we'll set this rat-infested crate aflame!"

Geoff kept his eyes on his prisoner, but he dearly wanted to walk over and take another shot at Killigrew's nose. The last thing he needed right now was to be challenged by one of his own men. "Shut up, Killigrew, else I'll toss you overboard!"

Undaunted, Pete Killigrew tried another tack. His Spanish was limited, but it was sufficient to reach *Magdalena*'s crew.

"*Cochino,*" he taunted a young sailor. The lad was barely twenty, and it was obvious that their defeat had galled him. Killigrew looked him over with contempt. "*Su madre es la puta? La prostituta, si?*" he provoked.

The Spaniard spat in his face, and Killigrew drew his cutlass. A cry went up among the Spaniards that was answered by the English.

"Hold!" Geoff shouted, but the command was lost amid the shouting of men and the rasping of steel. *Magdalena*'s crew leaped to their comrade's defense, and *Destiny*'s band joined the fray.

Diego cursed and, like Geoff, shouted to his men to desist, but to no avail. Cutlasses and swords rang, mingling with the cries of wounded sailors.

As before, *Destiny*'s men gained the upper hand, and the fracas was nearly at an end, when an uneasy tingle zinged down Geoff's spine. He turned quickly, stepping to the side just as his would-be attacker lunged with a blood-stained cutlass. He barely heard Giles's belated warning cry as he sank his own blade to the hilt in Pete Killigrew's chest.

It brought the last of the battle to a grinding halt. Even the Spaniards stood in stunned silence, witnesses to the clear attempted murder of the English captain by one of his own. Geoff gazed dispassionately on the man who had, quite frankly, become an irritant.

Killigrew's body slid from Geoff's cutlass to the deck, and Geoff gave the careless order to throw it overboard. The incident left *Destiny*'s crew edgy, filling the air with all the explosive tension of a powder keg in a lightning storm. The Spanish crew, sensing the uncertainty of whatever mercy they could hope for, stayed out of the way, watching in sullen silence as Madeira, exotic spices, precious fabrics, and their salaries disappeared into *Destiny*'s hold.

Bound so tightly to the mast that his wrists bled, Diego did not watch the process before him. Instead, he watched the other captain. The man was a mystery. He clearly took no pleasure in the day's events. Perhaps he was still shaken by his man's betrayal.

Without venom, Diego said, "I would not let it bother me. I do not suppose you can expect much loyalty from a pirate."

"Nor you much mercy," Geoff retorted, though he could not seem to summon much malice either.

But he had hit upon a nerve. Why had he shown them such mercy? Diego wondered. Why, in this one instance, had Capitán Hampton veered from what he claimed was his usual destruction of a ship that had dared to defy him?

The pirate who had captured Galeno earlier now directed the activity, keeping a careful eye on the cargo as it was unloaded. So, Diego thought, this man was the quartermaster. The man had long ago released Galeno, after Diego had given the boy strict orders to stay out of the way. Presently, Galeno helped the ship's doctor wash and bandage wounds. In yet another unexpected gesture of kindness, the quartermaster patted the child's head as the boy scooted past him in search of more bandages.

Leaning his head back against the mast, Diego closed his eyes. "So, Santa Maria," he whispered softly, "what I wished for most, victory, was not meant to be. Today was not yet my time to be a hero. What now? When does my time come?"

The only reply was the gentle groan of the mast as the wind pulled at its sails.

Chapter 14

Faith gripped the flintlock in white-knuckled fingers. She heard men going in and out of the hold, but they were eerily quiet. Perhaps this was the mood on a privateer ship when the captain had been lost in battle. Footsteps departed from the path to the hold, pausing outside the cabin door. She screwed up her courage as the door opened, and she raised the flintlock to her head.

"Good God, Faith, put that damned thing down!"

She was so relieved to see Geoff's face that she didn't even care that he had taken the Lord's name in vain. She dropped the gun to the desk and rushed into his arms, tears of relief spilling over her cheeks.

He held her tightly against him. She was a brave wench, he'd give her that. The determination in her eyes gave testimony to the fact that she had been prepared to die. No screaming, no hysterics, just a dignified end at her own hand. He took her anxious, beautiful face between his hands and gave her a thorough kiss, one that sent both their heads spinning.

"No time to tarry, love. There's much to do and a long story to tell you. You're safe, and I'm here, and I'll be back soon, for I'm wanting you a damn sight more than what we're loading up now." He smiled at her, and the quickening of his breath promised a reunion worth a few hours' more waiting. And he had called her love.

"I'll be waiting," she replied. "Do not keep me long, for I'd have you know how glad I am to see you."

For all their lighthearted banter, Faith still felt jittery inside. He could have been dead. It was only by the grace of God that he was not. But what about the next time, and the time after that? It was a sin, what he did for a living. He stole from innocent people. How much longer could he count on God's grace?

Every time that Faith's confidence flagged, each time that she wondered if she had sacrificed everything, her family, her home, her soul for naught, she assured herself that surely this was God's will. She had prayed for deliverance, and He had given her *Destiny* and her captain. Now she had to ask yet another question. What might Geoff have prayed for, had he any belief in the power of prayer? How was she his deliverance, too, and from what?

Geoff would never have wished for anyone like Faith. Well she knew that. And yet, was she not what he needed? She knew that she could give him the love he didn't believe existed, but any number of women could give him that. She could preach to him, teach him all that her church had taught her, but she was in such turmoil over her own religious convictions. Surely God could have sent him a far better missionary than her pitiful self.

It seemed that Geoff had been given to her so that she could ask the very questions that terrified her, defy all that she had ever accepted as true. Could she not be the same for him? It had all been too easy for both of them. She had been handed all the answers, and Geoff had been told there were none. Even as he encouraged her to seek the truth, could she not do the same for him?

Later that night, or really, early the next morning, Faith sat at the desk, holding up a delicate chain of gold filigree. Lamplight danced off the facets of a sapphire surrounded by diamonds that dangled from the chain. Her eyes were wide with wonder, but he could tell by the little tug of guilt at the corner of her mouth that she was about to refuse it.

"Now, Faith, 'tis not as though it cost me anything."

She cast him a look of dismay. "That's just it. It seems to me that to accept a gift I know is stolen is the same as stealing it."

"Where do you think I got the silk?"

Faith's conscience pricked her. The dress was finished, but there was no way to clean the delicate fabric on the ship, so she was waiting to wear it. "I guess I did not think about it. I was so busy worrying that it was sinful in and of itself."

Geoff laughed and pulled her up and against him. "'Tis a funny thing. I would think you had given up on all those commandments."

Faith flushed, but her smile belied any shame. "I cannot explain it. I know any minister would disagree, and mayhap I am only seeking an excuse for my behavior, but I cannot feel shame for what we share."

"I tell you, Faith, the rules you follow are the rules of men, not any deity."

She looked wistfully at the pendant. It tempted her, not for its beauty, though it was an exquisite piece, but for its value as a love token. Still, there were moral boundaries that went beyond the choices she made for herself.

"To whom do you suppose it belongs, and where was it going? What if this belongs to someone's mother, and she is sending it to her son for his bride-to-be? What if it is some last memento of a loved one lost? For you I am willing to risk my immortal soul, but I cannot take something from an innocent."

"Innocent? It belonged to a Spaniard."

"My uncle is a Spaniard. Why is that so terrible?"

"Ask the poor souls who have faced the Inquisition."

"Are we English without sin? Do we not justify the murder of savages in the name of God?"

"For God's sake, Faith!" At her wince he sighed in frustration. "I'm sorry. Damn your bloody command-ments! Must you make everything so complicated? Spain has been a thorn in England's side in these is-lands for over a century. Even the king grants us his blessings in plundering their greedy stores."

"Has the woman who wore this been a thorn in En-gland's side?"

Thrusting a hand through his hair, he sighed in frus-tration. He had never thought of himself as stealing from people. He had always stolen from Spain.

"If it troubles the king not that we take the entire city of Panama, what care you for a little trinket?" he grumbled. He felt another twinge of conscience over the whole affair of the Spanish ship, not at all liking it.

She shrugged and handed the necklace back to him. "It has oft occurred to me that the laws God gave Moses on the mountain protect us from doing injury to others. The Bible instructs us in many matters, and the more I think about it, the more I realize that much of that instruction is open to interpretation.

The Ten Commandments are not. They are clear and unambiguous. The eighth commandment prohibits me from taking this."

"Is the Bible ambiguous about fornication?" Geoff challenged, snatching the rejected offering from her fingers.

"Nay." Faith worried her lower lip with her teeth. In truth, she prayed every night that God would forgive her once she and Geoff were married. The fact that he had never given her any indication that he had changed his mind about marriage was something she refused to contemplate.

"'Tis simply that you are willing to break that rule?"

"This is unfair! You know why I have broken that rule, but if I try to actually talk to you about it, you get angry. You say that I am 'complicating' it."

Geoff rose and contemplated the darkness beyond the window. "Can you not see why we cannot continue like this?"

"Like what?" she asked, more bitterly than she intended. "I do but give you what you have, all along, told me you wanted, and I ask nothing in return."

"I wanted it to be the same for both of us!"

"It is. You're just too stubborn to see it. All my life, I have been told that this world and its ways are evil, and I have believed it because I had no way of knowing different. That belief made me afraid, and I worked ceaselessly to prove that I was good. Do you not see?" Geoff shook his head, perplexed. "We are the same, you and I. You see the world as evil, a place where you must take ere someone takes from you. No one has ever shown you any other truth, so you have worked ceaselessly to take all you could.

"You urge me to give up all that I have been taught,

and I am seeing it differently, that's sure, but what of you? Can you not open your eyes to a new truth? My love is real, Geoff, though you would deny it. All the world is not evil. We can choose to treat one another kindly, and to share the love we have, even with un-known Spaniards! I was always told that God is not moved by the works of men, but I have come to see that we move each other. He admonishes us to love one another. Perhaps that is the purest way we live His Word."

Geoff said nothing, only stared out of the port and into the night. The words she spoke were so full of hope that they left a hollow ache in his chest. Would that she could make them true, but she was young and naive. A few days in Port Royal and a few months on a sugar plantation would show her otherwise. She would give of herself, and those to whom she would give would cut her, hurt her until she learned that she must look to her own interests. How long would it be ere she would realize that life with a privateer would not serve her?

When he turned back to her, he kept his face care-fully unscrupulous. "There's a girl! God meant us to love one another, and if you'll not take my trinket, mayhap there is something I have that's more to your liking!" He reached for her, but she caught his wrists in her small hands.

"Nay, Geoff! You hate it when I hide my feelings from you, yet you think nothing of hiding yourself from me. If you cannot love me, at least do not lie to me."

Geoff pulled her close so that she could not see the depth of his own hurt. "Forgive me, my sweet. I have no head for this, but I would not try to hurt you. Come, let me soothe the hurt."

What he could not tell her with words he told her with his body, and because Faith knew this, she accepted what he could give.

Chapter 15

"All of it? You let them take the entire shipment?" Don Luis's face was purple with rage. "That pirate has pillaged two of my ships in as many months!"

"Don Luis," Diego protested, "we had already lost seven men to the fever, and even with a full and healthy crew, we could not have defeated the English. We did our best, I assure you, but in doing so, we nearly lost the ship as well. When we made port here in Cartagena, I was told that he usually torches the ships of those who challenge him."

Don Luis narrowed his eyes suspiciously. "So he does. But you fought him, you say?"

"With all that we had. We were greatly outnumbered."

"I will not have this! I want this man, this Captain Hampton. I want him here, in Cartagena, to face justice for the losses he has caused me!" He pinned Diego with his blazing brown eyes. "You captained *Magdalena* back to Cartagena. Do you want to keep your command?"

"Yes, Don Luis. I am a good captain. I tell you, I made the wisest choices I could under the circumstances. I am not a coward, sir. If I could meet Captain Hampton in an even match, I would do it, and I would win."

"Then you will have your chance. I will give you

three months and lend you *Marguerite,* my largest ship. If you deliver the English dog to me, I will return command of *Magdalena* to you, permanently. If you cannot find him, send the ship back to me, but you need not return with her."

"I will find him, Don Luis."

"I prefer him alive, but if you must kill him, then bring me proof."

Diego stalwartly ignored the sense of uneasiness that pulled at him. Yes, the pirate had spared his life and those that remained of his crew, but he had killed others. For that, he must face justice.

With a stormy mixture of dread and excitement, Faith caught her first glimpse of the island of Jamaica. This was the culmination of a daring voyage and a land filled with exotic promise. It was also, quite possibly, the end of her time with Geoff, and she felt as though her heart might burst with anticipation or shatter with grief. Which would come first, she couldn't say.

Beside her at the ship's rail, Geoff watched the island, too, his face an unreadable mask, a sign that never boded well.

"'Tis beautiful," Faith ventured, at last, unable to bear the silence any longer.

"Aye, 'tis," Geoff replied flatly.

The colorful tumble known as Port Royal lay scattered on a flat swath of land stretching between the Caribbean Sea and a long, narrow harbor. Beyond the harbor rose mountains choked with vegetation and swept by gray clouds and afternoon rain. There were woodlands aplenty in New England, but the glossy mystery of these forests surpassed anything she had known before. She knew, for Geoff had told her, that these dense, vibrant mountains were home to Maroons, those slaves who had managed to escape. It was a harsh existence, but a free one.

"Will we go ashore?" Faith asked, then held her breath waiting for his answer.

Still, there was no trace of emotion, either on his face or in his voice, when he replied. There was no way to know what he was thinking. "Aye. You'll want to do some shopping, I imagine. You've never seen anything like the stalls of Port Royal. And I know of a place where we can find a room for a few nights. It's toward the end of High Street, away from the worst of the taverns and," he paused, "other establishments."

"A few nights?" she asked.

"Aye." He gave her a terse smile, then turned abruptly away to speak with several crew members. Faith looked back out toward the island with no better understanding of what was between them than she had ever had.

Across the deck from her, Giles approached his captain. "Her heart is in her eyes, y'know," he commented, nodding toward Faith's back.

"Aye, I know," Geoff replied. "I could hardly miss it."

"And while most would never see it, we've been friends long enough that you cannot fool me. Yours is in your eyes, as well."

Geoff gazed impassively into Giles's serious countenance. "Is it, now? And what do you see, old friend?"

"That you're about to make the gravest mistake of your life."

"What would you have me do, Giles? Look out there. Do you see a town where Faith would make a

home? Am I to leave her there for months at a time
while I'm at sea? Nay, she'll be safe and sound with her
family, and they'll find her some pious, respectable
farmer or some such. It's better this way, Giles, and you
know it."

"Have you thought to ask her what she wants?
Mayhap she'd not mind a life at sea."

Geoff's mask slipped, and he gaped at Giles incredulously. "Surely you're not suggesting she sail with
us?"

"I'm saying that we've done well for ourselves,
Geoff. Mayhap it would not be so very bad to give up
this life and be merchant sailors."

There was an edge to Geoff's laughter, for all that
it was forcefully hearty. Faith's head snapped around
at the sound, and he lowered his voice. "Merchants,
you and I? Have you gone daft? Next you'll be suggesting I marry the wench and raise a brood of
children." At Giles's raised eyebrows, Geoff shook his
head adamantly. "Nay. That's not the life for you or
me." Even as he said it, he felt a little twinge. What was
it? Wistfulness? Well, a bit of regret, perhaps. He
would miss her, that was sure.

Unable to bear staying on deck with Geoff, only to
have him avoid her, Faith hastened below to change
her clothes. She was not going to greet this new land
in her hopelessly rumpled indigo cotton. For a moment, she banished all her worrisome thoughts and
allowed herself to savor the long awaited caress of silk
against her skin, softer even than she had imagined.
The skirts of her new gown rustled seductively
and shimmered around her, and she smiled in pure
delight.

But she hesitated before returning to the deck

above, her hand hovering at the cabin door. All the turmoil she had felt when she had first left her home returned full force, and for a moment, she felt dizzy. She was here, in this faraway land, wearing a gown she would never have dared to wear at home. She had learned much on the journey and lost her innocence. When she left *Destiny*, she well and truly left behind all that she had been and all that she had ever known.

Even if she ever could return to her family, what would they think of her? Her parents would be devastated, her brothers bewildered. In running away, she had risked everything, but she had had no way of knowing that she would be burning her bridges in many other ways, as well. She would never again be the girl they had known and loved.

But what was done was done. She could keep her somber cotton and wool, and still she could never recapture her old self, nor could she find it within her to want to. She forced herself to twirl carelessly, letting the silk twist and tug gently at her waist before it swirled back again and settled into place like a cloud.

Her ambivalence was only exacerbated by Geoff's reaction when she finally reappeared on deck. He glanced briefly her way, then looked back sharply. At first, his golden brows lifted in surprise, then furrowed as though he were perplexed. Finally, he smiled broadly and crossed the deck to her.

"Do you not like it?" Faith asked, nervously running her hands over the soft gathers of her skirt.

"Aye, 'tis perfect," he said, his face still lit with a grin. The silk was sensuous and vibrant, the style of the dress prim and straightforward. The dichotomy of the gown's luxurious fabric and sensible cut seemed the very essence of the woman who wore it. "Never

could I have imagined a gown that is so utterly suited
to my Faith."

His Faith? Suddenly, her heart felt lighter, and her
misgivings faded some. Mayhap all was not lost.

It seemed no time at all ere they sailed into the
crowded harbor and disembarked into the noise and
confusion of the docks. Faith's fingers bit into Geoff's
arm, digging deeply into the sleeve of the claret velvet
jacket he had worn when first they had met. Again, he
had donned a lace-trimmed shirt and his broad hat
with its flamboyant ostrich feather.

All around her the crowd ebbed and flowed, filled
with as many different kinds of people as Faith could
ever have imagined. There were slave ships that carried as many dark, lifeless bodies as living Africans. All
were chained and looked starved beyond endurance.
Some were angry, defiant regardless of the whips used
by brutal slavers to subdue them. Others looked
beaten, their spirits defeated, so much so that Faith
doubted that they would be long after their kin whose
bodies were manhandled with no respect for what
their lives had once been. Reverend Williams would
insist that their heathen souls were hell bound, but
Faith could not believe it was so. Surely the hell they
had suffered in the hold of the ship was more than
payment for eternal peace.

Interspersed among these scenes of misery, pirates,
ruffians, gentlemen, and naval officers moved together
in an endless tide of unlikely elements cast together.
Free Africans who sailed on pirate vessels walked
among their dark-skinned counterparts destined to
work in the cane fields. Women in dresses that fairly

glowed in the bright Caribbean sun brushed carelessly against the men. They obviously gave no thought to the luxury of a man's appearance, but rather to the gold that was as likely to be in the pockets of an unwashed buccaneer as in those of a dandified gentleman, perhaps more so. They would pause, laugh, touch as though they were long separated lovers, not just careless strangers. At times they would part. More often, they would stroll to one of the unkempt buildings that littered the streets of "the wickedest city on earth."

And if the merchants' stalls in Boston Harbor had awed Faith, those that lined the docks of Port Royal left her utterly flabbergasted. There were exotic pets, from colorful parrots and cockatoos to several varieties of monkeys. The smells of spices, perfumes, and unwashed bodies blended together, overwhelming the senses. Stalls filled with cheap baubles stood side by side with those selling priceless gold and jewels. And everywhere hawkers cried out the virtues of their goods, enticing would-be buyers.

Geoff led her through the throngs to a stall filled with fabrics and lace. "Here," he pronounced, "is just what I was looking for."

Amid the frills and finery, and looking very much out of place, a hulking man nearly a score of years older than Geoff stepped out to greet them. He had very little in the way of hair or teeth, and the smell of him cut right through the other scents of the marketplace.

"'Ampton, ye old dog!" he called out warmly. "'Aven't seen ye since old Morgan led all ye fools out on that raid. Thought ye'd been left be'ind, in Panama."

"Not me, Larken," Geoff boasted, clapping the man fondly on the back. "I've taken two Spanish ships since."

"Should 'ave known! Ye got more lives than any

cat." Larken noticed Faith, and a sly smile formed on his lips. "Ye've a fresh one, 'ere. Where'd ye find this pretty little piece?"

"Mind how you talk there," Geoff warned sternly. "This is Faith Cooper, and she's a lady."

"Is she, then? That's a shame. Ransom?"

Geoff shook his head. "I'm returning her to her family, no profit, out of the goodness of my heart."

Larken laughed loudly, as if he'd never heard anything so funny in his life. "Out of the goodness of 'is 'eart, 'e says," the older man chortled. "Ye've gotten somethin' fer yer trouble, I'll wager."

Faith couldn't decide which was worse, the fact that Geoff had just said he was returning her to her family or that this odious man was actually his friend. Suddenly the excitement of adventure faded, and she just wanted to flee the stifling press of people, colors, sounds, and smells.

"It was very good to meet you, Mr. Larken," Faith blurted, "but I'm afraid we've business to attend to." She gave Geoff's arm a tug.

"Cap'n, not mister," Larken corrected her. "What ye see 'ere is from me latest cargo."

"And this *is* our business," Geoff added. "You'll need new clothes."

Faith blinked back tears of frustration. He was leaving her, and all he could think of was her wardrobe? "I don't want new clothes," she protested. "I want to go back to the ship." Back to Geoff's cabin, where the rest of the world was an ocean away, and nothing mattered but the two of them.

"Trust me, *cherie*," a woman's husky French accent sounded behind her, "you need the clothes."

Faith whirled to see who had spoken to her, and

her jaw dropped in astonishment. The woman who had addressed her was beautiful, in a harsh and exaggerated way. Her hair was jet black, far darker than nature could have made it. Her wide, generous lips were tinted scarlet, as were the sharp cheekbones that dominated her tanned face. Her brown eyes were heavily lined in kohl, looking sultry and exotic.

But it wasn't her face that shocked Faith, or even her scarlet gown, cut so low that her very ample breasts nearly spilled out completely. It was the fact that the very same rouge that colored her lips and cheeks tinted the pair of nipples peeking out from the lace around her deep décolletage. The bright scarlet crests were blatantly obvious against the light lace.

The woman cast a haughty look at Faith and continued. *"Mon Dieu,* who designed that gown? *C'est tragique,* what they have done with all that gorgeous silk."

Faith registered neither the insult nor the blasphemy. She just kept staring, openmouthed, at the woman's chest.

"Do you like them, *cheri?"* the woman asked, leaning forward with a seductive smile. "With a tight enough bodice underneath, you might be able to make something out of *vos tétons petites."* She gestured to Faith's modest bodice.

"Veronique!" Geoff interrupted sharply. "This isn't a good time—"

Before he could finish his sentence, Veronique replied, "Then we should make it a good time." She sauntered over to him, her hips swaying provocatively. "A very good time." She breathed this last sentence, her voice even huskier. Boldly, she placed one hand on his shoulder, while the other caressed his broad chest and headed straight downward, over his flat belly.

Faith gasped, and no longer caring that she was in a strange place filled with pirates and criminals, she turned and fled up High Street. The road was lined with taverns, and drunken sailors called out to her, trying to catch her arms and skirts. Blinded by shame and anger, she shoved forcefully at the men who reached for her. Then someone grabbed her arm and yanked her sharply backward.

Chapter 16

Geoff's voice hissed in her ear. "Don't be a fool, Faith. You cannot go running off in Port Royal by yourself!"

"Then take me back to the ship!" she snapped. "Take me back, and then you can dally with your Veronique and brag to your Captain Larken!"

Instead of heading back toward the ship, he pulled her farther up High Street. "This is hardly the place for this conversation. The inn is just at the end of this road. We'll get a room there, and then we'll talk."

Faith eyed the people surrounding them and decided that perhaps there was some virtue in what Geoff suggested. The sooner they were off the street, the better. To her relief, she found that on the outskirts of town, there were some fairly respectable establishments. The inn that Geoff suggested was one of them. The room was small but clean, with a wooden chair, a comfortable-looking bed, and a washstand. The general din of Port Royal was dulled through the thick glass windows.

While she inspected the quarters, Geoff inspected her. His heart had been lodged firmly in his throat when she had bolted from his side at the harbor. Her shimmering blue skirts had disappeared instantly in the crushing throng, and for a sickening moment, he had thought he had lost her.

He could tell himself that he was only worried for her safety, but it was only half the truth.

She kept her back to him, staring out of the window into the street below. "I'm safe and sound, Captain. Please, do not let me keep you. Now that you are home, there are sure to be any number of people with whom you wish to renew acquaintance."

Refusing to be goaded, he asked softly, "Not what you expected?"

Through her tight throat, she answered, "I knew not what to expect. I thought your friends would be like Giles. I certainly didn't expect . . ." She let the sentence drift away.

Geoff doffed his hat and scratched his head. "Larken's not a bad fellow, actually. He's just a bit rough around the edges. And I must admit, it's not his fault that he jumped to conclusions. I've certainly never escorted a lady through the streets of Port Royal before."

She narrowed her eyes. "So I saw."

He had the grace to blush. God, Veronique had always been hard to manage. For years, every time he made port, he would eventually find himself prying her bold hands from his person. She was hardly his type. He had ever preferred less hardened, more costly women, ones who stayed in Port Royal only long enough to earn dowries that they took back home with them to England. Still, he knew that Veronique's life had been no easier than his, and so he tolerated her presence.

"She's just a friend," he protested. "Not even that really. An acquaintance."

"An acquaintance? I was under the impression that you had rather intimate knowledge of each other. Good heavens, *I* have intimate knowledge of her! Everyone who glanced at her neckline has intimate knowledge of her!"

Geoff shrugged lightly. "And then some."

A small sound of indignation caught in her throat. "How can you make light of this? Do you have any idea how I feel, knowing that you have touched me with the very same hands you used to touch her?"

"Nay, Faith! Never!"

"Do not lie to me!"

"How can you think that? Give me some credit! If ever I'd laid hands on Veronique, I'd pay for it with my life, in time. She may not have pockmarks, but I'll wager every scrap of booty that ever I've taken she carries something I want no part of. And she's a hard woman. But all the same, I'll not be cruel to her. We all do the best that we can in this world."

"You never—I mean, never with her?" Faith asked softly.

"Never with her. I swear it."

"Nay, do not swear. I believe you. But with others like her, you have."

"Not like her. Not so harsh or so crude, but none like you, either."

"But you're sending me away."

Geoff ran a hand through his hair and sank onto the bed. "You'd hate it here."

"I shall hate it anywhere without you. I shall hate knowing that others will replace me in your bed."

She thought of what Giles had told her on board the ship, how Geoff had never been given love and so had stopped wanting it. Surely that was the key. She had to make him dare to want love again. Words made him close her off, but actions he would accept.

"But no one ever shall replace me, not really," she added.

How could it be that Faith, who had once felt so timid and shy with this man, could bend her head to his and kiss him with the possessiveness she adopted as her tongue boldly explored his warm mouth? Was it some other Faith who tilted his chin and with her lips sought to send fiery trails of sensation down his slightly salty neck?

Geoff sighed and allowed his body to relax beneath her. He knew what she was about, knew that he should stop her ere she made it impossible for him to leave her, but her soft hands caressed him as her mouth returned to his. Passively, he allowed her to do as she would, even as his hands traced the curve from her delicate ribs, over her slender waist, to the gentle curve of her hip. She pushed him to the mattress and looked long into his face. There was a softness there, an ease that he allowed her to see only when they made love.

She rose from on top of him. It was hard not to feel a little shy, for the full light of midday shone through the window. But she knew that it was important that she not look away, so her eyes never left his face as she unlaced the bodice of her dress.

Geoff could not tear his gaze from the enchantress before him. Her cheeks were stained a becoming shade of pink, but she did not falter. She pulled the bodice from her shoulders, soft mounds pressing against her shift. The gown slipped away from her, falling in a shimmering pool around her feet. The thin fabric of her ivory linen shift skimmed her body, moved with her, hinted at curves without fully revealing them. Down the front was the neatly mended tear that he had made when first he had taken her.

She lifted the hem of the garment, revealing shapely calves and creamy thighs, then stopped.

"You must ask," she said.

He thought that she had gained a devilish grasp of teasing, for they had finished with his long-ago promise to Giles, but her aqua eyes were utterly serious.

"Ask?"

"Aye. You must ask me to give what I would, knowing it is more than you want."

"Faith— "

"Nay! I do not ask for forever, only this: You would not take me and pretend it was more than my body you craved. I will not give myself to you and pretend it is only my body I give. If this is goodbye, then there must be honesty between us."

Geoff let his eyes wander the length of her. Making love to her here, now, would only make parting all the harder. With a scowl he asked, "Is this where I'm supposed to be the one strong enough to do the right thing?"

Faith gave a little laugh, and tears stung her eyes. "Nay! My greatest fear is that you will lie there and tell me that you no longer want me."

"Aye, Faith, I still want you. I want all that you would give me and more, but selfish bastard that I am, I'll not offer what you would have in return."

"I want you, Geoff. It is enough."

She pulled the shift over her head, and his breath caught in his throat. God knew, he had seen her naked before, but only when he had undressed her, the heat of passion between them. Now she unveiled herself, selflessly offering her body to him ere lust could color her motives. Her muscles moved with supple grace, her arms and stomach taut. Geoff had always preferred full-breasted women, but with Faith he had come to understand what some men meant when they said that more than could fill the hand was a waste.

She pulled him up by the hand and helped him remove his own shirt. Then she settled in his lap again, her bare legs on either side of him, her firm backside cradled sensuously in his hands. Both knew that this was different than it had ever been. For Geoff, it was goodbye. For Faith, it was her only hope for keeping him. Their kisses were languid, and greedily they swallowed each other's sighs.

With his hands Geoff built a fierce but tender fire within her, luxuriating in the silken feel of her delicate skin. One hand in her hair, he gently coaxed her head back to feast upon the tight bud at the summit of each breast, gratified by her gasping moans of pleasure. Shifting his weight, he laid her upon the bed.

Her hair fanned over the pillow, and he watched her even as his hand trailed up the inside of her thigh. Her legs parted willingly, and her tongue moistened her lips. He began there, at her full, sweet mouth, but then moved to the end of the bed, bestowing a kiss upon her inner ankle. His lips wandered up her calf, stopped to tickle the back of her knee. Tiny bolts of lightning shot from along the back of her leg up the inside of her thigh to strike her most sensitive place. He did the same to the other leg with agonizing slowness, and she thought that she would scream if he did not touch her as she needed to be touched.

She tensed when his lips stopped short of the pale curls at the juncture of her thighs. "Geoff?" she whispered.

The musky scent of her tantalized him, and he whispered back, "Let me taste you, Faith."

Whimpering, she dug her hands into his hair. She was his, and she would hold nothing back. "Aye," she moaned, "oh, please, Geoff."

The first shock of his tongue against her was swept away in the tempest that followed. Geoff plundered the honey sweet softness she offered so willingly, her cries and the feel of her hands in his hair driving him wild. At last, she lifted her hips and strained against him, then relaxed with a husky moan. As she lay basking in the aftermath, he doffed his pants and lay beside her.

She smiled at him with feline contentment, then let her gaze wander over his sinewy chest and stomach to his tumescent manhood. Having lost all shame in the intimacy they had just shared, she studied him openly, touched him, and smiled at his indrawn breath. His shaft was firm, but the skin was as soft as velvet. He wrapped his hand about hers and set her to stroking him, his face a perfect reflection of rapture.

And yet, she wanted to give him more. Following his lead, she lowered her head and tentatively tasted the tip of him with her tongue. Emboldened by his guttural moan, she took him in her mouth, and he threaded his fingers through her hair, urging her to keep the rhythm her hand had begun.

Suddenly, his hands stopped her and pulled her face away from him. "Not yet," he groaned. With a patience he did not feel, he guided her above him, so that she again straddled the slim hips that tapered from his broad chest. Moving slowly, prolonging every sweet moment, she impaled herself upon him, lowering bit by bit until he had filled her. He was transfixed by the play

of the muscles in her stomach and thighs as she moved up and down, her hips making small circles because it pleased her to do so.

Her face was bathed in a fine sheen of sweat, her eyes lightly closed, and he watched the curls of her flaxen hair tease her tight nipples. Still, he kept his hands on her hips, helped her keep the tempo that drove them both inexorably upward, beyond all limits, until they shattered like glass and fell into a shower of diamonds that danced among the folds of the sheets.

Collapsing against him, Faith said nothing. She simply lay in the circle of his arms and breathed the warm, comforting scent of him.

His voice roughened by his earlier passion, Geoff murmured, "I want you to know something, Faith."

"Shh," she admonished, placing her fingertips to his lips. "You have told me fairly."

"Nay. I have not been fair at all. It will never be like this with any other." He felt her lips move into a smile against his chest. "I would not have you feel cheap or common. You are a treasure."

She idly wound a strand of his golden hair around her finger and smiled up at him. "What sort of privateer is it who lets a treasure slip from his grasp?"

He sighed. "What sort, indeed?"

"You have not yet sent for my aunt and uncle?"

"Nay, there has been no chance."

"Then there is no need to rush."

The lure of skin against skin proved too strong for doubts, and they moved together, pulling the moment around them like a mantle that protected them from the cold, uncertain future.

* * *

They lay together until darkness fell. The denizens of Port Royal were inclined to carouse long into the night, and the sounds of drunken sailors crooning lascivious verses poured in through the open window. Geoff grinned in the dark.

"Ah, the melodious sounds of my home," he commented dryly.

Bits and pieces of the words drifted through, causing Faith to blush, but the tunes were jolly, and she snuggled closely against him.

There was a brief pause in the merry making, and then the music took on a strange, unearthly quality. It was a genuinely harmonious blend of male voices, each one singing his own part in melodies that chased one another and called to her. Pulling on her shift, she rose and gazed out of the window, Geoff slipping in beside her.

In the street below, the revelers stood in a circle, uncharacteristically silent. In the center, a group of dark-skinned Africans lifted their voices in a mixture of pain and beauty that nearly made her weep, though the words were in a language completely foreign to her. The light of several lanterns wavered over ebony faces, so that the sound and the graceful swaying of their whipcord lean bodies conveyed the emotion more than their expressions, somehow weaving ever more tightly the web of enchantment.

A cursory look around proved that she was not the only one deeply affected by the strange music. To a person, the group was awestruck and speechless. Each note seemed to speak to the deepest, most forgotten place in each of their hearts and wrung from them their own pain, long buried beneath the futility of their lives. Hard, haggard faces softened as sailors, criminals, and prostitutes looked out into the night, watching their own troubles playing out across the darkness. Silence lingered long after the song ended. No one breathed, and the magic vibrated in the warm night air.

At last, Faith whispered, "How beautiful. It was so passionate and so melancholy!"

Geoff nodded in understanding, though she could barely make out his silhouette in the blackness. "Aye. 'Tis a wonder to me the plantation owners can bear it, the sadness in the Africans' singing." After a pause he added, "How many does your aunt own?"

"How many what?"

"Slaves."

A quick stab of shock jolted Faith. Slaves? "I do not think she owns any," Faith defended, despite her own doubts.

Geoffrey merely laughed as though she jested. "Now, Faith, no one can run a plantation without slaves. Most plantation owners boast their number of Africans as surely as they boast of their acreage and profits. They are considered financial assets."

Any reply stuck in her throat. Did truly all plantations have slaves? How many? Did they sing as these men had done? She could not bear it if they did! She could not understand the words, but she could well imagine they were of wives and parents, the simple joys of their village lives lost.

"Faith?" When she didn't answer, his curiosity pricked him. "Has she never written of her home? If she is a Puritan, like you, she's educated. What does she write of?"

Faith had carefully avoided talking about Winston Hall for fear that she would only strengthen Geoff's resolve to take her there. Now she was too disconcerted to evade his questions. "She was a Puritan, so aye, she is literate, but she does not write to us."

"You befuddle me. She was a Puritan, so she can write but does not?"

She would have to tell him sooner or later. How else would she explain the fact that her aunt and uncle would surely be stunned to see her? With a sigh, she confessed, "My mother and she have not written these past fifteen years. Elizabeth was disowned when she married my uncle and became a Catholic."

Geoff gave her an incredulous look. "Your mother disowned her sister?"

"Nay! She would have written, but her parents and my father forbade it."

"Your father? Your sainted father forbade his wife to write her own sister because he liked not her husband's religion." His voice was heavily laden with disgust as he offered up his summary of the situation.

"It is not as you make it sound. The Puritan church seeks a more pure, more true faith, one based upon the Bible and not the ambitions of men in a church gone corrupt." Geoff rolled his eyes in contempt, and Faith tried harder to explain. "I'll make no attempt to defend our church. Our good minister has shown me that we've corruptions enough of our own. Still, my father did only what he thought he must to protect my mother's immortal soul. As her husband, it was his duty."

"Just as he endeavored to protect your immortal soul by teaching you to hide your true feelings?" Geoff scoffed. "Oft you spoke to me of your father's great mind. If he is the intelligent man you say, then surely he knew that when he bid you cast your eyes down and hold your tongue, it was the same as a lie."

She shook her head, trying to deny the truth in what he said. His words almost made sense to her, caused her to doubt not just her church, but even her family, and it terrified her, sent the whole compass of her life spinning. "Nay! He loved me. He tried only to help me."

Geoff took her roughly by the shoulders. "Who are you, Faith? Whose words fall from your mouth? You've lived your whole life for someone else's approval, your father, your minister, and you try to make yourself believe the approval you seek is God's! When do you venture to set foot upon your own path?"

She drew back sharply. "How dare you! What do you think I have done? I am here, am I not? Have you any idea how far Port Royal is from my home, and not only in distance! I am trying to find my path, and aye, I dare to believe in and trust my God! Sometimes I am confused and scared, but I am doing all I can to make sense of my faith."

"Your faith makes no sense!"

"How easy for you to judge me! God's Word says it is easier to see the speck in another's eye than the one in our own. Whose approval do you seek, Captain Hampton? You looked to your mother and learned that women must be bought with coins and trinkets and pleasure, and you have paid those aplenty! Now you want a woman who cannot be bought so simply, and you know not how to give what she would have. You're no different than I!"

Geoff pulled back as though she had slapped him, pain he hadn't known existed in him slicing into his heart. "Enough!" he snapped and turned his back to her.

Undaunted, she addressed the broad expanse of tense shoulders. "Nay, it is not! You dismiss my beliefs as casually as my love. You pretend that you cannot understand my faith in God."

He whirled to face her again. "Pretend? Nay, Faith, indeed I have no grasp of it. Look around you!" He gestured widely. "How can you have spent over three weeks tossed about upon that vast ocean and believe that you have any significance, that there is any grand plan? And where is the wrath of your God in this modern-day Gomorrah?"

She blinked away tears, but her voice was strong and steady. "His very breath filled your sails across that ocean. His pulse rocked beneath your feet! How can you not believe in a divine force when we were somehow brought together just when each of us needed someone exactly like the other? Brought together on the deck of *Destiny?*"

Geoff fell silent. She was a romantic, a misguided religious zealot. Still, he had to admit there were times that he stood at the helm listening to the wind as it snapped powerfully in the canvas overhead, felt the roll of the ocean at his feet, and it filled him. It was not his mind, or even his heart, that swelled. It was something else, something Faith would surely call his soul.

The idea of a God, aloof and impersonal, who sat in judgment of mere men had never rung true to him, but the thought of a divine force that breathed life into his sails in the wind and whose passions tossed his ship at sea, these tugged at his imagination. The needle in his life's compass seemed to pull, for the first time, in some clear direction, and he rebelled against it.

"Go to bed, Faith," he said softly.

She had moved from the window's scant light, and he did not see her dash the tears from her cheeks. "You're lonely, Geoff," she whispered. "You need not be."

"Good night." His voice was heavy, as though he were weary and troubled.

Faith turned away slowly. They both had things enough to contemplate this night. Even as she climbed beneath sheets still warmed by their bodies, Geoff donned his clothes and quietly slipped out into the dark hall beyond. Faith did not fall asleep until the merest hint of first light began to seep through the window, and Geoff never joined her.

Chapter 17

By afternoon, Faith paced the floor of her room like a caged animal. Both breakfast and the midday meal had been sent up to her. "Upon the gentleman's orders," she had been told. The heat was stifling, and she paused sporadically to stand at the window and watch the street and try to catch a breeze.

Where was he? Her eyes searched the thoroughfare for Geoff's tall, familiar form. At last, she pounded a fist against the window frame. If she waited any longer, night would fall, and she dared not venture out alone after dark.

From her place at the window, she had watched the women who came and went below her. Men flocked around those who cast sultry looks from beneath fluttering lashes, and they jeered at and harassed nervous women who cast furtive glances around them. But those who held their heads high and strode with purposeful confidence were relatively unmolested. If a man still had the nerve to approach, fierce glowers seemed to improve the women's chances.

One woman, not much older than Faith, snapped, "Mayhap you seek a taste of my lover's cutlass. Cap'n Drake eats swabs such as you for breakfast!"

"No doubt ye've tasted 'is cutlass," the man shouted suggestively, but he let her be.

Faith squared her shoulders. She would walk out onto those streets, bold as could be. If her manner didn't protect her, she would call upon Geoff's reputation to keep her safe. One thing was sure. She would not stay in this room like forgotten baggage!

It wasn't easy to mask the terrified flutter in her stomach, but Faith refused to give in to the urge to glance fearfully around her. With all the bravado she could muster, she marched down High Street in the direction of the dock.

"Hey, love," a voice called out, but she ignored it.

"I've a lovely trinket 'ere," another called, "fer an afternoon's pleasure."

Faith sniffed and tilted her head a little higher. Ere she reached the market place that stretched along the docks, she had discovered that she could disregard the crude comments called out to her. With a thrill of accomplishment, she stepped up to Captain Larken's stall. She had made it without anyone's help!

Geoff's friend greeted her with a leer, but when Faith looked at him more closely, she saw that the lascivious expression didn't reach his eyes. They were, in fact, bright blue and twinkled merrily.

"Well, well," he said, his voice gravelly. "What 'ave we 'ere? 'Ampton's pretty little wench, is it? Come back to choose some silk after all?"

Faith smiled at him, her pleasure at seeing him quite genuine. Now she could relax, for she felt sure that the presence of Geoff's friend would discourage other men.

"Good day to you, Captain. I hope you'll forgive my behavior yesterday. I think I may have forgot to say goodbye." She shook her head in mock regret.

Larken chuckled. "That ye did, missy, that ye did.

Veronique, the little minx, she 'as that effect on other women."

Faith shrugged as though the incident hadn't mattered. "She was right about one thing. I do need new clothes. Of course, I need to find Geoff if I'm to do any shopping. Have you seen him today?"

Larken shook his balding pate. "Not today, though I saw 'is mate, Courtney. 'E was 'agglin' with some merchant over a shipment of wine, I think. Closer to *Destiny*, down that way." He gestured farther down the docks.

"Thank you, Captain," she said. "I'm sure that Giles will know where to find him."

Larken leaned close to her, and she held her breath against the smell of his body and breath, though she smiled politely. Had the man never bathed?

"If I was ye, I'd do me shoppin' now. Get all ye wants and charge it to 'im. I'll find 'im fer the money."

"Very tempting," she replied, her face a bit flushed for want of air. "But I really must find Geoff first." She took a step back and tried not to gasp for breath too obviously. "You've been very helpful." With a little wave, she set off once again, head up, shoulders back.

Giles quickly broke off his conversation with a local merchant when he saw Faith striding toward him. To her credit, she didn't spare a glance at the men who gawked after her. She walked with the same stalwart confidence of any of Port Royal's more seasoned inhabitants.

"Faith!" he called out. "I like not to think what Geoff will do if he finds out that you've been walking the streets here alone. Why did you not stay at the inn? He left plenty of coin for your comfort."

"My comfort?" she snapped. "I have spent the better

part of the day trapped in a tiny room with absolutely nothing to do!"

Giles winced uncomfortably. "I admit, I thought you might get bored. I should have come to see if you'd any needs I could fill, but we've a ship to unload and cargo to sell. What if I break off awhile, and we'll shop a bit? We're sure to find something to bide your time."

She crossed her arms and gave him a defiant glare. "And why should *you* come and see to my needs or take me shopping? Why must I 'bide my time' in that stuffy little room? Where is Geoff?"

Shifting his weight uneasily from foot to foot, Giles said, "He had a bit of business to attend to."

"All night?" She had no doubt that Giles knew much that he was loath to speak. Where could Geoff have gone in the middle of the night and still not returned? The image of Veronique's lush, scarlet-tipped breasts popped into her mind, but she banished it. He had told her that he did not sleep with Veronique, and she believed him.

"He'll not be back until the morrow," Giles replied. More softly, he added, "I'm sorry."

Faith studied Giles's face. His mouth was tight, and his gray eyes flashed with a trace of temper. "Why are you sorry?" she pressed.

He heaved a sigh of resignation. "I'm sorry that you were left all alone at the inn. I'm sorry that he didn't even have the grace to tell you himself."

"Tell me what?"

Giles lifted his eyes to the forest of ships' masts behind her, unable to look her in the face.

She tried to swallow, but the lump that had formed in her throat would not allow it. "He's gone to Winston Hall, hasn't he? He's gone to fetch my aunt and uncle."

Finally, Giles looked at her. "He woke me in the middle of the night, ranting about two people from two different worlds. I tried to tell him that you only needed time to adjust. If he could have seen you walk down here today, he'd know he was being a fool!"

Every time she had dared to think of this moment, the moment when she would know beyond a doubt that the affair was over, Faith had been overcome with despair. She expected that emotion to return with overwhelming force. Hence, she was entirely unprepared for the wave of rage that engulfed her now.

"Ha!" she barked, and Giles gaped in surprise. "*I* need time to adjust? Do you know what your best friend is, Giles Courtney? He's a bloody coward!"

Suddenly, Faith knew why people swore. She felt a pure, clean release when the vulgar word passed her lips. Raising her voice, she continued. "A bloody, bloody, damned, bloody coward! And—and he's a *bastard*, too, that's what!"

Giles's shocked expression melted into a grin.

"What are you smiling about?" Faith railed. "Two people from two different worlds? We're cut from the same cloth, we two. I'm the best damned thing that's ever happened in his whole bloody life!"

Laughing outright, he wrapped his arms around her and hugged her fondly, then set her at arm's length. "Do you know, Faith, I think that you are going to be just fine."

She stared hard into his face. "Damned right I am." This last curse lacked the conviction of all the earlier ones, and at last, the anticipated tears came. "Oh, God, Giles, he's done it, hasn't he? He's left me for good. You told me that he would."

"Shush now, Faith, don't waste your tears." Giles's face softened, and he pushed her hair from her face.

"*He* told me that he would. But I wouldn't listen. I thought—I thought . . ."

She lost the sentence in a torrent of sobs, and Giles pulled her back against him. "Don't cry, now, Faith. I cannot bear weeping. My sisters ever played me for a fool with their tears. I'll toss him overboard when he returns. Will that suit you?"

"Aye," she sniffled against the wet splotch she'd made on his shirt.

"There now," he murmured, and again, he pulled away from her. "Chin up. You've a whole new life ahead of you. You've but finished with one adventure so that you can start another. The countryside's nothing like here. You'll like Jamaica, and your family's plantation is one of the finest."

He stopped and looked at her miserable face. "He loved you, you know."

Tears welled up again in her eyes. "Why could he never admit it?"

Giles shrugged his shoulders as though to rid them of some ponderous weight. "In many ways, Geoff's the bravest man that ever I met. Who would have thought that he'd flee in fear from a mere slip of a girl?"

No sea breeze stirred the heavy, wet air in Faith's room. The curtains hung listlessly on either side of the window, though it was open wide. Another night and another day had come and gone. Giles had stopped by and taken her to one of the smaller, less seedy taverns for the midday meal. Otherwise, she had filled the hours affixing a ruffle of lace just under the hem of her

gown, giving it the appearance of having a fine petticoat underneath. She had just finished the task and
dressed again, for the light was waning, and she expected the maid would be in soon to light the lamp.

She was surprised to open the door and see that Giles
had returned. Then she looked over his shoulder at the
couple that accompanied him. The man was tall and
thin with long, dark hair streaked by silver. He wore a
coat and vest of silver and black, accented with fine
white lace, and a hat trimmed in silver braid. The
woman wore a breathtaking gown of emerald silk,
pulled back to reveal an underskirt of gold tissue, but
her face was hauntingly familiar. She looked very much
like Faith's mother.

For a moment, no one said anything. They simply
stared at one another with no idea what to do next.

"Faith," the woman whispered at last, and she held
her arms open to the niece she had never known. "My
dearest Naomi's Faith."

And Faith stepped forward to embrace her aunt
and her future.

"I brought these," Giles said, holding out the
clothes she had brought with her from New England.
"I thought you might yet need them awhile."

Elizabeth Fernandez de Madrid y Delgado Cortes
took the small bundle of clothes from the ship's quartermaster. Running her hands over the rumpled wool
and worn cotton, a thousand memories seemed to skim
across her face. Then she scrutinized the daughter of
the sister she had not heard a word from in sixteen
years.

"It is uncanny," she said. "You look so like Naomi,
but fairer, more striking with those eyes."

Faith self-consciously smoothed her silk skirt.

"God never granted us children, dear. At last, I can dote upon one of my sister's children. You cannot deny an old woman such a simple pleasure."

Elizabeth looked far from old, and 'twas clear she knew it. She smiled at Miguel, who quickly defended his wife's beauty, as though they had played out many a similar scene before. Faith could not imagine a comparable conversation between her parents. Surely her father would be shocked were her mother to display such vanity. Still, her aunt and uncle's relationship seemed easy and comfortable, and Faith felt a stab of longing.

This might have been her and Geoff if he hadn't been so stubborn. The thought filled her with sadness, dampening her enthusiasm.

"Well, you surely are a patient girl," Elizabeth said. "You look exhausted, and here I am dragging you all around the market. I do love to shop, as Miguel can tell you, but it's high time we were on our way. We won't make it there until tomorrow, but we've friends with a plantation where we can spend the night."

Once they had made all their purchases, they headed back to the inn to retrieve Elizabeth and Miguel's carriage. On the way, they had to carefully avoid the attention of a hard-drinking pirate in the middle of the street. He sat on a cask of rum, threatening to shoot anyone who refused to drink with him.

Elizabeth shook her head and took her niece's hand. "Not much like Boston, I think."

"Nay," Faith affirmed, thinking of Veronique. She couldn't suppress a smug grin at the thought of the temptress's indecent neckline obscured by heavy wooden stocks. Oh, what her Puritan neighbors would do with a woman like Veronique!

She didn't dare glance into any of the taverns. If she had, she would have spied the man who hid in the door of the Sea Nymph, the tavern where he had been half hoping, half dreading that he might see her pass by.

The blue silk gown was beginning to look the worse for wear, but he was glad that she had not resumed her old attire. Among the memories that he had so carefully stored away, this final glimpse would last the longest. It would be the one he carried with him until fortune saw fit to find him an opponent more skilled than himself.

Chapter 18

Winston Hall seemed to Faith far more than half a world away from home. The plantation was called after her mother and aunt's maiden name, as it had seemed unwise to keep the Spanish name it had borne before the English claimed the island. When Miguel had lived there alone, he lived in a small hut, just as most of his neighbors did. In deference to his English bride, he had had the manor house built of stones brought from England as ships' ballast.

The kitchen stood separately, behind and to one side. From the spacious veranda in front, they enjoyed an exquisite view of a small bay and the Caribbean Sea. In the shallows, the water was a cool aqua, just the shade of Faith's eyes, though she never made the connection. Farther out, where the water was deeper and all manner of sea life played among the reefs, it was the color of flawless sapphires, and sunlight danced upon a thousand facets.

The grounds were no less breathtaking. A spacious lawn with stone walkways surrounded the house itself. Dogwood, ironwood, and island mahogany provided shade, while ackee, wild lime, naseberry, mango, and almond trees added sustenance to their ornamental function. The gardens were brought to life by coral clusters of tiny, star-shaped ixora blossoms. Magenta pussy tails, long and fuzzy, like tiny boas, mingled with earth orchids in shades of crimson and fuchsia. Arbors provided shade along the walkway.

Cane fields stretched from the lawn to the sea, where sea grape and coconut trees provided shade along the edge of the water. Behind the house, cluster palms and other lush vegetation hid a wealth of bananas, plantains, and even more mangos and ackee.

Ackee, Faith discovered, was a curious, podlike fruit. The inner flesh looked like scrambled eggs, though it tasted nothing like them, and was fatally poisonous if eaten before the fruit ripened and popped open, exposing the pulp and black seeds within.

One morning, Faith dressed in one of Elizabeth's gowns and sat sewing in the gallery in a chair next to her aunt. A cool sea breeze blew through the open windows lining both the front and back walls of the long, elegantly furnished chamber. In the week since Faith had arrived, several black seamstresses had slaved day and night to complete the collection of gowns that would become Faith's new wardrobe. But Elizabeth insisted that she and Faith attach the trimmings of ribbons and lace.

"They'll steal bits and pieces, you know," Elizabeth explained, "and then they'll get into fights over them."

The thought made Faith sad. How little they must have to fight over bits of lace. She had wanted to talk to the slave women who had come to fit her for the dresses, but Elizabeth strongly discouraged it, and the women had quickly done their jobs and left. Likewise, her aunt kept her away from the kitchens and the women who worked them, and made sure that she never went near the field hands. Even with such limited exposure, it occurred to Faith that slavery was the serpent in this Garden of Eden.

Glancing at her niece's gloomy face, Elizabeth sought to cheer her. "Did Naomi ever tell you about the chickens we bartered for a long strip of lace?"

The statement snapped Faith from her musings. There were a few very wealthy women in Boston who trimmed their collars with a small amount of lace, but she had never seen her mother do such a frivolous thing.

"Nay, she never did."

"Oh, it was a delicate bit of finery!" Elizabeth said with a fond smile and a faraway look. "'Pretty enough for a fairy's wings,' Naomi said."

It was hard to imagine her mother indulging in such a fantasy. *"My* mother said that?"

"Aye! It was her idea, the whole scheme. We were still living in England at the time. A peddler came through our community, hawking fabrics and such. Our little village was made up of Puritans and farmers. They bought plenty of muslin, but no one had any use for the lace he carried with him, as well. While our mother perused sensible bolts of cotton, Naomi insisted that we simply had to have that lace."

"My mother?" Faith repeated dubiously.

Elizabeth only giggled. "Well, we hied ourselves home, and Naomi got this grand idea that we could barter chickens for the lace. The peddler would have to eat, she said, and he would be glad of a couple fine hens. I said that mother would not be so very glad to have lost them, but Naomi was certain that we could convince her that they had run off, if only we left the gate open."

"Nay!"

"Oh, aye! Well, we left the gate open. When all was said and done, we lost five chickens that day. Three we found in the woods, but two never did turn up." She winked at Faith. "Mother beat us both for our carelessness, but we had the lace."

"Mother *stole* two hens and *lied* to Grandmother?" Faith asked incredulously. "Are you sure we're speaking of *my* mother? Naomi Cooper?"

"Nay, Faith, we are speaking of Naomi Winston. And that was not the worst of it," Elizabeth answered. "There was not enough lace for each of us to use for anything separately, so we agreed that we would trim one of our petticoats. That way, we could share it, and no would ever need know because it would be under our dresses. But our mother knew everything. I often thought God spoke to her directly whenever we misbehaved."

Faith laughed. "My mother is like that now. None of us children could slip much past her."

"Mayhap it comes with children, that tattle-tale voice of the Almighty," Elizabeth chuckled. "Anyway, Naomi was the one wearing the petticoat when our mother demanded that we lift our skirts. My foolish sister tried to shoulder all the blame, but I'd my fair share to take. We took all our meals standing up for days!" She rubbed her backside in remembered pain.

"You must have been very close," Faith commented. At Elizabeth's sad nod, she asked, "Do you never hate them, your parents and my father? It breaks my heart when I think that I may never see my family again, but I made that choice knowing what I risked. What they did to you was so cruel."

"I made a choice, like you," Elizabeth answered. "And so did they. My parents hurt me, I'll not lie, but I know the teachings of that church. A more stiff necked, intolerant theology I've yet to encounter. There was little worse than Catholicism in their eyes. Black witchcraft, maybe, although perhaps not. The first time I genuflected before a statue in Miguel's church, I thought surely God would strike me dead for idolatry."

Faith smiled. "And yet, here you are."

Elizabeth surveyed her skirts and held her hands before her face. "So I am!" she exclaimed in mock surprise.

"I suppose 'tis foolish, when you think of it," Faith reflected. "We are all Christians. What can it matter to God that we worship somewhat differently?"

"Here in the Caribbean, we see people from everywhere. Have you ever met a Mohammedan?" Faith shook her head, and Elizabeth continued. "They are as fierce in their devotion to Allah and Mohammed as any saint to God and Christ."

Faith paused, deep in thought, before she said, "And so, in the name of their devotion, people have slaughtered each other in crusades and pushed loved ones away. Think you, Aunt Elizabeth, that 'tis possible that we all worship the same God, in the end?"

With a sideways glance and shake of her head, Elizabeth replied, "Not much of a Puritan, are you?"

"I was, once. I thought I was." Faith's brow was furrowed in thought. "I know what happened to me. I couldn't stand it anymore, swallowing my emotions, dutifully obedient to the point of nearly having to marry a man who despised me! But what happened to my mother? What became of the girl who took two beatings, all for a lace-trimmed petticoat?"

Elizabeth gave her a bittersweet smile. "Jonathan."

"My father?"

"Aye. We met him on Cigatoo. We took an immediate dislike to one another, Jonathan and I, but for Naomi, it was love at first sight."

"They are not like you and Uncle Miguel," Faith said. "But they love each other, that I know."

"Oh, I have no doubt of that, Faith. I may not ever have liked your father overmuch, but the man commands respect. If I know Jonathan, he loves you all fiercely."

"He does, and I've surely broken his heart," Faith agreed, her voice quivering.

With a harshness that was out of character, Elizabeth replied, "'Tis about time his faith cost *him* something."

"Then you do hate him for keeping you and Mother apart."

"I do not hate him," Elizabeth sighed. "Naomi wrote to me once. She could have done so again, if she had chosen to. I suppose I'll always feel a little hurt that she chose him over me, but I understand."

"You do?"

"Aye. Naomi needed Jonathan, even as I needed Miguel. My sister and I are on two different paths, and that is just the way of it. Do you really think yourself so unusual, a Puritan born and raised who eventually comes to rebel against all of the proscriptions, the hypocrisy?"

"No one I have known has ever spoken such rebellion."

"Only to face the stocks or be whipped? Imagine that," Elizabeth retorted, and Faith nodded in understanding. "Naomi and I spoke of it, though, in furtive whispers, in the dark of night."

Such a tale was inconceivable to Faith. Her mother

was a pillar of the church, an upright woman. She was very nearly as perfect as Faith's father.

"But while such thoughts made me long for escape, they made Naomi long for security. When I allowed myself to question the church, I felt free. Naomi felt terrified. I suppose the story of the lace sums it up well enough. After our mother discovered the petticoat and whipped us for our lying, stealing, and vanity, she marched us to the church. There we were lectured to for well over an hour. By the time we left, I was disgusted. It was only a bit of finery. But Naomi was utterly convinced that her desire for the lace was a sure sign that she was destined for the fires of hell. She struggled with such worries for a long time."

Faith could well imagine her mother's torment. Had she not wrestled with the very same fears?

"And then came Jonathan Cooper. A more solid, stable, self-certain man you'll never meet. He's a rock, that one. And he was handsome and hardworking, a man with a promising future. A man brimming with divine grace. When she fell in love with him, she changed. I almost wish I could say that it was for the worse. Our separation might have been easier to swallow if I could have believed that she feared him."

"Oh, nay!" Faith protested. "He is not a brutal man! He is forceful, and fearsome in some ways, but he would never really hurt any of us!"

Elizabeth reached over and patted her hand. "I know that, dear. As I said, I selfishly wished that Naomi had changed for the worse. Mayhap I was a little jealous. She married your father, and it was as though a light went on inside of her. He restored her. He gave her back her faith in the church, and in doing so, he gave her faith in herself. Who am I to judge that? He has made my sister happy. I cannot, for the life of me, hate your father."

"What did Uncle Miguel give to you?"

The older woman paused, as though she debated something in her own mind. Finally, she turned and arched a graceful brow at Faith. "Well, for one thing, he was devilishly handsome and a master of flattery. I must admit, having never in my life been told that I was beautiful, that meant a great deal more than it should have."

To her dismay, Faith felt her cheeks flame at her aunt's words. Even as she understood her mother's long-ago doubts, she understood Elizabeth's vanity. It was a heady thing, to be told of one's beauty and desirability.

"And he stirred within me feelings both forbidden and intoxicating. Sheltered as I was, I was ill prepared and overwhelmed."

Faith's face felt positively scorching.

Elizabeth continued, as though unaware of the girl's response. "We had a whirlwind romance, because my family was to spend only a few weeks in Jamaica until our ship came for us. My conversion to Catholicism was an impulsive one, born of passion, but I quickly came to embrace much of it."

"It spoke to you?"

"Not all of it. I saw the corruption I had been warned of since childhood, but having seen the flaws in my own church, as well, it mattered little.

"Forgiveness, Faith. Here was a God who had not already chosen my fate. I could ask forgiveness, and it would be granted."

"There is little enough of that in our church," Faith acceded.

"Even the very best people founder, Faith." Elizabeth looked hard at her niece, and Faith had the uneasy feeling that she could see right through her. "In the end, redemption comes through forgiveness. Forgiving others and forgiving ourselves."

When Elizabeth rose to check on the midday meal, Faith sat alone with her thoughts. Geoff's betrayal had cut her to the quick. She hadn't been able to decide which infuriated her more, the fact that he had seduced her and then discarded her, or the fact that she had allowed him to do so.

Wrapping her arms tightly around her waist, she walked to one of the front windows and gazed out at the bay and the sea beyond. Thoughts of Geoff always left her with a nauseating combination of frustrated ire and aching emptiness.

Where was he? Did he ever think of her? Had he any regrets?

She shook her head to clear it. These were futile questions. She could only hope that in time, she would be able to follow her aunt's advice and forgive both Geoff and herself.

Elizabeth had given her much else to think on. She had cast an entirely new light upon Faith's mother, and somehow it left her feeling somewhat differently about herself. Different paths, Elizabeth had said. Not one path of good and all others of evil, merely paths that were different. Where would Faith's take her?

Chapter 19

There would be many such conversations between Faith and her aunt in the weeks to follow. And the more they talked, the more certain Faith felt that despite the pain that Geoff had caused her, and despite her own fall from grace, *Destiny* had been the answer to her prayers, after all. Geoff's bold defiance of convention had shaken her loose from the grip of Puritanical fear. Now Elizabeth was helping her to find new places to take hold of hope.

Here was a woman who could forgive those who had denied her forgiveness. She could question churches without forfeiting her faith. Her thinking was adaptable, independent, admirable.

But Elizabeth was not without her own contradictions, and at times, they nearly split Faith's heart in two. She had quickly come to love both her aunt and uncle. They had welcomed her warmly and lavished her with the finest of everything they had to offer. At the same time, what she saw in the cane fields sickened her.

As on the ship, she could not understand the words of the Africans' songs, but the anger and sadness, ever colored by a fierce pride, spoke directly to her soul. It was a wonder they had the energy to survive, much less sing. Many did not. Those who did seemed to find that energy in the hostility and disdain that seethed just below the surface, impervious to the overseer's whip and the indignity of bondage.

The innocuous, sweet sugar crystals that had once been a rare treat could be had in abundance at Winston Hall, but Faith found that she had lost her taste for it. She drank her tea black and declined the luscious desserts prepared by the African women who served in the kitchen. Anything sweetened with sugar was made sour by sweat and sadness, bitter by blood and anger.

"Does it never disturb you, Aunt Elizabeth?" Faith ventured one afternoon, as she and the older woman rode in an open carriage. They traveled down the road, through recently burned fields, and out toward the beach. "All that you have costs them so much."

Faith inclined her head to a thin, young African boy not much older than her brother David. He moved among the blackened plants, cutting away the canes that stood strong amid the destruction. Fields were burned before harvesting to make them passable. Thick growth, snakes, wasps, and other hazards had to be destroyed before laborers could begin the work of harvesting. Fire eliminated these impediments without damaging the fruit of the canes.

Elizabeth smiled and patted her hand. "They look so human, 'tis easy to forget, but they do not have feelings like you and me, dear."

How could this woman who was so accepting of the differences between people be so unable to see past a mere difference in color? Faith wondered. Aloud, she answered, "They are not beasts."

Elizabeth sighed. "You must try to understand, Faith. When I first married Miguel, slavery appalled me, too, but 'tis a necessary evil. You'll grow accustomed to it.

The plantations simply could not run without African labor."

"Does that justify it?"

"They're savages, dear. Little more than wild animals."

"And kept so by their owners."

Elizabeth set her lips into a thin line. "There is naught that you can do about it. In this, 'tis better to just accept the way things are. Perhaps I have chosen not to see things anymore, but to dwell upon the Africans' plight only causes heartache. Once you have lived here awhile, you will come to understand."

Faith fell silent. In the last few months, she had learned that people could be either too rigid in their beliefs or too rigid in their denial. It seemed that they could be too willing to bend, as well. She doubted that anything could accustom her to the cruelty that plantation owners insisted was a necessity.

Her aunt's statement also brought to mind another quandary. She could hardly impose upon Miguel and Elizabeth's kindness forever. Elizabeth had subtly mentioned that several of their friends had fine sons who stood to inherit healthy farms, but Faith shuddered at the thought of one day becoming like her aunt, complacent at the suffering of the people who worked the cane fields.

As if that weren't enough, though she still felt much bitterness toward Geoff, she could not bear the thought of any other man's touch. Her hosts had been thoughtful, content with her tales of family and village life in Massachusetts, never pressing her for details of her voyage. That part had simply been too painful to speak of.

The two women arrived at the beach and alighted from the carriage. The slave who had driven them there laid out a blanket in the shade of palms on the fine, white sand and unloaded a hamper of food and wine. Faith smiled and thanked him, causing him to look at first startled, then suspicious, before Elizabeth sent him on his way to return in two hours' time.

"It does trouble you greatly, does it not?" Elizabeth sighed. "You have great affection for your uncle and me, but you cannot abide the way we live."

Realizing that it was a futile subject, Faith replied, "'Tis not for me to judge you."

Elizabeth shook her head. "Nay, 'tis not for any of us to judge each other. Life is not as black and white as we would have it."

"Some things are."

Her voice matter-of-fact, but without malice, Elizabeth replied, "So, there is a bit of Jonathan Cooper's steely will in his daughter, after all."

Faith gazed out at the excruciatingly blue sea. Ripples on the surface hinted at the eternal motion of wind and water, but otherwise it was as smooth as glass. Even as it had done when she surveyed it from the ship's rail, the ocean seemed to pull at her soul, and she voiced her thoughts aloud.

"Perhaps my father is not perfect, but as you said, he is solid and commands respect. I am not ashamed that he is a part of me. If only I could have his absolute certainty without sacrificing the freedom that I have found."

"For myself," Elizabeth replied, "I tend to be rather suspicious of those who seem convinced that they possess an absolute understanding of the Almighty."

"You sound a bit like someone else I know," Faith reflected.

At Elizabeth's suggestion, the two women tucked their skirts up above their knees and waded into the warm water, basking in the feel of the breeze upon their faces.

For all that she had let go of much of the hellfire and brimstone of her past, there was still a heavy weight upon Faith's soul. There were rules that were an intrinsic part of her, and she had broken them. She had begun to think that if she could but speak of it, then forgiveness might follow. Faith drew a deep breath and bolstered her courage.

"In many ways, Geoff is as certain as ever my father was. He is an atheist," she said, broaching the subject that had plagued her for weeks.

To the younger woman's surprise, Elizabeth didn't seem at all shocked by her pronouncement or the casual use of Captain Hampton's Christian name. "Is he?" she replied mildly.

"Aye. It troubled him, our different beliefs."

"Troubled him? I would have thought it to be the other way 'round."

"It seemed to me that we were not so very different at all. Neither of us could keep our philosophies if we examined them too carefully. He is as consumed by blind faith in nothing as I was in blind faith to the church of my childhood."

Elizabeth perused her niece with a look of heightened respect. "You are wise, indeed."

Faith looked down at the waves lapping at her calves. Wise? She doubted that.

"Interesting thing, that," Elizabeth commented.

"What?"

"What happens to you whenever you speak of your ship's captain. There is some deep turmoil there. It cannot be as bad as you think, my dear."

"We were lovers!" Faith blurted. She held her breath

and waited for her aunt's reproach, but again found she had worried for naught.

"Of course you were." Elizabeth took Faith's hand. "I wondered what had come between you."

"You knew?"

"Not when he came to tell us of you. He's a handsome man, that's sure, but he was so cold. I thought perhaps he harbored some grudge against you for stowing away on his ship, but he would accept no payment for your passage. I knew not what to make of him. As for you, you were obviously distressed when we met you, but that could easily be attributed to the loss of your family and all that you had been through."

"Aye," Faith agreed, "I had hoped you would believe that was all it was."

"In the weeks that you have been here, you have opened much of your heart to me, but whenever you speak of the ship, you lapse. Suddenly you are a guilt-ridden daughter of Eve. And you are miserable."

"Do I seem so? I try not to be morose."

"You are entitled to nurse your broken heart. Come, let us eat. We'll drink that bottle of wine, and you can tell me all about it."

Shadows moved across the pale sands, and Faith and Elizabeth laughed and cried and held each other. By the time the slave who had brought them there returned, Faith's face was tear streaked and her brain a bit muddled with drink, but her heart felt lighter than it had in weeks. The two women giggled while Faith managed to gain her seat in the carriage and pull her aunt in unceremoniously alongside her.

Elizabeth opened the second bottle of wine which they sipped slowly, staying somewhere short of truly drunk on the journey back.

Miguel was plainly shocked and dismayed when they tripped into the reception hall amid giggles at some private jest.

"*Querida*, you and our niece have returned!"

"We have!" his wife replied. Her eyes sparkled, and she draped her arms about him rather more affectionately than their lack of privacy warranted.

Miguel firmly extricated himself from her embrace, and his wife pouted. "How unlike you, Miguel, to be so prim and proper."

"I did not expect you to come home in such disarray and having had too much Madeira, I think."

"Oh, we had just enough," Elizabeth insisted. "I assure you."

"We have another visitor," Miguel announced, and a man with ebony hair, a dashing smile, and elegant, Spanish-style clothes joined them from the library. "Elizabeth, Faith Cooper, allow me to present my brother's son, Capitán Diego Montoya Fernandez de Madrid y Delgado Cortes. He was on his way from Spain to Cartagena when he was beset by pirates. He is here in Jamaica seeking the captain of the marauders. You will not believe it, but it is Captain Hampton he seeks!"

"I seem to be most fortunate," the captain added in flawless English, accented slightly by his native tongue. "By my count, Miss Cooper was aboard his ship at the time." He smiled hopefully at Faith. "You can act as a witness when I find him."

Chapter 20

The room spun crazily, although Faith was hard-pressed to tell whether it was a result of the wine or the situation. She was vaguely aware of her aunt's protest.

"Oh, nay! Surely you are mistaken. Faith would have told us if Captain Hampton had accosted a Spanish vessel while she was on it."

"I must confess," Miguel said, "I was bewildered by Diego's claim, as well, but he is certain he was attacked by Captain Geoffrey Hampton and the crew of *Destiny*."

Faith looked back and forth among those who gazed at her expectantly. What could she say? This man had seen the name of the ship, and Geoff was arrogant enough to have made sure that Capitán Montoya knew the name of the man who had raided his ship.

"He—he did it for me," she stammered. Then more passionately, she explained, "He wanted to let you go in peace, but his crew would not hear of it. They threatened mutiny, and he feared for my safety. Please, you must believe me."

Her uncle looked utterly dumbfounded, and Faith felt her face suffuse with color.

"This was a very important event to have left out of the tale of your journey here," he reproached. "You never told us that the ship you sailed on was a pirate ship. You were in grave danger, Faith!"

"I wasn't, truly! Geoff—that is, Captain Hampton protected me at all costs. I am so very sorry, Capitán Montoya, that the greatest price was borne by you. The fault is mine."

Diego eyed her with mild skepticism. "I can hardly fault you, Miss Cooper. Your presence on his ship was surely as much his reason for wanting to let us pass as it was his motive for attacking us after all. If you had not been there, he simply would have taken my ship with greater relish. *Magdalena* was by no means the first Spanish ship to be harassed by him."

Unable to refute the truth of his statement, she merely replied, "I doubt he is still near Jamaica. I cannot imagine where you might look for him. I am sorry, Capitán. The attack must have cost you dearly."

"It cost my crew and my employer far more. Several of my men died that day. And I do not own the ship or its cargo."

"But he spared the lives of as many as he could," Faith argued. "He told me so."

Diego seemed unmoved. "He killed one of his own men."

"There you have it!" Faith cried. "Proof that his men were near mutiny. The man he killed was about to kill him, was he not?" At Diego's begrudging nod, she continued, "He risked much when he spared your lives."

"How can you defend this man, Faith?" her uncle asked.

Elizabeth intervened. "It seems to me that her argument has some merit."

"Perhaps some," Diego conceded. "Nonetheless, I will find him and take him to Cartagena to face justice."

"Will you not send him to England, then?" Miguel asked.

"After the 'justice' that has been served to Henry Morgan? King Charles promised to arrest and try him, but he walks the streets of London as free as a bird." Diego made a small, disgusted sound. "Nay, I will take Hampton to Cartagena."

Faith's face paled, and Elizabeth addressed the men. "We spent too long in the heat, I'm afraid, and had a bit too much wine. Our Faith, here, is unaccustomed to spirits. I think I'll take her upstairs now, if you will excuse us."

Faith allowed her aunt to lead her upstairs, her mind awhirl in all that had transpired. In truth, it was relief to escape to the protective confines of her room.

Diego watched the women ascend the mahogany stairs to the upper gallery. His uncle's niece by marriage was a lovely girl, and well meaning, if misguided. Miguel had told him of her deeply religious background and of her heartbreaking departure from her home and family. It only made sense that she would see the English captain as her savior of some sort, hence, her misplaced feelings of loyalty.

Diego turned to his uncle and smiled. *"Su sobrina es muy hermosa,"* he said.

"Sí," Miguel agreed. His niece was, indeed, beautiful. *"Parece mentira, pero ella no tiene el esposo o novio."*

Diego's uncle spoke true! It was hard to believe that no fortunate man had yet laid claim to such a beauty. He doubted he sounded at all sincere when he replied, *"¡Es una lástima!"* A shame for her perhaps, but he counted himself lucky. If she had felt some infatuation for Hampton, well, the man was out of her life now.

Diego and Miguel exchanged quick, significant smiles and retired to the library again. He might come away from this excursion with more than just Captain Hampton and command of *Magdalena*.

The group reassembled to break their fast the next day, and Faith had recovered herself. In the wee hours of the morning, listening to the relentless songs of tree frogs, she concluded that it was most unlikely that the Spanish captain would find Geoff, and even if he did, Geoff had already defeated him once. Surely he could do so again. The comfort of these thoughts had finally permitted her to sleep.

Now she was dressed in a pale pink gown with a tight bodice that came to a low point in front and was covered in deep wine embroidery. The light silk skirts billowed over lace-trimmed petticoats, and the sleeves ended at the elbows with fetching, wine-colored satin bows. Though the neckline was modest, it was by no means prim, showing her ivory throat to full advantage.

Her aunt had chosen the gown, and she knew very well why. Perhaps Elizabeth was right to push her in this direction. It was time to accept the fact that whatever had happened between her and Geoff was over. It was time to think of the future.

Miguel and Elizabeth quelled their own garrulous tendencies, allowing their nephew to take center stage, and Faith had to admit, he was delightful company. He told colorful stories of outsailing pirates and encountering strange and humorous people in his travels. She allowed herself to consider him, much as she had once considered Aaron Jacobs. He was more pleasing to look upon than Aaron had been, and he was a ship's captain. Goodness knew, she had come to love the sea, and he kept no slaves.

Of course, there were a host of other things to contemplate. They came from different countries, countries that were hostile toward each other, at best. Her parents would never approve. There could be no doubt that she would suffer the same fate as Elizabeth, but for all she knew, that was already the case. She may well have sealed her fate the night she ran away. But even if she could never return home, she was not at all sure she could live in Spain or one of her colonies, which she might be expected to do if she encouraged Capitán Montoya.

There would be much for both of them to consider, but it was clear that her aunt and uncle hoped for a match. Faith smiled to herself. She and Diego hardly knew each other. She was certainly placing the cart before the horse with her thoughts of marriage and life in Spain!

"Ah, Diego!" Elizabeth cheered. "You have done what is ever so difficult with our homesick Faith. You have made her smile!"

Faith blushed furiously at her aunt's teasing, but Diego gave her a warm look. "I thought the room had gone suddenly brighter," he replied.

After breakfast, Faith pleaded a headache when her aunt and uncle took Diego on a tour of the plantation. When they gathered again for the midday meal, he resumed his flirtation. He teased her lightly and complimented her lavishly, and clearly she was expected to respond in kind.

For all that she was no longer a virgin, she was still

very inexperienced with men, and Faith was at a loss. She sensed that the capitán was perplexed by her bashfulness, but she knew that unlike Geoff, the purpose of his flirtation was not seduction. What, then, was the end objective of this game?

Hours later, Elizabeth and Miguel contrived to leave the two young people alone on the veranda to watch the sunset, and Diego finally lightened his suit.

"Do I offend you?" he asked. "I do not mean to press my attentions where they are unwelcome."

"Nay, I am not offended. I think you are accustomed to very different women. In my village, men and women do not speak so to one another."

"No? In Spain, a woman is expected to be modest and somewhat aloof, but you are more genuinely so. I am intrigued. How do the young people in your village express an interest in each other?"

"Well, they speak of crops and religious matters. They consider each other's standing in the church and among their neighbors. If the man believes they would be a suitable match, he petitions the woman's parents for her hand."

He frowned. "But how do they know if they are compatible?"

"The woman submits herself to her husband as the Bible demands. That makes them compatible."

"What if he wants her to be something she is not because he never really came to know her heart before they wed?"

Faith sighed. What had once seemed so simple and obvious now seemed slightly absurd. "If she has God's grace, she can be whatever her husband and parents expect her to be." At his dubious look, she elaborated. "'Tis not as though she has no voice. 'Tis simply that everyone knows what is expected from the start. Puritan women actually have quite a bit of say in the church, provided they are upright and adhere strictly to the tenets of the faith."

He considered this thoughtfully. "But how does the couple know if there is any fire between them?"

"'Fire,' as you call it, is a sin."

Diego grinned. "*Sí*, that is why there is confession."

"Not for a Puritan. God forgives the sins of those chosen by Him before their birth. He does this by granting them divine grace. Those with grace can resist their sinful natures and live in accordance with holy law."

His handsome face gaped in shock. "This is what you wish for in marriage? To resist nature?" He shook his head. "I have always thought that being allowed to give in to nature was one of the benefits of marriage."

Faith giggled at Diego's dismay. "Aye, well, that is one of the teachings of my church that I have come to question."

He smiled brightly. "You should be a Catholic!"

Faith laughed. "I have a good bit of thinking to do ere I commit myself to another faith."

"But Catholicism is not out of the question?" Diego's voice was a little too disinterested, as though he were trying very hard to make it sound as though it did not matter.

So, that would be an important question if there were ever to be any possibility of marriage. "Nay," she replied, thinking of her earlier question whether everyone worshipped the same God, in any case. "It is not out of the question."

They moved inside as darkness fell, and Faith was

delighted to learn that her fellow houseguest played chess.

"I must warn you," he told her, "I am a firm believer that all is fair in love, war, and chess! You have already seen that I am ruthless in love." His white teeth flashed in his dark face.

"Hold nothing back," she replied. "As you have seen, I keep my wits about me in all cases."

Whenever Faith had played with Noah, they would tease each other, trying to shake each other's confidence. "Are you quite sure you wish to do that?" they would ask each other. Sometimes they meant it, because one of them had made a foolish move, but at other times, they said it just to make the other one sweat. It was a taunt that she and Geoff had used, as well.

Diego moved his bishop, and Faith surveyed the board. The only purpose for such a move would be easily thwarted in two moves, when she should be able to take the piece. Try though she might, she could find no trap. Her brow furrowed, she asked, "Are you sure you wish to do that?"

Diego flashed her an arrogant grin, just the sort Geoff would have given before he pulled the rug out from under her. Carefully, she surveyed the board. No matter how hard she looked, she could see no other reason for his move than to take her knight, but her rook would intervene ere he would have his chance. She need not even move the piece yet. With a shrug, she moved her own bishop, patiently working her way toward Diego's queen.

Predictably, he moved his bishop again. She hesitated, but there was no imminent threat in taking it.

When she did, he pulled back as though surprised by her simple tactics.

"You are very skilled," Diego complimented.

Faith sighed. So, this was merely an act in order to perpetuate his flattery, she thought. He was letting her win.

"I assure you, Capitán, I am quite up to your best game. I have no need of your assistance."

Diego bristled and gave her a tight smile. "Of course. Well, since you have asked." He moved another piece, but his strategy was obvious, and Faith looked at her aunt in exasperation. To her surprise, Elizabeth frowned and shook her head slightly.

A single game with Noah or Geoff could last several days. Ere half an hour had passed, she had Diego's queen. He crossed his arms and glared at the board, and it occurred to her that perhaps this, at least, had not been intentional.

He cleared his throat and laughed weakly. "I had to sacrifice her. She was distracting my king." Gesturing across the board, he added, "Fair women are ever a distraction." Shifting in his chair, he perused the game. His king was in grave danger, indeed.

"Well," Faith suggested diplomatically, "perhaps 'tis a challenge reversing the damage from earlier, when you were letting me win."

"Aye, when I was letting you win," he agreed, swallowing hard.

"Faith!" Elizabeth exclaimed. "My, how time has gotten away from us! I think, mayhap, we should retire."

Faith waved her hand in dismissal. "The game is nearly over, Aunt Elizabeth. A quarter of an hour, at most."

Elizabeth rose and put her hand on Faith's shoulder.

"Look at you, dear. You can scarcely keep your eyes open," she said sweetly through her clenched teeth.

Faith cast a worried look at her aunt. She was clearly upset. With a sympathetic smile for Diego, she conceded, "Perhaps 'tis not quite fair. After all, you were not playing at your best the whole time."

"It is a terrible shame that you avoid sugar, Faith," Elizabeth said, far too blithely. "I can think of nothing you could use more, just now, than a mouthful of that wonderfully sticky honey and raisin pastry we had for dessert."

The remark stung and bewildered Faith. Embarrassed at having been unfairly chastised, she looked to Diego for support.

"Faith is right, of course," he said gallantly, but he rose from the table as though he had already dismissed the contest. "The game would have been over shortly."

For the first time, Faith realized that he was genuinely unnerved. He gazed down at the board, a dismal look on his handsome face. She glanced back at her aunt, who shook her head again. Had he been playing his best all along? If so, her remarks had been needlessly cruel.

"I'm so sorry," she began, but Elizabeth was now shaking her head vehemently. "That is, I am so sorry to end this now, ere we shall ever know who would have won. But I'm afraid my aunt is quite right. I'm too tired to keep my wits about me."

Diego didn't seem at all placated. It was clear enough that she would have won, and her attempt to soften her unintentional insults fell short.

"As you wish," he said, still staring at the board, perplexed.

"Good night, Aunt Elizabeth, Uncle Miguel." Softly, she added, "Capitán."

Diego lifted his eyes. Struggling to maintain his charm, he said, "Diego, please. We are all family here." Stepping around the table, he came to stand at her side and took her hand in his. "Although even a single word in Spanish sounds smooth and sweet as honey from your lips. Perhaps I could teach you a bit of my language."

She made no move to withdraw her hand. "That would be wonderful. I think I would like it very much."

Diego smiled, his ruffled feathers smoothed. *"Buenas noches,* Señorita Cooper."

"Faith. As you say, we are family. *Buenas noches,* Diego."

As always, night brought vivid memories that colored her thoughts. She listened to the frogs and the occasional sharp crack of an almond as it struck the roof of the kitchen beyond her open window. Who would have known such a small nut came in such a large shell?

It seemed to her that men were much the same. The outside hid too much of the man. Diego was subtler than Geoff had ever been. If Geoff had wanted from her what Diego wanted, he would have said, "I want you to be a Catholic and live in Spain and never to beat me at chess."

Spoken so plainly, it sounded awful, but then, what Geoff had told her so plainly from the beginning hadn't pleased her, so she had simply ignored it. He had told her in no uncertain terms that he wanted her body but not her heart. She had no one to blame for her suffering but herself.

What would any straightforward, honest man tell her he wanted? Faith, I want you to be yourself? I want your troubled spirit and your confusion? I want your intelligence and compassion? She had never been foolish enough to believe anyone would ever say such words to her. A man from her village would have required her body for begetting heirs and helpers to his business, her skills at the hearth and in the home, her unquestioning devotion to the church. One of her new neighbors' sons would demand that she ignore the suffering of the African slaves, look pretty and give him children, attend an Anglican church and behave respectably.

Geoff was right, she made things too complicated. She didn't want to be alone. She wanted children and a home. What did it matter what church she attended? But she didn't want to live on a plantation, and she didn't want to live in Spain. She would have prayed to God for an answer, but it seemed that the last time she had made such a request, He had told her in no uncertain terms to be careful what she prayed for.

She had to admit she was somewhat relieved the next morning when Diego told them that he must be about his business. That his business was finding and arresting Geoff was a thought she preferred not to contemplate.

Since there seemed to be little chance that Diego would press her toward any kind of commitment on such short acquaintance, she gave in to Elizabeth's suggestion that she wear an outrageously sumptuous gown to dinner. It was made of glossy black satin with a bodice ornamented by tiny pleats and pearls. The black overskirt parted to reveal an underskirt of white lace set aglitter by silver threads woven throughout.

She pinned her hair up, showing to advantage her fine features and high cheekbones, and atop the simple style sat a small cap of black lace and pearls. The deep, square neckline created the perfect setting for Elizabeth's pearl cross pendant. It rested against skin that rivaled the gems their creamy smoothness.

It had seemed a harmless indulgence until she saw Diego's reaction. His face lit with unrestrained pleasure, and he rushed to greet her at the door to the dining room.

"Why, you look the very essence of a Spanish lady, Faith. All this, just to bid Diego farewell? I am humbled."

A quick glance in her aunt's direction affirmed that this was precisely the response Elizabeth had hoped for, and Faith felt foolishly duped. They dined, and Faith found she dared not look up from her plate, for without fail she was the object of Diego's undivided attention. No matter how she demurred, he insisted she join him on the veranda to enjoy the moonlight after the meal. The lawn was thick with hundreds of dancing lights as fireflies frolicked, and though Faith was painfully aware of the romance of the image, she felt anything but romantic.

"You are shy," he said, as they stood in the night-time breeze from the sea in the dark void beyond. "I know that is why you blush so at my attention. I must tell you, I am utterly charmed. I thought perhaps you felt somewhat uncertain of me, but I see now that it was only your modesty. I will seek to quickly conclude this unpleasantness of finding the Englishman so that I may return and truly court you. I think our families would be pleased."

"Wait, Diego. I think you may make more of tonight than I intended."

"Of course, we must spend more time together ere we make any decisions. I only mean you to know that I will return as soon as I can to make this possible."

She tried to temper her dismay at this ardent proclamation of his intent. "You are, indeed, a handsome and charming man, but I must tell you, I do not think that I can move far from my aunt and uncle. I am already so far from home, you see."

A cloud passed over her companion's features, but he seemed to dismiss whatever thoughts had cast the shadow. "We will live in Cuba or Hispaniola. Perhaps Venezuela. A sea captain does not have to be difficult about where his wife lives, so long as it is a port he frequents."

"There is another matter! Will you not be at sea for months at a time?"

"Aye, but you can journey with me often. If you would like, you can visit here when I am away."

There was some sense in what he spoke. What was the harm in leaving the door open? "There is time to speak on these things," she conceded. Still, it pained her to see the hopefulness in his face. She sensed that he had set his heart on walking through that door.

He stepped closer to her and placed his hand gently against her face. "*Con permiso*—with your permission, I would give you some token of my feelings ere I leave."

His eyes had gone soft, and he was close enough that she felt his breath on her cheek. In reply, she lifted her face and closed her eyes. His mouth was soft and gentle, perhaps too much so. It occurred to Faith that it was not unpleasant, but something indefinable was missing, and she did not mind that he pulled away after the briefest contact. He smiled at her, and she smiled back, but she wanted nothing more dearly than to go back into the house.

"I should not keep you so long from the others. They will want to spend some time with you ere morning," she said.

"In a moment. I promise, I will take no further advantage of you."

He seemed content to gaze at her in the opalescent moonlight, which served only to make Faith fidgety. She tried to make conversation, but her every remark seemed to occasion some outlandish compliment, and by the time she could flee to the privacy of her room, she thought she would scream. Who would have reckoned that the only thing worse than censure was exorbitant approval?

Chapter 21

Geoff sat in the darkest corner of the Sea Nymph, slowly sipping from a tankard of bumboo, a sweetened drink of watered rum and nutmeg. What called to him from Port Royal for the whole of the two months he and his crew had prowled the waters of the Caribbean, he couldn't say. He had no stomach for the quantity of drink his men imbibed. Even the harlots had lost their appeal, though the Sea Nymph was known for its women, higher priced and a bit more select. He groaned inwardly as Giles beckoned two buxom wenches, a redhead and a blonde, to the table that he had chosen to avoid just such an encounter.

"For goodness sake, Giles, must you?"

Giles smiled at his friend's uncharacteristically soft tongue. "'Tis pathetic, really, Geoff. It's been two months since Faith went to her relatives', and you still never say 'God.' A sailor who says 'for goodness sake.' It's bloody embarrassing. You've pined too long, my friend." Giles turned to smile again at the two women, though he still spoke to Geoff. "If you'll not go to Winston Hall and fetch the woman you want, then you'd best go back to wanting the women at hand."

Geoff shot the other man a murderous look, but before he could reply, the blonde's warm, soft body filled his lap and two plump breasts presented themselves in front of his face.

"I tol' me frien' Molly 'ere," said the woman with a seductive smile, "well, 'e's not 'ere fer the drink. I'm thinkin' I might 'ave a bit o' what 'e wants." She laughed and wrapped her arms about his neck, drawing his face closer to her nearly naked bosom.

Molly, as was apparently the name of the redhead, had entirely captured Giles's interest, so Geoff had no choice but to look up at the wench in his lap. She was fairly young and fresh faced. Like most of the women at the Sea Nymph, she was probably staying only long enough to put together a nest egg. Then she would be off to seek a husband in the Colonies or back in London where her accent placed her home. She might even have a man waiting for her, one who would ignore the source of the dowry she would return with. Such an arrangement was not unheard of.

Geoff flashed her an obligatory smile. "And what does your friend Molly call you?"

The woman laughed again. "On a good day, she calls me Nell. I won't say what she calls me on a bad one."

Out of courtesy, Geoff chuckled and slipped his hand into her bodice. He had not touched a woman so intimately since the one who haunted his every dream at night. Perhaps Giles was right. Nell, here, might be just the cure.

"Well, love," he said, forcing himself to use the endearment he had banished from his vocabulary, "you're right. I'm not here for the drink."

She slid from his lap, and he allowed her to lead him up the stairs to the rooms above. Aye, it had been far too long since he had tussled with a willing wench, but he couldn't shake the feeling that he was breaking some kind of sacred bond. He laughed at his own musings. A sacred bond, for a man who held nothing sacred!

The laugh caught Nell's attention. "I do likes a merry fellow," Nell complimented over the bare shoulder that her sleeve had slipped from. "So many of the swabs 'ere is drunk an' surly. Molly and me, we picks and chooses. You and yer mate were the likeliest pair."

What would once have been a flattering statement made his stomach turn uneasily, but he squelched the feeling. He had wrestled with the needs of his strong, healthy body long enough. Surely it was his self-imposed celibacy that kept Faith so prominent in his mind.

Nell's room was cluttered, the sheets of the unmade bed rumpled, and Geoff tried not to think about who had lain there with her before and how recently. He had never been so fastidious before. He pulled her to him, would have run his hands through her dull blond hair but found it too tangled. She smelled of rum and other men's sweat, and with a muffled curse, he pushed her away.

"What is it, love?" she asked.

"I'm married!" he blurted, then brought himself up short. He couldn't have been more astounded at himself if he had told her he was the king of England.

Nell smiled. "'At's all right. Lots of fellows 'ere is. But yer wife's far away. England maybe?" She trailed her fingers over his arm. "No 'arm in gettin' the knots out o' yer riggin's. It don't mean nothin'."

It didn't mean anything. God help him, he didn't think he could ever again be content with a woman who didn't mean anything to him, and he didn't think any woman could mean more to him than Faith. His face split into a wide grin, and he reached into the pocket of his coat to draw out a handful of silver.

"For your trouble," he said. "You're right, I'm missing my wife, but you see, I love her."

Nell's face softened, and he could see in her a young wife, even someone's daughter. "I 'ope she knows 'ow lucky she is," Nell sighed. "I won't say I'm not disappointed. Yer as pretty a gent as a girl could wish fer, but I won't turn down the easiest silver I've earned in a good while."

She grinned at him, and he felt light of heart as he left her. He wished her all the happiness in the world.

His step was effortless as he descended back into the dark tavern. Giles was gone, doubtless being entertained by the wench called Molly. Having nowhere else to go, he walked down High Street toward the docks. He dodged drunks where they weaved or fell and smiled carelessly at whores without stopping to linger. He had thought to return to the ship, but he wasn't expected until late, so he headed west along the beach as the sun set.

A strange feeling of contentment overcame him as he settled the matter in his mind. He had always said he snatched what happiness he could where he found it. Why had Faith been any different? What was it about the happiness he felt with her that made him want to hold it close forever? And when had he started believing in forever?

As the gold disk of the sun approached the horizon, the light streaking of clouds around it took on a warm, golden glow that intensified to peach and finally orange, and the rippling water below reflected each hue faithfully. At the edges of the light, the sea turned to quicksilver, then blue satin scattered with diamonds. It was this sparkle, this scintillating, scattered light that delineated sea from sky more than any actual horizon, the reflection was so true. Air and water, so different, and yet only subtly distinguished. Each supported life. The creatures and plants that waved gently in the salty current would die as surely in the air above as he would in the depths below.

Mayhap this was what Faith had tried to tell him. Faith and faithlessness, men and women, air and water. What was God if not that barely perceptible line between sea and sky? Where was his soul if not in the love that had sprung to life where their two bodies, whole in and of themselves, and yet more so together, had joined? Was it his mother's voice that he spoke with when he told her that such things were fairy tales? When would he venture to set foot upon his own path, as he had once challenged Faith to do?

In the growing darkness, he realized that he had walked farther than he had intended. He had to chuckle to himself. Had he thought to walk all the way to Winston Hall in the dark? Nay, that was no plan. He would return to the ship. In the morning, it would take no time at all to sail to the bay on the outskirts of Elizabeth and Miguel's plantation. There he would beg, plead, do whatever it took to gain Faith's forgiveness and begin to rebuild the trust he had so stupidly squandered.

It was rare, indeed, that a man of Captain Hampton's experience allowed himself to become entirely lost in thought so close to the den of iniquity just beyond. If he had kept his wits about him, as any intelligent man did in this locale, he would have heard footsteps running at him softly through the sand, would have known he was in danger ere the stout club struck the base of his skull, blotting out his musings.

* * *

Diego joined his compatriot, the young sailor Killigrew had harassed, over the fallen body of the Englishman. He shook his head. It had been so easy; it was almost anticlimactic. He would have been disappointed, but knowing that he could quickly return the pirate to his employer and be free to pursue the fair Faith was ample compensation for the lack of a fight.

"It is another day, my friend," Diego said to the other man. "A better day to play the hero."

"Excuse me, Capitán?" the other sailor asked.

"Do you believe in destiny, Pablo?"

"Maybe, Capitán. I believe in justice. The pig who insulted my mother is dead. Now this one will be brought under the law. It was meant to be, was it not?"

Diego nodded. He and his man bound their prisoner, and Diego offered up his thanks to the saint upon whom he had come to depend. "Maybe you will give me my love, too?" he asked, certain that his lady would not fail him. Of all the saints, Magdalena would understand why a man would need to share his good fortune.

When Geoff awoke, he was bound hand and foot in the hold of a ship that rocked as though it were well out to sea. The hold was huge, close to a galleon in size. It was also nearly empty, a sure sign that the voyage would not be long. Unmistakably, it smelled like a Spanish vessel. He couldn't quite define why. Perhaps it was the spices they so often held, but he had been in the bowels of enough Spanish ships to know that he was in one now.

He had thought of just such an eventuality often enough. In moments of drunken bravery, his men could joke about the "hempen jig," that last dance at the end of a hemp rope, but when sober, the thought chilled the blood. To Geoff, it was an occupational hazard, a possibility one lived with in exchange for easy money and the thrill of battle.

He slammed his head back against the solid support beam to which he was tied and saw stars. Another blow to a head that already ached was foolish indulgence. If he were a weaker man, he thought, the irony of it would make him weep. For the first time in his life, he had something to live for, and his life was as good as over. And damn it all, there was something in his eyes, for they watered fiercely!

Somehow he had always counted on dying on another captain's blade. His body would be carelessly thrown overboard, and the world would go on as though he had never existed. If Giles survived the battle, he would have one friend to grieve him, but naught else. The wealth he had hoarded would be found in his cabin and divided among the crew. The indignity of hanging, and worse still, knowing that his body would rot in irons as a warning to others who would rob Spain in the name of England, set his teeth on edge. Of course, those were English customs. He knew not what to expect from the people who had set the wheels of the Inquisition into motion.

And what of Faith? Would the man who finally claimed her for his own be worthy of her? He indulged in a bitter smirk. More worthy than a libertine and privateer, that was sure. Still, what if she married

some staunch Puritan and resumed a life of ducking
her head and swallowing her passions?

Diego descended the ladder into the hold. "You do
not look so good, Captain. In fact, you look so sad that
for a moment, I could almost pity you. Then I remind
myself, you are the one who has gotten yourself into
this."

Geoff turned his head, recognizing immediately
the captain of *Magdalena*. Almost automatically, an accustomed look of bored disinterest masked Geoff's
hopelessness.

"'Tis empty in here," he commented. "We're not for
Spain, I think."

"You are very cool for a man on his way to his death,"
Diego said. "We are for Cartagena."

Geoff grinned with a humor he did not feel. "I
don't suppose I could convince you to simply run me
through now?"

Diego smiled back just as humorlessly. "It would be
a kindness, but my employer prefers you alive. Not
having Morgan, you will be paying for Panama and
every other indignity Spain has suffered at the hands
of your kind."

Shrugging carelessly, Geoff answered, "There's
some justice there, for I was part of that, as well."

Diego shook his head. "I would not offer that information in court. It would not go well for you."

"You're being remarkably civil. I don't know that
I'd be so friendly to someone who had plundered my
ship."

"I am being adequately compensated." Diego rubbed
the faint, dark stubble on his prominent chin. "I think
I know why you are so sad, and it is not just that you are
on your way to Cartagena to die. I am not a cruel man.

I would not torture you, but I think perhaps you would feel better knowing—about the woman."

Geoff felt the blood drain from his face. He knew, without a doubt, which woman to whom the Spaniard referred. "How do you know her?" he asked.

"Do you not remember? I am Capitán Diego Montoya Fernandez de Madrid y Delgado Cortes. It means nothing to you?"

Geoff's thoughts flashed back to the deck of the carrack where he had first met this man. The name had struck a chord then, but he hadn't been able to place it. Now he remembered. "It is very like . . ."

"Like Faith Cooper's aunt and uncle? Her uncle, Miguel, is my father's brother."

"She was not a part of any of it, I swear. She was but an innocent stowaway on my ship."

"*Sí*, I know this already." Diego paused again, uncertain whether or not he truly wanted to ask the question he must. Then he sighed. Better to know. "Tell me, did you care for her?"

"You said you were not a cruel man."

"I spoke truly. I would only know whether or not her fate troubles you. If she means nothing, I will not waste my time or yours."

Squeezing his eyes closed against another suspicious stinging spell, his voice rougher than it had been, Geoff replied, "Tell me."

"She was hurt. Was it by you?"

Eyes still closed, Geoff nodded.

"Did you rape her?"

Geoff didn't miss the tight anger in Diego's voice. The answer mattered to him beyond the interest of any mere gentleman in a lady's welfare. "Nay, I did not."

"Did you compromise her?"

"Would it matter?"

Diego pondered that but an instant. "It seems it is forever my soul's fate to be bound to fallen women. Nay, it does not matter. I mean to take her to wife. If she was yours first, 'tis of no consequence. She will be mine in the end, and I will love her as you did not."

Geoff finally opened his eyes and could almost feel relieved to see the proud honor that stamped his counterpart's face. "You will, won't you? Love her, that is?"

"I do already."

Geoff shook his head, a dark scowl on his face. "'Tis not enough to merely want her. You must be willing to die for her. To give up any foolish ideas you may have about being weak because she somehow makes life worth living. There must be nothing at all you would not give to make her happy."

Pity clouded Diego's dark eyes. "This sounds like wisdom you obtained too late."

"And at great price."

"What is to become of you is not pleasant, but you may die knowing that she is well cared for. I give you my word on this, Captain Hampton. You see, I learned long ago what you have only just discovered. Love and honor mean placing the needs of others before your own selfish desires. I think that for most of your life, you have taken what you want, but in the end, what do you have?"

Geoff leaned his head back against the beam, studying the raw wooden planks of the deck above him. "So, the final victory is yours."

Diego had enough compassion to keep from smiling. Though he felt no remorse at clearing the way for him and Faith, he could well imagine the other man's pain at having lost her, and all else, as well.

"And, Captain," Geoff added, "don't tell her about this conversation. Let her believe that you are the only man who ever loved her."

"You know, Captain Hampton, I think I could have liked you. You are more noble than you know."

A bitter sound caught in Geoff's throat. "Tell that to the judge, will you?"

Chapter 22

Faith and Elizabeth sat in the shade of an arbor. Embroidery hoops reposed in their laps with their still, white hands. The ocean and an exquisite hummingbird feeding upon a bird of paradise proved too distracting, and so the stitchery was forgotten. Faith could not help but think that Eden must have looked very like this place, yet she had come to understand why Adam and Eve might have sacrificed it for knowledge. In the three weeks since Diego's departure, Faith had carefully examined her relationship with Geoff and her future without him.

He had told her that making love with her was not the same as it was with other women, and it seemed unlikely that she would ever know such tempestuous passion with any other man, but perhaps that was best. The memory was sweet, but in the end, it had wrought her nothing but pain. Better to know that now, than to encounter such temptation later, when it could threaten any commitment she might have made.

And she needed a partner who could share in the sense of wholeness that consumed her here in this lush land with its verdant mountains, gentle rivers, musical waterfalls, and mysterious coastal caves and cliffs. She cared not whether he was Catholic or Protestant, Jew or Mohammedan; he had to be strong enough to face his soul and consider his place in the universe.

If she had had to sacrifice the paradise she had known in Geoff's bed for this new knowledge, so be it. Physical passion was not enough. She wanted something deeper. God gave man free will, but what was free will without knowledge? Perhaps Eve had sensed this. Perhaps in the sin that she had committed when she ate of the forbidden fruit, she had only deepened her love of God, loving Him not out of ignorance, but out of true choice. Never again would she blush to call herself a daughter of Eve!

Elizabeth sat quietly, watching her niece. "Lost in thought, I see," she said. "The island can do that to you, weave you into its magic spell. Have you found any peace, Faith?"

"I think I am coming to find some acceptance, even forgiveness, Aunt Elizabeth." She turned her head back to the sea and raised her hand to point to the vessel that sailed into view. "Who is that?" she asked.

Elizabeth shrugged and ran into the house to fetch a spyglass. Raising it to her eye, she said, "*Magdalena.* It looks like our Diego has come back."

For all her philosophizing, Faith's heart leapt into her throat. If Diego had returned so soon, then surely he had found Geoff. His desertion she could bear, but his death was another matter!

Presently, the handsome and decidedly happy Capitán Diego Montoya Fernandez de Madrid y Delgado Cortes waved to them as he hiked up along the road that led from the beach. "*¡Buenas tardes!*" he called.

"Diego!" she cried as she rose, her embroidery

falling, forgotten, beneath the arbor. "You are back so soon!"

"*Sí*, the expedition did not go exactly as I had hoped, but I think my employer was satisfied with what I could present. In any case, he has agreed to take over the matter for himself, and I may resume my position. I told him there was a personal affair I wished to attend to, so he is permitting me to take some time before I return to his employ."

He took Faith's cold hand in his and kissed her fingertips. "Ah, you are even more beautiful than I remembered. I thought of nothing but you the whole time."

"What did you give him? Did you find information on Captain Hampton's whereabouts?"

Diego's smile never faltered. "*Sí*, he knows where the man was last seen. I think it is fairly certain he has not wandered far. I wash my hands of the whole thing. Are you all right, *querida*?"

"I'm fine. 'Tis only, as I told you, he boarded your ship to protect me." Her pale face belied her words.

Nodding sympathetically, he replied, "You feel somewhat responsible, I am aware of this. But we both know, mine is not the only Spanish ship he has captured."

"Nay, I realize that." Belatedly, she seemed to realize that she must appear overly worried. "Where did you find him?" she asked more calmly.

Diego hesitated, then looked back toward the sea and his retreating ship. "He was at a tavern. He and his first mate were upstairs with two *prostitutas*."

She straightened her back and blinked hard. "I see. But you did not wait for him and take him?"

"He was with his friend, and then he set back toward

his ship. I am so sorry, *querida*. I know that this is hard for you. He was not unkind to you, and it is understandable that you are concerned for his welfare. If it eases your mind to believe he may yet escape Spanish justice, I will not argue. I only ask you to consider this: what befalls him in the future is his own affair. You ceased to have any responsibility for each other when he left you in Port Royal."

Faith tried to smile, but instead she nearly crumbled. "I need to be alone, if you do not mind," she murmured. At her aunt's understanding nod, they parted company, and Faith ran down the path and toward the sea.

Elizabeth gave Diego a studied, serious look. "You lied," she said.

Diego winced and raked a hand through his dark hair. "I skirted around a few things."

"And are you willing to live with those lies between you? If you get what you want, and she chooses you, will you be able to live with the things you 'skirted around'?"

"What would you have me tell her? Shall I tell her that he loved her? That he died loving her? That they could have been together, but I destroyed any chance they may have had? Or should I have let him go? *Sí*. Maybe I should have ruined my career so that your niece could spend her life with a pirate, one who would surely be caught by someone, somewhere. You know that he would have been executed or killed in battle, maybe after he had given Faith a few children to feed and care for. This is what you want for your niece?"

"Of course not," Elizabeth replied. "Still, there must be some way to tell her the truth so that she will understand."

"I do not think so. *Sí*, Elizabeth, I can live with these lies."

Faith did not spare a thought for her gown when she kicked off her shoes and stepped into the warm Caribbean waters. Her skirts floated around her as she knelt into the sea's embrace. The delicate silk was buoyed by air pockets, then slowly sank as it became saturated. Tears fell unheeded into the saltwater that tenderly clasped her waist. She sobbed without restraint, with all the passion she had thrown into her every joining with the man she had loved so fiercely.

Just as passionately, she wanted to hate Diego. He had, in effect, sealed the fate of the man she loved with all her heart. At the same time, she knew him to be gentle, a man of honor. What Diego had done had not been from spite. And of course, Geoff had known the risks he was taking. If it had not been Diego that pursued him for Spain, it would surely have been another.

Oh, Geoff! She could not imagine him gone. For months she had looked out upon the ocean and known that he was out there, somewhere. He may have been lost to her, but there was comfort in knowing he sailed upon the very waters that lapped upon the edge of Winston Hall's beach. Now he was doubtless in some dark cell, and soon he would be gone forever. The thought caused an ache in her chest so deep she could hardly draw breath for the pain.

This was where Diego found her, in the waning rays of the sun that sparkled on the crystalline surface of the tide. He pulled the boots and stockings from his feet, leaving his legs bare below his knee-length breeches, and waded out to her, helping her rise against the pull of her sodden dress.

On shore, he brushed away the flaxen hair that the breeze had loosed from its pins and wiped her tears. "I, too, have washed my sorrows in the sea. It can soothe a troubled spirit."

"Aye," she sniffed, "it can."

"I would help you soothe your hurts, as well, if you would allow me."

"Diego, I like you very much. *Yo te quiero mucho.*" He smiled at her efforts. "But, right now, can we just be friends? *Amigos?*"

Diego sighed, but offered her a warm smile. "I would be honored. We will be friends."

He took her by the hand and led her back to the carriage that had brought him there. They lit the lanterns that hung by the driver and slowly journeyed through the gathering darkness to the house. Diego held her hand, but other than that, he left her alone with her thoughts. The two alighted, and Elizabeth and Miguel rushed forward with worried faces, but they took in her ruined gown and the way she kept her hand trustingly in Diego's, and retreated into the shadows. It was enough that she was safe and unhurt.

They walked straight into the house and up the stairs, pausing outside the door to her room. Diego lifted her chin and looked deeply into her eyes. "I will not ask more than you would give, but I would tell you this. You English have two words, 'like' and 'love.' In Spain, we have one, *'querer.' Te quiero,* Faith. It is my dearest hope that someday you will say it to me as I say it to you, because right now, it is not the same for us, I think."

She had been right earlier. Diego was a good man, one who deserved to know everything about her ere he declared himself any more. "Diego, I have to tell you something. I have to tell you why I was crying."

He nodded somberly. "It is your captain."

She toyed with her wet, salt-stained skirt. "Aye, that, but there's more. You should know it ere you place too much of your heart in my care." She took a deep breath. "This is so hard. I wish I could say I regret it, but I do not. Neither am I proud, but I would not have a lie between us. I'm not—that is—if we were to wed . . ."

Diego held up his hand and shook his head. *"No es nada."*

"You have a right to know."

"No importa. The past is over and done with. If you would pledge to me your future, I would treasure it as much as any gift a bride would give to her husband. It is the only gift that truly matters, is it not?" Tears shimmered again in her magnificent eyes, and he allowed himself to drown in their depths. "No more tears, *querida.* Sleep well. Perhaps you will find room for Diego in your dreams tonight."

Surprisingly, there was no room, even for Geoff, in her exhausted and dreamless slumber.

West of the little Caribbean island, in the city of Cartagena, Geoff reclined on the floor of his cell in the Fuerte de San Felipe de Barajas, an imposing Spanish fortress. His was a small room with a heavy oak door, a tiny window that let in little air and less light, and a filthy pallet on the stone floor. He had long ago become accustomed to the smell of his own unwashed body, but he still wished for a fresh breeze.

Today he had a visitor, Father Tomás, and a small wooden chair had been brought in for the occasion. The thin, elderly priest and gaunt, young privateer eyed each other uneasily.

After a long silence, Tomás pulled his voluminous, brown robe about him, seated himself on the chair, and explained, "They sent for me because I speak fluent English. I do not know how much comfort I can give. I assume you are Protestant, but I will give you what comfort and counsel I can."

Geoff lifted an eyebrow. "You aren't going to attempt to convert me?"

"It has not been so very long since this was a seat of power for the Inquisition in the New World. Now the government is more concerned with piracy than winning souls for the Church. The zealots that remain hate your kind so thoroughly, they would just as soon let you burn in hell without redemption. No, I have no wish to convert you, unless you are moved to convert by your own conscience."

Geoff cast a despairing look at the cold floor. "It is too late for redemption, Father."

The priest put his hand on Geoff's shoulder. "It is never too late, my son, not so long as you have breath to ask God's mercy."

"My breath will not last long. I have yet to go to trial, but I know I will die, and the only mercy I would have asked of God is long lost to me."

"You must keep faith, my son."

Geoff gave a strangled laugh at the irony of his statement. "I have lost Faith, Father."

"You can find it again. Perhaps it is hard, here in a strange country, in a prison, but it is here that faith serves us most."

"Nay. I turned my back on Faith, and when I would have returned, God saw fit to intervene."

The priest furrowed his brow in confusion. "God does not keep us from our faith. It is our own selfish will and pride that come between the sacred and the temporal."

"Aye, you have the right of it there. Selfish will and pride. Ah, Father, what have I done?"

"God will forgive you, my son. You have only to ask in the name of His Son."

"God may forgive me, but will Faith? I suppose you will think it blasphemy, but to be honest, that matters far more to me." He buried his face in his hands, then raked his fingers through filthy, matted hair. "How can I forgive myself knowing that I turned my back on her, that I used her and cast her aside as though she were not the single greatest miracle of my life?"

"Faith?" The priest had never thought of faith as a woman, but having devoted his life to it, he found the notion appealingly romantic. A great miracle, aye, the satisfaction of living faithfully filled the soul beyond mere worldly gratification, but the forgiveness of faith? That he could not understand. Perhaps his English was in want of practice. "Do you ask if God forgives those who abandon faith?"

Geoff winced. "Abandoned, aye, that's just what I did. It doesn't matter now. The Spanish captain will take care of her, if she will have him. I only hope that I did not destroy her trust. Surely she will see that he is far more worthy of her than ever I was."

"I am sorry, my son. I do not seem able to follow your thoughts. A Spanish captain is more worthy of faith? Perhaps you do wish to convert?"

Smiling at his own folly, Geoff answered, "Nay, Father.

I spoke more to myself than you. You are wasting your time here."

Tomás smiled back. This young Englishman intrigued him, and at the moment, speaking with him seemed a more appealing use of his time than the mundane tasks that waited for him at the church. In the quiet of the prison they talked, and in ways that his more zealous brethren would never understand, he spoke of God as he experienced Him, beyond scripture, in the beauty of the earth and the goodness of the people he had come to know and love. It was this side of the sacred that seemed to speak to the young man whose soul was troubled and whose time was too short.

In turn, he learned of the woman named Faith, the one who had brought light into the darkness of the sea captain's world. He listened without comment to the confession that poured forth, and wished he could grant penitence and absolution as easily to Captain Hampton as he did to his parishioners.

"She sounds like she was a treasure."

"Aye. If only I had believed myself worthy of such wealth."

"But she has left you wealthy, indeed. She taught you that there is something to this existence beyond its brief flicker upon this earth. And you taught her. You taught her that faith must be examined and thought about, that mere rote practice is not enough."

At Geoff's look of ironic disbelief, Tomás laughed. "I know, it seems most of what we Catholics do is by rote. It is ritual. Through the practice of the familiar, that which comes as second nature, the mind can actually clear, and deeper examination becomes possible. I realize that not all Catholics use it for this purpose. Many a parishioner uses it as a time to go over her dinner menu or his duties in his work, but the truly devout pursue an endless quest for truth. You have been an important part in your love's quest, and you will live on in that. Keep Faith in your heart, my son. I believe, from what you tell me, she will always keep you."

"She gave me something else," Geoff answered. "She gave me the ability to find common ground with a priest, of all people, to seek a friend when I needed one most, in a place I would have once never considered."

Tomás rose and patted Geoff's shoulder good-naturedly. "You are a skilled treasure hunter. I will come again later in the week. Would you like me to come to the trial?"

Geoff nodded. "Aye, I'd like that. I have always believed myself utterly self-reliant, but I must admit, I would like a friend there when I learn of the time and manner in which I am to die."

Tomás bid him farewell and returned to the bright sunshine and pale streets of Cartagena, but the Englishman stayed with him. He would very much like to meet the remarkable young woman who had nearly reformed the hardened pirate.

Chapter 23

Faith and Diego strolled past the lily pond in the rear courtyard, and she idly brushed her fingertips over the deep green and violet leaves of the dragon's blood plants that edged the path. There was no breeze to stir the hem of her pale pink linen skirts, and sweat glistened on her brow and breast. She plucked a tiny, fluffy, magenta boa from a nearby pussy tail bush and twirled it absently. It seemed nearly impossible to concentrate on anything these days. She heard Diego's voice, but it meant no more than the drone of bees. To his credit, he tried not to press her too hard, but she was ever aware that he was courting her.

"Would you like that?" he asked.

He paused for her answer, and the break in his speech pulled her attention back to what he was saying. "What?" she asked.

"I said, I know it is a rather long journey, but I thought you might like to see your family again. It is an easy enough matter to find passage on an English ship."

Faith blanched. "Nay, I think that is not so wise. My aunt has sent them a letter to assure them of my safety, but I do not know if we will hear anything back or not. My father may well never forgive me."

"I am sure your father loves you and wants only what is best for you."

"I doubt he would think you are what is best." At Diego's crushed look, she rushed on. "You must remember that my aunt was disowned for marrying a Catholic. I may have cut myself off from my family forever. I wish I could know it was the right thing to do."

"You told me that you could not marry your village priest, and that you could not stay and still avoid this fate."

"Aye, that is so, but it has cost me much. I wonder if I shall ever find my place in the world."

"You know that I would gladly give you a place at my side."

"Diego, I wish I could tell you what you want to hear, but I cannot."

"Faith, I do not wish to press, but it has been over a fortnight since I returned to my uncle's house, and in less than a week my ship will come for me. I do not expect you to be so fickle that you can dismiss your captain easily. Your feelings for him were deep, and it speaks well of you that your heart can be so true. But it also says something that for once, it is not Hampton for whom you grieve. Perhaps it is time to move forward."

"My aunt says time heals all."

"She is a wise woman, Elizabeth, but sometimes healing requires some other balm." Faith turned to Diego with a quizzical look, and he took a breath and plunged ahead. "We have made good friends, Faith, and my mother once told me that in the long run, friendship is the most important part of a marriage."

"Diego, I do not think I am ready—"

"Nay, let me finish, please. I love you, Faith. I have already told you this. You like me, also, *sí?*"

"Aye. You have been a good friend, Diego, and patient, as well."

"You do not find me unpleasant to look upon?"

Faith laughed. "Nay, Diego. You are a most hand-some man."

A smile lit his face, and he drew her down with him onto a bench beneath the wide, scarlet-tipped poinciana tree. "Many a happy marriage has begun with less than this, Faith. I know I told you I would wait, but I must return to sea soon, and I would have you with me."

"Perhaps if we had more time . . ."

"My love, I must speak plainly, though it may cause you pain. We can spend every minute of the day with one another, and it will avail us naught if you con-tinue to lend your thoughts to a man who will soon be as much a ghost in reality as he is in your life. He left you. He is facing the fate that he has chosen. Your life must go on. I will work very hard to make you happy, Faith. This I promise."

He held his breath through her silence. He was right, of course. Her life would go on without Geoff, and it seemed to her that she would not be so un-happy with Diego.

"Where would I live when we are apart?" she asked.

As though he had anticipated this concern, he replied, "I thought perhaps Havana. It is an easy jour-ney by boat to Jamaica, so you could visit here often. Your Spanish is coming along. If you lived among those who speak it, you would learn quickly."

"But your family is in Spain."

"They see me seldom anyway. They will hardly notice a difference. Of course, I would take you to meet them."

"And my religion?"

At this, Diego's discomfort was hard to conceal. "You once said that Catholicism was not out of the question."

"Aye, but I did not say that I was certain."

"You will have things to think about. That is only prudent. You must decide whether or not you can pledge yourself to my church and whether you can be happy in Cuba, and these are not trifles. Still, I ask you to think on this. I would be a faithful husband. I would give you a good home and beautiful children. I would do everything in my power to make you love me and to provide for your happiness. Perhaps what you once found with your Englishman you could, one day, find with me."

"I will think on it," she replied. In truth, she was tiring of the limbo in which her life had become suspended. She felt restless, ready to move on. It seemed as though she teetered upon some precipice.

Diego leaned forward and tilted her face to his, pausing long enough for her to divine his intent. When she uttered no protest and made no move to retreat, he touched his lips to hers.

Some other balm besides time, this was Faith's thought as she allowed Diego's kiss to deepen. There was no doubt that there was a physical component to the love between a woman and a man, and if she was going to consider Diego, they should cultivate this between them as well as friendship.

She felt his warm lips upon her, parted her own to welcome his tongue, tasted the faint flavors of mango and masculinity. She heard his breath quicken, felt his arms embrace her, but she was an observer, strangely detached. Though she waited, expected some spark to ignite, it did not.

He pulled away from her, and the desperate disappointment in his eyes confirmed that he had noticed her failure to respond. "What you shared with Captain Hampton has wrapped itself tightly around you," he murmured passionately against her cheek as he placed light kisses along her jaw. "I would free you, if you would let me."

She straightened and went rigid. "What are you suggesting?"

He kept her hands in his and rushed to explain. "I would not ask this of you, but it seems you think only of him in my arms. I will marry you if you will have me. I am not asking you to be my mistress, but I would have you think only of me. If you would let me truly show you how I feel, I think you would see that you could feel it, too."

Pulling her hands from his and rising, Faith turned her back to him and took a few steps to place some distance between them. "You are asking me to sleep with you?"

"I would gladly wait, but I am afraid that if I wait too long, I will lose you. God will forgive us. My patron saint, she will understand. She will intervene."

"Your . . . ?"

"Never mind. We will talk later. Now is not the time for talk, Faith."

"What if it does not work? I have no desire to hurt you. I do like you, I do, but what if Geoff was the love of my life? What if I can never feel for you what I felt for him? It would not be fair to you. You deserve a woman who can return your love unfettered. You are worthy of more than a woman whose body betrayed you long before she met you."

He closed the distance and pulled her close. Looking fiercely into her eyes, he cried, "*¡No importa!* It does not matter! I told you that I do not care what happened before. I will gladly take whatever you have to offer, but give us a chance."

He kissed her again with reckless passion, and Faith forced her mind to go blank, allowed herself to be led, abdicated the responsibility inherent in conscious thought.

Miguel and Elizabeth were visiting a neighbor for the rest of the afternoon, and she doubted any of the slaves would dare to carry tales. He pulled her toward the house, and she followed. She looked at nothing but her feet as they peeped out from her skirts with her long strides, then counted the stairs and studied the pattern in the rug that covered the upper gallery floor. Anything to keep her mind from engaging in the moment.

When he pulled her into his arms in his room and sank onto the bed with her, she squeezed her eyes shut and banished the image of gilded hair and golden eyes that sprang before her. He kissed her skillfully, his hands roaming over her in gentle caresses designed to inflame without threatening. There was no question that her emotions were turbulent and wild, and she thought that perhaps she did feel some response, for her breath seemed to be coming in short gasps.

She had, indeed, removed herself from her feelings, for it was Diego who pulled away, realizing that she was sobbing.

"Forgive me," he murmured. He would have held her against him, but she pulled away and struggled to compose herself.

"I'm sorry, Diego. I'm so sorry."

His head dropped to his chest. "Nay, Faith, it is I who should apologize. I wanted you so much."

Guilt squeezed her heart at the pain in his voice. "'Tis not your fault! You are such a good man. You are handsome and kind, everything I should want. I cannot fathom myself, truly!"

"I can," he sighed. "You are steadfast and true, and because of that, you can never be mine." He walked to one of the windows in his room and looked out over the bay. When *Magdalena* returned, she would make a brief trip to Cartagena. "We must go on a short journey together, you and I, although it will not be the journey I had hoped for."

"I do not understand."

He turned and smiled at her with dark eyes that reflected his pain and regret. "I have a promise to keep, if it is not too late."

"Santa Maria," Diego prayed, "what have I done? I was so certain that I was doing the right thing when I took Hampton to Cartagena. I did not understand how deep this thing was between them." He stole a glance at the woman who stood at the ship's rail, searching for the coast of the Spanish Main.

"Now, whatever softness Faith has felt for me will vanish when she learns that I lied to her regarding the English captain's capture. If we arrive too late, she will see the blood of her beloved on my hands. We must arrive in time!"

Diego chastised himself. Oh, he had been a fine one to lecture the pirate about placing the needs of others before his own desires! Despite his honorable intentions, he prayed again. "Maybe we can save the Englishman's life, and he could be sentenced to prison or slavery. Faith would be grateful, but the two would yet remain apart. Better still, he might reject her again."

He dropped his head, ashamed of his own selfish thoughts. "Ah, but that is a fool's hope, is it not, Maria?

Diego and the lovely English Puritan were never meant
to be."

That night he closed his eyes and dreamed. Mary
Magdalene smiled at him with her full, red lips, gazed
at him with deep blue eyes, and whispered in her lyri-
cally foreign accent, "She is not the one for you, Diego.
You will sacrifice much for her, and for that sacrifice, I
will send you another. You will know her when you see
her."

Chapter 24

Geoff and Father Tomás sat quietly in the dark cell. The musty air seemed even more dense than usual, the silence more palpable. The trial had concluded only the week before. Spanish justice was to be swift. Captain Hampton would die on the morrow, hanged, as he should have been in England if Spain could trust English fair play. His face was unshaven, somehow making his eyes all the more imposing. It never ceased to amaze the priest that through it all, he had never seen fear in those golden orbs. Regret, yes, an impossible mix of self-loathing and pride, surely, but no fear.

"Are you at peace with your spirit, my son?" he asked.

"Aye, as much as I can be. D'you think I'm bound for hell, Father?"

"It is not for me to say. That decision rests in God's hands. Christ says that the kingdom of heaven can be reached only through Him."

"He also said, 'The kingdom of God is within.'"

The priest smiled slightly. "You have been reading the Bible I left you."

Geoff's answering grin was rueful. "There is naught else to do here." The smile faded as quickly as it had come. "I read. I do whatever I can to keep from thinking about the inevitable. I'll never see Faith again. If 'tis true, if there is a heaven and a hell, then I'll live with that single thought. I'll spend eternity knowing that she still exists, somewhere beyond my reach. God could spare himself the lake of fire and the brimstone. Existence without Faith would be hell enough."

"I think it more likely that hell is like that for everyone condemned to it. Existence without faith."

"I wish I could believe, Father. It would be so much easier."

Tomás nodded. He knew there were priests that would gladly take credit for the conversion of a man who professed beliefs that he did not truly hold in his heart, but he was not such a man. "I wish you could believe, too, my son."

A key turned noisily in the lock of the stout wooden door, and the guard who appeared addressed Father Tomás. *"Él tiene una visita."*

"There is someone here to see you. A woman," Tomás explained. *"Entre,"* he called. The guard stepped out and was replaced by the mysterious caller.

There was never a moment's doubt in the old man's mind as to the identity of the visitor. The woman wore a gown of white silk accented with silver ribbons and heavy white lace. Her hair was of spun silver, her skin opalescent, her eyes a startling shade of blue-green. She looked a very angel, and there could be no question, she was faith personified.

Tomás all but disappeared to the two people reunited in the dismal cell. Neither moved, neither breathed. That one last glimpse, one last moment both had hoped for, dreamed of a thousand times over, formed a bittersweet agony beyond words. All that they had lost hovered silently between them.

"Those eyes," she whispered at last, "they are surely yours, but this face is not." She ran her hands lightly over his thick beard, then moved them to his gaunt shoulders, encased in a torn, stained shirt. "Nor this body. Do they never feed you? Are you to starve for them?"

With a strangled cry he caught her, held her close, rained kisses upon her face before he captured her mouth and kissed her as though by this act he could bind them together forever.

His voice was husky with emotion when he spoke. "Oh, God, Faith, 'tis you. Ah, you are my redemption and my only taste of paradise."

She wept without restraint, holding him close and pressing her cheek fiercely to his hard shoulder. "I could not bear to never see you again. When Diego said he could bring me to you, I had to come, but now I think I will die if we must part again!"

He clasped her face tenderly in both hands. "'Tis glad I am to hold you one last time. I would have spared you the pain, but I am selfish enough to be glad to see you."

"Though it haunts my dreams the rest of my life, I'll never regret this moment. Diego and I thought to save you, but we cannot even gain an audience with the court. They say that tomorrow . . ." She stopped, emotion choking off the rest of the sentence.

Father Tomás watched on in silence, his own throat tight, his eyes blinking back tears of compassion. If ever he had seen two people who were meant to be together, it was this captain and his lady.

Geoff spoke tenderly to her. "We'll think of tomorrow later, but promise me this now. Promise you will not be there."

"Nay! You cannot ask that of me! I will die with you, though my body goes on. You cannot deny me the right to be there for you, to be the last thing you see when you bid this life farewell."

"Mayhap it will not be farewell for us. Mayhap there is another way." Geoff turned to Father Tomás, blinking him back into existence. "I do not know exactly what I believe, Father, but if I have a soul, I care not who gets it. It may as well be God as the devil. If there is any way that we can have another time, another place, I would have them. Will you wed us, here, now?"

The priest shook his head apologetically. "It is not so easy, my son. To begin, a marriage performed under these circumstances would not be legal. And I must tell you, I think God will not take a soul that is not well and truly His. So long as you doubt, salvation eludes you."

Faith's gaze carefully searched the priest's face. "Have you been sent to counsel Captain Hampton?"

Geoff smiled, and for a moment, the obligatory formalities made the situation feel absurdly normal. "Faith, this is Father Tomás. He has been my friend through all of this."

She curtsied. "If Geoff counts you as his friend, then you are a good man, Father. The legality of our union is unimportant. As for the destiny of our souls, I would follow this man into hell and have no regrets."

"My child, I cannot help to lead a faithful Christian woman astray."

"I have strayed already."

"God will forgive you! Do not act in a moment of passion, my child, and regret it for all eternity."

"Nay, Father, 'tis not only this man who has led me from the path I trod ere I met him. Indeed, the way was ever a slippery slope, and now, I have seen too much. I have come to love people who cause others the bitterest pain. I have questioned the faith of my childhood and somehow found myself. I have seen divine grace in a man who defies every absolute I once believed. I have been offered everything I should want and yet come away empty.

"I would bind my soul to this man in the eyes of my Maker, and I will trust the judgment of that Being. It matters not that neither the state nor the church will recognize this marriage. There is much I am unsure of these days, but this I know: God sees what is in our hearts. That is enough."

Her passionate words left Father Tomás with a mighty battle of the spirit. What these two asked of him went against everything he believed. To do as they asked, he jeopardized his own immortal soul. He closed his eyes and breathed deeply. "Heavenly Father," he beseeched silently, "grant me some guidance. What is Your plan for these two children of Yours? You have bound their hearts, but You do not soften them to You. To what purpose? Is he the test of the woman's faith? Do I help to tear her from You, or is it Your will that they stay together forever, whatever the price?" As he prayed, he listened to their hushed conversation.

"I never told you," Geoff began. "I thought I would die ere I could. I love you, Faith. Because of you, I believe in love. It is truly a miracle."

Her smile was both sad and wry, her voice gently teasing. "Nay, you lust for me. Just as 'tis the nature of the sea to reflect the clear blue sky, 'tis the nature of a rogue to lust for a wench. 'Tis no miracle."

"A saintly woman once told me that it was the nature of man to wonder at the reflection of the sky upon the sea, and mayhap that very wonder was the miracle. That it is my nature to love you, though once I believed there could be naught but lust, that is a mir-

acle, too. I know naught of God, Faith, but I know that
what we have is timeless and sacred in its own right."

Her fingertips brushed lightly over his brow and
traced the edge of his beard. "Saintly? Was she not driven from her village and her church as a temptress? She
is just a woman, Geoff, but she is a woman who loves
you."

"It seemed it was ever her fate to be faced with men
too shortsighted to see her grace. On the morrow,
and in the days to follow, remember that there was
one whose vision cleared and who loved you, too.
Though I may cease to exist at all, carry that with you.
It will prevail."

She sobbed softly, and something inside Tomás settled, found firm ground. "I will do it. I know not what
effect it will have in God's eyes, but I will give you this.
May God forgive me if I have not divined His will
correctly."

The guard remained in the hallway, watching the
door that had been left open so that he could hear
what took place within. Next to him stood Diego, and
as the couple in the cell exchanged vows, he slipped
silently away.

Time had only mildly altered the face of Juan Gallegos Lucero y Esquibel de Aguilar. The longtime
friend of Diego's father had left Spain nearly a decade
ago and risen quickly to a position of considerable
power in Cartagena, but the weight of responsibility
became him. His mahogany hair had grayed slightly,
but good-natured kindness still lit his dark eyes. He
embraced Diego warmly, despite the late hour and
the younger man's unannounced arrival.

"Forgive me, Don Juan," Diego said in his native Spanish. "I do not mean to bother you so late, but I was unsuccessful in contacting you earlier, and the matter is urgent."

"The days are full, that is true," Juan replied. "The hour is no matter. I regret that we missed each other the last time you visited Cartagena."

"It was unfortunate. My visit was hasty, as is this one. I plan to sail tomorrow."

"I see, then it is urgent, indeed, or we would have missed one another again." Juan's hearty smiled caused a small pang of guilt to stab Diego.

"Of course, I wanted to visit with you, Don Juan, but as the hour is late, I will be direct about my purpose. I have come to claim the favor you have often insisted that you owe me."

Juan's eyebrows shot up in surprise. "This is most unexpected, Diego. For many years, whenever I have suggested that I owe you a debt of gratitude, you have rebuffed me. Thirteen, no, fourteen years ago, when you saved my son from drowning, I would have funded your education, purchased a ship for you, whatever you asked."

"I knew all this, Don Juan, but truly, it was an honor to save Francisco. It was never my intention to seek a reward, but I find myself in dire need."

"Naturally," Juan said, "if it is in my power to grant you what you seek, I will do it, but I must confess that you puzzle me. What has caused this change of heart?"

"If it were not of grave importance, I would ask nothing of you. This I ask on behalf of another."

"What is it you would ask?"

"There is an English pirate sentenced to die tomorrow."

"Captain Geoffrey Hampton. I know of him."

"You have great influence in both the government and the court."

"I do," Juan affirmed, his eyes narrowing.

"Do you think that you can obtain a pardon for him?"

Juan contemplated the man before him. "Are you in earnest? Even I can see that it costs you dearly to ask this favor. Do you owe this man something?"

"Yes, I suppose you could say that."

"Why?"

"I made him a promise."

"What was this promise?"

"There is a woman. We both love her."

"But she loves him?" Juan guessed.

"Yes."

"Then why do you not let him hang and claim her for yourself? What is this promise, and why did you make it?"

"It was I who brought him here to die. I told him that I had fallen in love with the woman who was once his. He asked only that there be nothing I would not give for her happiness. I loved her. At the time, it was an easy promise to make."

"You are a good man, Diego," Juan replied, placing a fatherly hand on the younger man's shoulder. "I have no doubt that you could make her happy."

"I thought so, once. The captain thought so, too, and gave me his blessing to try."

Juan simply nodded and waited for Diego to continue.

"She wanted to love me, Don Juan. She was willing to give herself to me, but despite her best efforts, she could not give me her heart. She had already given the whole of it to Captain Hampton. It seems they were made to be together. How can I compete with that? If he hangs tomorrow, she will grieve for him until the day she dies. If she is to be happy, I must give her my rival. I am bound, sir, by both my promise to him and my love for her."

Juan shook his head. "He is a pirate. If she is as good and loving as you say, is he worthy of her? Often women love men who are not good for them. They are drawn to the danger or they hope to change them. Have you considered this?"

Diego nodded his head. "I hoped that was the case, but in his own way, he is a man of honor. He understands her, as I do not. They share a quest. I overheard them today, talking to an old priest. What lies between these two is even deeper than love. I know this is what must be."

Juan paused to consider Diego's request. "There is a bloodlust for English pirates among the Spanish colonies that will be hard to placate with anything but the death of one of them."

"I ask only that you try. If you do not succeed, I will know that you did all that you could."

"Well, false modesty aside, if anyone has the power to spare this Captain Hampton, I suppose it is I. Still, it seems poor payment to reward you for saving my son by robbing you of the woman you love. Are you certain this is what you want?"

Sadly, Diego shook his head. "It is what is right. It is not what I want."

"I will do what I can. If I cannot spare him, perhaps you are wrong, and she was meant to be yours. If I am successful, I pray that it is because there is another out there for you."

Diego nodded, his face filled with the depth of his certainty in the promise of his saint. "There is another, Don Juan. Somewhere out there, there is another."

Juan's smile lit his face and lightened the mood for them both. "Preferably a *Spanish* maiden," he added.

Chapter 25

The pale beginnings of dawn slanted almost imperceptibly through the window of Geoff's cell. Still, he was entirely aware of it. He had not slept that night and was grateful for Tomás's quiet presence. Neither had spoken since midnight. It was as if by speaking they would make this day real. Silence could hold on to yesterday indefinitely, couldn't it?

Nay, that was not so, and the lightening sky laughed at their folly. Shades of warm gold and peach mocked the men who steeped in a cloud of gloomy despair.

"Why are these things not always done at sunrise?" Geoff complained. "It seems I have always heard that men are condemned to die at dawn. Whatever could the judges have been thinking when they set the time for noon?"

It was a rhetorical question, and Tomás doubted that Geoff would have liked the answer. It gave Geoff more time to stew, just as he was, making the event all the more terrible. It also insured a greater audience. But he was there to comfort, not to introduce cold, hard reality into a situation already too cold and real.

Instead he asked, "Was it better that she came?"

Geoff paused, seeming to search for the answer somewhere beyond the tiny window. "It was a mixed blessing to see Faith again, but aye," he said, at last.

"Though 'twas hard enough to leave her the first time, and this is harder still, 'tis glad I am that I leave nothing unsaid and that we have done what we must to come to terms with this parting." He squeezed his eyes shut against the light.

"To weep would not make you less of a man," Father Tomás suggested.

Geoff spun, his golden eyes molten. "I refuse to give them that! They'll not get a drop from me. The Spaniards have gained victory enough here!" He brought himself up short and added, "No offense, Father."

The priest waved the comment aside. He, too, felt that he had done what he must, though he must confess and answer for it later.

"I do wish I could keep Faith from coming today," Geoff added. "There's no sense in making her live with the memory. What I endure will be over soon enough for me. She needn't be there for my sake. I can see her in my mind's eye, the wind and sun drying her hair on the deck of my ship. Mayhap the next hours will be tolerable if I spend them thus, taking out and polishing to perfection every memory of the time I have known her." As though he could almost smell the tantalizing scent of her, he inhaled sharply and smiled.

"Aye, that should help," Tomás replied. "Dwell on pleasant memories for a time."

The smile faded, and Geoff turned to him again. "I've been thinking of my mother, as well."

"A natural thing, my son. At such a time, you must seek whatever comfort you may."

"I'm not sure I'd call such thoughts comforting, Father. There was very little love between us. Still, if

I'm ever to reconcile with her, or rather, the memory of her, 'tis now or never. Faith is a wonder there, as well. She has every reason to be angry with her family, and yet she loves them still, defends them fiercely. Would that I could know such loyalty to the woman who gave me life. She was, after all, the only family I have ever known."

"I think you need not hear from me that nearly everyone has some redeeming qualities, whatever their sins."

"Aye, well, my mother's sins were plenty, especially by your standards. Even so, she taught me to find joy where I could, though there was little enough of it for either of us. Until Faith spoke of it, it never occurred to me that my mother suffered for the life she led. It seems to me now that it was not entirely of her choosing."

A small, ironic grin spread across Geoff's face. "D'y'know, just now, I find I can actually think tenderly of her, remember rare moments when we were simply mother and son. I cannot decide if I've gone soft in the heart or soft in the head."

Father Tomás chuckled quietly. "These are hard times, my son. A bit of softness is a blessing in either case."

"She was a beauty. I'd have given her that even when I hated her most. Well, we may see one another again all too soon, and if we do, the place will be hot enough without anger and regret."

Tomás shuddered. It did not rest easily with him to hear the Englishman speak so blithely of God's eternal wrath.

Though they both knew that it would be hours ere a guard would come to escort Geoff to the gallows, both men jumped at the sound of footsteps in the corridor and the scrape of a key in the lock.

"*Vamos,*" the guard commanded in a flat voice.

Geoff had heard the command often enough that he did not need Tomás to translate.

"*Yo no comprendo. ¿Qué le pasa?*" Tomás asked the guard.

"*No sé.*"

Geoff gave Tomás a quizzical look, and Tomás replied, "He says he doesn't know what this is about."

Geoff and Father Tomás were ushered into a small, tidy office with simple furnishings, where a distinguished-looking gentleman awaited them. He was dressed in velvet and fine muslin, and spoke like a man who was seldom opposed. He introduced himself as Juan Gallegos Lucero y Esquibel de Aguilar, and Father Tomás explained to Geoff that he was an influential member of the government, well known and highly respected.

Geoff bowed slightly, but was unimpressed. Another official, another Spaniard to lecture to him on the evils of England and her privateers. Sarcasm laced his voice when he replied, "Forgive me for not dressing for the occasion. My wardrobe is limited, and there seemed little need to buy anything new. I wouldn't get much use from it."

Though Don Juan spoke in Spanish, leaving Father Tomás to translate, he looked at Geoff. "I do not need to tell you that there is very little time left. What I would like to know is how you feel about it all, now that it is nearly over."

"Feel about it?" Geoff asked. "About dying?"

"About living—" Juan explained, "your life, as you have lived it."

"As you have observed, my time is limited. Father Tomás's counsel has been sufficient. What purpose does this conversation serve?"

Juan Gallegos shrugged carelessly. "I have not been a part of the proceedings. I wish to know you better. I would know what manner of man dies at the will of our justice. As a member of our government, it concerns me."

Aware of his ragged appearance and the fate that awaited him, Geoff lifted his chin a notch. He would be damned if he would be judged yet again and found wanting. "I have done what seemed necessary to survive. And I'll tell you this, I have no love of the Spanish. Your atrocities have left a bad taste in the mouths of much of Europe. As for your place in the New World, England has as much right to profit by it as Spain. What I have done has served my king and my country, as well as myself."

"Then you have no regrets?"

"I make no apologies."

Gallegos pinned him with an all-too-perceptive gaze. "Regrets and apologies are not always the same thing."

It was on the tip of Geoff's tongue to say that it was none of his damned business, but he only sighed, his shoulders dropping a fraction of an inch. "Who can die with no regrets? Will you, when your time comes? What I find utterly ironic is the fact that this should have come just when I had begun to see another path for my life."

The Spanish official raised his eyebrows. "You are

reformed? Is this how you will plead your case in these last hours?" he asked, his voice laden with contempt.

"I plead for nothing. I only give you an honest answer to your question. Call it a conversion, of sorts," said Geoff. He smiled at Gallegos. "I met a woman." The other man returned a half smile of his own. "I would have left privateering for her."

"Would you? Why?"

"She would have insisted on it. 'Thou shalt not steal' and all that. She told me that I should think of the people I stole from, not just the country."

"And this simple argument moved you? Forgive me, it is somewhat difficult to believe that such an obvious observation would sway a hardened pirate."

"Privateer," Geoff corrected. Then he looked away, trying to put his thoughts into words. "I know it sounds strange, but I rather liked the captain who brought me here. He's a good man. There was a time I would have laughed in your face if you told me that I would trust the only thing that has ever mattered to me to a Spaniard, but I am. And Father Tomás, here." He gestured to the man who had become a lifeline in the weeks that had passed, and who smiled as he translated. "He is not only a Spaniard, but a Catholic priest. He is also my friend, and that is another fact I would have once found implausible."

"So you are telling me that you *are* reformed? If we would let you go free, you would 'go forth and sin no more'? Do I understand your words?"

"I am not so pathetic that I would fall to that hack-neyed plea. 'Please spare me. I've come to Jesus. I'll ne'er do evil again.' I doubt me that would move you to mercy."

"Your fate is already decided. I only thought to

learn what manner of man you are before your sentence is carried out."

"I am an honest one. If I had yet many years before me, I would be no threat to you, though I realize that, of course, that matters little now."

Don Juan rose and scrutinized Geoff carefully. "As I had been led to expect, there is much to admire in you, pirate, and life is infinitely more complicated when one has to face one's enemies as human beings."

"You speak like a man inclined to grant clemency," Father Tomás said, a telltale tremble of hope in his voice.

"I have no doubt that were it in my power to grant, a second chance would not be wasted on this man, but I yet doubt it would be fully deserved. Tell me truly, Captain, why this change of heart? Would you have me believe you would change your whole way of life for a mere woman?"

"She is no mere woman."

"I have thought that myself, more than once, about more than one woman. These feelings often fade."

"Because of her, I have come to see the world and how I live in it differently."

"But you say that you have not found God?"

"Nay, I found faith."

"The woman?"

"Nay. Oh, I found her, but more than that, I found faith in others, faith in myself, faith in the general rightness of things." He stopped and regarded the Spanish official more carefully. "How did you know the woman's name was Faith?"

Gallegos ignored the question. "Then it would not be your intent to resume your former occupation. What would you do?"

Uneasiness crept up upon Geoff, raising the hair on the nape of his neck, and he wondered anew at the purpose of this inquiry. Nonetheless, he answered honestly. "I have a substantial fortune available to me, provided my crew has not already seen fit to dispose of it. I would buy *Destiny* from the crew and set up an honest business. I would spend my life with the woman I love. Aye, I suppose I would 'go forth and sin no more.'"

"This fortune, would there be enough in it to compensate Diego Montoya's employer for the cargo he lost to you and your crew?"

His patience at an end, Geoff nearly shouted, "What is this about?"

"Answer the question."

"Aye! It would make the purchase of a ship somewhat harder, but it could be done. Why do you ask?"

"What would you do if you were not left with enough funds for the ship?"

In frustration, Geoff raked his hands through his hair and began to pace. "I suppose I would talk to my first mate about establishing a partnership. He has no taste for the killing that often goes with taking Spanish vessels."

"Would you be willing to sign a statement to the effect that you would pose no threat to Spain or any of her people or property?"

He stopped and faced his inquisitor. "Are you asking me to?"

"Would you?"

This could be a trick, some final cruelty. Cautiously he answered, "Aye."

"Upon pain of the most gruesome death?"

"Aye."

"And would you legally marry the woman, in fact, swear you would not touch her until you have accomplished this?"

Anger bubbled up inside of Geoff, and he gripped the back of his chair to keep himself from throttling the man who seemed to hold freedom tantalizingly close before him, but stopped short of actually offering it to him. It seemed that nothing more than sordid curiosity could motivate such an interview.

"Why are you asking me this? Aye, aye, I would do it all, not to spare my life but because it is the life I would have if it were not to end in a few hours' time! Is it somehow more just that I die with the salt of my regrets rubbed into the wounds the hemp will inflict? There, you have it! Now let's call an end to this ridiculous charade. Put the damned rope around my neck and get on with it!"

Father Tomás repeated Geoff's outburst, translating faithfully, but wincing at the grim demand for an end to the horrible wait.

"Although it pains me to admit it," Juan Gallegos said, "I can see why Diego Montoya has such respect for you, Englishman." He drew a deep breath and handed a sheet of parchment to Father Tomás. "I ask these things because they are the conditions of your pardon. Father Tomás can read the contract and verify it for you."

Dumbfounded into silence, Geoff only stared at him. Finally, he turned to the priest, and Tomás confirmed the contents of the contract.

"Is this true?" he finally asked the man who had presented it. "You are offering me a pardon?"

"The offer is sincere. If you agree to these conditions,

you will sign the contract and be sent immediately to Port Royal on board a Portuguese ship."

A sudden, acute awareness of life swept over Geoff. He breathed deeply, intensely conscious of the air that moved powerfully in and out of his lungs. He could actually feel the blood pumping through his veins and flexed his hands, struck by the simple miracle that he could do so. These were things he had not thought to do another day, and it occurred to him that he would never again take his breath or body for granted.

"Why? Why would this be done?" he asked. "It all seems real enough, but it makes no sense. Well I know the court was pleased to finally have an English privateer at its mercy. Why this sudden leniency?"

"You say you have found faith," Don Juan replied. "It was not misplaced."

At noon, Geoff stood on the deck of a Portuguese ship, the wind in his hair, his arm draped over the shoulders of an angel, and wondered how the crowd that awaited his execution was faring. It seemed he should feel more elated, but part of him still didn't trust the smell of the sea and the warmth of the woman at his side. Mayhap he had fallen asleep, and he would yet wake to find himself in his cell, awaiting the end.

As for Faith, she thought perhaps she had never met anyone as selfless as Diego. God willing, he would find the woman who was meant for him. She wondered about the man beside her. He was quiet and seemed a thousand miles away. Did he wish that marriage had not been one of the conditions? Marriage was one thing if you didn't actually have to live with it, but this was another matter.

"Have you any regrets?" she asked.

He laughed softly. "That seems to be the question of the day." At her confused look he smiled and shook his head. "What have I to regret?"

"You once told me that you preferred willing wenches and the heat of battle."

"Did I say that? Nay, that was another fellow. One who only thought he knew the meaning of passion."

"Not you?"

"Nay. That man was never content, ever searching for something he could not name. He knew not the joy of finding his heart's desire. He thought it didn't exist."

"And you? What do you prefer?"

"Love, a love that can be counted on, one that will last forever."

She thought her heart would burst as it swelled within her. "I thought forever was a fairy tale," she chided softly.

"What thick-headed lout e'er told you that? 'Tis a mystery, not a fairy tale. That man I once knew, he saw no mysteries. Nothing existed that he could not see, but the poor fellow never knew that he was blind."

"I knew a woman very like that. Oh, she believed in the mysteries of life, but she believed she had solved them all." Faith frowned, then amended, "Well, she thought others had, anyway."

"Really? What became of her?"

"She is only now beginning to understand the questions."

Chapter 26

Mayhap the building was filthy and run down, but such was the state of nearly every available structure in Port Royal, and neither Geoff nor Giles had funds enough remaining to build anything new. Giles smiled optimistically in the gloomy light that trickled through the grime-encrusted windows.

"Why such a dark scowl, old friend?" he asked Geoff. "There's nothing here a bit of plaster, soap, and a strong hand cannot remedy. God knows, we've each of us lived in worse." He took another glance around and amended, "Well, at least as bad."

"Aye, but neither of us thought to bring a wife into such a mess." His gaze swept the small office space. One long window looked out onto the street, or rather, would look out, once it had been cleaned. Plaster fell from the walls and ceiling in patches, and there was actually enough dirt and rubbish on the floor for the two men to leave footprints. It was devoid of furniture, another quandary, given the fact that having paid Geoff's debt to the Spanish merchant and bought *Destiny* from the crew, neither man had much left in his purse. Well Geoff knew that the room above, the one he intended for their living quarters, was in no better shape.

He had felt such bright confidence when he and

Faith set sail from Cartagena. They were together, and they had the rest of their lives before them. Now the truth of the matter seemed far less romantic. There would be many years of hard work to come ere they replenished the money he had spent getting them to this point. He ran his hand through his hair and thought of his beautiful Faith in these dingy apartments. It just didn't seem right.

Giles was undaunted. "We'll have a go at it before you bring Faith here. It won't look so bad then, you'll see."

Geoff smiled and shook his head. How had he ever been so fortunate as to find such a friend, and how was it he had never seen before just how important this friendship was?

"Do you never think you would have been better off just leaving me to my own devices? I could have gone broke alone paying off that damned Spaniard, and you'd have been the captain of *Destiny*, plundering ships and getting rich."

"Aye, and met my demise at some sea dog's cutlass or the end of a hangman's rope. Well I knew that if they caught you, I had no better luck. Nay, I'm of a mind to settle down a bit. Mayhap I'll find me a wench to grow old with. It seems to suit you."

"You'll be hard-pressed to find a wife here," said Geoff. "There's plenty of women, but few enough of the marrying kind."

Giles kicked absently at the rubbish at his feet, raising more of the dust that already formed a gritty coating in both their mouths. "Mayhap one will fall into my lap, as Faith did in yours."

Geoff grinned. "She put herself in my lap, as it were."

"Dumb luck!" Giles argued. "She knew not whose

lap she had landed in, else she would have run back home ere we left port in Boston."

"Aye, Boston," Geoff echoed softly.

"We're bound to return there, sooner or later," Giles said. "Think you she'll join us? Will you two ever face her fearsome father and sainted family?"

Geoff left the question unanswered, floating with the dust motes in the stale air.

Despite his every effort to convince her to stay at the ship while he and Giles cleaned and made repairs, Faith insisted that she accompany them the next day. He made one apology after another for the scene that would meet her, but Faith waved them all away. It still took him aback, her lack of concern for luxury and comfort. Although he knew her to be a strong woman, he expected her to burst into tears at the sight of the wrack and ruin he and Giles had purchased.

But Faith simply assured the two men that it was a point of great pride among Puritans that in addition to their modesty, they were known for their capacity for hard work. In less than a fortnight, the trio had the office and accompanying apartment sparkling clean and furnished.

The opulence of Winston Hall had been an exciting, new experience for Faith, but she had to admit that she preferred the simple home that she and Geoff shared in Port Royal. The tiny room boasted a small hearth, a sagging bed, a nearly empty cupboard, a wobbly table, and four equally unsteady chairs.

It mattered not, for she had unflinching faith that they would work hard and build a better life, and Geoff found her confidence infectious. They had put many hours into it, and if the place was not as splendid as Winston Hall, nor as finely crafted as the home of her youth, it was clean and tidy and filled with love and laughter.

At times, Faith did look around her and puzzle where they might put children when they came, though the thought tugged at her heart. She had ever thought to have her mother there to guide her when it came to raising children of her own. She had always seen them bouncing on her father's knee.

And there were smaller aspects of their humble life that plagued her. The tendency for their chairs to fall apart was one of them. Having examined one that morning, and coming to the inescapable conclusion that something must be done ere the entire seat disintegrated, Faith decided that she was not the daughter of a cabinetmaker for nothing. Mayhap she had never actually built anything, but she had spent countless hours watching the men in her family.

There was a cabinetmaker four doors up from them named Stuart Abrams. He was generally known to be a cantankerous sort, but he never failed to smile at Faith when she came and went to market or on some errand. She ought to feel some remorse for what she planned to do, but she was a desperate woman. Shamelessly, she smoothed the lavender skirts of one of her most flattering gowns, checked her hair in the mirror, pinched her cheeks for color, and strode downstairs to the shipping office.

Geoff was gone, out with a potential customer, Giles said as he wrote in a ledger at the broad table that served as a desk for them both. She told him she would return soon and marched out the door. Outside Mr. Abrams's joinery, she forced herself into a more relaxed demeanor and sailed through the entrance as though she dropped by to visit all the time.

Had anyone cared to ask, Stuart Abrams could have told him the cause of his sour disposition. Though his wife, Mathilde, was reigning matriarch of decent society in their neighborhood, she was a shrew behind closed doors. For a moment's reprieve, there were whores aplenty, all friendly as could be and good enough, but they were also crass and rather hard looking. The sea captain's lovely, young wife was a breath of fresh air, so although he had been donning his coat to leave, Stuart didn't protest the delay.

"Good morning, Mr. Abrams," Faith said cheerily.

"Mistress Hampton. Aye, it is a fine day, isn't it?"

Immediately he realized that he must have appeared a complete fool. It was, in fact, overcast and sure to rain before noon. But his visitor smiled kindly.

"Aye, Mr. Abrams, fair indeed. Do you know, in all the weeks we have been neighbors, I have never been in your shop."

He wondered briefly if his hairless head was as shiny as always. Perhaps his wife was right and he should take to wearing a wig. Shrugging self-consciously, he said, "I don't suppose my shop is of much interest to a young lady like you."

"Oh, but that's not so. You see, my father is a cabinet-maker in Massachusetts."

Stuart smiled broadly. A pretty woman with some knowledge of wood—'twas a fine day, indeed! "Then mayhap you'd like to see this," he suggested, holding up a round case upon a pedestal for inspection. "I've just finished this knife caddy, here. See—the knife blades fit into these slots, the top comes down like this, and it locks. 'Tis for the mistress of one of the plantations. Have to keep the knives away from the slaves. They've been known to take a blade to themselves, you know."

"Or an overseer. Aye, I know. Sad, is it not?" He noticed that she spoke with the kind of compassion seldom wasted on slaves, and he found it touching. "Still," she continued, "this is ingenious, Mr. Abrams! And the craftsmanship is superior!"

He swallowed nervously, the approval in her extraordinary eyes leaving him feeling boyish and unsophisticated. Unfortunately, the thought of her husband, the sea captain, intruded. Word had it that he was a privateer and a man who had sent many a sailor to Davy Jones's locker without a grain of remorse.

"How fares your husband's business?" he asked.

"Well. Ere long, he will have enough in his hold to set sail. Is that a new coat?" She reached out with one of her elegant, white hands and lightly touched his cuff.

Stuart straightened up a bit and tugged at the coat. "This? Nay, 'tis an old rag." But he flushed and preened despite his words.

The lady graced him with another winning smile. "'Tis a most flattering color, and the cut suits you."

He sucked in the paunch that lately kept him from fastening the front of the coat. "You are too kind. My wife insists 'tis out of date."

"Nay, Mr. Abrams. The style is quite classic. Were you going somewhere?"

Though the besotted cabinetmaker was loath to end the conversation, he did have an appointment to keep. "Aye. I've several deliveries to make. I was about to close the shop for the day."

"How fortunate that I should stop by! I have several pieces of furniture that require repairs, and though I'm sure you would do the finest job on them, I've no coin to pay you. I have to be thrifty until my husband's business finds success. Still, I have decent knowledge of tools and cabinetry. Might I borrow a few things for the afternoon?"

Now, Stuart Abrams's tools were his pride and joy. More than that, they were his very livelihood. Even Mistress Abrams, though she henpecked him fiercely, dared not touch his prized implements.

It was with genuine regret that he replied, "Why, Mistress Hampton, I should very much like to help you, but you see—" The good carpenter stumbled over his words. It was rare, indeed, that he was the recipient of such a sunny smile, and he would rather not cause it to fade just yet. Nonetheless, his tools were his tools!

Those captivating blue eyes widened hopefully. "I shall take very good care of them, I promise, and I should be able to finish the work this afternoon. You shan't even miss them."

"Well, that is—"

She breathed a disappointed sigh. "It is a lot to ask," she conceded, and he couldn't help but notice that her pout was as fetching as her smile.

Mr. Abrams heaved a sigh of defeat. "Now, Mistress Hampton, don't distress yourself. Mayhap I could lend you a few things."

"Oh, thank you!" she cried, her face lit by joy, and Stuart found he was hard-pressed to give a damn about the bloody tools. She listed the pieces she needed and accepted his offer to help her carry them back to the apartment.

When they walked into the neat, almost austere office, Mistress Hampton paused and looked around. Her face showed a hint of trepidation.

"My husband's partner was here when I left. He must have run an errand."

Glancing around, Stuart asked, "What is it you'll be using these on?"

Her worried look grew more pronounced. "Some things upstairs. But I can manage from here, I'm sure."

"No, no," Stuart protested. "I can take them up the steps for you." Before she could demur, he started up the narrow staircase. Like the apartment above his shop when he and Mistress Abrams had first lived there, this was one room. He smiled at the ramshackle state of things. It reminded him of when he and Mathilde were first wed, when passion and enthusiasm had meant more than appearances. He sighed heavily. They had since built on to theirs, adding rooms filled with fine furnishings and fashionable whatnots, and he would give it all up if only Mathilde went with it.

Stuart set the tools down, very much aware that he was alone with a beautiful woman who had been flirting with him, but the sight of a cutlass leaning casually against the bed brought him 'round quickly.

"I shall be back for them around four," he said, his Adam's apple bobbing beneath his cravat.

She was visibly relieved to have him on his way, but still favored him with another smile. "That should be plenty of time. Thank you, Mr. Abrams. We are, indeed, fortunate to have such a generous neighbor."

Stuart gave her a last, wistful look, and she blushed,

casting her gaze to the floor. In that brief instant before she looked away, he saw the look of guilt that clouded her blue eyes. His customarily dour face broke into a wide smile. Funny thing, he had forgotten how much better one's face felt with the corners of the mouth turned up.

"Do not let it weigh too heavily on your conscience, mistress. It's sure you're not the first pretty woman who used a bit of flattery to persuade a man to do her a favor. We all do what we must in this world. Just be thankful that if God didn't see fit to make you rich, at least He made you comely."

When he left, Faith set her conscience and shame aside and picked up a plane. She quickly discovered that using the instruments was not as easy as it looked. It took a while for her to figure out just how to get the best results, but she knew what to do, and soon they began to feel natural in her hands. She puzzled a bit over poor-fitting joints, but found that a few small pieces of the company's best stationery, trimmed flush with the wood, tightened them up nicely.

Her father had oft spoken of the way that working with wood calmed his spirit and soothed his troubled mind, and she found that she understood how this was so. The smell of wood shavings, the sharp crack of the hammer, these things brought crisp, clear memories to her. She could see Noah and Isaiah as they worked together and teased each other. She thought of David's childish hands carefully performing some small task, mayhap smoothing a rough edge or tapping a tight joint into place with the help of a brother, striking fingers as often as wood.

She thought of her school days, when she would sit upon a high stool in the joinery and practice reading from the Bible while her father listened. Whenever she paused, unable to even begin to pronounce some difficult word, he would supply it without looking up from his work, and she was ever amazed. He seemed to have the whole of the Good Book memorized.

Once, she had wanted to be like that. In an effort to grab hold of her parents' unshakable faith, she had memorized countless pages of scripture. In the end, it had availed her naught. It was not her religion that she missed. It was her family.

Chapter 27

Geoff found her on the floor, next to their upside-down table, plane in hand, as she industriously shaved the bottom of one of its stout legs. God, she was a fetching sight.

"Where did you get the plane?" he asked. Her resourcefulness never ceased to surprise him.

"I borrowed it from Stuart Abrams."

"Abrams? Why, he's the surliest man I've ever met, and avaricious as well. What did he charge you?"

"Nothing. I smiled very sweetly at him and told him that my father was a cabinetmaker so I knew how to use and care for the tools. And I may have mentioned something about how very fine he looked in his coat. He was only too happy to help."

Geoff shook his head and grinned. "What's this? Using your fair face to bend some hapless man to your will? It sounds like wicked, wicked pride to me."

"I think there's little Jesus Himself would not do to hold this table steady." To prove that it had been worthwhile, she accepted his help in upending the thing, and they stood back to admire its level surface and solid stance.

"'Tis a miracle," he said.

She looked with pride upon her handiwork, but the look faded, and sadness replaced it. Seeing the tears that misted her eyes, Geoff wondered if perhaps the shabbiness of their home bothered her rather more than she would say.

"What was it like, your home?" he asked, guessing rightly what occupied his wife's mind.

"I have oft spoken of my family," she said, and moved to fetch a broom to sweep the shavings.

"Aye, but what of your house?"

She leaned on the broom and looked off into some distant memory. "Well, 'tis a sturdy clapboard house. Father built it, so 'tis snug and warm, every plank fitted tightly so that the winter chill is hard-pressed to find its way in. There is a keeping room with a hearth and sitting area to one side, and a table and chairs on the other. Many a lively discussion took place 'round that table, and many an argument between siblings mediated by Father."

Geoff tried to imagine her life, so very different from his own. He had lived in a gaudy brothel, surrounded by squabbling women and boisterous men.

"Is it large?" he asked.

"Comfortably so, downstairs. At first, Noah and I shared a big chamber upstairs, and Mother and Father had one of their own. We shared that room with a screen for privacy until we were seven and Isaiah came along. Father walled off a little room, more like a cubby, really, and that became mine. 'Twas fortunate that the fourth and last child was a boy as well, for my room would never have fit a sister!"

"Did it bother you, having to take a much smaller space?"

"Oh, nay! 'Twas cozy and comforting. I think I would have been afraid to sleep in a big room without my brother, but there was no room for monsters and demons in my little cubby."

"Then this does not strike you as so very poor a home?"

"Nay, Geoff! Whatever made you think it would?"

"'Twas not what I had envisioned for us."

"Patience, my love," she chided while she resumed sweeping. "In time you'll build your company and we'll find another home. I assure you, I am happy to be with you; the place matters not. Still, I would be lying if I did not say I would as soon live a bit farther from the noise and bustle someday."

"That reminds me—I have good news," he ventured carefully. Her face brightened, and she looked at him expectantly. "Giles and I have taken the last order we need to fill *Destiny*'s hold. We're bound for Boston by the end of the week."

For a moment it seemed her heart stopped beating. Boston. Home. Geoff and Giles had both made it clear that she was welcome to sail with them whenever she would. She could not help but wonder, would she be as welcome with her family?

Her aunt and uncle had heard nothing, but of course, letters were slow and uncertain. 'Twas possible a reply was on its way. 'Twas possible there would be no reply, no further word, ever. Many a night, on the voyage to Jamaica and at her aunt and uncle's, Faith had tossed and turned sleeplessly, wondering whether she had made the right choice. Now, gazing at the man who seemed ever delighted with her, scowling in disapproval only when he sensed that she was not being true to herself, she knew that she would make this choice a thousand times over, whatever the cost.

"What troubles you?" he asked. "We needn't be apart. You'll come, too, won't you?"

"Aye. 'Tis only that much has happened since last I saw Boston Harbor."

"Aye, that's so, but think of all you'll have to tell your family."

"Then you had thought to visit them?"

Geoff sighed, exhaling his own doubts and uncertainties. "To be sure. I am of two hearts about it, I confess. I rather imagine they will want to know that you are well and to meet your husband." The thought that had plagued him all week surfaced, and he gave her a guarded look. "Perhaps you are not eager for that meeting."

Faith sighed, too. "Not entirely. I told you of my aunt. She was disowned for marrying a Catholic. You do not even count yourself a Christian."

He shrugged. "Tell them I am Anglican. Mayhap they will not be perfectly content with that, but surely 'twill satisfy them."

Faith sank into a newly repaired chair. There were still times when their separate upbringings opened a chasm between them. "I am not even prepared to count myself Anglican, much less you. Lying is a sin, Geoff."

"Mayhap they will not ask," he offered. She arched her brows at him. "There's naught we can do about it now," he said tersely.

"And naught else I would do. There's nothing I have done that I would change. What I have gained will simply have to help me accept what I may have lost."

He stood behind her where she sat and eased the tension from her shoulders with firm but gentle hands.

His touch, as ever, sent delicious warmth coursing through her.

"It may be that all is not lost. Even as you miss them, surely they miss you, and though they may be rigid, you have oft told me of the love among them. They may yet yield to see you well and happy. Either way, know this, whatever you face at home, you do not face alone."

"If only they could know the depth of contentment I have found with you, they would know this is as it should be." She paused and placed her hand on his. "I do not know if I can ever convince them."

"Come to bed, love. We'll yet find some way to take your mind from your worries."

Leaning her head back, Faith smiled up at him. "I think I will ever feel a little thrill when you call me that."

He gave her a seductive smile. "What? Love? Well then, come with me, love, to our shabby but ample bed, love." He pulled her up and across the room. "Where I shall show you, love"—he tugged on the laces of her gown—"just how much I mean it, love."

Together they sank onto the bed. He took her mouth against his, and his warm hands pushed her gown and then her shift from her shoulders. Those hands moved on, lightly grazing the sides of her breasts, and her nipples hardened in response. In her ear he murmured delicious suggestions, every so often breaking the rhythm of his speech as he repeated the endearment over and over, causing her to giggle against the side of his neck.

Both groaned in frustration when they heard Mr. Abrams enter the office below and call out.

"A moment, Mr. Abrams," Geoff replied loudly.

Faith moved to tug her clothes back on, but Geoff stayed her hand and smiled at her in a way that set her heart thumping. Making no effort to straighten his own disheveled garments, he tripped hastily down the stairs.

Faith blushed and buried her face in the sheets. Surely their neighbor would discern her husband's dishabille, and it was likely he would reason out why. 'Twas the middle of the afternoon! What would he think?

When Geoff returned, he pounced playfully onto the mattress, immediately picking up where he had left off.

"I believe Abrams was disappointed that I was the one who returned the tools," he commented, shoving her skirts down past her hips.

"I'm quite sure he knew what we were doing," Faith chided, though she made no move to stop him. "You should have tucked your shirt in."

"Poor devil," Geoff commented. "I s'pose I shouldn't rub it in. He can only dream of this." He nipped at her breast, but she pushed him away, her cheeks pink again.

"Did he say anything?" she asked.

Her husband grinned. "He asked if you had accomplished everything that you had hoped. I told him that we were in the middle of one last task, but that I had just the tool for the job."

She cried out and struck him on the arm. "Nay, you did not!"

He laughed and pulled her into his arms. "Nay. I did but tell him that you had wrought wonders with our pitiful furniture."

She relaxed in his arms, and, indeed, let him take the worries from her mind.

Chapter 28

The voyage back to Boston was entirely unlike Faith's journey away. Of the original crew, only the cook, Mr. Bartlett, chose to stay with Geoff and Giles. The others were either unsuitable for a legitimate merchantman or had no desire for such an unexciting vocation. The new crew consisted of men who liked not the rigors of navy life nor the danger and bloodshed of piracy. There was no doubt that they were a coarse lot, but they worked hard enough and were somewhat more trustworthy.

It seemed that thirty-six hours of seasickness would be a predictable part of Faith's traveling, but beyond that, her body adjusted. It was far less traumatic when she could stay above deck, her eyes fixed firmly on the horizon to minimize the effects. As the captain's wife, she was afforded every courtesy and the highest respect. Far preferable to spending four weeks in but two gowns, she embarked upon this adventure with two trunks of clothes. A wide-brimmed straw hat and cotton gloves protected her fair skin from the sun, allowing her more time on the open deck. At night, the lower decks were not strewn with the sleeping forms of sailors. Far fewer were required when fighting and possibly capturing another ship was not a consideration. The men all fit comfortably into the hammocks hung in the crew's quarters.

The cozy familiarity of Geoff's cabin had its own differences. There was nothing shy or desperate between its occupants, only the natural conclusion of days spent by a man and a woman seduced by mild breezes, sapphire waters, and warm rains.

With the help of both Giles and Geoff, Faith learned to use the backstaff, sextant, compass, charts, and stars to map their course. In time, they hoped to be able to buy Giles a ship of his own, and Geoff would welcome a new navigator, especially one who warmed his bed, as well. Best of all, this new training gave her plenty to do to occupy her time, and she soon found herself falling in love with the sea. Geoff laughed and said they would make a sailor of her yet, if only she would learn to give a proper cussing. She and Giles exchanged sly looks. If only he had heard her one day on the docks of Port Royal.

Where they had once traveled from the chill of an early New England spring into the warm embrace of the Gulf Stream, now they left sunny climes and rounded Cape Hatteras, with its inhospitable waters, to meet the crisp beginnings of autumn. The weather changed in other ways as well. Storms were more worrisome in the hurricane season, so when the ocean waves became violent, and the horizon before them dissolved into a solid gray mass of sea and sky, the crew worked diligently to skirt the worst of it. Trusting Geoff and Giles to keep them safe and on course, Faith rode these storms out below, saying a little prayer for good measure.

At last they neared the Massachusetts coast. Though Faith had come to love the lush tropics with their exotic flora, her blood quickened at the sight of dense forests licked by tongues of autumn flames that colored the leaves. Soon, the woods would erupt into a conflagration of reds, oranges, and golds, ere winter stripped them bare. It was a crisp time of tart apples to eat and leaves to crush underfoot. Aye, for all the beauty and blessed warmth of her new home, she would ever miss the changeable land of her birth.

The homesickness that had hovered somewhere deep within her became an intense ache, and yet she dreaded what must come. When they at last arrived in Boston, she hesitated to stroll the docks as she once had. She stayed close to Geoff and Giles as they arranged to sell the rum, sugar, indigo, and other goods that filled *Destiny*'s hold. Days passed, and she had yet to even shop among the merchants who daily gathered outside the Boston Town House, much less visit her home.

"Are you not sick to death of endless talk of prices and deliveries?" Geoff asked her as they ate the third meal in as many nights at the inn where they were lodging.

"If I'm to be your helpmate on voyages, I must know all aspects of your business," she replied.

Geoff rolled his eyes. "You cannot fool me, love. You are hiding. Can we not at least take our meals at some other establishment?" He glanced around the nearly empty common room. "There are plenty to choose from, and this place is not the best, I assure you."

Faith studied her hands, which clasped and unclasped with a will of their own in her lap. "I know. I'm well aware that no one who knows Boston well eats here. But what if someone I know should come to town and take a meal before they return to their home? 'Tis a common practice."

"Is that not a part of why you came here, to see people that you know? Look at me, Faith. This cold New England air seems to be turning you back into a Puritan."

"Nay, not a Puritan, but what? 'Tis so very different here, Geoff. Religion is everything. What am I?"

"You are Faith."

"Faith the faithless."

"Because you chose not to have your beliefs handed to you by pompous, arrogant clergymen? Good God, is this about that insignificant little speck you were betrothed to?"

She winced a bit, hoping that he didn't see, but he caught the tiny gesture. "I'm sorry," he said. "I'm much better about it these days."

"I know, and I appreciate it."

"Well, there you have it, love. You may not have found a church that suits you, and you may not always know exactly what you believe, but you keep your commandments and hold me to them as well, like it or not. You're a Christian, Faith. More Christian than many who sin all week, then sit in a pew every Sunday and consider that adequate homage to their God. What more can they ask?"

"I suppose I had better find out," she said, her voice resigned. "If you can spare the day, mayhap we should take a ride tomorrow."

It was still dark when Faith rose and chose a modest and relatively simple gown of deep violet raw silk. The neckline was high and edged with lace that concealed much of her throat. Long sleeves were gathered into three puffs and banded with black satin ribbons, the same ribbons that also trimmed the bodice. The effect was both fashionable and subtle. She wore her hair in an uncomplicated knot and finished the outfit with a small cap that matched.

Geoff made fewer concessions, wearing the elegant lace and fabrics fashion demanded. Still, his royal blue coat and black breeches would not be entirely out of place, despite the fact that they were of luxurious velvet. He pulled his hair back into a queue, downplaying its sensuous texture.

They hired a coach just after sunup and rode in silence while the familiar road passed by the window. It seemed to Faith that she knew it only from some fantasy and not from years of having traveled it. When she saw the first little cluster of buildings at the edge of her village, she drew back from the window. Better to see her family and gauge her welcome before anyone saw her. If she was waylaid by a neighbor, someone would surely alert her parents ere she could speak with them, and that might go badly.

They passed the church, a solid clapboard building that dominated the main road running through the center of town. To her relief, Owen Williams was inside or absent altogether. A quick glance at her husband's face suggested that he shared her sentiments.

All around them, the village bustled with activity. Even those who lived in the town proper kept some animals, chickens, goats, perhaps a few pigs, and the air was pungent with their presence. Women tended to these while their husbands and sons tended to business. It was mid morning, and the sounds of hammer and anvil rang out from the smithy.

Although Aaron Jacobs's wood mill lay on the outskirts of town, the sound of planks being cut from raw timber carried to the coach, and Faith wondered if Aaron had found a suitable bride.

Faith focused on her surroundings rather than allowing her mind to wander a few short minutes into the future. Her nights had been wracked with happy dreams of warm homecomings that dissolved into nightmares of rejection and anger. Which would it be? She would know very soon.

The coach drew up to the end of the short road that led to her family's home. The house sat back from the road at the edge of several acres of forest land, the source of wood for her father's business, and at her nod, Geoff knocked on the roof of the coach, signaling the driver to stop.

Faith sat, unable to bring herself to alight, and Geoff tilted her face to his to bestow a long and gentle kiss. "Whatever happens, we have each other," he told her. "I truly hope this is a happy occasion, but no matter what, you will never be alone in the world."

She gave him a tremulous smile. "I cannot say which would be worse, to never know how they felt or to have them tell me to my face that I am a disappointment and a disgrace."

"Right now, ere you face their judgment, do you feel disgraceful?"

"Nay."

"When you leave here today, you will be the same woman who sits here beside me now. Remember that."

She nodded. "I will."

Other than the fact that trees that had once held but the promise of buds were now filled with leaves just beginning to turn, her home looked just as it had when she left it. She might just as easily have dreamed the last six months but for the very real man who walked reassuringly beside her.

From the joinery came the industrious noise of hammer and saw, and Isaiah's distinct laugh floated musically through the open door. Chickens scurried out from under the couple's feet, and the milk cow in the pasture beyond the house watched their approach with complacent eyes. David appeared in the joinery doorway carrying a bucket, and he paused to assess the visitors who strolled along the path.

"Faith!" the boy called, his face breaking into a dazzling grin that Geoff immediately recognized as his wife's. "Father, Noah, Isaiah, 'tis Faith!" He dropped the bucket and ran to her, arms outstretched, and she knelt, toppling over when his little body slammed into hers. "Mother said you were far away in the land of pirates and black slaves! We thought you'd never come home anymore. I'm taller! Can you see that? I'll be tall as Isaiah ere he knows what happened. That's what Mother says. Who's the man?"

Faith laughed and tousled his blond hair. She accepted the strong hand that appeared before her and rose to her feet. This would be Noah, Geoff thought of the young man who embraced Faith silently, tears sliding down his face. He recognized him from the harbor the day he had offered her the silk.

"See, Noah, I told you. She's come back! Faith?" he tugged insistently at her skirt. "Faith? Who is the man?"

Another boy, apparently the middle son, Isaiah, clasped her from behind, having tried but failed to displace his older brother, and she twisted to place a hearty kiss on top of his pale hair.

For a moment, Geoff seemed invisible to them, but not to the older man who watched from the joinery entrance. The one who must surely be Jonathan Cooper made no move to join his children. He merely stood, clearly taking measure of the stranger who had accompanied his wayward daughter home.

Geoff took a step forward. He would rather meet the man head on, on his own terms, than wait, but the father his wife so admired turned away and disappeared into the shop. He looked to see how she would take this blow, but she was still caught up in her reunion with her brothers.

He looked down at the tug on his coattail.

"Sir? Excuse me, sir? Did you find my sister and bring her home to us?"

Geoff smiled at the boy, but his answer was cut off by another cry that came from the steps leading to the front door of the tidy clapboard house.

"Faith! Oh, Faith, my baby girl!" The woman running to join the group looked very like Faith, though older and more severe in her coif, her face lined by time and labor.

"Mother!" Faith cried, and the boys at last relinquished her so that their mother could embrace her, as well. "Oh, Mother, I have missed you all so!"

"We missed you, too, dear! More than you can know. I thank God Elizabeth found you. Did you get my letter?"

"Nay, I did not, but I have been hard to find—first at Winston Hall, then Cartagena, then Port Royal."

"Cartagena? Indeed!" She turned to Geoff and swept him with a glance that took in his elaborate dress and too casual air. "And who is this gentleman?"

"I have asked and asked, Mother, and no one will say!" David whined.

"Shh!" his mother scolded.

Faith's elation slipped a notch, but she would have to face this sooner or later. "This is Captain Geoffrey

Hampton, my husband. Geoffrey, my mother, Naomi Cooper, and my brothers, Noah, Isaiah, and David. I would introduce my father, but he seems occupied elsewhere." The hurt in her voice said that she had not missed seeing him after all.

Geoff bowed slightly. "Mistress Cooper, gentlemen, 'tis a pleasure."

For the first time, the older boys seemed to really notice him, and they inspected both Hamptons, taking in every aspect of their appearance.

Naomi recovered first. "The pleasure is ours, Captain. Well, I think we shall have to declare it a holiday, for there will be little work any of us will be good for until we hear every detail of your story. Come, we'll sit awhile and talk."

"And Father?" Faith asked.

Naomi's smile faltered but slightly. "I think it would be best to let him work. I will go to him later."

Later, Faith thought. When her mother had all of the details and could think of some way to break the news to her husband and try to convince him to speak to his only daughter. She swallowed her bitterness and allowed David to lead her inside, his little legs skipping merrily.

Chapter 29

Naomi's smile did little to mask the concern in her eyes as she gazed at the newest member of the family. She quietly sipped her tea while her two youngest exclaimed in excitement.

"A privateer?" she commented uneasily. "My, that must have been very exciting."

Geoff shifted uncomfortably. There was something about the woman's scrutiny that unnerved him.

"I wonder if you may come to find the life of a merchant captain unbearably dull by comparison," she added.

"'Tis the sea I love," he said, "and I still have that. I've found I've lost my taste for so much adventure. There's a contentment in this new life we've chosen." He was rewarded by the tiniest spark of approval in his mother-in-law's eyes.

Faith decided to skirt any more uncomfortable issues for a time. "All we have spoken of is us. Noah, surely I am an aunt by now!"

Noah's face brightened, and the mood of all gladdened with it. "Aye! My Esther has given me a fine son. We named him Matthew. You must come and see him before you set sail. He's a strong boy and full of smiles. And Esther will want to see you and meet Geoff, here."

"Of course," Faith answered. "Mayhap on the way home this afternoon. I have told Geoff all about you and Esther. You'll be fine parents, I know!"

Naomi seemed to weigh her next comment, then said, "You'll stay for the midday meal, I think. That is, if you have the time."

Faith nodded hesitantly. "We have set the whole of today aside." She rose and looked out the window to the joinery. "Are you quite certain we should stay?"

Naomi joined her daughter, wrapping her arm about Faith's waist. "Aye, I think you should stay." Turning back to the men, she told them to continue with the stories. "I'll see how Jonathan fares. I believe he will be able to break from his labors and join us."

That Noah and Naomi exchanged doubtful looks did little to boost anyone's confidence, but Geoff forced a cheery tone when he turned to David and asked whether he liked being an uncle, and the boy's enthusiastic response covered the tension.

Naomi crossed the yard with a spine of steel and stepped into the joinery. Jonathan did not look up when she entered, but picked up an awl and began to carefully carve the chest before him. There was no telling how long he had been sitting idle.

Leaning against the workbench, she said, "I know not whether I prefer your absence or your anger. I think you will simply have to master your emotions, Jonathan."

"Do I seem out of control, Naomi?"

She gave him a stern look and crossed her arms. "We have a son-in-law."

He continued to work. "A son-in-law? We have no daughter."

"That is strange. I remember a long night's labor that produced two babies, a boy and a girl. I remember kneeling at your side, each of us begging God to keep her in the palm of His hand when a fever wracked her tiny body. I remember you working here, like this, listening to her read her lessons to you. Do you remember none of these things?"

"For all the good those prayers did us."

"Jonathan, you do not mean that!"

"All that labor, all those hours of prayers and teaching and worrying, and how did she repay us?"

"I love you dearly, my husband, but I will not be a party to the same mistake twice! I saw all too well how it hurt my own mother to turn her back on Elizabeth, and I will not be forced into a similar position."

"Elizabeth forced your parents' hands. 'Tis Faith who is repeating the mistake."

"Nay! In this, we are at least partially to blame. Faith was right, as we both know. Time has not softened Owen Williams. The man is a tyrant and on the verge of being driven from his pulpit. That we nearly bound our daughter to him gives me nightmares! I know that Faith hurt you, but you must forgive her."

"Is she here to ask forgiveness? Is she here to make amends? Is that why she is here, married to some man we know nothing about?"

"She trusted us to keep her safe and to protect her welfare, and we failed her. Would you see her married to Reverend Williams just to prove her obedience? She is happy, Jonathan. Captain Hampton loves her and protected her when we did not."

He turned to face her, at last. "Captain Hampton."

"Geoffrey Hampton."

"An acquaintance of Elizabeth's?"

"Nay, though she has met him. They were married in Elizabeth and Miguel's church."

He rose and brushed sawdust from his knees. "Where did she meet him?"

"She sailed with him to Jamaica."

"The letters from her and Elizabeth made no mention of him."

"'Tis a long story. He is her husband. 'Tis a little late to be inquiring into his background or the manner in which they met. They are staying for the noon meal. Will you join us, or will you stay here and sulk?"

"I like not your tone, Naomi."

"You shall regret it, you know. They will not be here long. Will you let her sail away with so much unsaid between you two?"

"I have nothing to say to her."

"Lying is a sin, Jonathan Cooper."

He heaved a sigh and looked past her through the open door. "I will be in, in a moment."

Naomi returned to the house, and Faith reveled in the simple joy of preparing a meal with her mother again. They laughed easily and automatically fell into their former division of duties, Naomi cutting vegetables, Faith making small adjustments in the seasonings. David set the table with haste, complaining that the task would cause him to miss some thrilling tale, despite the fact that every word of the conversation carried from the hearth to the table.

Naomi remained carefully aloof from the newcomer

who spun those tales, but she smiled at him from time to time, and Faith felt encouraged.

"He is a good man, Mother," Faith assured her. "And so is Uncle Miguel."

Her head bowed, Naomi murmured, "She's well then, and happy, my sister?"

"She is, but she misses you."

"And I her," Naomi confessed. "The passing of time softens things. I should very much like to see her."

Geoff partook with wonder in the comfortable family life his wife had so oft described. Aye, he could be content with a lifetime of this with his Faith in a home of their own.

The sound of Jonathan's footfalls on the steps outside penetrated the conversation and brought immediate silence. Even David seemed to know that this would not be an easy meeting and held his breath waiting for his father.

Jonathan entered the room and surveyed its occupants with a grave face. At last, his gaze settled upon Faith, and she resisted the urge to drop her gaze, keeping it steadily on his instead. He frowned, and she found that she could not swallow for the lump in her throat, but she held her ground.

"Father."

"Faith."

Five pairs of eyes watched, and Geoff cleared his throat, breaking the strained exchange. Faith introduced him, and the two men greeted each other, Jonathan's face guardedly hostile, Geoff's carefully bland. Faith knew both men well enough to know that neither expression boded well. Her father had made up his mind, and her husband was preparing for battle.

The merriment of the moments before evaporated,

and everyone quietly took their place at the long oak table. After the blessing, Noah made a brave attempt at a doting story about little Matthew, and Isaiah laughed obligingly, though he had heard the tale several times before. His gesture reminded others to do the same, and they forced themselves to follow suit, but the laughter quickly faded when the family patriarch remained silent.

Faith stared at her plate and seethed, even as her heart grieved. He would not forgive her. So be it. Why, then, did he not just stay in the joinery? Why not let her visit awhile and leave with no inconvenience to him?

What he did next was worse.

"So, you're Anglican, then?" he asked. He waited for his new son-in-law to answer.

Geoff looked at Faith, hoping she would give some indication that he should lie after all, but she seemed to be concentrating on swallowing the mouthful of squash she had taken. "Nay, sir. I am not."

"Nay? I thought the two of you were married by an Anglican priest."

"We were. 'Twas convenient."

"Convenient."

"Aye."

Jonathan took a spoonful of beef and chewed thoughtfully ere he spoke again. "There are still Puritan churches in the Caribbean."

"Aye, there are. There are all manner of churches, though they are few enough in Port Royal."

"You live in Port Royal?"

"Aye, when we are not at sea."

Jonathan nodded curtly. "When you are not at sea. And though churches are few, you have found one that serves?"

"We are at sea much of the time."

"Without a church, you are at sea all of the time."

Geoff bit back his reply. Give him a good, honest sword fight over this verbal battle any time.

"In what faith were you raised?" Jonathan asked.

"Your grandchildren will be raised honest Christians, Father. You need not fear on that account," Faith interrupted, but she fell silent again at her father's glare.

"Is there some reason we should not discuss this?" Jonathan asked.

"Some consider religion to be a highly personal matter," Naomi supplied. "Mayhap these questions offend."

Jonathan turned to Geoff. "Forgive me. 'Tis only that matters of faith are much a part of this family's conversation, and you are family, are you not?"

"Jonathan," Naomi warned.

He appeared to acquiesce. "How long have you been married? My wife did not say when she came to fetch me."

Faith breathed a sigh of relief. "Just over two months. Geoff wanted to meet all of you as soon as possible."

"Aye," Geoff pasted a smile on his face and looked around at those faces that were less hostile. "Faith had told me so much about all of you, and she has missed you terribly."

Naomi smiled. "We have missed her, too. It was good of you not to keep us waiting. This is much better than learning of you through a letter."

"'Tis a long voyage from here to Jamaica," Jonathan commented.

"A month or so," Geoff replied. "I have sailed longer stretches."

"A month. And when she journeyed to Jamaica, there

were other women on the ship to keep my daughter company?"

"Ah, well, my ship was not exactly prepared for a female passenger."

"No?"

Faith jumped in, hoping to change the course of the conversation. "I stowed away, Father. He did not know there was a female on board until after he set sail."

He raised his brows at Geoff. "You must have been rather upset to discover an unexpected traveler on your ship."

"It was understandable, given the circumstances." He was tired of the game, and Geoff did nothing to soften the intentional barb.

"That is a long time for an unaccompanied woman on a ship of men. We must thank Providence, indeed, for placing her into the hands of an honorable man who would not take advantage of the situation."

She couldn't help it. The cider she swallowed took the wrong path in Faith's throat, and she choked, her face turning deep red.

Jonathan gave his wayward daughter a piercing glare, and she found she could not, by any bent of will, look him in the face. "I have lost my appetite," he announced, rising abruptly. "I will be in the joinery the rest of the afternoon. Good journey to you both."

He walked out the door with surprising calm, but Faith dearly wished he would fly into a rage. All her life his calm, rational disapproval had kept them all neatly in line. Somehow it was far more effective than any display of temper could have been.

She finally dared to look at the others around the table and cringed. Her mother dabbed her eyes with the corner of her napkin. Noah and Isaiah looked positively sick. David gazed at her with fear and confusion, not understanding what terrible sin his sister had committed, but knowing full well that she had, indeed, committed one.

Only Geoff looked her in the eye, his face silently conveying, "Well, are you just going to sit there?"

She stood without excusing herself and ran to catch up. Jonathan did not break his long strides, and Faith had to take two steps to his every one to keep up.

"We cannot part this way! Father, please, I have traveled a month to see you."

"We have nothing more to say to each other."

Running beside him and breathlessly keeping his pace, she spoke quietly but firmly. "Mayhap you have nothing more to say, but I have yet to speak my piece."

He turned on her in the doorway of the shop, blocking her from entering. "Much has changed, Faith Cooper. I well remember a time my daughter would not have dared to challenge me."

"Am I your daughter?" she asked. He glared at her in stony silence. "Am I?"

"Nay, not anymore." He turned his back and entered the joinery, Faith upon his heels.

"So be it. Then there is no commandment that bids me hold my tongue."

He did not acknowledge her but began to sweep the dust from the floor.

"What was I to do, Father? I could not marry Owen Williams. I was desperate. You saw no way to protect me from him, and 'twas clear you would never grant me permission to escape to Aunt Elizabeth's."

Somewhat bitterly she added, "She's well, by the way, and sends you her greetings." The comment brought no response.

"Are you the one human who is without sin, Father? God will judge me, this I know, but not you. When I was a child, it seemed there was never a question but that you had the answer. Well, answer me this, if Jesus can love the sinner though he hates the sin, can I never be worthy of your love, just as I am?"

"How dare you!" Jonathan tried to bellow his indignation, but his throat constricted around a sob. "How dare you accuse me of not loving you? I love you more than life. Would that I could have died ere I saw what has become of the child I have ached for, worried about, eaten myself up over at night."

"What has become of me? I am well and happy! You worried for naught. Can you not be glad for me?" she pleaded.

"Happy for the heartbeat of time you spend upon this earth. Have you lost all care for your soul, Faith?"

"Nay, I have not. I cannot think God would give me such joy and all the while stoke flames beneath my feet."

"Are you so sure that God is the source of your joy?"

"Why would He not be? We are well and truly wed. Whatever mistakes we made we redeemed."

He gazed out the window, a mighty struggle playing across his features, and Faith waited. In the past six months, she had come to understand such struggles, and she respected his need for thought.

"Are you with child?" he asked.

"If I am, it was conceived after we were married."

Jonathan ran his hand through his hair, and it occurred to Faith that it was yet grayer than when last she had seen him.

"You do not go to church, either one of you, do you?"

He sounded tired, but they were talking. It was a step in the right direction.

She sat upon the high stool that had occupied a place in her father's shop for as long as she could remember. "I have gone a few times to the Anglican church, but it does not speak to me. You were not far off earlier. I am somewhat at sea where my faith is concerned."

"You know where to seek a guiding light and a safe harbor."

Faith nodded. "Aye, but I must reach them on my own. You cannot do that for me."

"I thought that I had charted your voyage for you when you were a child."

"No one can chart the journey of another's spirit, Father, but you gave me fine tools."

"So you would still look to God to guide you?"

"Aye, I look to God, but He is not always as clear as I would hope." He looked profoundly sad, and Faith guessed his worry. "You think that I struggle because God has not deemed me worthy of His grace."

Tears welled in Jonathan's eyes, and for once, it was he who dropped his gaze to the floor. "'Tis not for me to say."

"In my life," she said, "I have ever acted faithfully, with the best intentions."

"You must act as God intends. 'Tis not for us to rely upon our imperfect impulses."

"Nay, I have not acted upon impulse. What I have done, I have done with intent." He blanched, but Faith knew that he must know everything if he was ever to understand. "Aye, even that. I thought long and hard before I gave myself to Geoff, even though he made it very clear he had no intention of marrying me."

Jonathan sank down upon the chest he had been working on, his shoulders slumped in defeat, and Faith joined him. They sat with only a small space between them but did not touch.

"Why did he, then?" Jonathan asked.

"Because it was meant to be. If I had not known him in that way, he would never have seen that what he felt for me was not what he had felt before. I would have been but a passing regret, a minor curiosity left unsatisfied. You must ask Geoff how he feels about me, but I think you would find that I have changed the course of his life. I offered him hope and love. These things which our family has ever taken for granted, he has lived his whole life without."

"And what role does he play in yours? What do you receive in return for risking your immortal soul?"

It was Faith's turn to deliberate for a moment. "Freedom. Geoff does not presume to know the mind of God."

That he was not entirely sure there was one was a point that could wait until another day.

"I am presumptuous, then," Jonathan replied, obviously hurt.

"I find Owen Williams presumptuous. I find our church presumptuous. Geoff lets me search. He accepts me. I do not have to be someone else when I am with him."

"I have never wanted you to be anything else."

"You would have worried, even as you do now."

"Have you always had these questions?"

"I think, perhaps, I have."

Jonathan looked at her, baffled and sad.

"I wanted you to be proud of me," she explained. "I

wanted to be what everyone seemed to think I was. But underneath, it somehow did not fit."

"I would have loved you no matter what."

"Aye, I believe that, but would you have encouraged me?"

"To stray?"

"To search."

He looked into her eyes but still made no move to touch her. "They have not changed, those eyes of yours. They are the very eyes I dried after countless mishaps, the ones that sparkled whenever I offered some praise. Through it all, you are my child. How can I turn my back upon you? You are a part of me. You always will be."

"As you will be ever a part of me, Father."

"You say you have needed to search. What have you found?" he asked.

"I am coming to hear what speaks to my heart. No one is perfect, Father, and God created us so. Why condemn humanity because we are as He made us? We grew up. I grew up. Even as Adam and Eve had to leave the comfort of paradise, I had to leave the comfort of my home. Since the fall of Adam, 'tis our nature to make mistakes. The church says that this is proof of our wickedness, but 'tis only proof that we are not God. None of us."

"The church tells us that we may find redemption through Christ."

"Our church also tells us that only the elect will be redeemed. God is not moved by the will of men, and so it matters not what we think and do."

"And you question this?"

"It leaves us so powerless. It seems to me that God may move through the will of men. We make choices.

We make mistakes. Mayhap Christ redeemed us by showing us how to redeem ourselves. He taught us to live among each other with love and compassion. I think salvation has less to do with how Christ died than with how He lived."

Jonathan shook his head. "Am I to choose between my daughter and my theology? 'Tis too much to ask. Both are dearer to me than breath."

"God is a father, too. Would He ask you to make such a choice?"

At last, he put his arm around Faith's shoulders, and she leaned her head against him. They sat thusly for some minutes before he said, "'Tis heresy, but then, some called John Calvin a heretic, as well."

"Then can you forgive me?"

"There is nothing to forgive. As others have reminded me, I am not blameless in your decision to leave."

"And what of my questions, my doubts? Can you love me in spite of them?"

"You have given me much to ponder, Daughter, but of course, I love you. I must have faith that you will find your own way."

She turned her face to his shoulder and wept with relief, and he held her, soothing her as he had ever been able to. When she calmed, he wiped her cheeks with his sleeve, as he had oft done when she was small.

"I think I have not made a good first impression with your husband."

She sniffed and smiled. "Well, then we had better return. I would have him meet the man I told him of, the one I still hold in the highest esteem."

They left the joinery hand-in-hand, and Faith finally relaxed enough to drink in the familiar sights and

sounds of home. It felt so good, so natural to walk with
her father the well-known path from the shop to the
house.

Halfway down the trail, Jonathan froze, his gaze
caught by something beyond the house. Faith stopped
with him, her eyes following his to fall upon a most
unwelcome visitor.

Chapter 30

The Reverend Owen Williams also paused on his route from the main road to the Cooper residence and regarded the two that exited the joinery. All three slowed their steps, no one eager to initiate the inevitable.

Jonathan shook his head grimly. "There must be some way to send this one on his way without incurring one of his accursed temper tantrums. The man is famous for them."

Faith just nodded and stayed at her father's side as they resumed their pace, set to meet the minister together.

In due time, Reverend Williams called out, "I see the rumors were true. The prodigal daughter has returned!"

They closed the space between them, and Jonathan replied, "Rumor has swift wings in this village."

Williams nodded. "Aye. Goodwife Little was upon the road this morning and spied our long-lost Faith with your family." He turned to Faith, and his eyes perused her, noting with a frown of disapproval her rich clothing. "I am told you arrived with an escort, and yet I see only you two."

Faith wiped at her cheeks to be sure that no tears yet remained. She was certain her face was red and her eyes swollen, and it seemed vastly unfair that she should have to face this man when she was already so unsettled. Still, she lifted her chin and looked him squarely in the eye.

"I arrived with my husband, Captain Geoffrey Hampton."

"Captain?" he replied with the sneer she remembered all too well. "A seafaring man. He is wise to bring you with him while he is at sea. I should imagine there are all manner of temptations in the Caribbean for a woman left to her own devices."

"Actually, she comes with me because I cannot bear to be without her. If ever there was a woman who could rise to the challenge of temptation, 'tis Faith."

The small group had been so intently focused upon one another that none had heard Geoff's approach, and Faith was pleased to see an embarrassed flush stain the minister's face. Even so, he recovered himself quickly.

"I know you," he said, after he had taken a moment to examine the newcomer.

Geoff stepped uncomfortably close, and his cold, calculating smile was the very one few men had survived to tell of. "We have met. You do not know me. They are not the same thing."

Williams stumbled back, and though this time 'twas anger that reddened his countenance, he wisely held his tongue.

Jonathan struggled to keep a somber look about him, but the merest hint of a grin slipped through upon witnessing Williams's discomfiture.

Avoiding the intimidating figure in front of him, Williams addressed Faith. "I thought you to be a liar when you said that he had accosted you in Boston. I see now I was fully justified in my conclusion. How came you to know a rough sailor when you lived the life of a pious daughter in our village?"

Geoff would have responded, but Faith raised her hand to stop him. "I confess, I was not entirely honest, but neither was I the crafty deceiver you say. I had only just met him when you saw us. When Geoff lied and said that he bought the silk for his sister, I did not contradict him, as perhaps I should have. Even so, I did not ask for his attentions, and I was, in fact, chastising him for his impropriety."

"And yet, somehow, here he is."

"Aye," she answered, "here he is. Providence works in mysterious ways."

The minister cast a dubious glance at Geoff, but could not hold his gaze. "Providence delivered you from a minister and placed you in the hands of a common sailor?"

"Delivered?" Faith reflected. "Aye, that is precisely the word I would have chosen, and as you can see, he is anything but common."

"Your time away has but sharpened your tongue."

"Aye, my tongue and my sight."

Jonathan marveled at his once meek daughter who now managed to look down her nose at a man several inches taller than her. Subtly, he straightened a bit, pride written on his lean face.

"Will you allow her to speak to me with such disrespect?" Williams demanded.

Jonathan shrugged. "She is her husband's subject now."

"She is the king's subject," Geoff corrected. "She is my wife."

"A woman is like a child," the reverend lectured. "She

requires guidance and a firm hand. One has only to look to Eve to see this."

"Ah, Eve," Geoff replied. "Well, one has only to look to Adam to see how ill prepared men are to provide such things."

At Jonathan's laugh, poorly disguised as a cough, Owen Williams turned upon the only one over whom he still had any authority. "Is this some new interpretation of scripture, Goodman Cooper, or do I detect that you are amused by their blasphemy?"

"He has a point," Jonathan ventured.

"Does God command wives to obey their husbands or does He not?"

Jonathan turned to his son-in-law, and the two formed an unlikely alliance. "Do you wish her to speak more respectfully to our esteemed minister?" he asked.

Geoff turned to Faith. "Is this man due more respect than you have shown, Wife?"

Her eyes sparkled, but she feigned careful consideration. "I do not think so, Husband."

He turned back to Jonathan. "Nay, I do not wish her to follow any course but that which she has chosen."

"It would seem that she is in complete obedience to her husband, ill prepared though he may be to command her," Jonathan said.

"I will not be mocked! The Lord is not mocked!" Williams shouted. "I knew all along that you were a wicked, wicked woman, Faith Cooper. I see now that even a devout man of God such as myself could never have hoped to bring you to the path of righteousness. It is we who are delivered! I thank God that He saw fit to remove you from our hallowed haven ere you could contaminate it with your sinful nature!"

"Look you to your own sinful nature!" came Faith's firm reply. "Tell me truly, what compelled you to ask for my hand? Did you seek to quell my wickedness or satisfy your own? I should very much like to know, Owen Williams, are you the only man besides Christ to enter the world free from the guilt of Adam's fall?"

"Prideful wench! You are not the temptation you think!"

"Faith," Geoff inquired, "have you not oft reminded me that lying is a sin?"

"Aye," she answered, glaring daggers at the minister. "Even that which we will not admit to ourselves cannot be shielded from God's eyes."

Williams spluttered, his eyes blinking spasmodically, but no intelligible speech issued from his throat.

In a tone tinged in some pity, Jonathan said, "Much has happened since last you saw Faith, and it seems that your paths have well and truly separated. Mayhap it would be best if we bid you good day, Reverend. My wife, sons, and I will see you at meeting on the Sabbath."

"If her path turns from me, it turns from her church and thereby you, as well, Goodman Cooper!"

Jonathan regarded him through narrow eyes. "You have no dominion over this family, sir."

"I am the ultimate authority over this family, sir!"

"God is the ultimate authority."

"Through me!"

"You cling to your pulpit and your authority by a slender thread, Reverend. Do not presume to interfere where you have no moral or legal right. I tell you this now, I feared you once, and that fear nearly cost me my cherished Faith. It will not be so again."

"Which faith do you cherish most?"

"God gave me my faith, even as He gave me this child. There is no choice to make. Good day."

Williams eyed his stubborn parishioner, then the couple who stared coolly back. His face had maintained a consistently ruddy hue, and now it but deepened. "Do you leave today?" he asked Geoff.

"Nay," Jonathan answered, surprising Faith and Geoff, "they stay the night and return to Boston on the morrow. When do you sail?"

"The day after," Geoff replied.

"Well, then," Williams said, "I will speak to you again at meeting, Goodman Cooper." He nodded curtly and took his leave without a backward glance.

"He walks as though he sat on large stick and keeps it with him still, in a most uncomfortable place," Geoff observed casually.

Faith's hand flew to her mouth. Her husband and father had formed a fragile bond. She could not believe he would so stupidly jeopardize it with such a statement.

Her father's response was more shocking yet.

He rubbed his chin and contemplated the retreating figure. "Aye, I have oft noticed that."

The afternoon passed quickly and ended far more cheerfully than it had begun. Noah went home and fetched Esther and Matthew, a healthy butterball of a boy. The lamps burned later than ever they had before in the Cooper house, but at last weariness won them all over and they retired above.

Faith took her old bed and Geoff Noah's. She missed his warmth, but did not believe she could have shared a bed with him in her parents' house. How long had it been since she had fallen asleep in such quiet? She had grown accustomed to a creaking ship, raucous sailors, or singing tree frogs.

It was nigh onto midnight when the family awoke to a loud banging on the front door along with shouts of alarm. "Fire! There's a fire in the village! Jonathan, come along!"

Jonathan pulled on a shirt and breeches and raced down the stairs, his new son-in-law a step behind. "Why do I not hear the church bell? It should be ringing the alarm!"

"'Tis the church itself, and the rectory, as well!" their neighbor cried.

Chapter 31

The two men flew out the door and had gained the road ere Faith and Naomi finished donning their dresses. Isaiah followed, dragging a wide-eyed and bleary David behind him.

Every available man and woman, as well as older children, had begun to form a bucket brigade, but it was clear that the buildings could not be saved. The streets were bathed in a flickering kind of twilight glow from the holocaust, despite the darkness of the sky. The best that could be hoped for was to save the structures around them. Faith and Naomi joined the line while their husbands climbed to the roofs of neighboring houses, pouring the buckets of water handed to them over the shingles to guard them from flying sparks.

The labor of passing buckets blistered the hands, but it required no real concentration, and Faith sadly watched glowing beams of wood collapse and crumble within the blackened ruins of the church. It mattered not that the structure belonged to a religion she no longer embraced. The church had been a second home to her, a place of welcome and calm contemplation. As for the rectory, well, it held little meaning for her, but Owen Williams stood before it, weeping bitterly and wailing at the top of his lungs that he had been poorly served by the One to whom he had devoted his life.

Her mother took in the spectacle and shook her head. "The Lord gave, and the Lord hath taken away."

"Blessed be the name of the Lord," Faith agreed. She did not miss the fact that her husband and father valiantly fought the burning embers that swarmed around them while the village leader threw a tantrum and railed at God.

The heat from the conflagration blasted the people who battled it, and those closest had to soak their clothes to keep from being set aflame themselves. The labor was backbreaking, and though it took surprisingly little time for the fire to consume what had taken many days to build, all were blistered, sore, and exhausted ere it burned itself out.

The villagers stood before the charred rubble from which wispy tendrils of smoke rose. The smell was acrid and burned noses and throats. This place had sheltered them in times of joy as they forged new families in marriages and baptisms, as well as in times of sorrow, when beloved elders and often even those but newly baptized were sent into God's care from this harsh land. Women wept softly, children stared in frightened awe, and men scratched their heads, wondering what they had done in their tiny village to so incur God's wrath.

The minister had been sitting, his head cradled in his arms against his knees, snapping at anyone who dared to offer succor, but suddenly he jumped up and looked frantically about him.

"You!" he screamed, his red, swollen eyes fixed maniacally upon Faith. "You are to blame for this!"

She had been standing among old friends, offering

softly murmured words of comfort, accepting subdued congratulations on her marriage. The little
group around her dispersed in alarm, and for an instant, she stood alone. Without hesitation, her family
joined her—her husband, parents, and brothers.
With her father on one side, Geoff on the other, each
with an arm wrapped protectively around her, she
could almost pity the wretched man before her.

"Calm yourself," Jonathan chastised. "Surely you're
not saying that Faith set fire to the church."

"Aye, she did! The very fires of hell your godless
daughter has brought upon us! We were purged of
her, and now that she has returned, God's wrath
smites us all!"

"That's a lie, Owen Williams, and well you know it!"
Goodwife Hobbes, the blacksmith's wife, stepped forward from the crowd that had formed a circle around
the scene.

She turned to address her neighbors. "My youngest
is yet recovering from that stomach ailment that swept
my poor family, and I was awake and cleaning up after
him. I was at the pump, and I noticed that a light
burned in the minister's window. Doubtless up con-
cocting another serving of that hellfire and brimstone
he dishes every Sabbath! The fiery torment that
awaits all but him, to hear him tell it," she added with
disgust. "I saw the flame overturn in the dim light,
then a sudden brightness as it caught the curtains."

She advanced upon the minister and poked an ac-
cusatory finger at his chest. "Anyone with an ounce of
sense would have sought to douse the fire while it was
small, but you screamed like a foolish chit being
chased by a mouse and ran out of the house. While
you stood in the yard flapping your arms and howling,

waiting for others to tend to the situation, the fire spread. If you had acted upon it yourself, the church would never have caught."

All eyes turned to the minister, whose face went purple with rage. "What was I to do?" he shouted. "Would you have me stay in the rectory and burn with it? I tell you, 'twas the hand of the Almighty overturned that candle, a hand moved by contempt for that creature there!" He pointed to Faith, who stood in her wet, soot-stained gown that had once been so rich.

"Then why did He not strike my father's house or my husband's ship? Why do I stand here, soaked and sore for helping my neighbors, while you stand unscathed, useless even to yourself?"

"You are a pathetic excuse for a man, much less a minister!" shouted Roger Smith.

George Mayfield chimed in, as well. "We've had enough of your holier-than-thou preachin' and meddlin'! We'll have a meeting in the village, but 'tis a fair bet you'll be looking for a new position ere the sun sets. Imagine, a man of God blaming an innocent woman for something he knows full well he did himself!"

Williams stalked over to this latest parishioner to speak his mind. "Look who is changing his tune! When first I came to this village, you and Smith were the earliest to tell of this woman's pride and wantonness. Now you defend her?"

Roger flushed a little guiltily. "Do you not know two poor losers when you see them?" It would cost him much in the eyes of his neighbors, but he faced those around him, his face contrite. "I've searched my soul since I helped drive my friend and neighbor's daughter from her home. I thought myself a wealthy man of some importance, and it irked me that she would pass me over. If she was prideful, I was the more so." He turned back to his friend George. "Can you not admit the same, George?"

"Aye. Roger has hit the mark in that. You seemed to me an ally to soothe my wounded pride. That didn't last long! Time has shown you a pompous busybody, Williams!"

The clergyman looked about him, but in the multitude could not find a single sympathetic face. What he saw was a collection of people to whom he had grown tiresome and singularly uninspiring. Mayfield was right; they meant to turn him out.

"Will you send me into the wide world with naught but the clothes upon my back?" he whined. "All I ever owned was in that house!"

There was general murmuring among the throng. Mayhap they were not the world's most forgiving lot, but they were not callous. Indeed, the man was entirely bereft.

"I'll give you a horse and saddle," volunteered Timothy Hobbes. "After all, it was my wife set these wheels in motion, however deserved."

"Aye, that's good," said Roger Smith. "And we'll take up a collection among us for your severance."

"Severance! I have lost everything in the world, man!"

"'Twas no one's fault but your own," Jonathan answered. "We will give as generously as we may. That and God's grace will have to suffice."

"If God's grace you have," Faith muttered under her breath, but her mother scowled, and she fell silent. Justice had been served. It would be far better not to carry a grudge. Besides, if it had not been for the odious preacher, she would never have met her beloved Geoffrey. Aye, she could well afford to be charitable, and the Hamptons were the first to contribute to the minister's severance.

Williams had been sent packing, and Faith and Geoff had finished one last meal with her family. The couple stood by the wagon, where Noah waited to drive them back to Boston.

"Write often," Naomi admonished Faith. "And give Elizabeth my love."

"I will," Faith assured her. "And, Father, do not forget that you promised to send a new table. I would be so proud to have something of yours in our home."

Geoff and Jonathan exchanged smiles, and Geoff said, "'Tis not goodbye just yet."

Faith gazed at him, baffled. "Nay?"

"Nay. I have decided to delay our departure a few days. I trust Giles will understand."

"Well," Faith said, her voice still puzzled. "Then I guess we shall have another visit ere we leave."

"Actually," Jonathan said, "we shall have many long visits in the weeks to come."

"Jonathan?" Naomi asked, her face tenuously hopeful.

"Aye, Naomi. Our son-in-law here has granted us a few days to make arrangements with Noah to care for the animals and the shop while we are away. I think we shan't much miss the snow this winter."

"You're for Jamaica?" Noah asked, his face mirroring the surprise in his voice.

"If you'll mind our home and the business," Jonathan said, and his oldest son nodded enthusiastically.

"Never worry, Father. I'll take good care of it all."

Isaiah and David let out whoops of joy, and Naomi threw her arms around her husband. Then she pulled back and looked deeply into his face. "Perhaps . . ." She stopped, but her eyes pleaded with him.

He hesitated only a moment, then said, "'Tis a long journey. It would be foolish to come so far and not see how your sister fares. Too much love has this family missed for differences in religion."

Amid smiles and laughter, plans were made to meet in Boston in two days' time. Once in the wagon, Faith took her husband's hand and felt its warm strength. Aqua eyes met golden brown and held steady.

There would be no more second-guessing of a Being beyond her comprehension, only certainty of a loving presence that she could ever trust. Her life stretched before her with the promise of love, laughter, and family. Eternity could take care of itself.

For a sneak preview of Paula Reed's next romance,
FOR HER LOVE,
Coming in October, 2004,
please turn the page.

From time to time, Grace had traveled in one of her father's rowboats. Several strong-shouldered slaves would row her family up the coast to a neighbor's plantation for a visit and then back again, just as they now rowed her and Giles to *Reliance*. But the ride today was different. For the very first time in her life she was being rowed out to a tall ship, the kind that sailed clear across the ocean, and her heart pounded with the adventure of it.

Sitting next to her on the narrow wooden seat, Captain Courtney smiled and said, "We'll weigh anchor and sail out a ways—not all that far, but probably farther from shore than you've gone before."

Grace laughed, feeling a little foolish about all her excitement. "Undoubtedly farther than I have gone before. Your ship looks big from the dock, but from so close, it is truly enormous!"

"Once you sail from the sight of land, it gets much smaller," he quipped.

His jest only confused Grace. "What do you mean?"

"No matter how big your ship is, the ocean is much bigger. When you leave sight of land for months and then finally spy a new and distant shore . . . well, you understand life a little better."

Grace looked up at him, her eyes wide with wonder while remaining serious but not cynical. "Do you?"

"Aye, life is like that. Sometimes you sail with nothing to trust but the stars and your sextant and compass—nothing really tangible. You think of all the miscalculations you might have made, and you wonder if you will die there in all that cold blue emptiness. Then you see it, pale and indistinct on the horizon; another place, different people, a new experience. It all works out if you plot your course carefully."

"But if you are rash," Grace argued, "if you do miscalculate, then you *may* die out there. Or even if you do everything right, there are storms, and mutinies, and a dozen other things you might not have anticipated."

"Aye, all of that is true. Sometimes a good sailor must act quickly and rely upon his instincts."

"Have you good instincts, Captain?"

"Call me Giles," he replied.

As he had many times in the past twenty-four hours, he wondered about his instincts. They were usually sound, but Geoff's were often better. What he wouldn't have done to have his friend here to talk to about all of this. Still, sometimes the weather had blown them off course, and Giles was as skilled as Geoff at finding their way again.

He studied Grace, who was gazing at *Reliance* with the dancing, eager eyes of a child. Damn! It had all been very amusing when he was the one watching Geoff's world turned upside down by a woman. Grace was blowing his ship off course with all the unpredictability of a hurricane.

"How shall we get from this boat onto yours?" she asked.

His eyes widened. "My what?"

She pointed. "Your boat."

Giles gave her a look of mock indignation. "Pardon me, madam, but did you just call my *ship* a *boat*?"

She grinned mischievously and fluttered her lashes. "Forgive me, sir. How shall we get from my father's tiny little boat to your great big boat?"

He laughed and shook his head. "I daresay you'll have a bit more respect for my *boat* once we've hauled you up the side of it on a wooden plank tied to rope thrown over a pulley."

He had wondered if Grace would be afraid of being carried up the side of the ship by a rope, but she only sang out, "Really?" An eager grin spread across her face, and she jumped up and leaned forward, craning her neck to see the apparatus by which this would be done.

Unfortunately, her enthusiasm well nigh capsized the rowboat. With a little shriek and flailing arms, she nearly went backwards into the water, but Giles caught her by the skirt and pulled her onto his lap.

"Careful, or you'll have us all in the drink and we'll not have our little adventure after all." He laughed even as he admonished her.

Grace leapt from his lap, nearly upsetting the boat again. She didn't know which was the greater cause for her mortification, the fact that she had been on his lap or the fact that she had nearly drowned them all. But embarrassment could not sustain itself under the onslaught of her excitement. She put a little more distance between them and beamed at him.

"It shall be just like a swing, only way up there!" She pointed to the ship's deck. "I had a swing when I was a little girl. 'Twas tied to a poinciana tree. As far as I was concerned, my father could never swing me high enough."

Giles laughed again. "I shouldn't like to swing over-much in that thing. 'Twill send you right into the side of the ship, and you'll be back to the very fate I saved you from—waterlogged in the Caribbean Sea."

Still, when they reached the ship, and each pull from above carried her higher and higher, Grace squealed in delight. She didn't give an instant's thought to propriety as she climbed over the rail, hiking up her skirts and petticoats to show a shapely calf. Giles took a moment to appreciate the sight from the boat below her and smiled happily. For the first time since he had arrived at Welbourne Plantation, he felt like he was actually courting Grace.

Once she was firmly aboard, Grace stared up at the tall masts. There were two, something Captain Courtney (no, Giles, she corrected herself with a slight blush) had told her was true of brigantines. He had said that his company owned two such ships, and that this one was new to them. There were also a series of ropes and rolls of canvas that stretched high above her. She watched several men climbing around up there, inspecting ropes and canvas. Her gaze was so intensely locked upon them that she didn't realize she was stepping backwards until she tripped over a bucket and landed hard on her bottom, her skirts drenched in dirty water.

Giles hauled himself from the plank that had just pulled him up to the deck, vaulted the rail, and was at Grace's side. "Are you all right?" he asked, his eyes full of concern.

She gave him a wry grin. "Well, you see, I *wanted* to get wet one way or another today, and you kept *saving* me. I had to be creative."

He chuckled and lifted her into his arms. "Well,

had you but said so . . ." he replied. He carried her to the rail and swung his arms back as though to hurl her overboard.

"Nay!" she squealed, hardly able to get the word past her convulsive laughter. She wrapped her arms around his neck and held on for dear life.

God, she smelled sweet, Giles thought. The heady scent of jasmine and the feel of her light but nicely rounded body begged an immediate response from him, and he had to fight the urge to kiss her long and hard.

Grace grinned up at him, pleased to see the lines on his face deepen with laughter rather than worry. Then his eyes left hers, dropping to her mouth, and she could feel the heat of his gaze upon her lips. Something happened inside of her, a peculiar pull that made her pulse quicken. Her smile faded, and she said primly, "You may put me down."

"Of course," Giles said, doing so. He cleared his throat and tried to clear his mind.

Averting her gaze, she resumed her scrutiny of the deck while she gathered her wits.

'Twas big, and peopled with very few crewmen. Seven, by her count. There was a hatch in the floor leading to the lower decks, and stairs leading to a higher deck at the rear of the vessel. Up there was the great wheel used to steer the ship.

"May I?" she asked, pointing to the wheel.

"Certainly," Giles replied. He followed her up the steep stairs, both to protect her from taking a tumble and to enjoy the way her hips gently swung her skirts to and fro. He felt lighter, certainly more himself, here on familiar territory. He called out to his men, and the sails were unfurled to the brisk breeze. The canvas filled quickly, and in no time they were gliding away from Welbourne and all its sorrows.

Grace didn't know which was more fascinating, the sea or the man. He was back to his former self; dark hair back in a tight queue, impeccably smooth shirt and jacket, and boots polished. He called out orders and the men instantly obeyed, but his voice was not harsh; indeed, it was quite merry. He held no whip, and it was obvious that the men felt no fear. He shouted to a particularly young sailor to pick up the bucket and swab the puddle that Grace had left behind, but the lad was so entranced by the sight of Grace that he slipped in the water and went down as hard as she had.

"Poor sot," Giles said with a grin, "dazzled, no doubt, by the sight of you." Then he made a point of gazing at her with a thoroughly smitten air and tripping lightly over an imaginary impediment. She laughed softly and had to admit to herself that she rather liked being outrageously flattered.

She looked back down at the crew. "They are all white," Grace commented.

"Pardon?" Giles asked.

"Your men, they are all white. And there are so few. I saw many more than this when you were loading my father's goods, and he pointed out your Negros. Where are they?"

Giles shook his head. "This was but a short pleasure trip. I've no need of a full crew. Doubtless the rest are carousing the streets of Port Royal, spending their wages on vice and sin."

"The Blacks, too?"

"Aye, them, too."

"Do they not fear that they will be sold as slaves while you are gone?"

"A free Black is not uncommon in Port Royal, neither are slaves."

"I cannot imagine it."

"I doubt you can. One has to see Port Royal to believe it." So it was on to more serious matters. "I've an apartment above my office. If you come back with me, I'll look for a house outside of town. Mayhap I can find something near Geoff and Faith."

Grace looked up at him, and some of the mistrust that seemed ever a part of her clouded her gaze. "Your business partner and his wife?"

"You'll love Faith," he assured her. "I'm sure you'll be fast friends."

All of her life, she had lived as a white woman, but Grace had never had a white friend. She'd had Matu, and Matu was all. She and Iolanthe had socialized with the wives and daughters of other planters, but she had never become close to any of them. Iolanthe had friends in Saint-Domingue to whom she wrote, and she often visited with the wife of their closest neighbor. They compared embroidery stitches and designs for gowns, exchanged beauty secrets, and complained about their husbands and servants. Grace felt a little sick. She did not want to become Iolanthe.

"*If* I go back with you," Grace said. "If I marry you."

"Would you like to take the wheel awhile?" Giles asked.

They had things to talk about, but the prospect of steering the huge ship was too tempting. She smiled at him and said, "Oh, aye! But what if I make some error?"

"We're not far out and the trip is short. At this point, you can't make a mistake of any consequence."

There was substantial wisdom in that statement. She grasped the wheel firmly and followed Giles's instructions, steering the ship this way and that for no reason but the fun of making it go where she wished. He stood close beside her, and she found that she didn't mind it at all. In fact, she found his presence reassuring, and she rather enjoyed the tingle she felt when his arm accidentally brushed against her shoulder or when he leaned down to murmur a suggested course in her ear. The sun was warm and the breeze refreshing. Water glided under them in shades of sapphire and turquoise. The sky was a brilliant azure, though dark clouds gathered in the mountains above the plantation. In time, they would sweep to the sea.

After a while, Giles suggested that they let one of the men take the helm while he showed her the rest of the ship. They toured the galley, and he showed her the passengers' quarters. The lower deck was dark and the chambers cramped, every bit of space used with the greatest efficiency.

"Our other ship, *Destiny*, was never meant to take passengers, so it has no cabins but those for the first and second in command. Since we've started our business, we've taken a few travelers, but it meant the first mate must give up his quarters to females. *Reliance* has no such problem."

"Then why did you buy it?"

Giles furrowed his brow. "*Reliance?*"

"Nay, *Destiny*. I should think you would want a vessel that was versatile and could be used for goods or passengers."

"Ah, we did not buy *Destiny*, at least not until after

we had commanded her. Back then she belonged to the whole crew, more or less."

Grace frowned. "The ship had to belong to someone."

"She changed hands a few times. You see, Geoff and I and our old shipmates—we took her. Then the two of us bought her from the rest."

"Took her? From whom? Why?"

"From another captain and crew. I haven't always been a merchant sailor, Grace. Geoff and I were privateers."

Grace's delicately curved jaw dropped and her eyes widened. "Privateers? Like pirates?"

"Nay! We didn't prey upon ships willy-nilly. We took Spanish ships for the king. And as for *Destiny*, the Spaniards we took her from had stolen her first from an English crew."

"But you didn't return her to her English captain?"

"He was dead, killed by the Spaniards."

"And what became of the Spanish captain?"

"We killed him."

Grace stared at him, thunderstruck. Then, to his astonishment, she burst into laughter. "Oh, Giles! For a moment I actually believed you!"

"And now you don't?"

"Oh please!" she shook her head vigorously. "You could never kill anyone."

A tiny muscle in his jaw ticked. "As you have oft pointed out, Grace, we do not know one another well." Turning away from her and retreating down a tight passageway, he called back, "There's not much to see in the hold, for 'tis empty, and 'twould not be proper to show you my quarters. Shall we go above again?"

Grace didn't move. She watched his retreating back

and realized that he walked differently on a ship: though the rocking should have sent him off balance, as it did her, Giles only moved more gracefully, rolling with the vessel. He paused at the hatch, looking back at her. In the shaft of illumination from the deck above, she saw him in a different light. Shadows were cast downward over his face and the gray eyes that had always struck her as being soft, now seemed hard as steel.

Was no one ever what they first appeared, she wondered.

Wordlessly, she joined him at the ladder, and he motioned her up first, following behind her. Once again they stood at the deck's rail, this time watching the shore grow closer and closer. Grace knew that she had to be the one to patch the strained rift that had come between them.

"You still have not told me when you decided to marry me," she prompted.

He scanned the horizon and replied tersely, "Does it matter?"

"Aye, it does."

Giles looked down at her, and now she fancied his eyes were more like the sea in a storm than hard steel.

"Would you even consider marriage to a man with my past, a 'pirate'?"

She cocked her head coyly. "Nay, not a pirate, but mayhap a privateer. And I'll tell you something else, Giles Courtney. I do know you. You may have killed men, but every one weighs upon your conscience. I can see it in your face." She set her hand on the deep blue velvet of his sleeve. "We all do what we must to survive in this world. We see things and do things that we pay for a thousand times over."

"The Spanish are no more merciful to the English, I assure you," he said laconically.

"I believe you."

He breathed deeply and spread his hands to encompass the horizon. "There was so much freedom. I'd served under captains I'd no love for, for so long. At least with privateering came wealth. Geoff and I could swagger into Port Royal as men of means with all the liberty that entails."

"And yet you became merchants."

Giles grinned, and Grace breathed a sigh of relief. "Well, that was sort of Geoff's fault. 'Twas one of the conditions of a pardon he obtained when he was captured by the Spanish. Still, I was ready to settle down." He carelessly brushed a wispy ringlet away from her face where the wind had blown it, such a harmless, intimate gesture that Grace forgot to breathe. "You're right. I'm not a man to whom killing comes easily.

"And now, as for when I decided to marry you, it was in that hut, with that little girl." Both of their faces sobered at the memory. "That weighs heavily on *your* conscience. You don't see yourself as any different from them, and you suffer when they suffer."

She watched the shore, unwilling to look into his eyes. "And that is what you have always desired in a wife, a woman who thinks herself no better than a slave?"

"Good God, did it sound so to you? Heavens, no. I just feel ready. I've a ship of my own and a prosperous business, but a man wants more. There comes a time for a family."

"For heirs, you mean. Someone to inherit your business."

"Mayhap, if I've sons with any desire for it. But nay,

that is not what I mean. I want children, not heirs. I want a wife, not a slave."

Oh, the words were all so right! Grace squeezed her eyes shut, then opened them into the dazzling sunlight. *Keep your eyes wide open, you foolish girl*, she scolded herself. "And you chose me because I am beautiful, intelligent, and honest."

"And modest," Giles teased. He took her chin in his hand, forcing her to look at him, and in her eyes was all of the bitter cynicism he had come to expect. "You *are* all of those. But they were only the reasons I chose to call upon you. I asked your father for your hand because you deserve better than this. How old are you, Grace?"

"Twenty-two."

"Twenty-two. I am thirty. I live in a city of sin and villainy, have served on crews peopled by common criminals, and killed more men than I care to count, and yet I see more pain in your eyes than ever I have seen in my own mirror."

"And so you pity me?"

"We two, Grace, are in need of a balm. What say you? Together might we make a corner of the world just as we wish it?"

Her heart ached with the beauty of the thought. Children, not heirs, not poppets, not dolls to be dressed prettily and then alternately coddled or abused, never knowing which or why. A wife, not a slave. She thought of her father and stepmother. Had Father ever wooed Iolanthe with such pretty words, or had they snapped and sniped at one another from the very beginning, each maneuvering for power?

And what if he did not say cruel and frightening things to her before he took her? Aye, in truth, Jacques's

words were the true source of her terror. Giles was not a
man to hurt people. He must hurt her, of course, to
make the children that he wanted, but surely he would
be as quick as possible and soothe her if she wept. And
she was bigger now. She could bear a man's weight without suffocating, and would probably not tear so badly.
In her mind, a silky French voice whispered, *"It is a
shame that the breaking can only be done once."* Only once,
and the worst of it would be over.

"Grace? I'm sorry. Have I said something to upset
you?"

Giles's face, not Jacques's; kind concern, not mali-
cious delight. "N-nay, I'm fine. I think that we might
make such a corner."

"Then you're saying . . . ?"

"Nay! I am not saying anything. Not yet. Only that I
will think on it."

In all honesty, it was a relief to Giles that she had not
said aye. On the deck of his ship, it felt like they were
rushing, going too fast. Here, they had all the time in
the world to get to know one another and to proceed
carefully. But by the time they reached the plantation's
bay, the clouds had begun to roll in and he had to row
swiftly to get them to shore and shelter ere the rain was
upon them.

Embrace the Romance of
Shannon Drake

By Best-selling Author
Fern Michaels